*Will she say "yes"
to his intoxicating desire?...*

Until now, she'd never wanted to kiss a man. Oh, there were handsome men in New York, those who worked with the abolitionist movement. Some of Bruce's friends were good-looking as well, except they all thought they were and made no pretense of modesty.

But Duncan MacIain made her think of slumberous looks and long mornings abed. Of kisses in dark hallways and a hand reaching out to stroke her arm in passing. A quick look, a playful smile, and promise in the word, "Later," accompanied by a gentle laugh.

Regret lodged in her chest like a brick. The time wasn't right. The circumstances were against her.

"I'm very tired."

He shocked her by reaching out and touching her cheek with two fingers. No more intrusive than that tender touch. As if he measured the heat of her blush. She felt like her cheeks were aflame, warmth surging up from her toes.

Finally, he removed his hand, dropping it to his side.

An American in Scotland

KAREN RANNEY

AVONBOOKS

An Imprint of HarperCollinsPublishers

This is a work of fiction. Names, characters, places, and incidents are products of the author's imagination or are used fictitiously and are not to be construed as real. Any resemblance to actual events, locales, organizations, or persons, living or dead, is entirely coincidental.

AVON BOOKS
An Imprint of HarperCollins*Publishers*
195 Broadway
New York, New York 10007

First Avon Books mass market printing: March 2016

Avon Trademark Reg. U.S. Pat. Off. and in Other Countries, Marca Registrada, Hecho en U.S.A.
Avon, Avon Books, and the Avon logo are trademarks of Harper-Collins Publishers.
HarperCollins® is a registered trademark of HarperCollins Publishers.

Printed in the U.S.A.

10 9 8 7 6 5 4 3 2 1

To looking up and looking beyond. To always keeping your sense of humor, no matter what. To believing in the rainbow even in the midst of rain.

An American in Scotland

My darling sons,

When you each came into the world, I marveled at the miracle that created you. I held you in my arms and knew I would cherish you until the breath left my body.

Now I must bid farewell to all three of you at once.

The Almighty has indeed challenged me this day.

I know you go on a great adventure and do so with eagerness and enthusiasm. The Highlands offer less opportunity to you of late. I know this and mourn the circumstances of your leaving even as I know you will do honor to the MacIain name.

When someone asks me about my sons, I'll speak proudly of you. My eldest son, I'll say, remained in Scotland, a few days' journey away. But one of my sons traveled to England to make peace with the conqueror, while the other set sail for America.

You will have children of your own, each of them carrying the MacIain blood and name. Tell them about our history, how we dreamed of an empire. Tell them about the place from which we came, a corner of Scotland known for its men of greatness and nobility.

Mention your mother, if you will, who bravely relinquished her sons to the future.

The Almighty has not given us the power of foresight, but I cannot help but think years from now, your children and your children's children will be proud MacIains, as formidable as their ancestors.

Love sometimes means sacrifice, and I feel that truly on this day. I sacrifice you to honor, to your heritage, and to a future only you can create.

Go with God, my darling sons. May your dreams be realized and may He always protect you.

> Anne Summers MacIain
> Scotland
> June, 1746

Chapter 1

Glasgow, Scotland
May, 1863

$\mathcal{R}$ose thanked the driver as she exited the carriage and made her way down the path to the door. She didn't know what she expected, but the three-story structure with its curved front surprised her. The bay windows, one on each side of the house, were curved as well. She had the thought that it was a friendly place, that the windows were almost like eyes. The two columns on either side of the front steps created an open mouth, almost as if the house were saying: *Who are you? A stranger? Welcome anyway.*

What if he refused to see her? What if he sent her away?

That couldn't happen. She couldn't allow it to happen.

She'd come so far.

Scotland surprised her, almost as much as its people. Everyone, from the porter to her fellow travelers on the train, had been a delight, genial and exceedingly helpful. While it was true they were curious, almost intrusively so, she didn't mind repeating that, yes, she was an American. Yes, the war was a terrible thing. Thankfully, most of the discussions of her country ended there. She didn't have to explain where she came from, what she truly thought about the war, and why she wore mourning. Because she was unaccompanied, no doubt most assumed she was a widow.

Assumptions were wonderful things. They kept her from lying.

Rose had expected a country filled with unique vistas: tall, craggy mountains and heather bedecked glens. She saw those and more, heart-stopping bridges that arched over gorges and rivers crashing over rocks to settle in placid pools. Sections of Scotland were green and verdant. Other places were brown, gray, and black.

When they arrived in Glasgow, her opinion of Scotland underwent a transformation.

Here was a place as bustling as New York. Cranes and spires filled the horizon. The sound of hammering and shouting obscured the call of the seabirds overhead. Docks and ships, long buildings and bustling people, wagons and carriages, all gave the appearance of frenetic activity.

She had no idea Glasgow was so large, so hilly, or so crowded.

After carefully consulting the letter in her reticule, she gave the hired driver the address to the MacIain house.

How odd that after all these weeks, all she felt was an incredible urge to sleep.

The voyage from Nassau to England had been relatively swift, and a great deal less stressful than running the blockade from Charleston outward to the Bahamas.

The train from London had been a marvel of

speed and efficiency. Had she been on a different errand, she would've enjoyed herself immensely. As it was, each day sounded like a gong in the back of her mind, a deep-throated noise to alert her to how long she'd been gone.

Time was not on her side.

She had debated finding lodgings before calling on the MacIains. But the carriage driver said he might be able to help her in that regard, so she needn't worry. The only thing that concerned her was her dwindling resources.

He must agree. He simply must. If he didn't, she was faced with having expended the funds on the voyage with no results to show for it. Even worse, she would have wasted the time it took to come to Scotland.

No, that wasn't the way to think about the situation. Surely Mr. MacIain would see her since she was related by marriage. After all, the three branches of the MacIains had originated from the same family. She knew that because Bruce was forever repeating the MacIain family tree. He was absurdly proud of the fact that he had been descended from Highland warriors.

Her own family history was not so illustrious. Her great-grandfather had nearly starved in Ireland and found passage to the New World and a new life. Evidently, being an Irish laborer held no esteem. But her great-grandfather worked hard, put away his money so that his son had a small inheritance when he died, a habit that set his descendants on the road to prosperity.

Good fortune, however, had a way of turning on its head. She knew that only too well. She also remembered her great-grandfather's words, repeated by her father often enough: "Opportunity must be met with effort." That's exactly what she was doing in Scotland. She had made the effort, because Mr. MacIain had provided the opportunity.

She steadied herself before the door, adjusted the string of her reticule, fiddled with the bow of her bonnet. She fluffed out her skirts and peered down to check if there was dust on her shoes.

Perhaps she should have found accommodations first and prepared herself better for this meeting. She should have washed her face, at the very least, put on a little pomade because her lips felt chapped. But she was very much afraid that if she had seen a bed, she would've fallen atop it and not awakened for a few days, at least.

Before she rested, however, she had to meet with Duncan MacIain.

He must agree. He simply must.

She dared herself to grab the knocker and let it fall, hearing the echo of the sound inside the house.

She had envisioned the man she was about to meet so often, especially after having read his letters to Bruce. He would be a distinguished individual, perhaps the age of her father if he'd lived. He'd be a sober and responsible person who would immediately feel the bonds of family. He would agree to her terms not only because they were fair, but because she represented the American MacIains.

She didn't mind if he was avuncular with her, if he lectured her as to the dangers of her trip here. He would, perhaps, put her in the care of his wife, who would cluck over her like a mother hen, ask all sorts of questions about her journey and issue her own share of warnings.

How long had it been since she'd been cosseted? Never by her mother since she'd died at her birth. Her father had done so, but he'd died years before.

She shook her head at herself, let the knocker fall again, and arranged her face into an amenable expression. She had quite a bit of experience at that. She could smile through almost anything, and had.

"Yes?"

The woman who opened the door was a matronly sort, dressed in a somber blue that nevertheless was a pleasant color for her complexion. Her smile was an easy one, as if she had long practice at being pleasant.

"May I help you?" she asked. "If you're a friend of the missus, she's dining with her family now. Like as not it'll go on for a few hours. Do you need to see her?"

The smell of food wafted out of the house. Rose was so hungry she could define each separate scent: fish stew, freshly baked rolls, roast beef, and something that smelled like fruit cake.

Her stomach growled, as if she needed reminding she hadn't eaten a real meal in two days.

"Mr. MacIain," she said, pushing aside both her hunger and her fatigue. "Is he here? I need to see him."

"You've business with Mr. Duncan? Well, he mostly transacts his business at the mill, miss. Wouldn't it be better to call on him there?"

She didn't know where the MacIain Mill was. She'd taken his home address from the letters he'd written Bruce.

"I've come from America," she began, and had no more said those words than she was dragged into the house by her sleeve.

"Well, why didn't you say so from the very first? From America? All that way? And here I let you stand on the doorstep. Is that your valise? And your carriage? We'll take care of both right away."

The woman, matronly only a moment ago, had turned into a whirlwind.

Rose found herself being led through the house, following the scent of food until she thought her stomach would cramp. In moments she found herself standing in the doorway of a small dining room.

Dozens of people, it seemed from her first glance, were seated at the table, all of them attractive and well dressed. Some of them were smiling as they looked up.

"Duncan? This lady came all the way from America to see you."

She couldn't think for the hunger. She couldn't even speak.

A man stood, and she thought that hunger must surely have made her hallucinate. Tall, brown-haired, with the most beautiful blue eyes she'd ever seen. He smiled so sweetly at her, so perfectly handsome and kind, that she wondered if he was real.

He was broad-shouldered, with a face that no doubt captured the attention of women on the street. They'd stop to marvel at that strong jaw, that mouth that looked as if it could be curved into a smile or just as easily thinned in derision.

She hadn't expected him to be so arresting a figure. No doubt that's why she wavered a little on her feet.

"Yes?" he said, coming around the table toward her.
"Mr. MacIain? Duncan MacIain?"

He regarded her with a direct stare so forceful she felt as if her will were being drawn out of her with that glance.

She reached out one gloved hand toward him. Suddenly everything changed. The air around her grayed. The floor rushed up to greet her instead of him. Yet he somehow caught her when she fell. As he did so, she had the strangest thought, one that troubled her even as darkness enveloped her.

This was why she'd come all this way.

DUNCAN CARRIED the woman to their spare room, his mother and Mabel following close behind.

His mother had already removed the bonnet that nearly obscured the woman's features, revealing hair that was as red as the sunset over Glasgow. Although swathed in black, she was young, with precise features and the porcelain complexion English beauties have.

She was pretty, but he thought she might be beautiful when she was happy and smiling.

The mourning didn't suit her. She should be attired in bright colors, something in emerald or ruby or peacock blue, a shade that wouldn't clash with her hair. He'd only gotten a quick look at her eyes before she fainted, but they'd looked as green as the pines surrounding Hillshead.

"Put her on the bed, Duncan," his mother said. "We'll unlace her. The poor thing might have fainted because of her corset."

"Or hunger," he said, examining her features.

Her nose was delicate but well defined. Her

mouth was full, but her jawline was too sharp, as was her chin.

She nodded and turned to Mabel. "Perhaps we should prepare a tray for her."

Mabel nodded and left the room.

"Who do you think she is?" Eleanor asked.

"I haven't the slightest idea," he said.

"Under the circumstances, would it be acceptable to look?" she asked, glancing down at the woman's reticule in her hands.

He stared down at their unexpected guest. Her cheeks were white, but her red hair escaped like fire, tumbling over the pillowcase. A woman of mystery had suddenly appeared at their doorstep wanting to speak to him, but she'd collapsed before she could say a word.

He understood his mother's curiosity. He felt the same.

"I know it's utterly rude, but wouldn't she want us to know? The poor dear didn't even get a chance to say a word before she toppled over. Do you think she's sick?"

"I hope not," Duncan said. "She isn't running a fever." He placed the back of his hand against her cheek. "She's almost too cold. I would be willing to bet she's exhausted."

"Well, whether it's rude or not, I'm looking." With that, his mother pulled the drawstring open on the reticule and peered inside.

"There isn't a very great amount of money, especially not for one traveling so far. There's only a small jar of lip salve, one of pomade, a tiny flacon of perfume—almost empty—and a letter."

She pulled out the letter, unfolded it, then stared at him. "It's one you wrote, if I'm not mistaken."

"Me?"

Eleanor nodded as she handed it to him.

He read it, then gave it back to her. "It's one I wrote to Bruce MacIain about buying his cotton."

"Then she's a MacIain," she said. "That's a relief. But the poor thing is wearing mourning. Do you think she's his widow?"

"A reasonable assumption," he said. "But I think it would be better to ask her before we jump to any conclusions."

"Then Mabel and I will care for her."

Duncan smiled. His mother was one of the most generous and giving people he knew. Of course the stranger would be welcomed as a long-lost relative and given the status of family.

The woman was probably a widow, not surprising since America was still immersed in their civil war. But he'd never expected to meet one of his American cousins, let alone be fascinated by her appearance.

He would leave her to his mother's care. For now, the woman would have a place to rest and recuperate before they questioned her further.

"*THERE YOU* are," a voice said. "A bit of potato soup, that's what I thought I'd give you. I asked myself, 'Mabel, what would you want to eat coming out of a long sleep?' 'Why, potato soup,' I said, 'with cream and onions and a bit of cheese sprinkled on top with a wedge of just baked bread.'"

She had died and gone to heaven, and the woman who'd been at the door—Mabel—was an angel.

"I imagine you'll want to use the necessary, having been asleep for nearly a day and a half."

Rose sat up, brushed her hair back and stared at Mabel.

"A day and a half?" she asked. "I've been asleep that long?"

Mabel nodded and pointed to a screen behind which was a door leading to a modern lavatory. After washing her hands and face, Rose returned to the bed and climbed back onto the mattress, realizing she was still tired. She could easily have slept another day.

"Aye," Mabel said. "My gran always said a safe conscience makes a sound sleep."

"Is that a Scottish saying?"

"It is, at that."

She tried to smile. Her conscience was anything but clear.

"My father always said that a good laugh and a long sleep are the best cures in the doctor's book."

"Did he now?" Mabel asked, smiling. "Would that be an Irish saying?"

Rose nodded.

"A strange thing to go from being an Irish girl to Mrs. MacIain," Mabel said. "But for the best, I'm thinking. You tuck yourself into bed again and I'll arrange the tray."

"It isn't Mrs. MacIain," Rose said.

"Aye? No it isn't, is it? Not with your husband's death. A sorrow for you, poor dear. It brings it back, doesn't it, calling you Missus? Then I'll call you by your given name if that's all right with you. And what would it be, you poor dear?"

She stared at Mabel, wondering where she'd

gotten the idea that she was widowed. She really should explain before any more time elapsed, but perhaps explanations could wait. The soup smelled so very wonderful and it had been days since she'd eaten.

Hunger, always a beast temporarily at bay, roared up and overpowered any other thought.

She folded down the sheet and took the tray with eagerness. She began to eat, savoring each spoonful.

The journey to Scotland had been filled with guilt, the food she'd acquired the cheapest she could find. But this meal, unexpected and free, tasted better than anything she'd eaten in months.

"It's Rose," she said, taking a bite of bread.

Mabel was a wonderful cook. When she'd told her as much, the woman smiled brightly.

"Rose it is, then, although with that hair of yours it should be Red, I'm thinking."

"My brothers always said that," Rose said, continuing to eat. She was so hungry she could have eaten the pattern off the bowl.

The soup was glorious, as wonderful as Mabel had portrayed it, with lots of cream and a pat of butter swimming in the middle of the potatoes and cheese. She ate the bread almost as fast, and when Mabel asked if she wanted seconds, she eagerly nodded.

"You poor thing. How long has it been since you've eaten?" another voice asked after Mabel left the room.

She turned to see an older woman at the door. She vaguely remembered seeing her before collapsing.

"I'm Eleanor MacIain. I'm so very sorry that you fell ill on your way to visit with us."

It was more like not having proper food or the money to buy it, a comment she didn't make to Eleanor.

"I've been insufferably rude," she said, before the older woman could continue. "Taking advantage of your hospitality without explaining. I've come from America with a business proposition for Duncan MacIain."

Eleanor nodded. "There's time enough for that," she said, stepping aside when Mabel entered the room again, this time bearing not only another bowl of soup but a piece of fruitcake.

"Once you're rested and fed is time enough. Besides, you're family. You're our American cousin. It's a delight to have you here. What a pity our English cousins couldn't have extended their visit. We would have had all three branches of the family reunited at once."

She smiled brightly at Rose, who had no choice but to return the smile. At the same time, she felt like a cheat, someone who was taking this lovely woman's hospitality under false pretenses.

Would Duncan understand when she explained?

Chapter 2

$\mathcal{B}$y the morning of the third day, Rose felt wonderful. Why wouldn't she? She'd been treated like a princess, a very welcome guest in this lovely home.

Every hour on the hour, it seemed, Mabel was bringing her another treat: a piece of fruitcake or a cup of chocolate or an entire plate of ginger cookies. The guilt she felt at not being able to share them with her niece or the others at Glengarden lasted only a few minutes. What she was doing here would ensure that all of them would eat in the future.

She felt well enough to leave the comfortable bed and dress. Only once did she get dizzy, when she was bending over to tie her shoes.

Lily caught her and chided her for even that small act. The maid had become as protective of her as Mabel, checking in with her a few times a day, making sure she didn't need anything. Eleanor was as solicitous. All the women acted as if she were an invalid. She wasn't. She'd just been exhausted and nearly starving. Thanks to their kindness, she was neither now.

Lily, however, was having nothing of it. "You'll be falling in a faint next, and leaving Mabel and me to pick you up."

"I promise I shan't," she said. "But I'm all slept out, Lily."

"Could you eat a bit?"

That question was always answered with an affirmative yes. After weeks of not knowing when her next meal would be, she wasn't about to turn down food.

Lily was a thin slip of a thing with a large mouth that seemed to overwhelm the rest of her face. She was almost always smiling, which was contagious; you couldn't help but smile in return. Her white apron must have been changed several times a day. It was always spotless, as was the cap she wore, although her bushy brown hair escaped it in a joyous fashion.

Rose's hand was taken and she was spirited down the hall, where they turned left and descended a steep set of stairs.

They passed a lovely small parlor, entered another hallway, through a dining room, but instead of entering a kitchen they went down another corridor before finding themselves in another parlor, this one larger.

This house was strangely laid out, a comment she didn't make aloud. She was in no position to criticize the Scottish MacIains' home, but it surprised her that it was so small in comparison to Glengarden. Not only that, but it didn't seem to have any consistent design, making her wonder if it had been added onto over the years.

Finally, she found herself in a large kitchen with windows open to the bright spring day and directed to a round table where Mabel was sitting.

"You're up and about, then. How lovely. The

missus is at one of her meetings or she'd be happy as well to see you."

"Her meetings?"

Curiosity was only a desirable trait in mousers and physicians, Rose. She could hear Susanna's words now. Susanna MacIain was the matriarch of the American MacIains and had definite rules about southern womanhood, none of which she followed very well.

She was, after all, from New York. A New Yorker, according to Susanna, had no breeding.

"Aye. She works to help the poor, she does," Mabel said now, pulling out a chair for her. "She's forever doing good work, is the missus. A kinder, sweeter person you'll never meet."

She knew that firsthand. Anyone else might have tossed her out the door the first day. Eleanor MacIain had tucked her up in bed and ensured she was cared for.

Mabel and Lily were as sweet and kind. The only person she hadn't seen after that first night was Duncan. He was the one person who hadn't come to her room, but then it wouldn't have been proper, would it? Still, she'd come all this way to meet with him. Besides, she needed to know if her hunger had made her foolish. Was he truly as handsome as she remembered?

Time was not her friend, and she'd taken three days that she didn't have. She needed to finish her errand and return to Glengarden as soon as possible.

"I need to see Mr. MacIain. Do you know when he normally returns from work?"

"He sometimes comes home for lunch," Mabel said. "Not all the time, but most days."

Rose consulted her brooch watch. Eleven-thirty. Would he be able to meet with her this afternoon? Or would he want to delay until this evening? She needed to speak to him as soon as possible.

If he didn't say yes, she would be faced with returning to Nassau empty-handed.

Her stomach abruptly rumbled, loud enough for Lily and Mabel to hear.

She felt her face warm. It was the smell of Mabel's scones cooking, no doubt, that prompted her hunger.

"They're almost done," Mabel said, smiling.

Lily grabbed another cup from the sideboard as Mabel went to the oven.

Rose tried not to look as eager for the scones as she was. She'd already eaten breakfast and she was ready for lunch. The aroma was more than tantalizing. She felt as if she were being led by the nose to the stove.

"If he doesn't come home for lunch, what time will he come home tonight?" She really did need to talk to him, as quickly as possible.

Mabel placed the tray of lightly browned scones, plump with raisins and smelling of spices, on the table. No human being could possibly resist them. When Mabel gave her two on a plate and Lily poured her some tea, she thanked both women.

She folded her gloved hands around the hot cup. She hadn't accustomed herself to the strong tea she was served at every occasion, but perhaps it was an acquired taste. Another comment she wouldn't make. She was a guest in this house and was grateful for anything she was given.

Two teaspoons of sugar—another luxury—made

it bearable. Coming to England, to Scotland, meant reacquainting herself with all the creature comforts that had been lacking at Glengarden for a while: sugar, endless food, and the comfort of caring people.

Bruce had believed in waking at dawn, and it was a habit the entire household had assumed. She was grateful that the Scottish MacIains didn't wake at five, but an hour or two later.

Nor was that the only difference in the two branches. This home was run so much more informally. She'd heard Eleanor call out more than once and overheard laughter coming from the kitchen. The servants seemed almost members of the family.

At Glengarden, no one helped each other. The slaves were there to do their bidding. At least, that had been true until January.

She reached for her fork, trying to pace herself, but it was nearly impossible. The smell of the pastry was beckoning her. The first mouthful made her close her eyes in bliss.

"Mabel makes the best scones in Scotland," Lily said.

She opened her eyes to find both women smiling at her.

"It's truly wonderful. It's like biting into heaven."

Mabel's laugh swirled around the room and incited her own smile.

"I'll remember that as being the best compliment I've ever received, Rose MacIain, and I'll be thanking you for it."

For the next several minutes the only thing she did was concentrate on eating.

"I knew I smelled scones," a voice called out. "It's

almost like following a trail, Mabel, all the way from Hillshead."

A woman stopped into the kitchen doorway and stared.

Her face was triangular, ending in a pointed chin. Her eyes, a soft blue, possessed a dark circle surrounding the iris, as if to accentuate the shade. She reminded Rose of someone, and in that instant she knew who the woman was: Glynis, Eleanor's daughter.

"You must be our American cousin," Glynis said.

Before she could prepare herself, the other woman came to the table, leaned over and gave her a hug.

"You're Rose, am I right?"

She nodded.

"I'm Glynis and I've been waiting to meet you. I'm so glad you're up and about. Now you can come to Hillshead to visit. We'll have high tea. It's a practice we've been doing for about a year now. It's an excuse to drink whiskey in the afternoon and have all sorts of fattening foods. Nothing like Mabel's scones, however. You dear, you knew I was starving for them, didn't you?"

With that, she gave Mabel a hug before taking the empty chair.

"How is Dora?" asked Glynis.

Rose sat there, eating her scone, trying to process the whirlwind that was Glynis. She'd heard of her, of course. Both Mabel and Lily had been forthcoming. Glynis had been married and widowed before marrying Lennox, the love of her life, and now lived in the big house on the hill.

"She's fine. The little one looks to have the colic, though. The missus told her to stay home and tend to him."

"While she still pays Dora, of course."

Both Mabel and Lily nodded.

"You'll find my mother is the most generous person in the world," Glynis said, turning to her.

"Who's Dora?" Rose asked.

When will you demonstrate any breeding, Rose?

Susanna was an ocean away yet she was still being troublesome.

"Dora works for us and helps Lily. She had a baby not too long ago, but the poor dear hasn't had an easy go of it."

Rose had the feeling she was one of Eleanor MacIain's charity cases, too.

"Well, what do you say?" Glynis asked.

"About what?"

"Coming to Hillshead for high tea tomorrow. Or our Scottish version of it. About three, long enough from lunch that you'll be peckish, but not that long until dinner."

She might be on her way back to America by that time, or at least to London.

"I don't know if I'll still be here," she said.

Mabel's mouth dropped open. Lily's eyes widened. Only Glynis seemed unaffected.

"Of course you will," Glynis said. "You've just gotten here. You can't leave so suddenly. I want to talk to you about America and of course you must meet Lennox. My father and sister-in-law are the most delightful people and you can't leave without getting to know them."

"I can't?"

"Absolutely not."

How did one refuse Glynis anything?

"What do you think of Scotland, Rose?" Glynis

asked as she refilled her cup from the pot in the middle of the table. "Or haven't you had a chance to see anything of your homeland?"

"It's not actually my homeland," she said. "My family is Irish."

Glynis smiled again. "I guessed that from your hair."

At least the woman didn't use a disparaging tone or hurtful adjectives to describe it. What did you do when you were born with hair the color of flames? You couldn't very well wear bonnets inside. Susanna had actually suggested she might try dyeing it black like all her dresses.

"A gesture of mourning, my dear," she said when Rose had looked agog at her.

"I'm so sorry to hear you were a widow," Glynis said.

In her eyes was the same look of compassion she'd received from Eleanor MacIain. Both of them had been widows. Both of them had known sorrow. Neither of them deserved a lie.

All of them, every single person in the MacIain household, had been more than kind to her. They'd taken her into their home and their family without a single thought. From the day she arrived in Scotland she'd felt welcomed, and all she'd given them in return had been falsehoods.

The sound of the door opening made them all turn.

"That'll be Duncan for sure," Mabel said.

She was both suddenly relieved and absolutely terrified.

Chapter 3

Rose stood, brushing away the crumbs from her dress, waiting for him. Would he come into the kitchen? Or was he one of those men who insisted that he be waited on in the dining room?

Suddenly, he was there in the doorway, making her heart do a dance like tiny feet jumping in her chest. What on earth was wrong with her? The tea, that's what it was. It was really too strong. Her reaction had nothing to do with the fact that his face fascinated her, with his eyes drooping on the outer corners a little, making him look entirely too charming.

He might be as vile as his American cousin.

Dear God, anything but that. *Please don't let him be like Bruce.* That fear had been with her all the way to Scotland.

Yet neither Mabel nor Lily had ever indicated that he was anything but kind. Surely they would have said something.

Mabel spoke before she could. "Miss Rose needs to talk with you, Duncan. Would you like to sit here? You can have your lunch and talk, too."

"I think in the parlor, Mabel. I'll have a few of those scones for now."

"I'm glad I beat you to the kitchen," Glynis said, smiling at her brother.

He grinned back at her.

"Are you trying to convince Mabel to come to Hillshead again? She won't. I'll make sure of it." He turned to Mabel. "Marry me, Mabel, and live with me here forever."

Mabel's face turned a hearty shade of red. "Go away with you now, Duncan MacIain. And scones are not enough for a meal and well you know it."

He only grinned, leaned over and kissed her cheek while stealing two scones in a napkin.

He motioned Rose to follow him and she did, grabbing another scone for herself, to Mabel's delight.

They retraced the path she and Lily had taken earlier through the maze of corridors and into the dining room and out of it to reach the parlor.

A settee rested against the wall opposite a large window. Next to it was the chair, and between the two, a small round table equipped with a lamp. In front of the settee was a long rectangular table on which there was a stack of books. She wanted to examine their titles to discover what the Scottish MacIains liked to read.

The parlor was small, an almost intimate room. As a widow, people wouldn't look askance at her being alone in a room with a relative, even a distant one.

What would they say if they knew that she and Duncan weren't related at all, even by marriage? Or that she'd never married?

The room was cozy, with worn but comfortable furniture. The view from the windows was of the enormous hill nearby and the house at the top of it.

"Hillshead," he said, catching her glance. "It's my sister's house now. Or hers and Lennox's."

He indicated the settee and she sat, nibbling on the scone while he sat opposite her in the matching chair.

For a few moments they ate in silence.

"How are you feeling?" he asked after he'd finished and blotted his mouth with his napkin.

"Wonderful," she said. "So much better. Thank you for your hospitality. And your kindnesses."

"Is that what you wanted to talk to me about, Mrs. MacIain?"

She shook her head, wondering how to begin. First, she should correct him as to her identity, but that wasn't the most important part of this conversation.

Besides, the lessons she'd learned in Nassau were still with her. There, the factors had argued with her about her ability to sell the cotton in her possession. She didn't want the same problem with Duncan.

"When you fainted, we looked in your reticule," he said. "I apologize for the invasion of your privacy, but we were only trying to establish your identity."

She nodded.

"You had a letter in there. One I'd written to Bruce MacIain."

Again she nodded.

He began to smile, but the expression didn't reassure her one whit. There was another emotion in his eyes, one hinting that this man wouldn't be like most of the southern men she knew: more than willing to be charmed by a belle armed with grace, a pleasing manner, and a voice thick enough to remind her of New England maple syrup in the dead of winter.

"Why have you come to Scotland, Mrs. MacIain? Why did you wish to speak to me?"

Her New York nature had nothing on Duncan. He was blunt, yet it was so refreshing to talk to someone who didn't take the long way around to reach a point that she almost smiled.

"You were interested in cotton, I believe."

He didn't say anything, so she continued.

"Are you still?"

She folded one gloved hand over the other, keeping them immobile. She raised her head, leveling her gaze on the man opposite her, all the while maintaining a pleasant expression.

Two years of living at Glengarden had made her adept at hiding her emotions.

"Your letter indicated that you were," she said.

"Mrs. MacIain, your husband didn't seem interested in providing me with any of his cotton."

There was something about the man that was both alluring and frightening. It might be his penetrating gaze or the stillness about him, as if he had all the time in the world, and the patience, too.

"Please call me Rose," she said. "Otherwise, we sound like echoes, don't we? Mr. MacIain. Mrs. Mac-Iain. The reason for being here? I have cotton. I have a great deal of cotton that I need to sell."

"Do you have the ability to act for your husband, Rose?"

There. The very reason she had to keep up this charade. No, she didn't have Bruce's authority. In fact, Bruce had specifically instructed his factor that his cotton wasn't to be sold in his absence. Instead, let it rot in warehouses in Charleston while his family starved.

"Bruce is no longer able to make those kinds of decisions," she said. "Would you be interested in buying it?"

"My condolences."

She scanned his face, but there was no way to

read the message in those direct blue eyes. He didn't sound especially sad about Bruce's implied death.

"I would have been interested at one time," he said. "I was planning on running the blockade myself."

"Were you?"

"If I'm not mistaken, Rose," he said, "you did as well. Otherwise, you would not be sitting here with me."

"I did," she said. "The outward-bound trip is rumored to be easier than approaching Charleston."

So far, Providence had smiled on her. Her money and her courage had lasted during the voyage to England. Now all she had to do was convince Duncan MacIain to purchase the cotton he evidently needed and she had to sell.

She had to make him see that it would be an arrangement to their mutual satisfaction.

He sat back in the chair and smiled at her. "Are you cautioning me against running the blockade? Perhaps it's best that I changed my mind."

Oh dear. She certainly could not begin negotiations with an irritated man. She shouldn't have spoken. Susanna always said that her New York nature was grating on a person.

You'd be better served, Rose, to be a bit more southern in your approach. Southern women do not demand. We are more clever than that.

She had never, in the two years she'd lived in the South, attempted to be more like her South Carolina relatives. Now might be an interesting time to try.

"I'm a mere woman, Duncan. Who am I to caution a man of your strength and resolve?"

His laughter startled her into smiling.

He really was quite attractive, and the burr of his voice did something to the back of her neck, but she would not allow him to see that she was affected in any way by his appearance or his accent. To do so would be to weaken her bargaining position.

"You'd once expressed an interest in Glengarden's cotton," she said, getting back to the subject at hand.

"An interest your husband didn't seem inclined to pursue, Rose." Something about his tone interested her. An emotion that shouldn't have been there.

"Unfortunately, Bruce believed that selling the cotton to anyone other than the Confederacy was disloyal."

"You don't feel the same, I take it?"

"I believe the Confederacy would have been a great deal more solvent now, Duncan, if they'd based their currency on cotton. At the moment, however, they've no idea how to leverage the crop to their advantage. That's why factors are making millions and the blockade has become so successful.

"You won't be able to find any cotton in Nassau," she went on. "Most of the cotton that's run the blockade has already been sold to either Fraser Trenholm or the other factors."

He didn't say anything for a long time. She sat back in the corner of the settee, placed her gloved hands one atop the other and regarded him with patience.

The two years she had lived at Glengarden taught her a great deal about people and herself. She had finally managed to quell her habit of saying what was on her mind. People didn't have an inkling of her opinion or thoughts. Unfortunately, most of the time the people around her didn't care to know, either.

She had, in those miserable two years, learned how to deal with vain and irrational women and stubborn men.

A stubborn man sat opposite her. He might speak in an entrancing accent and be handsome, but his mind was not easily changed. The fact that he was actually listening to her was a surprising development. She had thought that she would have to convince him of her knowledge of the cotton market before he would.

Or perhaps he was getting ready to banish her from the room. That was possible as well.

"I've been in contact with several factors, Rose. I agree with your assessment of the situation. The factors have effectively closed off the market, unless planters are willing to sell their cotton at a forty percent discount."

His knowledge surprised her, but it shouldn't have. He ran a mill that was dependent on cotton to survive. Of course the world market would be of interest to him.

"I have nearly a thousand bales of cotton," she said. "I am not willing to sell it for almost half of what it's worth. I'm assuming you still need cotton. If you do, I have it. It occurred to me that we might come to an agreeable arrangement."

Before he could speak, she held up her hand. "I am not trying to take advantage of a familial connection, Duncan. I only want what is fair."

He had to agree. He simply had to. If he didn't, she had come all this way for nothing. She'd spent money that she barely had for a lost cause. If he didn't agree, she would have to go back to Fraser Trenholm with her pride in tatters and agree to their horrendous price. That is, if they would even buy the cotton from her. The money she'd make would be half what she'd originally calculated and only suffice for a few months. If the war ended in that time, fine. If it lasted longer, they'd be in the same predicament, but without cotton to sell.

She had one other alternative left to her. She'd heard of caravans of cotton going north, organized by women in a similar situation to what she faced. They'd sold the cotton to the Union in order to buy supplies.

The problem was, she'd have to fight both her sister Claire and Susanna to do that. And if they were suspected of doing such a thing, they would be considered traitors to the Confederate cause. Glengarden might be put to the torch and the inhabitants of the plantation ostracized, or worse.

Still, she might not have a choice.

She occupied herself in arranging her skirts, tugging on her gloves, trying not to hear the ticking of the mantel clock.

THEY WERE interrupted by Lily, who entered with a tray. "I've brought more scones, sir, and Mabel says she made you cold roast beef and mustard on a slice of bread for lunch. Oh, and tea."

He smiled at the maid. "Thank you, Lily." Turning to Rose, he asked, "Would you like some more tea? Or something to eat?"

"No, thank you." She waited until Lily left and he'd served himself before continuing. "Glengarden cotton is among the best in the South. I'm offering you the price you'd pay delivered to Glasgow, less twenty percent."

"Is twenty percent the familial discount?"

She shook her head. "No. It's because you're going to have to retrieve the cotton yourself."

He held up his teacup as if in salute. "At least you recognize that."

"Another proviso. I need the money in gold. Not Confederate dollars, Union currency or English pounds. Gold will keep my family fed and give us some hope for the future."

He sat back, replaced his teacup on the table and regarded her steadily. "You don't sound very optimistic about the Confederacy winning, Rose."

In her answer, she could at least give him the truth. "It's my belief that the men of the South went to war on a romantic notion, intent on keeping their way of life the same. Nothing ever stays the same, Duncan. Everything changes in life. That was their first mistake. Their second was allowing the thrill of war to blind them to the facts. The South may be passionate and eager to fight, but they are no match for the Union."

"Would your attitude have anything to do with the fact that you didn't grow up in the South?"

"My attitude has everything to do with the fact that I didn't grow up in the South. How did you know?"

He smiled. "You don't sound southern, Rose. I suspect it's a northern accent. New York?"

She nodded, surprised.

"Isn't it uncomfortable for you to live at Glengarden?"

Her stomach fell to her feet. This was not going at all the way she expected. She had come to discuss cotton prices, transport costs, and percentages, not her views on the South.

"Yes."

With any luck, that terse answer would satisfy him. It seemed it didn't, because he smiled at her again. This time his expression was almost chiding.

Perhaps the only thing left for her was the truth, except, of course, that she wasn't ready to tell it.

"You're very opinionated, Rose. Have you always been so?"

"Yes," she said, giving him another bit of truth.

She didn't add that she rarely expressed her opinion because she didn't want to be met with derision or that strange, southern way of acting that her sister had embraced. A woman was not supposed to have any serious thoughts. That's what men were for.

He finished the lunch he'd been brought and she sat there, waiting for his decision. Finally, he stood and strode across the room to stare out the window. After several long moments of silence he turned to face her.

"Your husband is dead."

She was so startled she only stared at him.

"Otherwise, you have no legal standing to sell anything, isn't that true?"

What on earth did she say now?

"I imagine life has been very trying for you lately," he said.

He didn't know the half of it.

"Do you have documentation about this cotton of yours?"

"Yes," she said, nodding. "Certificates from the warehouse and inspection stamps, plus the latest inventory."

"May I see them?"

She nodded again and stood. "They're in my valise," she said, and left the room, her heart lighter than it had been for days.

He wouldn't want to see the papers unless he was interested. Or did he doubt her word?

Duncan MacIain wasn't as sweet and compassionate as his female relatives. He was, however, as handsome as her first glimpse of him. Plus, he knew more about the cotton market than she'd expected.

A few breathless moments later she returned to the parlor, handing him the papers she'd brought from Glengarden.

"I'd decided against traveling to America," he said, folding his arms in front of him. "I'd decided it was too risky an adventure, that I might not be able to obtain any cotton at all, especially since learning that the Confederacy is buying up space in the holds of a great many steamers."

He was very up-to-date on the news. She had only heard that on arriving in Nassau.

If she couldn't tell him the truth about her identity, at least she wouldn't lie about other things.

"My views are not aligned with those of the Confederacy, Duncan. They would have my family starve for the cause. I've lived the life they would preserve at all costs. I find nothing about it to admire. I neither think it noble nor enlightening to enslave vast numbers of people."

"You're an abolitionist," he said.

"I proudly wear that label," she said. "But I think I'd rather be called simply human. I cannot abide the idea of one person setting himself up above others and calling himself master."

He smiled. "I hold your views," he said. "I'd be more comfortable if the Confederacy lost. I dislike having to subsidize slavery in order to keep my mill solvent and my family protected. At the moment, however, southern cotton is what we need."

She was straddling a strange line. She was pretending to be Bruce's widow, but she couldn't emulate Claire's behavior.

"How did an abolitionist come to live at Glengarden?"

She should really tell him now, before this ludicrous situation continued any longer. She took a deep breath to do that very thing when he continued speaking.

"You fell in love with Bruce to the degree that your beliefs no longer mattered?"

She narrowed her eyes. "Is it only women who do that, Duncan? Are men never similarly affected?"

"It's been my experience that love, once it borders on obsession, is a dangerous emotion."

Perhaps it was love bordering on obsession for Claire. She felt torn in this odd position in which she'd placed herself, pretending to be her sister. Granted, Claire had fallen deeply in love with Bruce, enough to give up her home and her family for him. But Claire hadn't expressed any deep and abiding belief in the abolitionist movement. Claire had truly never been interested in anyone but Claire, another disloyal thought.

Yet how could Claire have tolerated slavery without a word of protest? A question Rose had asked herself almost every day she spent at Glengarden.

"There would never be a woman in existence who fascinated you enough that you would do something contrary to your nature?"

"No," he said simply.

The answer dumfounded her. "Not ever?"

"I doubt it."

She shook her head.

"As to how an abolitionist came to live at Glengarden," she said, giving him the truth, "I never thought it would be as terrible as it was. Nothing I said ever swayed Bruce."

Or Claire. She'd addressed her concerns to her sister first. Nothing she ever said to Claire seemed to make a difference.

"It's just the way it is in the South, Rose," Claire had said. "You'll just have to get used to it."

Her sister was surrounded by servants. Someone was always there to do her slightest bidding. If she dropped something and needed it picked up, all she had to do was flick a finger toward the offending object and it was fetched for her. Effort was simply not necessary. Her smallest wish was granted and money appeared to be no object, at least until the war started.

Claire never seemed to notice—or care—that the people who served her never looked her in the eye. They weren't free. They were chattel, according to Bruce and his family. They were simply belongings, like a horse or dog.

"If you'll pardon me for saying so, you must have been an annoyance to your husband with your abolitionist's views."

There was that tone again.

"You didn't like him, did you?" she asked.

Instead of immediately refuting her question, he remained silent. When the answer came, she knew it was the truth.

"I never met him," he said, "but no, I was not disposed to liking your husband."

"May I ask why? He was well regarded in Charleston," she said. "And in other places in South Carolina. It was not at all difficult for him to assemble his own regiment."

"Did he award himself a title? General MacIain?"

The comment was so unexpected and yet so pointed that she couldn't help but smile.

"Colonel. Bruce didn't like people to think he was taking on airs."

"Yet for all his popularity, I do not doubt that there were people who did not like your husband, Rose. You asked why I didn't like him. He bragged about his life, including how many slaves he owned. The number seemed especially important to him. He never once seemed to think it morally repugnant or wrong."

She walked to the fireplace, admiring the small figurines assembled there.

"No, he wouldn't. It was a point of honor to him."

"I am tied to southern cotton although I don't want to be. He, on the other hand, went to war to keep his way of life the same."

"You're right." She glanced back at him. "I didn't like Bruce very much, either."

How very odd to confess the truth and wrap it in a lie. She despised Bruce MacIain and had worked against him every day she'd been at the plantation. She was so grateful she hadn't been the man's wife. It was bad enough to be his sister-in-law.

DUNCAN CONCENTRATED on the documents in front of him, perusing the certification from the warehouse, the statement of the inspection of the bales. From time to time he glanced at her.

She'd returned to the settee and was as still as any of the bric-a-brac in his mother's parlor. Her cheeks were rosy, though, indicating that waiting for his decision wasn't as easy as it appeared.

Until a few months ago, he'd planned on running the blockade. Then he learned from the factors with whom he was in communication that cotton production had fallen drastically in the last two years as planters were urged to grow wheat, corn, and beans to feed themselves and the Confederate armies. The result was that the cotton crop was a fifth the size it had been before the war began.

Not only were the southern states not producing as much, but there was so much demand for cotton that prices were astronomical. It was the reason he'd chosen not to go to America.

Yet now the price Rose had asked was more than fair. He could easily pay her more and still make a profit.

His English cousin, the Earl of Rathsmere, had purchased the *Raven* from Lennox for just such an opportunity. Duncan had sold all his English properties and converted the proceeds to gold in preparation for the adventure. But why go through all the trouble, not to mention the danger, if he'd just come back with an empty hold?

He still had the ship. He had the resources. He had the time, and he certainly had the inclination. He'd do anything to save the mill.

Rose had a thousand bales of cotton.

All the documents looked in order. From what he'd learned, she was right. Glengarden cotton had a good reputation.

"Will you give me a few days to consider?"

"Of course," she said, standing.

Her smile trembled and he wondered how important his decision was to her. Would it make the difference between life and death? He had the feeling it would.

He watched the door long after she left, wondering what it was about the Widow MacIain that intrigued him so much. He had the feeling she was hiding something. If he said the proper word, would all those secrets come spilling out? Or were they trapped behind her beautiful green eyes forever?

Chapter 4

$\mathcal{T}$he next afternoon, at exactly two-thirty, Rose was led to a lovely carriage parked outside the Mac-Iain house. Glynis had come to escort her herself, which meant there was no demurring, no excuses, no last minute illnesses to concoct. Glynis, as pleasant as she was, had a backbone of iron.

She had a feeling both Glynis and Eleanor got their way when they were adamant. In this, Glynis was most definitely insistent. Rose was going to tea at Hillshead and would, no doubt, be questioned endlessly about Glengarden.

She dreaded the afternoon.

Glynis, however, was oblivious to any of her fears.

"I want you to meet my father-in-law. He's the most amazing man and so talented. Then there's Mary, my sister-in-law, the sweetest person in the entire world, besides my mother, of course. She's finally in love and being around her is delightful. It's been entirely too long for dear Mary to find someone companionable. She kept saying that she would be content to be a spinster for the rest of her life."

Good heavens, what would Glynis say if she knew about her true circumstances?

Hillshead was a three-story house at the top of a hill. All its white-framed windows looked like so many eyes, spying on the terrain and below, to Glasgow itself. Built of red brick, the house was surrounded by green hedges that also lined the paths winding to the double front door. Around the house were giant pines leaning protectively over the roof, as if Hillshead were a tiny creature and the forest determined to protect it.

For all its size, with its two wings stretching out in the back and framing a series of gardens, it was only a third the dimension of Glengarden. But Hillshead had no slave cabins concealed behind a line of trees.

She was given a tour, and expressed her genuine awe at the ballroom, the Italian gardens, and other treasures of Hillshead. The house was more richly furnished than Glengarden, and more lavishly decorated, but in ways that startled her. It had a definite nautical theme. The carvings on the doors were of ships, waves, or sea creatures. The paintings in the hallway were of famous ships. Even the tiebacks on the curtains were done with nautical knots.

It wasn't until tea that she understood why.

What Glynis called high tea in the Scottish fashion was a buffet set up in a sunny parlor on the west side of the house. The upholstery on all the furniture was a yellow and red flowered pattern. The walls were lined with a red silk, making the room a bright and cheery place to be.

Crimson carpet woven in an oriental pattern lay in the middle of the room.

The mantel and fireplace surround were carved with deer gamboling among the thickets, with acorns on vines thrown in for good measure. At least here, unlike the rest of the house, there wasn't a ship or sea creature to be seen.

When she entered, four people were already sitting on the various chairs and settee.

A tall man with black hair that curled at the ends stood up and came forward. His gray-green eyes crinkled at the corners as if he thought life was a great jest. His cheeks were already shadowed by a beard that gave him a swarthy look. He reminded Rose of her brother Montgomery, who had to shave more than once a day.

Pain shot through her. Not unexpectedly, because she was often reminded of her brothers in odd ways.

"You're Rose," he said. "I'm Lennox and my chief claim to fame is that I'm Glynis's husband."

"And the very best shipbuilder in the world," Glynis added, standing on tiptoe to kiss her husband on the mouth in front of everyone.

That display of affection took Rose aback, but so did Lennox easily wrapping his arm around his wife's waist and pulling her close.

"Well, not quite the best," an elderly voice said.

She turned to see an older gentleman sitting in an adjoining chair, gripping his cane and staring toward them.

"Almost the best. He'll be the best when I go off to that great shipyard in the sky."

Lennox laughed. "My father, William Cameron, who is the best shipbuilder in the world."

Glynis smiled at both of them. "But we're being rude. We should have introduced everyone properly. This is my sister-in-law Mary and Robert."

Rose's eyes were drawn to a couple sitting on one of the settees. Mary had Lennox's black hair, but her eyes were noticeably greener. Rose immediately had the impression of a fawn, even though Mary looked nothing like a deer. Perhaps it was the gentleness in her eyes, the sense that she could be easily wounded, that had her thinking such a thing.

Rose smiled at the other woman and said something innocuous about how fine a day it was.

Robert, who had stood at her entrance also, bowed a little toward her, adding that you could never be certain of Scotland's weather.

The weather was always a safe topic, but it was too quickly exhausted.

She smiled, disposed to like Robert because of his awkwardness. He glanced back at Mary as if for approval, his brown eyes as earnest as a child's. Two gentle people had found each other, and she hoped they continued to be as happy as they looked right at this minute.

She sat on the settee closest to Mr. Cameron.

"It's all a mess, isn't it?"

She looked to her left. He was staring toward the center of the room, and it was only then that she realized he was blind.

"Coming in when you don't know anyone can be daunting," he said. "I know the feeling well. For the longest time, I didn't want to be around new people. I couldn't see them, so I was always confused."

"I should think that not being able to see people would be an advantage," she said softly. "You don't know when they're looking at you. If they consider you an object of scorn or pity, you're ignorant of it."

The elderly man tossed back his head and laughed as if she'd made the most brilliant comment.

"You're delightful, my dear. A true American. Not afraid to say exactly what she thinks."

She could feel her cheeks warm. She hadn't been herself for more than two years. These days in Scotland would always be precious, not simply for the memories, but for reminding her of who she'd once been. The girl who'd argued with Jeremy, her brother, who attended abolitionist meetings every week and cheered and applauded the speakers. That girl had disappeared, and until these days in Scotland, she thought she'd been banished for good.

Conversation swirled around Rose like fog. She grabbed tendrils of it when people tried to include her from time to time and answered as she could. Glynis was right. William Cameron was a fascinating man who spoke of Russia as if he'd spent a great many years in the country.

When she questioned him as to his expertise, he admitted that he had lived in St. Petersburg for some time.

"We had our own shipyards there, Cameron and Company, before we sold it and devoted our time here in Glasgow."

"What sorts of ships do you build, Mr. Cameron?"

"I won't have that. William it is, or I'll find myself talking to the trifle instead."

She smiled, charmed by him.

"We build blockade runners, Rose," Lennox said. "We've sold quite a few to Fraser Trenholm."

She was startled enough that she stared at him. Before she could comment or ask a question, Glynis interjected with a remark of her own.

"Which means, Rose, that we sell them to the Confederacy. The War Department is not very fond of us."

"An understatement," Lennox said. "We have

Union operatives everywhere in Glasgow. They don't even make an effort to hide themselves anymore."

"I had no idea that the war had come to Scotland," she said, genuinely surprised.

"Unfortunately, it has," Glynis said. "However did you meet a man from the South, being from New York?"

Her accent was not that distinctive. At least not since she'd lived in South Carolina for two years.

Although she hadn't expected the question, it was easily answered.

"Bruce was a friend of my brother's. They both attended the Military Academy."

"So you moved from New York to South Carolina?"

"Yes," she said.

"It must have been a difficult transition for you," William said.

It was like moving from heaven to hell, but how did she say that?

"Yes," she said.

The paucity of her answer may have hinted at how she felt, because William smiled, reached over and patted her hand.

"Are you hungry?" he asked. "I hope you brought your appetite with you. High tea's an excuse to eat anything we want to. You can have trifle and cake or roast beef or simply biscuits if you want. "

She had been hungry for most of the last year. She wanted to tell him the truth, something that rarely occurred. She was not given to sharing her thoughts with strangers, especially when they were of such a personal nature.

"We've all sorts of treats, plus cheeses and fruit. Wine and whiskey and ale."

It was the most outlandish collection of foods she'd ever seen. She could have fish if she wanted—she didn't. Or porridge with honey. There was leek soup or cucumber sandwiches or cookies—biscuits, they were called. She ended up having some sandwiches that tasted of salmon, a slice of the most delicious chocolate cake she'd ever eaten, and something called a Tipsy Laird, which reminded her of the tipsy cake the cook used to make at Glengarden.

It was the most beautiful dessert she'd ever seen: layers of pretty sliced fruit over custard and cake. The cake had been soaked in whiskey, until she was certain she was going to be the tipsy one.

She was feeling gluttonous and certain she wouldn't be hungry for dinner.

"Has the war reached where you live?" Lennox asked.

She shook her head. "Not yet. Glengarden is not far outside Charleston," she said. "On the Wando River. There's a bend in the river that nearly encircles the land. We're almost an island. We've not experienced anything, although from time to time we can hear gunfire. In Charleston it's much worse. The Union navy is constantly trying to close the port."

"Tell us about the American MacIains," Glynis said.

"What would you like to know?" she asked.

The dreaded questions had begun.

"What's your household like?"

Perhaps it was the spirits she'd imbibed that made her answer so honestly.

"Unusual," she said. "But perhaps like most plantations lately. Susanna is the matriarch and in her sixties. In the last year she's been very confused. Some days she thinks it's an earlier age, before the war began. Then there's Claire, my sister, and Gloria, my niece."

"You have no men in your household?" Glynis asked.

She shook her head. When no one said anything, she continued.

"Women are doing remarkable things nowadays. They're keeping plantations running, growing food and raising their families while men are gone for months, sometimes years."

She could just imagine Bruce's reaction to that.

When will you get it into your head, Rose, that I don't care about your opinions? You're a woman, for God's sakes. It's time you acted like one.

How many times had she gotten that lecture? How many times had Claire looked on with a helpless expression? Strange, she could never remember her sister being so silent in the past. When Claire didn't like something, she was the first to voice her disapproval.

Had love changed her sister that much? If so, she didn't want anything to do with it.

Claire had changed. The metamorphosis hadn't been the least bit gradual. Within a day of arriving at Glengarden, she'd noticed that Claire had begun mimicking her mother-in-law's affectations, the strolling walk, the slow speech patterns. Other changes were just as visible, but more troubling: the fact that Claire didn't seem to notice the dozens of slave cabins behind the house or the fields where men, women, and children worked, bent over in the hot South Carolina sun.

Claire had affected a helplessness she'd never demonstrated in New York. It was as if moving south had stripped her of every bit of intellect or initiative. What Bruce said was law.

Rose had first met Bruce when her brother brought him home on leave from West Point. Robert and Bruce were best friends and fellow cadets. Bruce had always seemed a pleasant sort, a young man with more than a little confidence, good bearing, and a bright future. As the MacIain heir, he had a fortune at his disposal, and showered Claire with presents and promises.

Claire was smitten, transformed from a girl who'd once spoken about marrying one day, to a woman who was suddenly head over heels in love. She couldn't talk about anyone but Bruce. What Bruce thought, what Bruce had written in his last letter, when Bruce was due to arrive, what Bruce might think of her new dress.

It was enough to make Rose roll her eyes and escape from her sister's presence as often as she could.

Susanna, Bruce's mother, was a creature from a novel, an overbearing personality with a sly smile, keen eyes, and a voice capable of delivering a tongue-lashing with a dose of honey.

She'd only met Susanna at the wedding, an event that should have, in Susanna's words, taken place at Glengarden, where tradition dictated that all weddings of a MacIain occurred.

Her father, a strict traditionalist as well, decreed that if his daughter was going to live so far away, she'd at least have her start in married life in the same church where her parents had been wed.

What might have been a showdown ended happily with Susanna conceding the point. Her father had as much charm as Bruce when he wished. Her father's character, however, didn't have a dark side, one that showed the instant the charm stopped.

Claire hadn't been interested in the running of Glengarden even after Bruce had gone off to war. The overseer, a man Rose had despised from the first moment she met him, had been tempted away to another plantation, a decision she heartily endorsed.

He hadn't been replaced.

There was no need to punish people who simply wanted to be free. Besides, by the time the overseer had left, the final cotton harvest was over. Glengarden's fields remained fallow and probably would for some time.

"Do you have slaves?" William asked.

The five of them were looking at her.

Her stomach clenched. Maybe she should have had more spirits and less trifle.

"Yes, until a few months ago. One hundred seventeen men, women, and children."

"Children?" Mary asked, her voice shocked.

She nodded, but she wouldn't tell them tales of life on the plantation. Those stories were not for such places as this lovely parlor and these innocent people.

"The family has never forgotten their heritage is Scottish," Rose said. "The males in the family all have Scottish names. Donald died when he was a child, but there was Bruce."

"What a pity for a mother to lose her son." Glynis looked at the far wall as if seeing something from the past. "The war is making widows of a great many women. Did my mother tell you that I lived in Washington for a time?"

Rose shook her head.

"I can remember when the war began. We thought it would only last a few weeks."

"I remember hearing the same," she said.

Bruce's friends had been the first to declare themselves victorious in the war against the Union. They'd shot their pistols into the air, gotten drunk on Glengarden's whiskey, and peed in the rose-bushes. She'd stayed in her room for days, praying they would take themselves off to war. Instead, they waited nearly a year, during which Bruce had special uniforms sewn and his own flag designed.

She often wondered if real war was as exciting as the pretend war he played with his friends. Was shooting at the enemy as exhilarating as scaring the slaves with their guns? Were their fancy uniforms still spotless?

"Are you enjoying your stay in Scotland?" William asked her.

Thank God he'd changed the topic. *Please, don't make me go back there, even in my thoughts.* This time in Glasgow was a purge, of sorts. She was cleansing her mind and maybe her soul. Anything but remembering those years, her helplessness, and her hatred.

Chapter 5

*D*uncan halted at the entrance to the dining room. Rose was already there, just as she was every morning for the last week. Just as he had every morning for the last week, he felt a surge of something curiously like excitement.

He wasn't behaving like himself and that fact both confused and amused him.

For a moment he debated whether he should skip breakfast. They'd managed, for the last week, to eat most of their meals together, but in the morning they were alone.

He was finding himself in the odd position of being fascinated with a woman. The more he learned about her, the more he wanted to know. He wanted to understand why she got that far-off gaze in her eyes from time to time. Was she recalling Glengarden? Did she yearn to return there? Or was it sadness for Bruce he saw?

"Do you like beets?" he asked as he entered the dining room.

She stopped in the act of extending the napkin across her lap and looked over at him.

"Is that what we're having for breakfast?" she asked.

He had the feeling that if he said yes, she would

have planted a perfectly acceptable expression on her face and forced herself to eat them.

The way she moved was as if each action was deliberate: the placement of a hand, the extension of a finger. She kept her elbows tucked into her sides as if afraid to take up too much space. Even her walk was set and defined. Her skirt never belled like Glynis's, revealing her ankles when she raced from place to place. Instead, Rose reminded him of a statue come to life, unfamiliar with the freedom once she was no longer bolted to her pedestal.

He was tempted to grab her hands and swing her in a circle, just to make her laugh or to set her free from her precision.

Her eyes were level and direct. She rarely looked away from the object of her conversation, as if she had once been told she'd be punished for inattention.

She fascinated him because she was a porcelain doll like the one Glynis had as a girl, the same one his mother had kept all these years. He'd always thought the doll a little bizarre, but Glynis had set him straight.

"It's because you don't love her, that's why. You just see that she's a doll. You don't see Betty."

He wondered if he were making the same mistake with Rose. Was he just seeing what Rose wanted everyone to see, and not the woman beneath?

"No beets, thank heavens," he said, sitting opposite her.

The rectangular table could be expanded with several leaves, but for normal occasions it sat four comfortably. Since his mother was absent, it meant she was either abed, which was a foreign occurrence, or off doing something nice for someone else, which was more likely.

Lily bustled in a second later with two laden plates, each piled high with Mabel's choice of breakfast. Between the blood pudding, sausages, toast, and eggs, it was enough to keep him full for most of the day.

Rose studied her plate.

"Then why did you ask me about beets?"

"I suppose it was a test, of sorts," he said. "They taste like dirt to me. I have tried, on numerous occasions, to acquire a taste for them. I've not been able to do so."

"Do you have more affinity to those who dislike beets, is that it? What if I asked the same thing about peas? Do you like peas?"

"Not particularly. Do you?"

She nodded, then surprised him with a smile, one so bright it took him aback.

"I don't like beets, though. Does that put me in your good graces?"

"I don't believe you've ever been out of my good graces, Rose," he said, smiling. "Disliking beets only solidifies your place there."

She stared down at the plate in front of her.

Rose was above average height, perhaps even taller than Glynis. Her stillness made her appear smaller. Yet this woman had crossed the ocean on her own in order to barter with him. And barter she had. She'd ticked off every single advantage to purchasing her cotton, even considering the very large drawback of him having to go and procure it.

She was a born tradesman, a comment he had made to her when they sat in the small parlor one night.

She'd startled him by smiling in delight.

"My father was a greengrocer," she said. "He was so successful he bought out all of his competitors. He always said that it was because most people expected an Irishman to only know about cabbages. He could pick up any vegetable or fruit and tell you how it would cure you. How ginger helped the stomach and celery the breath. I think people came to his stores not only because of the quality of his produce but to be entertained by his knowledge. He said you couldn't sell what you didn't know."

She'd taken a deep breath and exhaled it.

"He was a grand man and I've missed him every day he's been gone."

"I feel the same about my father," he had confessed. "I always ask myself what he would think of my decisions."

"I know exactly what my father would say," she said. "He wouldn't be happy with me, so I'm not for asking him."

"What have you done that he would have disapproved of?"

"Lied," she said, staring down at her gloved hands. A second later she'd transferred the look to him. "I've sworn at God, I'm afraid. I've been angry at Him, and my father would not be pleased."

The more she said, the more he wanted to know.

"You can't have been all that evil," he said.

Would she tell him what she'd lied about? The rage at God was easy to understand. She was a widow. Why wouldn't she have been angry at the Almighty for taking her beloved husband from her?

Except that Bruce wasn't her beloved husband, was he?

"Why didn't you like Bruce?" he asked now. "I'm assuming your feelings about him changed after your wedding. Was it slavery?"

She looked up at him. "Yes."

He remained silent, wondering if she would expand on her answer. Getting information from Rose was a patient project, but he was willing to give as much time as it took.

She looked away, toward the small breakfront, as if fascinated with the display of his great-grandmother's china.

"On my arrival at Glengarden, I was given a personal maid, a girl of thirteen. She, too, was a slave, as were all the servants. I asked Bruce to free her. He refused. Instead of a birthday present or a Christmas gift, all I wanted was Phibba's freedom. He always steadfastly refused."

She hesitated and he waited again.

"I soon found out that Phibba was pregnant. Being my maid was easier than sending her to work in the field. A few months later she died in childbirth."

"Were slaves allowed to marry that young?"

"Slaves weren't allowed to be married. Phibba was assaulted by someone before I arrived at Glengarden."

"Did you ever find out who assaulted her?"

She turned her head and regarded him steadily.

"No. Even my questions were treated with derision. Why was I so concerned? She was only a slave. She was replaceable. She wasn't important."

She stared down at the plate in front of her. "The only comment Bruce ever made about her was that it was a pity her child hadn't lived because the boy could have fetched a good price."

He stared at her. In her story was disgust, sadness, but also the same sort of horror he'd felt reading Bruce's letters.

He'd had the sense that Bruce MacIain was firmly fixed in his role as owner of Glengarden, whatever prestige that brought him. In one letter the man had listed the acreage he possessed along the Wando River, what a landmark his plantation was, and how many slaves he owned.

That one comment had made him hold the letter away as if the pages held a contagion.

Ever since he was old enough to understand how cotton was grown, he'd had a sense of disgust for the process. He disliked being complicit in the continuation of slavery, but the fact was, the mill needed cotton and there were few places to get it, the best being from the southern states.

Yet until Bruce had bragged of his ownership of other human beings, he'd never been ashamed. A relative of his, a MacIain, owned slaves.

He didn't say anything for a long while, merely began to eat a breakfast he no longer wanted.

"I'm surprised Mabel hasn't fed us oatmeal," she said, changing the subject, for which he was grateful. "She seems very fond of it."

"She always has been," he said. He leaned close to her. "I warn you, however, she also likes beets."

He was grateful for her sudden smile, even if it was forced.

"I understand you went to Hillshead yesterday. Did you like it?"

She nodded, then smiled again. "I think I got a little tipsy."

Amused, he said, "Did you do anything shocking?"

"I don't think so," she said, putting down her fork. She reached for her cup but didn't pick it up, her eyes direct on him.

She was wearing her gloves again, and it occurred to him that he'd never seen her without them.

"It's all right if you did," he said. "We're family and would forgive you."

He was watching her so closely that he caught the flicker in her eyes, the look toward the door of the dining room, as if she wished to run away.

"By marriage only," she said, bringing her attention back to him.

Her marriage to Bruce.

He should be showing her respect as the widow of a man who'd died in war, not watching for her smiles.

But for the life of him he couldn't pretend to have any regard for Bruce MacIain. Nor sadness for his death.

As their breakfast continued, they spoke of commonplace things, topics that would be perfectly acceptable should anyone overhear them. He wanted, however, to ask her about Bruce, to have her tell him about her marriage. Was that the reason she was so cautious in her mannerisms? Was that why she sometimes seemed so brittle and at others so vulnerable?

He applauded his mother's good works and admired her for her compassion toward others. Perhaps he felt that same emotion, but his was more narrowly directed toward the people who depended on him to make the MacIain Mill a success and keep them employed.

Yet at this very moment he wanted to do something he'd never felt compelled to do before: stand and embrace an almost stranger, place his hand against the back of her head and hold her still in the safety of his arms.

Somehow, he would find words to comfort her and ease her fears. Words he couldn't fathom at the moment but hoped would somehow find their way to his lips.

He would promise to keep her safe, to give her freedom, to reward her for every extemporaneous act. He wanted to see her race through the glen like Glynis had once done, skirts and petticoats flying. Or even climb a tree. Perhaps that was too much for such a dignified woman, but he'd like to hear her voice a wish to do something daring and untoward.

"Have you come close to a decision, Duncan?" she asked, her voice soft.

Her eyes, green and clear and direct, had the effect of silencing his mind for a moment.

"I really must return to Glengarden soon."

Don't go. Stay here instead of returning to South Carolina. Don't go back to a war. Don't go back to that place.

"Soon," he said. "Very soon."

He abruptly stood, realizing he was being rude, but felt compelled to leave her as quickly as he could. He said something about a meeting at the mill, grabbed his coat, hat, and greeted Charles as if his driver was the most welcome sight in the world. He hadn't thanked Mabel for breakfast or Lily, and the way he'd left Rose had been unlike him.

A sign, then, that he was well on his way to doing something idiotic, and all because of Rose MacIain.

Chapter 6

$\mathcal{T}$he garden attached to the MacIain house was a lovely place, small and secluded, set near the herb garden outside the kitchen door. Someone had planted roses in a rectangular pattern, and a bench sat in the middle near a cleverly designed bird-bath in the shape of a tulip. Rose loved flowers. At home in New York she'd kept an extensive garden. Flowers didn't make her bite her lips in frustration. When you toiled in a garden, you were rewarded by beauty and order.

A chilled breeze swept over the lawn, smelling slightly of the sea. The Clyde River wasn't far away, and from time to time she could hear bells toll. Had the sound originated from the ships moored along the docks, or from one of the many churches in Glasgow?

"There you are," Eleanor said, peeking over a hedge. "Has everyone deserted you?"

"I think it more like I've deserted everyone else. I saw this lovely place and just had to sit and read for a few moments."

Eleanor joined her on the bench.

"It's been my favorite place for years. The light is right and people aren't apt to find you. Except, of course, Glynis and Duncan, Mabel and Lily."

Being the recipient of Eleanor's smile, the woman's blue eyes twinkling at her, was like being bathed in the sun's warmth.

"It's been so lovely having you here. I think you're very brave. Like my Glynis, traveling across the ocean on your own. Her first husband was with the British Legation in America, you know."

"No," she said, "I didn't."

Eleanor nodded. "I didn't like him. A confession I made to myself on this very bench. You'll find that it's very receptive to confessions." Eleanor patted her hand. "But you wouldn't have many of those."

She wasn't nearly the paragon Eleanor MacIain thought her.

"Did you enjoy your visit to Hillshead?"

Rose nodded. "I did. Your daughter is a lovely person. I think she and Lennox are a wonderful couple."

Eleanor's laughter startled her.

"Glynis claimed him from the time she was a baby. Lennox was five years older, but I guess she decided he was hers. Even as a toddler her eyes lit up at the sight of him. It took some time, but they're finally married. Now all they have to do is provide me with a grandchild and I'll be eternally happy. And Duncan to marry as well, but he's had a burden on him for the last few years," Eleanor said, sighing. "The mill has been struggling and he feels such responsibility for it. Perhaps if he married, his wife would take his mind from his worries from time to time."

She really didn't want to talk about Duncan and his future wife.

"Well, I'll leave you to your reading," Eleanor

said, standing. "I've agreed to attend another guild meeting. I'm beginning to think we should stop with all the endless meetings and simply do more work."

"Thank you for everything," Rose said. "You've been so kind to someone who just appeared on your doorstep."

She didn't know how it would turn out between her and Duncan, but she knew that she'd always remember these days in Scotland and the generosity with which she was treated.

"Oh my dear," the older woman said, "it's been our pleasure. You were a delightful surprise and the very best gift we could ever receive."

She bent to kiss Rose on the forehead before leaving the garden.

Eleanor was the type of woman Rose wished she'd had as a mother. Or perhaps her mother had been as kind and loving. She'd died when Rose was born. Claire had been six and their three brothers seven, eight, and nine years old.

She wondered if Glynis knew how very fortunate she was. Eleanor believed that her daughter could do no wrong. She felt that way about her son as well, but mixed in with her affection for Duncan was a large dose of pride. You could see it shining through her eyes when she looked at him.

These MacIains were nothing like the people she'd left behind at Glengarden. They were generous and genuinely caring people. She couldn't imagine any of them acting like Bruce or Susanna.

The deception disturbed her. She'd been in Glasgow for a week now and in that time had been treated like a beloved member of the family.

She couldn't continue like this. Either she had to tell them the truth or leave, one of the two.

DUNCAN REMOVED his hat and coat, hanging them both in the foyer. He could hear Lily and Mabel in the kitchen chattering away, the sound of their laughter a background for life here in this house. They weren't servants as much as friends he paid. They each worked very hard, were beyond loyal, and had no qualms about telling him what to do at any time of the day or night.

Threading his hand through his hair, he surveyed himself in the mirror, then brushed off a few pieces of cotton fiber from his jacket.

"You need to get yourself a good girl as a wife, Duncan. It's time you thought less about the mill and more about yourself. Here, have another piece of tart, there's a good boy." That advice had come from Mabel.

"I've had a dream," Lily told him not too long ago. "I saw a girl with bright blond hair and blue eyes, and you'll see her on the street and make Charles stop right there to say hello to her." Lily was forever having dreams about his romantic encounters, but he doubted he'd ever ask his driver to pull over so he might accost a stranger.

What did Rose see, looking at him? According to Glynis, he was getting a bit long in the tooth. Settled in his ways, she'd said more than once. He'd found a gray hair at his temple the other day and plucked it out. Thankfully, it hadn't been followed by a dozen or more of its brethren. Otherwise, his hair was brown and thick. His eyes were blue, not a remarkable shade or as striking as his sister's.

Perhaps he was just average. Neither ugly nor with the looks to make a woman swoon. Did they do that when thinking about men? He wasn't about to ask any of the females in his life. They'd laugh their heads off.

He was only in his thirties, which didn't make him a doddering old fool. Granted, perhaps his interests had narrowed in the past years to making the mill prosperous again. Even when he couldn't sleep his mind had been on the mill. In the wee hours of the morning he'd taken to designing a new loom he'd like to build.

He was hardly as interesting a figure as a dozen other men he could name.

What could he offer a wife? He wasn't wealthy like his brother-in-law and best friend, Lennox. He didn't have a fortune tucked away to use when things got difficult financially. He'd always worked and if he ever brought home a wife it would be to share in that uncertainty.

Why the hell was he thinking of marriage now?

He had a decision to make and he'd considered it long and carefully.

A few short months ago he'd had himself convinced to run the blockade, acquire a hold of cotton in the *Raven* and sail back to Scotland a hero of sorts. Then the dearth of cotton made such a venture foolish. He'd talked himself out of it in favor of restructuring the mill itself.

He had ideas about scaling back production, using Indian cotton to produce not high quality cloth as they'd always done but particular pieces, items that were specifically ordered. It would mean changing their business model from a volume producer to one that was deliberately targeted to certain applications. He could see MacIain Mills producing patterned cotton to be used in a variety of industries.

He'd have to invest in several new pieces of equipment that he didn't have now, but he had the money if he spent it wisely and didn't go off on an adventure he'd once considered the only way to save the mill.

Yet in the past two days that's all he'd thought about, pushing his ideas about reorganizing the mill to the back of his mind, accepting Rose's challenge, whether she knew it to be one or not. She'd dared him with her proposition.

The parlor was empty, which meant she was in the garden.

He found himself outside before he consciously thought of seeking her out. Or perhaps that was a lie he told himself, one of many when it came to Rose.

He was too interested in her. A warning bell sounded deep inside his mind.

She sat on the bench, the last of the sunlight filtering through the newly born leaves of the oak above her. Everything around her was green, lush, a promise of spring, but in her mourning she was a warning that even in the midst of life, there was death. Her hair was uncovered, a bright flame against the black of her dress. A contradiction, but Rose MacIain was a study in contradictions.

She was both young and worldly, possessing an aura of maidenly reserve yet was a widow. She espoused the abolitionist cause, but married a man who proudly owned slaves.

Rose MacIain was spirited and courageous, daunting, and the most beautiful creature he'd ever seen. She was also his American cousin's widow, a point he'd do well to remember.

He stood there waiting for her to acknowledge him, not making a sound or announcing himself. Her head was bent, her eyes intent on the page of the book she held in both hands.

What was she reading? What words kept her so intent on their meaning that she was lost to the world, to him?

The leaves above her, kissed by the breeze, were more mobile than she. Her hands didn't move to turn the page. Her eyes didn't look up to see who had disturbed her solitude.

For a moment he wondered if she was ignoring him on purpose. Should he simply turn and walk away? Should he apologize for intruding on her? Would she understand that, despite himself, he was almost compelled to see her?

She'd been in his home for a week, and in that time she'd altered his life. He was coming home sooner from the mill and leaving later in the morning. He found himself returning for his noon meal every day. He spent more time in the small parlor where he knew she and his mother took tea and discussed books, New York, and embroidery, of all things.

What the hell did he know about embroidery? Even less than he wanted to learn.

Now she sat only ten feet away from him with a breeze blowing the scent of newly birthed flowers around her, encapsulating her and confusing the hell out of him.

He had never once been tongue-tied. Never been devoid of words, especially in his own garden, yet here he was, wanting to stretch out his hand, take those few steps between them and touch her in some manner. Perhaps on the shoulder. Or her hand, always gloved, always shielded from prying eyes.

That was another mystery.

Rose, a contradiction and a delight, someone who reduced him to boyhood.

He should banish her as quickly as possible, before she made him stand before her and babble about the weather, the smell of the Clyde, and anything else that floated through his fevered brain.

No, one woman could not do this to him, yet she did, sitting there so silently.

When she looked up, tears swimming in her green eyes, he almost surrendered there and then. He wouldn't have been surprised to find himself falling to his knees before her.

Take pity on me, he might have said, had his brain being able to form the words. *Leave this place. Leave Glasgow. Go somewhere safe, where I'll know you're protected, but don't do this to me.*

He never said those words, of course.

Instead, he went to the bench, sat beside her and said, "Rose, what's wrong?"

She smiled a watery smile that had the effect of a spear straight into his heart.

"The words. They're so very beautiful. And heartfelt, don't you think?"

She held out the volume of Robert Burns to him.

He would call Burns a great many things: bawdy, filled with life, amusing, but he wouldn't have called his poetry beautiful.

"I'll buy your cotton, Rose." He heard himself saying the words before he consciously thought them.

Her eyes widened.

"I didn't think you would," she said. "I thought my coming here was a terrible mistake."

He stretched his hand across the book and she put hers atop it.

They weren't being entirely proper at the moment. Nor, as he looked into her eyes, was he sure he ever would be again. She touched something inside him, some wish, perhaps, to be a hero or some need to be a protector. Something even greater than wanting to keep the mill alive. The mill was a creation, an enterprise, an entity, and Rose was so much more.

Was he being a fool for deciding to sail to America? He was taking a chance, that was certain. He was taking a gamble.

A long time ago his ancestors had left the Highlands after the '45, looking for a way to make a name for themselves, seeking their own fortune away from a section of Scotland that was being punished and put to the yoke. Had they hesitated as well or simply shrugged aside their misgivings and gone on with their adventure?

Who was he to do less?

He had the feeling that his bargain with his American cousin would benefit her more than him. Still, it wasn't a decision he would reverse.

Like it or not, he was off to America.

ROSE MADE her way back to the lovely guest room she'd been given, grateful that she didn't see any of the MacIains or Mabel and Lily. She needed to be alone right now, to rinse off her conscience.

She'd done what she came to Scotland to do. She'd made arrangements to sell Glengarden's cotton to

Duncan MacIain. It was a very fair bargain. Anyone would agree, yet in doing so, she'd manipulated and outright lied.

Everything she'd said about Glengarden cotton had been true. It was the finest in South Carolina, perhaps in the entire South. Their factor had always been able to command the best price.

Everything else was a lie, though.

She was not the widow MacIain. Nor did she represent Bruce, away at war.

How much more glorious to fight for the Cause than to make provisions to protect the people at home. A wife who was slavishly devoted to him, a mother who could hear nothing bad ever said about him, a daughter who was being shown her father's daguerrotype each day in the hopes that she would recall the man who Maisie told her hadn't even bothered to be home for her birth and, when he first saw her, made no pretense of being pleased that his first child was a girl.

Bruce had evidently thought everything would remain the same while he was away at war.

Duncan MacIain's terms had been fair. He'd been honorable in their talks. He'd done nothing to indicate he was willing to take advantage of the situation.

A weight had dropped from her heart, leaving her feeling almost buoyant. Her gamble had paid off. She had saved them, at least until the war ended. Perhaps, by that time, Bruce would have returned. Or news would reach them that he would never be coming back.

Before she'd left Glengarden, Claire had accused her of wishing for the latter. She'd been so surprised, she wasn't able to respond. She hadn't known what to say because, God forgive her, it was true.

Life at Glengarden would be almost bearable without Bruce's tyrannies and cruelty.

She'd liked Bruce when he was her brother's friend at the Military Academy. When he'd been their guest in New York, he impressed her father and was friendly to her. At his marriage to Claire, her only sister, she'd felt the first tinges of unease, but had only grown to know the real Bruce MacIain while living in South Carolina.

At Glengarden, Bruce was the scion of the MacIains, feted and praised from the day of his birth, never corrected, never criticized, never given boundaries. In a way, he was Caesar. He could, and did, order the whipping of a slave for an imposed infraction without seeming to give a care. He sold off young children, ignoring the silent tears of their parents.

She was certain that some of the children born in the slave cabins were his, but she'd not once voiced her suspicions to anyone.

Thankfully, Bruce finally marched off to war, aglow in Claire's worship, telling anyone who would listen that he and his regiment of friends were certain to bring those Yankees under control within a fortnight. He'd never made mention of the fact that his once best friend would probably meet him across the field of battle. Or that his wife was from New York. Claire was somehow absolved, but Rose's identical heritage was suspect. She was one of those Yankees Bruce now hated.

She'd watched him ride down the road beneath the tall oaks with his friends and prayed he'd never return. Yet here she was, pretending to be Bruce's widow. Of all the uncomfortable, hideous masquerades to perform.

Had she let the MacIains think Bruce dead because that's what she wished? How horrible was she? Even a tyrant no doubt had good qualities. She'd spent time looking for Bruce's. Perhaps, in the privacy of their marital chamber, he was gentle with Claire. He modulated his words and never spoke with sarcasm.

Perhaps, in the dark of night, he crept into his daughter's room, stood over her cradle and spoke to her in tender tones that revealed his joy at her presence. Maybe he sat beside her as she slept and told her about the history of Glengarden, how she would be its princess one day.

No, Bruce would rather be present at the whipping of a slave, or raping one.

Now she closed the door and leaned against it, saying a series of prayers: thanks that Duncan had agreed to buy their cotton. Secondly, that she'd be forgiven for the lie she was living, and third, that God would understand her unremitting hatred of Bruce MacIain.

Chapter 7

"*I* knew it. I knew it. I told Lennox this morning that I had a feeling you were going to do this thing."

"How did you find out?" Duncan asked. A moment later he shook his head. "Do Mabel and Lily listen at keyholes?"

"Rose told me. She's overjoyed, but you and I both know this is foolhardy," Glynis said. "This is probably the most foolhardy thing you've ever done, Duncan."

Standing, he went to the window overlooking the mill. Once, each of those buildings had been filled with people industriously working. Now only a few of the looms were operating while the others sat idle, waiting for cotton.

He'd taken a loan from Lennox and it had gotten them through the last months, but he wasn't about to allow his brother-in-law and friend to continue to give him charity.

What would his father have done in a similar situation? He didn't know, despite the fact he'd asked himself that question daily for the past two years. What he did know was that his father wasn't the type of man to simply pretend the situation would resolve itself. He would have gone out and done what he needed to do to care for his family and those in his keeping.

"We can keep the mill going with Indian cotton, Glynis, but not like it has been. The price is too dear and there's not enough of it."

"Then send someone else to America."

He glanced back at his sister. "If Rose can run the blockade, I certainly can. Besides, I'm not going to send someone else into danger, Glynis, just because you're afraid for me."

She sighed. "I like her, truly I do, Duncan, but I wish Rose had never come."

The comment surprised him. Glynis was exceedingly kind, especially to someone in an unfamiliar situation. She'd been in similar circumstances when married to her first husband, a career diplomat.

"You'd changed your mind before she came. You weren't going to continue with this foolhardy plan. It's her red hair."

"I beg your pardon?"

"Red hair," she said, waving one hand in the air. "Men love red hair, for some reason. They do idiotic things for women with red hair."

"I haven't," he said.

"Then it's her green eyes. You have to admit they're striking."

"Yes, they are."

"See?" she said. "I knew it was because she's beautiful."

He took a deep breath and exhaled it.

"It's not because of Rose, Glynis," he said, coming back and sitting on the chair beside her. "It's not even for me. I could do with Indian cotton. We'd have to change direction, perhaps eliminate even more jobs, but it would keep the mill alive. This might be a last resort, but I can't afford to ignore it."

"How long would a few hundred bales of cotton last?"

"Not just a few hundred, Rose. Nearly a thousand."

She frowned at him. "You are going to do it, aren't you? You've always been stubborn."

"I'm not the stubborn MacIain. You are."

She shook her head. "Maybe once, but I'm a Cameron now, and you've taken up the trait."

"I don't know what you'd call it, Glynis. Stubbornness, pride, determination. But it's not just my life. It's the hundreds of people we still employ."

He grabbed her hand. When they were children they had a game of trying to grab each other's thumbs, but now she let her hand rest in his.

"How am I to tell a mother that she won't have the money to feed her children? Or that she can't pay her rent? What's a little danger compared to that?"

What's a little danger compared to that?

The words circled in his mind, a caution floating on bat wings. He could leave Scotland and go to his death. He'd never see any of them again. They'd be ghosts in his mind until he, too, became nothing more than a specter.

"Are you sure you're not doing this just because you want to look like a hero in her eyes?"

He dropped her hand, surprised.

"Of course not."

"Are you sure? I've seen the way you look at her. As if you've never seen a woman with red hair before. You need to take another trip to Edinburgh, I think."

What the hell did she know about his trips to Edinburgh?

He felt the back of his neck warm. He was not about to discuss Edinburgh with his sister.

"I appreciate your concern," he said, nearly desperate to change the subject. "But I've decided."

She sighed, then pressed her hand against her waist. "Then you'd better do everything in your power to keep yourself safe, Duncan. I want my child to know his uncle."

Startled, he stared at her.

"Yes," she said. "I'm going to have a baby, and I hadn't intended to tell anyone other than Lennox just yet. But it's a bribe to make you come home, safe and sound."

"I can promise you that," he said. "If you'll keep yourself the same."

She nodded, tears filling her eyes.

He knew better than to say something foolish, such as her condition was making her irrational, so all he did was hug her and remain silent.

Glengarden Plantation
South Carolina

MAISIE SAT at the rocking chair on the edge of Glengarden's veranda, catching the best of the afternoon light. Her eyes weren't what they had once been. The brighter the day, the easier it was to thread a needle.

She was almost finished hemming a dress for Miss Susanna. Age had done taken its toll with her mistress just as it did with everyone. Miss Susanna still liked to think of herself as young, even though decades had passed since that word could be rightfully used.

As Maisie aged, she'd begun to think of getting older like the Holy Trinity. Not the Father, Son, and the Holy Ghost, but Time, Age, and Death.

Age brought with it the need to shorten dresses, let out waists, dispense with such fripperies as extra wide hoops and shoes with heels. Instead, Miss Susanna had added a walking stick to her wardrobe, pretending that she didn't need it. When she walked through her room and held onto the backs of chairs, she tilted her chin up in a way that dared anyone to forget she'd once been a young beauty. That was a lifetime ago, but Miss Susanna would likely always be vain, even up to the day she died.

It would be a race to see which one of them would make it to see St. Peter first.

When she was a younger woman, she might have asked Miss Susanna if she believed there was a heaven for white folk and one for slaves. She suspected that Miss Susanna would have brightly replied, "Why, yes, of course, Maisie. How silly of you to ask."

So when the time came—and she had a feeling it was coming faster than she wanted it to—she was supposed to believe that she would be transported by angels to a separate place, one where the manacles she always imagined she wore would be released by a golden key.

Now she knew there was only one heaven and one hell for slave and white man alike. She wasn't all too sure she was going to meet most of the MacIains at St. Peter's desk, but she was certain she was going to hear the screams of some of them from below.

The air was quiet. One or two tree frogs were announcing that they were going to be loud tonight.

If the temperature was cool enough, she'd shut the window against the sound. They always seemed so happy in their noise, as if they were talking with each other about the party they were having. Or planning another get-together soon enough.

If her Phibba had been around, they would have laughed about the idea of tree frogs talking to each other. Her Phibba was one of those who could see whimsy in the everyday world. When she was a little girl, Phibba had once knelt on the paving stones leading to the gravel drive, watching as a line of ants crossed and asked, "Where do you think they're going, Mama?"

"I don't know, child, now get up before you get yourself all messed. It's Sunday and the Lord will not be pleased if you're all dirty."

"Why not, Mama? It's the Lord's dirt."

She smiled now at the memory, and for a second, just a blessed second, the pain was blunted a little. Like having a toothache took your mind off a broken arm.

Losing Phibba wasn't as simple as a broken arm. The loss of her daughter was like having every single one of your bones broken slowly. Then, when the first one healed, it was rebroken so the pain and the memory of the pain never left you.

She'd never known how deeply she could hate until Phibba died. She'd never known how strong she was, either, with the ability to push that hate so far down that no one could ever see a hint of it.

"Yes, sir, Master Bruce."

"No, sir, Master Bruce."

"Whatever you want, Master Bruce."

He'd killed her Phibba as certain as he'd taken one

of his guns to her head and shot her. But his weapon of choice had been lust. He'd used her daughter before she was a woman, when she was just a child. When God, the white man's God, had laughed and gotten her with child, Bruce only smiled and said that if the child was a boy he'd just made himself some money.

It had been a boy. A perfect little boy whose birth bred a little more strength to push the hate down a little deeper. Neither he nor Phibba had lived, no matter what they'd done to try to save her.

No one ever spoke of Phibba, of how she was still a child when she died. Her death was like the rest of Glengarden. Nothing bad showed on the surface. None of the slave cabins were visible from the lane up to the house. Nor was the whipping post visible. Everything was beautiful and perfect and terribly, terribly false.

That's why she always sat on the veranda in the afternoon, a place she was most definitely not allowed. But Bruce was away at war and the MacIain women rested and didn't notice. She stored away that small victory to gloat over when the tree frogs partied and the doves cooed.

Glasgow, Scotland

"WHAT DO you mean, you hadn't planned on me accompanying you?" Rose stared at him as if he'd suddenly turned green. "Surely there's room for me on the *Raven*."

"It's not a passenger vessel, Rose," Duncan said, the reasonableness of his tone irritating her.

"Do you know of any other ships leaving Glasgow in the next week headed for America? Or to the Bahamas?"

His silence was an answer.

She was so annoyed at him that she could barely speak. By refusing to take her, he was relegating her to another train ride back to London. Heaven knew how many days she would have to wait to find a ship going to America. Not to mention the expense of the voyage.

She folded her arms in front of her and stared at him.

"I have to return home as quickly as possible," she said, giving him the truth. When she left, they were down to their last resources. "Please," she added.

He walked closer, stretching out his hand to touch her arm.

"There's no room, Rose. There's only the captain's cabin and I've appropriated that. The captain is bunking with his first mate."

"I'll take up a corner. A pallet. A cot. You'll never know I'm there."

"Would you have me ruin your reputation for the sake of expediency?"

She truly wished she hadn't thought him attractive or fascinating, or easy to talk to. He was determined to protect her, and in doing so, was making the situation so much worse.

Very well, she'd tell him the truth.

"Your gold is going to save them," she said. "All the people at Glengarden. There's no food and no funds to buy it. What the blazes does my reputation matter when people are starving?"

He studied her for a long moment. Did he want her to go into the details?

Bruce had donated all of their horses to the Confederacy and converted most of Glengarden's assets into Confederate currency. They had plenty of greybacks, but they were now only worth pennies on the dollar.

Susanna had been used to reigning over a prosperous household but didn't know how to practice economies. Claire, even when Bruce was away at war, was so burdened by thoughts of her husband's opinion and desires that she couldn't do anything. Rose was left to keep the household running, to salvage what was left of their resources, slaughter their remaining livestock and keep them all fed.

"By the time I return I'll have been gone a month. I have to get back."

"Running the blockade into Charleston is harder than the outbound voyage, Rose. You said that yourself."

She nodded. She knew that.

"You'll be in danger. How can I put you in harm's way?"

She threw her hands up in the air.

"I have to get back to Glengarden, Duncan. Don't you understand? They're depending on me."

None of them had been equipped to handle the sudden deprivations in their lives, though Maisie knew where to look for mushrooms, which to leave behind and which to harvest. She gathered up wild onions by the basketful, set nets for fish. Without her skills, they would have starved.

As it was, Rose had barely been able to tolerate another serving of fish.

They had no more livestock. They'd gone through all the flour and sugar, the kitchen gardens hadn't been tended and nothing was growing there. There were no vegetables to be had and no one would give them credit for seeds because the merchants in Charleston had to live, too.

No one had thought to lay up seeds for hard times. There'd never been hard times at Glengarden, and the idea of it had never occurred to Bruce.

She'd taken the last of her inheritance to make the voyage to Nassau and on to Scotland, reasoning that the food it could have bought would only last a few weeks, and if she were successful in Scotland, she would be able to provide for them for months, if not years.

"Do you have any doubt that I'll get home in my own way if you refuse to take me?" she asked Duncan now. "I'll buy passage on any ship. All you'll be doing by refusing to take me is delay me from reaching Glengarden and force me to spend money I can't afford to waste."

He didn't say anything, just turned and walked back to the chair he'd occupied.

"Please," she said. "If you won't take me to Charleston, then take me to Nassau. At least as far as there."

"I can't leave you in Nassau to fend for yourself."

"I won't be alone," she said, forcing a smile to her face. "I have friends there. I will stay with them until I obtain passage to Charleston. Of course, you could make it easier for me and take me all the way."

He regarded her for a moment.

"To Nassau, then. And only there."

She nodded. She'd have the duration of the voyage to convince him to take her to Glengarden.

It was enough for the moment.

Perhaps she should emulate her sister in her adoption of a southern woman's charm, bat her eyelashes at Duncan MacIain and make herself so fascinating that he wouldn't think of abandoning her in Nassau.

She smiled at the thought of attempting such a feat.

"What's so amusing?"

"I was just thinking that I needed to be more like my sister," she said, knowing that the remark wasn't going to explain her sudden humor. She would never be, could never be, like Claire.

But she was going to do everything she could to charm Duncan MacIain.

Chapter 8

$\mathcal{D}$uncan sat back in his seat, took a sip of wine and considered the group around him.

Glynis, his irrepressible sister, sat with Lennox at her side, probably in defiance of proper dinner table seating. No one cared.

His mother sat beside him, occasionally placing her hand on his arm. He glanced over at her and smiled. She was doing that a lot lately, as if to reassure herself that he was still there. Eleanor had surprised him, however, in not cautioning him about his adventure. Perhaps she recognized that it was the only chance to bring the mill back to its former success.

Tomorrow he'd be sailing away from Scotland and toward war. Ever since blurting out his agreement to Rose, he'd been recalling a conversation with his English cousin.

Dalton, the Earl of Rathsmere, had gone to America to fight, an idiotic decision he readily admitted.

"There isn't one waking hour that you're free of danger," Dalton had said. "There's not one moment you feel safe."

Yet his own ancestors have done the same, coming down from the Highlands, making something of themselves. Strong men, they'd each gone on to found a dynasty, representatives of which had thrived.

It was his turn now to face a challenge.

This felt like a MacIain family venture. They would be sailing on the *Raven*. His English cousin had purchased the ship, a blockade runner Lennox had built. His American cousin had sold him a warehouse filled with cotton. It wouldn't solve all his raw material problems, but it would certainly go a long way toward keeping the mill solvent.

All he had to do was finish the voyage.

They had a fine captain in Captain McDougal. The man had once been employed by Fraser Trenholm, the same company that originally purchased the *Raven*. Captain McDougal had made ten successful blockade runs to Charleston and back, which was good enough recommendation in Duncan's eyes.

He'd felt a little guilty about pushing the captain out of his quarters, but now that Rose was accompanying him, he didn't know what else to do.

"I didn't expect to be there all that often, sir," McDougal said. "Besides, you represent the owner of the *Raven*, and it's fitting you should be in the stateroom."

Thankfully, the captain's quarters consisted of two rooms, a parlor and a stateroom. He planned on giving the larger cabin to Rose while he had a cot moved to the parlor.

Their crew of twenty-two consisted of the captain, the mate, the pilot, two engineers, eight seamen, seven firemen, a cook, and a steward. All the men were either Scotsmen or had some experience with running the American blockade.

A burst of laughter made him realize that he

hadn't been following the conversation. If his concentration was on all the details still left to be done before he set sail, that was to be expected. But this might be the last time he was around the people most important to him.

Was this voyage ill-fated? Was he being a fool? No doubt a great many people would answer in the affirmative.

He caught Lennox's frown and shook his head slightly, a mute repudiation of his friend's concern. Perhaps his somber mood was due to nerves. Or maybe he felt anticipation for the journey. Sooner started, sooner over. Only hours to go now.

Rose glanced at him and for a moment their gazes clung and held. Was Glynis right? Was he fascinated with this red-haired woman? Was this why he'd decided to take her to Nassau?

She was a relative by marriage only, but the bonds of family were still there. She deserved his respect and his concern. He'd care for her as assiduously as if she were his sister.

Hardly his sister, though, was she? But she was a widow. He needed to remember that. Despite the fact she'd traveled all this way, she was no doubt fragile emotionally. Did she still love Bruce?

It wasn't just Bruce's bragging about the number of slaves he owned that Duncan disliked. The tone of Bruce's letters had been autocratic, as if he'd deigned to answer Duncan's letters only because he was otherwise bored. He'd grown tired of Bruce's pontificating about the southern cause and he'd taken umbrage to the man's way of demeaning anything that wasn't rooted in South Carolinian culture and Confederate ideals.

The American Civil War had decimated the textile industry in Scotland and nearly brought the MacIain Mill to the edge of bankruptcy. Causes meant less than the lives of the hundreds of people dependent on him.

I didn't like Bruce very much, either.

He hadn't been able to get Rose's story of her maid out of his mind. What had the rest of her marriage been like? Were there other instances of Bruce's cruelty? Did she genuinely grieve for the man or was she relieved that he was dead?

He glanced over at his sister. He wished she'd tell everyone the news so the rest of the dinner could be a congratulatory one. Glynis with a child. Whether it was a boy or girl, he knew the child would take after Glynis. He or she would be a handful, a hellion with a mind of his or her own.

Lennox would be the happiest man alive.

Duncan wasn't beset with envy often, but he found himself feeling that emotion now. Glynis and Lennox were happy, and even though their happiness had been paid for with pain and loneliness, he suspected they would have many more years of joy than the ones they'd spent alone.

What about him? Perhaps, one day, he might have a significant announcement of his own. A marriage, a birth, some life change that now seemed to elude him.

"I expect you to keep my brother in line, Rose," Glynis said, looking at him with a smile.

He couldn't let that comment slip by without an answer.

"That's a little ironic coming from you. You're the one who used to scandalize Glasgow. Lennox and I did what we could to protect your reputation."

"Oh pish, you were just as bad. Kissing Margaret Sullivan after church."

"That was a dare," he said, sending Lennox a look. His friend had evidently told Glynis about that day. He'd thought himself in love and Lennox had dared him to kiss her.

"When was that?" Eleanor asked.

Glynis really did need to share her news.

"Or when you put a frog in Mr. Trumbull's carriage."

"Duncan, you didn't!" His mother glared at him.

He was on the verge of leaving Scotland, and all his sister could do was bring up instances of his misdeeds? He shook his head.

"For the sake of our mother," he said to her, "I will not recount everything you did in your childhood."

"He's known to tell gigantic falsehoods as well, Rose. Be prepared for outlandish tales."

"I'll keep that in mind," Rose said, smiling.

He glanced over at Lennox. His childhood friend had acquired a habit of smiling a great deal lately, ever since marrying Glynis, as a matter of fact. If they'd been alone, he would have congratulated him on the upcoming birth of his child. He noticed, however, that Lennox wasn't doing anything to curb Glynis's enthusiasm for maligning him.

"And he's famously penurious. He isn't charging you for the voyage, is he?"

He stared at his sister.

Rose's smile grew. "No, he isn't. Of course, I don't know what my chores are to be on the voyage. Do you think he'll make me do the washing?"

"At the very least," Glynis said. "Or his darning. He's notoriously tough on socks."

"Glynis." He was not about to talk about his socks with Glynis. Next, she'd bring up his visits to Edinburgh.

At least her conversation had lightened the mood. Nobody was talking about the dangers, and for that he was grateful, even if he was her target.

"WHY ARE you smiling?" Duncan asked, joining her in the parlor after dinner.

"Because your conversation with Glynis reminds me of me and my brothers. Especially after Claire left home. We were forever haranguing each other."

He came and sat beside her, studying her in that way he had. So much went on behind his eyes, thoughts he never revealed. She wanted to know what he was thinking when he looked like that.

"Sisters can be a burden," he said, "but not more so than brothers, I suppose. Which one teased you the most? Jeremy? Robert? Or Montgomery?"

She looked away, staring at the fire lit against the chill of the spring night. She'd told him about her brothers and he hadn't forgotten. Not even their names, which was more than Bruce had ever remembered.

"Each of them at different times," she said. "Strange, how they could make me so mad. I'd give anything to have that time back again. Instead of being irritated, I'd just hug them."

He reached out and grabbed her gloved hand.

He seemed to know how she felt, how grief would come upon her at odd times. There were moments when the yawning emptiness almost overwhelmed her. Her heart should have been filled with memories of their years together, but they'd been shortened by war.

She turned her hand in his and their fingers linked. He gently squeezed as if to let her know he understood the depth of her loss.

He was nothing like Bruce or any of his friends. He didn't boast. He didn't act in a grandiose manner. He didn't brag of his achievements or his horses. He treated everyone within his keeping with kindness. His affection for his servants was as obvious as his love for his mother and sister.

She liked him. Moreover, she was growing to respect him. He kept his word. When he said he would do something, he did it. There was nothing hidden in his character, nothing about him that was unsavory. He was honest and decent.

More than she could say for herself right now.

"Why do you always wear gloves?" he asked, studying the black kid leather. "Was it a fire?"

"No."

She pulled her hand back and stood.

"Must you go?" he asked, standing as well.

"Yes." Oh, yes, before she was tempted to tell him all her secrets. Before the masquerade ended.

She wanted to be honest with him. She wanted to tell him that she wasn't a MacIain. She wasn't a widow. She hadn't been a wife.

Until now she'd never wanted to kiss a man. Oh, there were handsome men in New York, those who worked with the abolitionist movement. Some of Bruce's friends were good-looking as well, except they all thought they were and made no pretense of modesty.

But Duncan MacIain made her think of slumberous looks and long mornings abed. Of kisses in dark hallways and a hand reaching out to stroke her arm in passing. A quick look, a playful smile, and promise in the word "Later," accompanied by a gentle laugh.

Regret lodged in her chest like a brick. The time wasn't right. The circumstances were against her.

"I'm very tired."

He shocked her by reaching out and touching her cheek with two fingers. No more intrusive than that tender touch. As if he measured the heat of her blush. She felt like her cheeks were aflame, warmth surging up from her toes.

Finally, he removed his hand, dropping it to his side.

His jacket was open, revealing the snowy shirt beneath. She wanted to touch him, and she'd never before wanted to do anything of the sort. But now she wanted to place her hand flat against his chest and feel his heart beat against her palm.

"Are you leaving because I asked about your hands?"

She was staring straight at his throat, at the pulse beating there. She couldn't look at his face, she just couldn't, not with heat flaring on her cheeks and shocking thoughts coming one after the other.

"No." Yes. Perhaps.

How was she to bear a voyage to Nassau with him? The days had been interminable on the *Intrepid*. What would they be like on the *Raven*?

Maybe she should tell him now that it would be better if she took passage on another vessel, but that would only delay her arrival in Charleston. From what she'd heard of Lennox's ship, it was one of the fastest blockade runners built.

No, she would just have to guard herself, mind her emotions, and keep her thoughts under control.

Chapter 9

"*D*ear heavens, is that the *Raven*?" Rose asked, approaching the gangplank.

They'd said good-bye to everyone the night before; this dawn boarding would be a discreet one. There were still Union operatives in Glasgow, each of whom would be overjoyed to telegraph the news that the *Raven* had finally set sail.

The ship had been brought up from the Cameron and Company shipyards, where she'd been berthed for the past year. Stretched along the bank of the Clyde, she was an impressive sight to behold.

The *Raven* was a side paddle wheeler with twin smokestacks painted gray, her hull the same color, with a black line indicating where the iron cladding began.

"According to Lennox," Duncan said, "she's three hundred feet long and has an eleven foot draft, in addition to five watertight compartments and four boilers. He swears that, even fully loaded, she can outrun anything sailing today."

"I didn't think she'd be so large."

"She can carry all the cotton you have in Charleston, Rose, and still fly past any Union ships."

"She's absolutely beautiful."

He glanced down at her. "Lennox builds beautiful ships."

He didn't tell her that the *Raven* was thought to be

cursed. Her original captain, Gavin Whittaker, had been murdered on the top deck. A few weeks later a fire had destroyed the wheelhouse and part of the captain's quarters. Both had to be rebuilt. An additional circumstance that fueled rumors of a curse was the fact that the *Raven* had been sold to the Confederacy. After the damage to the ship, Lennox bought it back in order to make the repairs. When they were completed, representatives for the Confederacy sent word that they were no longer interested in owning the ship.

She was, according to shipbuilders—a group of men as superstitious as sailors—a ghost ship.

When his English cousin purchased the ship a few months ago, the talk didn't stop, because the *Raven* had never gone to sea. This would be her maiden voyage, and a long one, across the Atlantic Ocean and back again.

If anyone else had built the *Raven*, he would have worried about her seaworthiness, but he knew Lennox. He knew the care with which his friend built his ships. He also knew that Lennox had made a point of taking the *Raven* down the Clyde once a month, not only to test her out but to try to put a stop to the rumors about the ship being cursed.

This voyage was being financed by Dalton MacIain, the English MacIain. In addition to purchasing the *Raven* from Lennox, Dalton had paid the captain and crew and given Duncan credit to buy the cotton he needed. Adding his own contribution meant Duncan could also fill the hold of the *Raven* for the inbound voyage. Even after paying the price Rose had demanded, and paying Dalton back plus a percentage, the profit would be substantial.

A good business arrangement for everyone all around, with the added benefit that the *Raven* would lose her reputation as a ghost ship.

Once on board, he introduced Rose to Captain McDougal before taking her to the two rooms of the captain's cabin.

In the parlor, two bolted bookcases with rails sat against a far wall. The bookcases were filled, and he couldn't help but wonder who had taken the time to do so. He bet it was Glynis and some of the books had been selected for Rose's tastes.

A settee and table faced an iron brazier that looked capable of warming the entire space.

He opened the door and stepped aside for Rose to precede him into the stateroom. A large square bed was bolted to one wall. The second wall was taken up by a porthole and two bureaus, no doubt fastened to the wall as well.

She peeked behind a screen painted to resemble branches with flowers on them to find a tall wooden chest with brass hinges.

"What is this?"

He smiled when he saw it, unfastened it from the wall and lowered it.

Once it was nearly to the floor, it was obvious what it was.

"A bathtub! How wonderful."

"One of Lennox's additions," he said.

She smiled when she saw the twin wardrobes.

"Did you arrange for two of them?" she asked. "One for your clothes and one for mine?"

"Actually, I didn't," he said.

"A good thing." She picked up the valise sitting beside one of the wardrobes. "That's all I have." She looked around the room, at the door with a porthole overlooking the deck and a porthole on the opposite wall with a view of the ocean. "It's twice as big as the cabin I had on the voyage to London."

"If you'd like to come into the parlor anytime, please feel free."

She nodded.

He'd had a cot brought in and placed behind the settee in the parlor. It wasn't going to be as comfortable as his bed at home, but it would do.

"You should be comfortable here," he said. "Are you a good sailor?"

She turned to smile at him, her smile as radiant as the morning sun. She'd fixed her hair so it was in a bun, but a few tendrils had come loose and were framing her face.

"To my surprise, I am. The voyage from Charleston to Nassau was difficult only because I was so nervous. From the Bahamas to London, the ocean was placid, the surface resembled glass."

"You're a more experienced sailor than I. You've traveled across the Atlantic. The most I've done is accompany Lennox on sea trials and in his dinghy."

"I've never thought to travel on such a beautiful ship, though. Or one so large," she added, looking around her.

"The better to carry your cargo," he said.

"I suspect your hold is already full."

It was, but he didn't want to discuss the munitions they carried or the other items like the fifteen hundred French wool blankets and a thousand pair of English double-soled copper-pegged shoes.

Captain McDougal had come up with the list, acquired from his contacts in Nassau. Duncan could understand why they were carrying the weapons, but the cobblers' tools—awls, rasps, and hammers—confused him. If he didn't know better, he'd think someone was intending to set up a shoe shop in Charleston.

"We'll be casting off soon. We have the Clyde to navigate, but we'll be out to sea before you know it."

She smiled at him, an expression he took as dismissal.

He closed the stateroom door, stood there looking at the settee. First of all, it was too damn short. Secondly, it was upholstered in something scratchy, and thirdly, the horsehair made the cushions lumpy. He was going to have to learn to like sleeping on the cot.

What about undressing? Would she come into the parlor wanting a book and interrupt him in a state of nakedness? Not that he'd mind all that much, but there were her sensibilities to consider. But, as a widow, surely she'd seen a man without his clothes? Perhaps they should make sure to knock before entering the other's room. That would solve the problem.

As to meals, that was easily arranged. If she didn't want to have her meals with him, they could easily do so on deck. Or he could choose to eat with the captain or the crew.

He was worrying entirely too much about this.

She was simply his relative who was accompanying him to Nassau. That's all this was.

DUNCAN STOOD on deck staring back at the land they were so quickly leaving. Had his ancestors felt the same as he did now? Had his uncle, generations past, stood just as he was, feeling a tug of sadness as he left everything that was precious to him?

The splash of water against the hull, the horns, bells, and the cawing of seabirds were all sounds accompanying them on their journey down the Clyde.

They passed the cranes of the shipyards, half-built ships being given life, finished vessels awaiting their sea trials, docks and offices like Cameron and Company. Scenes he'd seen all his life but never from the vantage point of leaving them.

Would he see them again?

The ship plowed through the water as if excited to be free, the Union Jack mounted above her bow flapping in the wind.

They passed a castle perched on a crag of rock, a train trying to catch up to their speed, the tall spire of a church.

He stood there, uncertain how much time passed.

This part of the Clyde smelled of oil and decaying vegetation. Soon they'd be past Rothesay then into the Firth of Clyde, headed for the Atlantic Ocean.

The river widened, the distance to the shore became farther. Soon, the hills in the background, forested or striated in grays and blues, would be only shapes on the horizon. The seabirds grew less frequent as the waves grew deeper.

Rose didn't speak when she joined him. She was comfortable with silence and didn't talk simply to fill a gap in conversation. They stood there at the railing, hearing the splash of the powerful paddle wheel, smelling the coal fumes belching from the *Raven's* two smokestacks.

Finally, it happened. Civilization was only a shadow on the horizon. The *Raven* was alone on the stretch of water, Captain McDougal in command.

"I did like Scotland," she said. "It was nothing like I expected."

"Why is that?"

"For all their pride in their heritage, the American MacIains would have you believe that Scotland is still a rough and wild place with men who wear kilts and carry around cudgels. They think themselves far advanced."

"Advanced enough to own other men?"

She turned to look at him.

"We Scots fought against England to prevent being enslaved," he said. "I find it odd that my American cousins would forget that lesson."

She didn't say anything for a moment. "Yet you took their cotton readily enough," she said.

When she wielded a verbal spear, it was tipped with poison.

"Yes, I did. I have no excuse for it. I could explain myself by saying it was business. That I was just doing what other mills were doing."

"Did you never think that by buying the South's cotton you were encouraging an economy dependent on slaves?"

"Yes," he said, giving her the truth. "I did. Yet I had little choice. I still don't. For that reason, I pray the Union is victorious."

"What I'm selling you is Glengarden's last crop. There's every possibility we'll never produce another cotton crop. And we can't be the only plantation with that future."

"Then perhaps it's right that it happens," he said.

To change the subject, he told her a story he'd once heard from Lennox.

"Did you know that sailors' wives and mothers often make a sacrifice to the sea before their men begin a voyage?"

"A sacrifice?"

"It's in the way of a bargain," he said, staring down at the waves. "Whatever she gives to the sea has to matter: a favorite pot, a kettle, a bit of embroidery she fancies."

"And in return, the sea won't keep her man?"

"That's what's supposed to happen."

"Perhaps we should give it something as well, a token of respect, a sacrifice for a safe voyage."

Before he could stop her, she'd unpinned the cameo at her neck and tossed it into the ocean.

"Why did you do that?"

"Love itself is sacrifice, don't you think?"

He studied her until she turned her gaze to the sea.

"No," he said. "Not just sacrifice. It should also be devotion, compassion, understanding. You should be given to as often as you give."

Her eyes returned to him. Her smile was faint, as if she forced it. Instead of commenting on what he'd said, she turned the conversation back to the cameo she'd tossed overboard.

"I lied a little. Do you think the sea will know? It doesn't pain me to part with it."

Her smile had disappeared and in her eyes was an expression he couldn't read.

"Did Bruce give it to you?" he asked.

She shook her head.

"No, my sister."

With that, she turned and left him, leaving him staring after her.

Glengarden Plantation
South Carolina

"*I WANT* my shawl, Maisie. The blue one with the gold thread shot through, Maisie. Not the plain blue one."

"Yes, Miss Susanna."

"And my pot of rouge. I could do with some color."

"I can't remember where I put it," Maisie said. "I'm sorry, Miss Susanna, but this old mind of mine isn't working like it used to."

She wasn't going to help that poor woman look silly at her age. Susanna thought that old age could be held back with bright colors and slathering on rouge.

"Find it," Susanna said, her voice uncharacteristically rough. "I don't want Bruce to see me looking less than my best. He's been gone a year, Maisie."

She knew exactly how long Bruce had been gone. Slightly more than a year. Thirteen months, three days, and a few hours. Time in which a bubble had seemed to descend on Glengarden. One of, if not happiness, then certainly contentment. No one held back their words, although it had become a habit to do so. If someone laughed, it wasn't followed by a guilty look toward the corridor or sudden silence to listen for the sound of boots on the carpet.

Dinner was spent in conversation, not silence. In the morning, Gloria would come racing down the front steps and out the door as if to embrace the whole of life at Glengarden. Not one soul would stop and caution her. Or guide her away from the stables because her father was there.

Without Judge Wellington telling them, they'd have no idea Bruce was on his way home. Or that he'd lost a leg.

The devil does take his due.

Every night she said a prayer to the Almighty that the South would lose, that all those men who'd paraded around on Glengarden's veranda dressed in their fancy uniforms would fall in battle. Every night she also prayed to be forgiven her hatred. Not spared of it, because it was the only thing that kept her moving each day. Otherwise she would have wakened in her bed outside Miss Susanna's room, remembered that her Phibba was dead, and wished herself dead as well.

Michael had been one of the few slaves who could read. He'd recited passages of the Bible to them and she'd memorized the ones that gave her the most comfort.

Vengeance is mine, I will repay, was not one of them.

"I'll go and look for the rouge now," she said.

"Be quick about it."

Rouge was not going to make Susanna look twenty years younger. Nor was it going to soften the signs of age. The last year had not been kind to the woman known as a beauty in her youth. The skin on her face was so thin it barely concealed her bones. Her nose, once aquiline, was now as sharp as a knife.

None of them had had enough to eat in the last few months. Susanna was the thinnest of them all. Once, she'd bragged about her girlish figure. Today it resembled a skeleton.

Did Bruce know that the slaves had left? In other years they would have finished sowing cotton seed long before now. Did he know there were only three of them still at Glengarden? She took care of Susanna. Old Betsy, who had been old twenty years ago, still lived where she always had, in the last cabin in the third row. Benny, twenty-seven now, would always be a child since he'd been struck in the head by a horse's hoof as a toddler.

Once she'd heard Bruce complain about the incident. The boy was worthless now and couldn't fetch enough at market.

"If he was a damn mule I could put him down."

She'd added another prayer that afternoon to be forgiven her hatred.

The others were gone, off to freedom with Miss Rose's help. Sometimes one or two. Once, ten of them had left together. They'd been cautioned that although Mr. Lincoln had freed them, they still needed to get to the North before they were safe.

Anywhere was safer than Glengarden.

Something else Michael said stuck in her mind. Not a verse from the Bible, but some other place. Another book written by a man with time to think and wonder about life. She couldn't remember it exactly, but it reminded her of something Old Betsy said. No man is completely evil, even the Devil. Wasn't he once beloved of God?

Bruce loved Glengarden. She'd seen him many times standing on the veranda, his eyes cast over the fields and the approach to the plantation. Or sometimes he'd turned to look at the river, lapping at the sloping lawn. His proud smile had left no doubt of his feelings. He loved his friends, those young men who clustered around him like he was a princeling. He loved his horses, although he treated them badly. He loved his mother because she was his mirror in all things. Her son could do no wrong.

Most of all, he loved himself.

Did he still love himself with one leg missing?

They'd soon find out, wouldn't they? The dread she felt was growing by the day.

Sighing, she went to the small bureau in the dressing area next to Miss Susanna's room. There, beside the chest, was the cot on which she'd slept for most of her life. She pulled out the bottom drawer, removed the stockings, and grabbed the pot of rouge she'd hidden.

The coloring would make Susanna look even worse than she did now. If she were in her right mind, Susanna would know that. But, of course, none of them were in their right minds, were they?

Bruce was coming home.

Chapter 10

Aboard the Raven

Once they were out to sea, Rose and Duncan shared a lovely dinner with Captain McDougal in the parlor. A collapsible table hinged on the wall beneath the porthole was set up, and they feasted on something the captain called Mediterranean stew with hard crusts of bread and apple tart.

After dinner the captain taught her several terms she'd never before heard. A wall was evidently called a bulkhead. The floor was a deck and a door a hatch. By the time the evening was over she had a list of at least twenty new words and hoped she remembered them all.

As the captain left, he glanced at Duncan and then back at her.

"I've a favor to ask you, Mrs. MacIain. I muster the men first thing in the morning. I've sailed with some of them. They're fine men, ma'am, but they're not used to traveling with ladies."

"Would you like me to avoid the deck, Captain?"

"Not at all, ma'am. Just first thing in the morning."

"I'll give you the all clear, Rose," Duncan said.

They considered her a lady, but the definition evidently differed greatly between South Carolina and Scotland.

The two men had no idea what she'd seen at Glengarden. A man was often naked when whipped, the better to humiliate him completely. She'd witnessed slave auctions when traveling to Charleston with Claire. A good piece of merchandise, as Bruce would say, needed to be stripped to ensure the quality of what a buyer was purchasing.

But she would pretend to be as reserved as they evidently thought her. And as sheltered.

A few moments later she said good night to Duncan and entered the stateroom. She sat on the edge of the bed, overwhelmed with loneliness. The dinner had been enjoyable. The time in Scotland so different and pleasant. Now she was on her way back to Glengarden and she had to face the future.

The ocean suddenly rolled beneath her. She had the sensation of being on a child's hobbyhorse, with the same drop in her stomach and none of the excitement.

The lantern above the bureau was secured to the wall, but it swung with the increasing movements of the ship, making her think it might go out any moment. Beside the bureau was a cunning wire cage for the basin and pitcher. The cage must have been bolted to the deck. Otherwise, the china would have slid off the top of the chest and crashed to the floor, especially since the sea was getting rougher.

She wound her arms around her waist and bit her bottom lip. *Don't be ridiculous, Rose. You're perfectly fine.*

Her stomach rolled a little with the pitch of the ship. She'd had no difficulty with her stomach on the voyage to London. Surely she could tolerate the sea outside Scotland.

The storm had come up so suddenly. She certainly

wasn't prepared for it. She fervently hoped Captain McDougal was. He was such a genial man, with a close-cropped beard and flashing brown eyes. He was often smiling, but his voice was somewhat loud, making her wonder if he was used to calling out commands.

At that moment it felt as though the ship hit a trough and then reemerged on the crest of a wave. The storm and the *Raven* were engaged in a battle, and she didn't have any idea which would win. If the *Raven* did, they would all be saved, but if the storm was triumphant, none of them would ever see their families again. Memorials would be said in their names. Maybe some kind women would toss roses into the surf as if laying wreaths on their graves.

She had never been so dour before, a word she'd never heard before visiting Scotland. It seemed to have a perfect meaning now. Even in the most difficult days at Glengarden she'd been optimistic. She'd had hope in the future, in the little victories she'd accomplished. Small things, really, that meant nothing to Bruce, but everything to those with no freedom. Being allowed to attend religious services, have their own gardens, be given enough cloth to make their own garments.

The problem with Bruce was the same as with the other plantation owners she knew. They thought their slaves were dumb, little more than oxen, while she knew just the opposite.

Once the announcement was published about the Emancipation Proclamation issued by President Lincoln, she did everything she could to help people escape. The proclamation wasn't legal yet—that

would require an amendment to the Constitution—
but it was incentive enough for those who were desperate for their freedom. They slipped away from
the plantation by the twos and threes, armed with
what small amount of money she could spare and
directions on how to contact organizations who
would help them further.

A low growl of thunder was accompanied by a
rolling wave. The hobbyhorse had begun to gallop
and she was losing her composure. She tried to
think of something else, anything other than the
rising storm.

Susanna's birthday had been yesterday, and no
doubt there was a celebration at Glengarden. There
were no raisins or flour left, but perhaps Benny and
Maisie had been resourceful again. Whatever came
of their efforts, Susanna would never have noticed
or cared about the sacrifice.

A MacIain didn't barter. How many times had
Susanna said that to her, her head at a regal angle,
her brown eyes narrowed at the effrontery of a New
Yorker giving the matriarch of Glengarden advice?

"We've no money, Susanna. We can't buy supplies. We have to do something."

Evidently, a lady was not to mention that they
were poor, because Susanna's face became florid,
her eyes flashing dislike.

"That's as it is. Bruce will solve the difficulty."

Bruce wasn't there. Bruce had pranced off to war
on his favorite stallion, his friends outfitted in identical uniforms, less the braid and epaulettes.

They had a fortune in cotton they weren't allowed to touch because of Bruce's orders, but no
other usable funds.

Susanna didn't bother herself with the day-to-day realities of the plantation. She remained, for the most part, isolated in her suite of rooms on the second floor of the main house. Occasionally, she deigned to come down to the parlor for a celebration in which she reigned over the festivities: Bruce's birthday, the hundred-year anniversary of the building of Glengarden, or Gloria's baptism.

Thunder shook the ship as if the Almighty was annoyed at the idea of her returning to South Carolina. If there were any other way, now was the time for divine intervention, but she didn't mean dying.

She was not afraid. Of course she wasn't. After two years at Glengarden, a storm wasn't going to terrify her.

Maybe she was feeling the storm so strongly because the *Raven* was so large. Perhaps a smaller ship would have skipped over the waves while the *Raven* was carried along almost like an offering to the gods. Here, Poseidon, here's a toy for your amusement.

She needed to undress, get ready to sleep, yet how anyone could sleep through this storm was a mystery. The shouting outside the door wasn't reassuring, either. Lightning cracked so close that she was blinded for a moment and nearly rendered deaf by the thunder immediately following it.

Determined, she stood, wavered with the ship's movement, then grabbed the wardrobe to the left where she'd put her few clothes. She pulled her wrapper and nightgown from the valise, nearly fell when the ship tilted again, and wished she could remember one of the prayers from her childhood.

All she could recall was something Old Betsy

said every day. She closed her eyes and recited it, remembering the old woman as she rocked back and forth in her chair.

"Jesus, hear us, King, in our sorrow. You know, King Jesus, that we wander in the wilderness, the poorest of the children of Adam. Give us the shelter of the oak tree in the daytime and a roof over our heads at night."

She added a postscript: "And keep us safe on the ocean."

Her hoop was easily disposed of; it collapsed once it was removed, and could be tucked into the wardrobe, the two petticoats along with it. She could have unfastened her bodice more easily if her fingers weren't shaking so much. She reached to unpin the cameo, then remembered she'd tossed it into the ocean.

Evidently, that hadn't been the wisest choice she could have made. Maybe the stories were right and she should have sacrificed something she'd genuinely loved. Not the cameo Claire had given her, done in such a way she couldn't help but be insulted and hurt.

"You're not the least attractive in black, Rose. The least you could do is wear something pretty."

Claire's gift was further tainted by the fact Bruce had given it to her, but she found herself wearing it on this journey to hide her threadbare collar.

Claire had never worn mourning for their brothers. Bruce evidently didn't approve of her grieving for the three of them because they'd been Yankees, even though one of them had once been his best friend. She'd never understood Claire's refusal to stand up to him on this point. They were her brothers, too, and had grown up with them just as she had. For far longer, in fact.

Rose hadn't sought Bruce's approval, merely asked the laundress if she could help her dye her day dresses. When she'd appeared wearing her mourning, Bruce hadn't said a word.

Claire had, though. She'd shaken her head and said, "Oh, Rose."

Perhaps she was being unkind and too judgmental. She'd never come out and asked Claire if she mourned them. You didn't have to wear black to be filled with grief. It was quite possible that Claire wept for their brothers in the solitary confines of her room or in the small chapel on the grounds of Glengarden.

If the sea demanded something of value, the only things left were her memories. Perhaps she should sacrifice some of those. The day Jeremy presented her with a white and black spotted kitten they'd named Whiskers who'd been her constant companion, especially when she was reading. Or how Montgomery used to tease her about her singing. Robert knew she had a sweet tooth and would sometimes surprise her with a bag of horehound candy.

Which one of those memories would she give up? Not one of them. Nor would she ever stop remembering them. She didn't care what army they belonged to or what battle they'd been in when they died. Those facts weren't important. What was important was who they'd been, what they cared about, and that she'd loved them.

The thunder was directly above them now. The voice of God was displaying his irritation at them in a language of explosions and arcs of light.

She couldn't swim. There'd never been a need to learn in her childhood, and although Glengarden was bordered on three sides by the river, she hadn't wanted to go near it.

God, I don't want to be cowardly, but I am afraid.

There, the truth as she finally finished unbuttoning her bodice and removed her dress.

Her soul and her conscience should be clean, but they weren't. She was guilty of so many sins, and now was not the time to die, not before all those black marks could be removed. She'd lied to the nicest family she'd ever met. She was guilty of hate, so dark and evil an emotion that it felt like a monster curled up in the pit of her stomach.

Not to mention that she was a virgin and it hardly seemed right to go to her death without knowing what passion was like. She hadn't wanted a religious life. She hadn't cared about the purity of her body. Circumstances had simply declared that she was unmarried and unloved.

The ship punctuated that thought by rising in the air like a horse having a tantrum.

She hung up her dress in the wardrobe, fell back onto the bed and unfastened the busk of her corset.

There was nothing she could do about her soul, conscience, or virtue at the moment. All she could do was get below the covers, pull the sheet over her head, and pretend she was going to live until morning.

Her corset unfastened, she tucked it in the drawer beneath the bed, sparing a moment from her terror to admire the extra storage. Her shift and pantaloons were next, and she folded the garments and put them beside her corset, closed the drawer and donned her nightgown and wrapper.

She really should wash her face and brush her teeth, but did those things matter when the ship was still rolling and rocking?

A STORM at sea was a wondrous thing, as awe inspiring as it was soul reducing. The dark storm clouds seemed to be only a curtain to display the fiery fingers of lightning. Or a screen on which a tableau was being performed for his amazement. Instead of shadow puppets or a selection of silhouettes, this was a portrayal of nature's ferocity.

During the first few minutes Duncan felt enlivened by the experience. After that he started to worry.

He'd never considered himself a coward. Granted, his daily routine was such that he didn't often encounter physical danger, but he'd been in difficult situations. Still, nothing he had experienced had been close to this storm.

He couldn't stand without holding onto the furniture as the ship rocked back and forth. He finally made his way to the chair beside the settee and sat.

All the ships that Cameron and Company built and Lennox designed were seaworthy, but he found himself wondering if they were stormworthy as well. Captain McDougal was shouting at the men, but as inexperienced a sailor as he himself was, he didn't know what the man was demanding. Were they taking precautionary steps or had something gone wrong? Even worse, had someone fallen overboard as the ship tilted precipitously to one side and back again?

Since he couldn't actually do anything to help, all he could do was remain calm, out of the way, and leave the men to do their jobs.

He wished he were an experienced traveler like Rose. She'd probably experienced a storm at sea before. Had it been one as vicious as this, with the lightning flaring every few seconds and thunder coming down on them like a clenched fist?

The wind had risen to a gale. The *Raven* was rolling to one side then the other, the ship's stability in danger. They were helpless, pitching in the darkness, at the mercy of the rough sea.

How would they survive if the *Raven* capsized?

Their death by drowning seemed entirely possible in the next quarter hour, and he held onto his balance only by gripping the arm of the chair with one hand and the bolted bookcase with the other.

Rain washed in beneath the doors as if seeking him out. He pitied the men on deck, doing whatever sailors did.

He had worried about running the blockade. He had been concerned about somehow getting embroiled in the middle of the American Civil War. He had even questioned his eagerness to assist Rose and buy cotton no experienced factor had seen.

Not once had he confronted the idea that he might not survive crossing the Atlantic.

He had a general idea of where they were, just past Ireland, heading into the shipping lanes. If they continued on the same latitude, they would hit Nova Scotia, but their course was a more southern one. That is, if they survived the storm.

He clamped his hands on the end of the chair arms and stared at the door leading to the stateroom. He hadn't heard anything from Rose since they separated after dinner. He sincerely hoped he hadn't agreed to take her to Nassau only to have her drown on the voyage there. Perhaps she would have been safer on a commercial vessel, something designed to handle passengers. No doubt they would have stewards running throughout the ship, reassuring passengers that all was well, they weren't in danger of plunging to the bottom of the ocean.

He couldn't reassure anyone right at the moment.

A good thing she was a widow, otherwise her reputation might be tarnished by accompanying him without a chaperone or at least a maid in attendance. A strange thing to concentrate on appearances now, when they might die at any moment. Propriety was a habit and no doubt an integral part of his character. Although, ever since Rose came into his life, he'd been thinking less about propriety and more thoughts that had no business being paired with a respectable widow.

What a pity he hadn't taken advantage of the moment in the garden when she'd been reading Burns. He could have gently put the book aside, leaned over and kissed her.

Perhaps she'd not been weeping about poetry as much as grieving for her dead husband. What would that make him, an opportunistic satyr?

The ship rolled again as if it had fallen into a trench and righted itself. At least he had a strong stomach. That was one good thing to concentrate on, as well as the timing of their dinner. The kitchen fires would have been extinguished with the storm. Why, though, hadn't he thought to bring a bottle of whiskey? Hadn't there been a crate in the provisions they'd arranged?

If they survived until tomorrow, he'd be sure and ask Captain McDougal.

Chapter 11

The swinging lantern was abruptly extinguished, leaving her in the darkness with only the flashes of lightning to illuminate the room.

The storm was growing. God stretched out His hand and jagged streaks of fire flowed from His fingers, causing the waves to rise. Thunder growled like Cerberus, the dog of the underworld.

She wrapped her arms around herself as the ship rocked from side to side. They were going to capsize. Even from here she could hear the *Raven*'s massive engines whine with the strain.

Dear God, she didn't want to die. Not this way with the ocean swallowing her screams.

She stood, grabbed her wrapper and made her way to the door, holding onto the end of the bed in order to keep her balance. Cowardly or not, she needed the reassurance of another person. If nothing else, Duncan would tell her that her fears were unjustified, that the *Raven* could withstand this monster storm and emerge unscathed.

She tapped on the door but doubted Duncan could hear her over the roar of the wind, as if God blew his breath in spite and incited the waves to rise even higher.

Pushing open the door, she stood there for a

moment, until the rocking of the ship catapulted her into the parlor. Thankfully, Duncan was still dressed and awake.

He sat in the chair facing the door to the stateroom, his hands clenched on its arms, his face tense. She knew, in that instant, that he was as afraid as she.

"We're going to die, aren't we?"

"I haven't much experience of being on the ocean in bad weather, but I would have to say that this is no ordinary storm."

"That isn't the least reassuring," she said, holding onto the back of the settee in order to make her way to him.

At least the furniture was bolted down. Otherwise it would have slid from wall to wall. The lantern at his side swung wildly on its hook, but at least it still illuminated the room in a golden glow.

"I'm all out of reassurances at the moment," he said. "However, I can muster up a few lies if that's what you prefer."

Even though lies might have been preferable to a horrible truth, she shook her head. Better to know what was ahead than to pretend it didn't exist.

A sudden surge sent her careening close to him. Duncan kept her from sliding farther by reaching out and grabbing her. A moment later she was on his lap, her arms around his neck.

She was only in her nightgown and wrapper. If nothing else, she should get dressed. Or perhaps it didn't matter. Would their bodies ever be discovered or would they sink to the bottom of the sea?

Burying her head against his shoulder helped ease the fear a little. Smelling his bay rum and the sandalwood that seemed to scent his clothes didn't take her mind from the fact they were in terrible danger, but at least she wasn't alone.

"I don't want to die," she said, her lips so close to his neck that every word was like a kiss.

"I concur with that sentiment," he said.

Was he always so proper and restrained? She was ready to cry, but his behavior was that of a man only mildly inconvenienced by the weather.

She was trembling while he was warm, solid, and *there*.

"Tell me about your worst fear," she said. "Something you've never told anyone else."

He reared back and looked into her face.

"My worst fear?"

She nodded. "I'm afraid of the cold house," she said. "It's where Bruce locked me up."

"I don't understand," he said, frowning. "He locked you up?"

Another blast of lightning illuminated the porthole in a blinding white light. She closed her eyes.

"No, you first. Something you're truly afraid of."

"That I'll fail," he said. "That I won't be able to save the mill."

She shook her head. "No. Not that. Every business owner is afraid of failure. Something personal."

"Like being afraid of spiders, that sort of thing?"

She opened her eyes. "Are you afraid of spiders?"

"No."

She grabbed his shoulders when the ship pitched to one side. Screaming might help. At least it would defuse her terror a little. Because she was with him, she kept silent, but she held onto him a little tighter.

"The mill closing down is the one thing I'm afraid of," he said. "Although if this continues much longer, being at sea during a storm might replace it. Now tell me what the hell a cold house is."

"It's where we keep cream and butter. It's lined with straw so it stays cool in the summer, or as cool as anything can be in the South Carolina heat."

He didn't say anything, but she could hear his curiosity in the silence. How much to tell him? It seemed foolish to hide the truth when she might be dying in this storm, and from the sudden frightening pitch of the ship that might be sooner than she expected.

"Why would your husband punish you?"

Here she was, again, trapped in a lie. It hardly seemed proper to continue that lie at this moment, when she might be so close to heavenly judgment, so she told as much of the truth as she could.

"Bruce put me in the cold house to teach me a lesson." There, not a lie. In fact, those were Bruce's own words.

"Why?"

"I disobeyed."

"You disobeyed? What did you do?"

"I wasn't supposed to go near the slave cabins, but I did."

She looked away, mesmerized by the swinging of the lantern and the strange shadows it was casting on the walls. One looked like a dragon, then nothing more than an oval, before shifting into a shape resembling another fierce creature, one created by nightmares.

"I was supposed to ignore what I saw. It was the way of the South. It was what happened at Glengarden. I didn't understand. But how could I? Above all, I was never to lift a hand to help a slave."

"What did you do?"

"What didn't I do?" The list of her infractions was long and varied.

She remembered sitting in the dark, thinking about those insects that must share the space along with all matter of snakes and rodents. Sitting on the dirt floor, she was a good eight feet deeper than Glengarden's foundation. Even deeper than a grave.

At least nothing scurried in the darkness. Once, something had hissed at her and she'd stood, spun in a circle, arms flailing to keep the monster at bay. She hadn't heard the sound again. Nor had she ever told anyone how terrified she'd been.

A lesson Bruce had taught her: any weakness she showed was used as a weapon against her.

The first time he locked her in the cold house, she'd been too stunned to cry out until she heard the click of the lock. She'd spent a long time banging against the door and screaming for Bruce to release her, only to learn later that no one had heard her.

"Have you learned your lesson?" he asked when he'd finally opened the door hours later. She'd climbed up the four steps, blinking in the glare of the lantern Claire held in one hand. Her sister had just stared at her wordlessly, tears puddling in her eyes.

She'd done nothing more onerous than treating one of the slave girls for the whip marks on her back, yet Claire behaved as if her behavior had been traitorous.

It wasn't the last time Bruce had chosen that kind of punishment. Her greatest sin, in his eyes, was talking to the slaves or going to the slave cabins.

She hadn't given up, despite how many times he put her in the cold house. Even though Claire begged her to respect and obey Bruce, to be a good and dutiful sister, she couldn't find it in herself to ignore what she saw each day. She was stunned to realize that her sister had acquired blinders of a convenient sort.

She had no difficulty rebelling. She had always been a dutiful daughter where her father was concerned. After his death, she had occasionally challenged her brother, Robert. Then, after he'd gone off to war, Montgomery. She and Jeremy, however, had almost never disagreed, since they seemed to have the same nature. Only once had she argued with him, and that's when he followed his two older brothers to war, leaving her alone and faced with the most terrible decision of her life: where to live.

She'd made a terrible mistake choosing to live with Claire. She'd known that the day she arrived.

"And he punished you?" Duncan asked now.

She nodded. "To remind me who was in charge at Glengarden." Bruce's words again.

"I'm glad the bastard's dead," he said.

Tonight might be when she met her Maker. God surely wouldn't approve of her falsehoods. She'd told lies for the right reasons, but that didn't make them the truth.

The lantern was suddenly extinguished, the smell of oil overlaying that of the stew they'd had for dinner.

She hugged him tighter, her cheek against his. He was warm, his cheek bristly yet oddly comforting. She wouldn't have to die alone. They would, at least, be together.

She'd made so many mistakes in her life and had no chance to repair them. There wasn't any time now to make up for irritations and annoyances that had once seemed so important. *Easy is the descent into hell, for it is paved with good intentions.* She really didn't need to remember Milton right now.

Tell him. The voice wasn't simply that of her conscience, but had the force of celestial fervor.

Both of Duncan's hands were on her back, one stroking up and down in a rhythmic, soothing gesture, the other held firmly at her waist to keep her anchored there. If it were an ordinary moment, she would have been embarrassed to be straddling him, her knees on the outside of his legs, her arms wrapped around his neck. This wasn't an ordinary moment, but one of perfect clarity.

With her breasts pressed against his chest, she could feel him breathe. Their hearts beat in furious time, as if they raced together in fear. Her nose brushed against his ear, nudged his earlobe. Her cheek was welded to his, the heat of their conjoined skins warm and comforting in the increasingly fearsome night.

The darkness only heightened the senses. She could smell his bay rum, stronger around his neck, less so at his temple. His hair was silky beneath her fingers, his shirt finished with starch, the skin below the open collar soft, pebbling when she stroked it.

When the thunder cracked at the same time the bony fingers of lightning scratched the sky, they reacted as one. His hand pressed more firmly against her back as her breath exhaled against his neck. Her lips brushed his skin; his embrace tightened.

"Tell me about the mill," she said, her voice faint and thin.

"I'd rather hear about Glengarden. A pretty name for what must have been hell."

She pressed a kiss to his neck in gratitude. No one else had ever realized that's exactly what it had been. Two years of it, the last year only made partially bearable by Bruce's absence.

"It's very large," she said. "The house itself is only part of the plantation."

The ship lurched, the engines' scream that of a wounded animal crying out in its death throes.

Duncan tensed, and she, who had reached the limits of her terror, simply squeezed her eyes shut and began to pray.

"What's the house like?" he asked.

She shook her head. "I don't want to talk about Glengarden," she said. "I don't want the last thing I say to be about that awful place."

"Then choose some subject."

She reared back, wishing the darkness was not so absolute. Placing her hands on his cheeks, she leaned in and kissed him.

For a moment he didn't move, and then his mouth opened beneath hers. He slanted his head, deepened the kiss, and banished the storm.

If they were to die, let it be like this, with Duncan giving her the first kiss she'd ever received. Let him show her how a man kissed, how he could coax her mouth open and her tongue to touch his and then retreat. Let him heat her body from the inside out, cause stars to dance beneath her eyelids and her breath to halt not because of fear but delight.

At least her last act would be inspired by passion, not fear. Joy her final emotion.

He was kissing her chin, her cheeks, the place below her ear that had never been touched by another human being, let alone a man with bristly cheeks who murmured her name as if it were a benediction.

Finally, his lips returned to hers and she learned so much in the minutes that passed. How to touch the corner of his mouth with her tongue. How to sigh into his mouth or smile when his skin grew warmer beneath her hands.

He cupped her breast and she gasped in surprise. When he would have moved his hand, she reached down and pressed hers against it. No one had ever touched her before. No one had ever stroked her breast with fingers that felt magical or thumbed her nipple.

She wished she had buttons on her nightgown so she could unfasten them. She wanted his hands on her bare skin.

Adrift in his kisses, she threaded her fingers through his hair and gave herself up to pleasure. She lost all track of time, all notion of where she was or even who she was. Her name wasn't important, her past was irrelevant. All that she knew was that she never wanted to move.

Duncan murmured against her lips. "Rose."

Gently, he placed his hands on her shoulders. A moment later he was pushing her away.

She blinked at him, coming back to herself. She was Rose O'Sullivan, a woman who'd deceived and lied to this man who'd introduced her to passion. Slowly, she pulled her wrapper into place, conscious of two things: the ship had stopped rocking so fiercely and Duncan MacIain would never again be a stranger.

"The storm has eased," he said.

How long had they been kissing?

She could hear shouts from the deck. They'd survived. They'd come through the storm.

Rising from his lap, she went to stand behind the settee. Thank heavens it was dark in here. She couldn't see his expression and he couldn't see her blush. She was shocked, bemused, and didn't know whether to apologize or act as if nothing monumental had just happened.

He'd kissed her. She'd kissed him, enthusiastically, passionately. He'd kissed her for minutes, maybe longer. She'd lost track of everything but him. He'd touched her breast, the feel of his palm against her nightgown one she wouldn't soon forget.

She should say something, explain herself, but all she could do was turn and make her way to the cabin door, closing it firmly against temptation.

HE'D KISSED her.

Worse, he'd wanted to do much more. He'd wanted to strip her of that soft wrapper and nightgown and see her naked. If he couldn't light that damn lantern, he would experience her in the darkness. His hands would stroke over her skin, feeling every indentation and plump curve. His lips would follow his fingers until he learned her as well as he knew himself.

Not only had he treated her with disrespect, he hadn't been in control of his own faculties. His emotions had been those of a youth, delighted, ecstatic, and overjoyed, discovering that everything he had imagined about a woman was doubly so. For a few moments he'd been thinking that they could use the floor as a mattress if they couldn't make it to the stateroom. He had been more than willing to tumble Rose to the deck and take her right then and there. The storm would hide her screams of pleasure and his shouts of triumph.

What the hell had happened to him?

Ever since she'd come to Glasgow, he'd been on the verge of losing himself. He wasn't even sure who he was anymore. The man he had always known himself to be, focused, determined, on a set path, had disappeared. He wasn't as interested in the MacIain Mill as he was Rose MacIain. He wanted to know everything about her. Not only her body, but her mind. What was she thinking? What did she feel?

Had she been as enthralled with their kisses as he had been? He hadn't cared about the damn storm as long as she was in his arms.

He had to stay away from her.

He'd be friendly, but no more than that. Above all, he wouldn't let himself be alone with her.

There, that ought to solve his problem.

Chapter 12

She couldn't face him. She couldn't see the look in his eyes. She wasn't sure what she would see there, either confusion or contempt. She was supposed to be a widow yet she had acted the part of harlot. An eager one, at that.

Her first kiss had been more astounding than anything she had expected. Her body had been on fire. Her mind had been numbed by pleasure. Her lips had known exactly what to do. How had her tongue learned all of those talented things?

She wanted to inhale his breath again. She wanted to feel the warmth of his cheek against hers. She wanted to breathe against his ear, know the contour of it. And his neck—she'd kissed him there repeatedly.

What was she going to do? How was she going to face him?

She had avoided breakfast by simply calling through the door that she didn't feel like eating. She had remained in the stateroom, grateful that the storm had left them only with placid seas. Everything was tranquil, giving her nothing but time to think.

Was she supposed to excuse herself from the noon meal, too?

She had come too close to starving at Glengarden. Therefore she had a choice, to be hungry or to face him.

She couldn't possibly explain herself. She had been in her nightgown and wrapper, practically naked.

He'd touched her breast.

Perhaps he should feel badly about his own actions. In fact, she should probably expect an apology from him. After all, she was supposed to be a widow. And there he was, his hand cupping her breast, his thumb gently abrading the nipple.

She should have screamed in affront. She should have slapped him. Instead, her hand had curved around his cheek, her fingers sliding through his beautiful hair. She had kept his head still for a kiss.

It would be so much better if she could claim that she had been overcome by his baser instincts.

Instead, she had instigated everything. After all, she had planted herself on his lap. She had straddled him like he was a horse and then, to make matters worse, enfolded her arms around him. The man had no choice but to place his hands on her back. If one hand crept around to her front and touched her breast, perhaps it was merely because of the motion of the ship.

That was it.

The kiss was an accident, brought about by the pitching and rocking of the vessel. They were each complicit and each to be excused.

So, when the noon meal arrived, she was prepared to enter the parlor and face Duncan, only to discover that he had decided to eat with the captain, leaving her alone.

AFTER HER lunch it was safe for her to go on deck. Before she did, she perused the bookshelves in the parlor. She wasn't in the mood for philosophy or geography or anything to do with ships after last night, thank you very much. She wanted something that was light and charming, so she selected one of Mark Twain's books.

She opened the door to the deck, expecting there to be debris on the deck or some damage. Either there had been and the crew had industriously removed any trace of it, or the *Raven* simply sloughed off any signs of the storm. The decks were swept clean, the grayish white paint gleaming in the afternoon sun.

The paddle wheel was churning through a submissive sea while the two smokestacks pumped out clouds of smoke. From what Captain McDougal said last night at dinner, once they berthed in Nassau they'd change to anthracite, a different type of coal that burned cleaner and didn't produce noticeable smoke.

"If you've got a gentle breeze abeam," the captain said, "smoke from the chimneys will give away your location. That's why once we run the blockade, we'll have men watching the skies even in the dark. It's easy enough to see smoke from a ship burning soft coal."

If she hadn't experienced the storm of the night before, she wouldn't know it by the glorious day. The sky was a cerulean blue, the air so clear she felt like she could see for hundreds of miles. There were no other ships on the horizon, no sign of land anywhere. They were in the midst of the Atlantic, alone and subject to the ocean's whim. Now it acted tame, almost subservient, but it might rear up at any moment and show its awful teeth.

Last night she'd thought they were close to dying. She'd never been as afraid in her entire life, even when Bruce locked her in the cold house. She'd known that, eventually, he would come and let her out.

The routine was always the same. Hours would

pass until he returned, and when he did, he'd recite a litany of her sins for which he passed judgment.

"Have you learned your lesson, Rose?"

She was always supposed to answer, "Yes, Bruce, I've learned my lesson."

The few times she hadn't followed the unwritten script, he'd turned around and left, locking the door again, shutting her in the dark.

After her apology, he would say: "Are you going to do it again, Rose?"

"No, Bruce." She'd learned to repeat that by rote.

Every time he punished her, she promised not to repeat her sin. Sometimes it was days before she did, or even weeks.

Most of her activities were unseen or unnoticed because she had the collusion of the one hundred seventeen slaves at Glengarden. None of them would ever have reported her. Once, it was the overseer who'd done so, because she'd interfered with a whipping of a very young boy. Another time, Susanna told Bruce that she had taken some of her own bedding to one of the cabins. Or that she'd been seen delivering food to one of the older men who was feeling poorly.

Both Susanna and Claire saw her involvement—or even her acknowledgment—of the slaves as abhorrent.

Had Claire ever spoken to Bruce about her activities? She wasn't certain, but she did know that her sister had never defended her.

A thought to put a blight on the day, if she let it.

One of the seaman approached her.

"Would you like to sit, ma'am? I could roll a barrel over there in the corner. You could read and get a little of the sun."

"Thank you, I would like that," she said, smiling at him.

The corner turned out to be a place where she could see all the activity on the deck yet be out of the way of the spray from the paddle wheel.

The *Raven* was churning through the Atlantic, making her wonder how many days until they reached the Bahamas. Her voyage to London had taken nine days, ten if you counted how long it took to dock. They could easily make Nassau in eight.

She opened her book and began to read, glad she'd chosen a humorous volume. Mr. Twain had a way with words and she was soon smiling in delight.

Her father had told her that she'd taken to reading like her brothers had taken to rough-and-tumble sports. Claire had been the delicate one, the perfect lady, always reciting rules to her or criticizing her deportment. *Deportment,* a word she heard a little too much from Claire. She was too jerky in her movements. She had no grace. Her table manners needed to be improved. She lacked the wit to make sparkling conversation.

She hadn't cared much about learning the rules of womanhood, but give her a book and she was enraptured. She found, over the years, that it was easier to read if she hid herself away, and often did so in the attic of their New York home. There, the winter afternoons were almost warm and cozy, with the heat wafting upward from the snug kitchen. When she did venture downstairs with her current book, it was to endure teasing from her three brothers and an exasperated look from her only sister.

"You're always reading. One day, you're going to look up and find that life has passed you by, Rose.

You'll be a spinster with nothing to cuddle up to but a book."

That comment had caused her brothers to laugh, as if the thought of her ever cuddling up to anything was uproarious.

Claire still gave her that look from time to time, enough that when she read it was in the silence and peace of her room at Glengarden before she was sent off to live in the slave cabins. When she did venture outside, when the heat became oppressive, she chose one of the massive oaks to sit under, someplace far enough away from the fields that she could pretend she was somewhere else.

Yet she was never as adept at pretense as the people who lived in the big house. Those same people, dulled to their own experience, had no difficulty whatsoever condemning her actions.

"I can't believe that you would willfully bring scandal to the family," Claire said before she left. "Traveling all that way alone."

"No one has to know," she answered. "If anyone notices my absence, simply tell them that I've gone to visit friends."

Susanna believed their duty was to suffer any indignities of their position in stoic and ladylike silence. Even if that meant they starved to death. As long as it was gracefully done, they wouldn't shame the MacIain name, the heritage of Glengarden, or her beloved South.

Yet however much Susanna might have disapproved of her errand, she was the only one to give her any practical advice about running the blockade out of Charleston.

"If you're boarded," she'd said in an accent that

was as thick as the air on a summer day in South Carolina, "claim to be an ex-pat. Tell them you were escaping from the South for your home in New York. Greet those long-lost Yankees as if they were your brothers come to life."

She'd only stared at Susanna for a moment. The matriarch of the MacIain family had never gone out of her way to have a relationship with her and she'd acted in kind. They were exceedingly polite to each other, but they'd never had a conversation more important than the weather or the flowers.

Standing there, watching as Susanna tapped her cane imperiously on the beautifully waxed floors of the Glengarden foyer, she'd abruptly wished that they had meant more to each other, that the older woman could have come out of her protective shell or that she herself might have tapped on it once or twice.

Would a closer relationship have changed anything? It was too late to wish for that.

Twice, a shadow obscured her view. Twice she ignored it, knowing full well that Duncan was standing there. When she ignored him the first time, he walked away. The second time, he picked up a crate and returned to her side, placing the crate next to her barrel.

She put a finger in her book to mark her place.

"Do you think we'll have another storm?" she asked.

She'd scanned the sky, but it had been almost cloudless. The few clouds that had scuttled overhead looked friendly enough. Yet they'd had no hint of the storm last night, either.

"I've never known anyone to be able to foretell storms, especially on the ocean, so I can't answer that question."

"Do you ever lie?" she asked, smiling. "To save someone's feelings or to ease someone's fears?"

"I've been known to bend the truth on occasion," he said, "for those reasons, but I don't like doing it. It seems to me that the truth is better under most situations. Are you afraid?"

She thought about her answer for a moment. "Not afraid. Cautious, perhaps. I don't want to go through something like that again."

"Shall I apologize?"

Her cheeks immediately heated.

He really shouldn't look so fixedly at her. His gaze had the effect of warming her from the inside out.

"No," she said.

"Are you certain?"

"We are both to blame, don't you think? The storm was no doubt the cause for us acting so foolishly." She held out the book to him. "Have you ever read this? It's quite amusing, yet at the same time it's profound. I've read some of his work before, but it was nothing like this."

"Are you certain, Rose? I shouldn't have taken advantage of the situation."

He was not going to be deflected, was he?

"I don't think you're the one who took advantage," she said, trying to be as honest as he. "I believe I was the one who kissed you first."

Could her cheeks get any hotter?

He took the book from her and turned it over in his hands.

"I shouldn't have taken advantage," she said. "You were being very kind to me, very understanding."

"I wasn't feeling kind or understanding," he said,

handing the book back to her and leveling that look on her again.

He really had to stop doing that.

They needed to talk about something else.

She hugged the book close to her chest and stared out at the endless ocean.

"Are you really planning on leaving me in Nassau?"

His smile altered character and that flat look was back in his eyes. Evidently, Duncan didn't like to be challenged as to his dictates.

That was really too bad. She had absolutely no intention of changing her personality to suit him. Bruce could give him countless examples of her sedition.

"We've discussed this before," he said.

"You know that if you do," she said, "I'll simply have to book passage on another ship. They're charging two hundred fifty dollars on every blockade runner. That's two hundred fifty dollars I could use for seeds, Duncan. Or livestock."

"Why not return to New York instead of remaining in South Carolina?"

She smiled. "I'm a woman without a country. The southerners look at me as if I'm an enemy in their midst. Here I am, from New York, a Yankee in their bosom. Yet if I return to New York, having lived two years in the South, can you imagine the reaction of my neighbors?"

She looked away again, focusing on the wires leading down from the masts.

"Besides, there's no reason to return to New York. My brothers perished in the war. They were the last of my family. My sister lives at Glengarden with me."

"Don't you realize how much more difficult life is going to be at Glengarden, the longer the war carries on? It's been two years, Rose, and it doesn't look like it's going to end any time soon."

"I know exactly how long the war has lasted, Duncan. I can mark the day of every major battle."

"Stay in Nassau with your friends and I'll join you later. We could return to Scotland together."

"What would I do in Scotland, Duncan, without family?"

"You have a family, Rose. One who's already welcomed you."

His family didn't know the truth about her. They'd welcomed an imposter, but she wouldn't tell him that.

"Why go back there?"

"My sister and my niece."

"I'll bring them to Nassau," he said.

Oh, if it were only that easy. As for returning to Glengarden, there was no other choice.

"In the last several months the plantation has fallen apart and a portion of that blame is mine," she said.

"Why?"

Once again she told him the truth.

"I did everything I could to help the slaves escape once Bruce left for war. Slaves weren't allowed off the plantation without a note from their owner. I forged dozens of notes, sent people north with letters of introduction to organizations that could help them. They left by the twos and threes. A few at a time, they were barely missed, until suddenly they weren't there."

She met his eyes. "I let them know about the Emancipation Proclamation, that they were free. I didn't tell them that it wasn't legal yet. It was enough to give them hope, and they hadn't had hope in a very long time."

He didn't say anything, just watched her steadily.

She hadn't expected the plantation to collapse or for the remaining inhabitants to be helpless without the constant presence of their slaves. The kitchen garden was left to wilt. The livestock weren't cared for and had to be slaughtered early. None of their flour or sugar were rationed or even inventoried.

It was as if Susanna and Claire were adult children living in a massive dollhouse where they were posed periodically. They had no actions of their own, no thoughts, and no initiative.

Without Maisie and Benny, she didn't know what would have happened to them.

"I can't leave the rest of the family to their own devices." She had to make sure the remaining inhabitants of Glengarden had some protection against what was surely to come.

"I'll get the gold to them," he said. "You can remain in Nassau."

She shook her head.

Claire and Gloria were her only living relatives. As far apart as Claire and she had grown, she still couldn't walk away from her sister without trying to convince her to leave Glengarden. They'd find a place to live as far from war and the taint of the plantation as they could, where everyone was free.

"You mustn't worry about me, Duncan. Remember last night? We survived."

"And the war, Rose? What about the war?"

She didn't have an answer for that.

He stood and left her without another word.

Chapter 13

*S*he was just a door away. Just there, tucked away in the captain's bed, the comforter warming her from the cool sea breeze. Was she sleeping? Was she dreaming?

Did she dream of him, of Bruce? Did she weep in her sleep for her dead husband? Or did she fear him still?

The man had been a tyrant. What kind of man imprisons his own wife? What kind of husband treats his wife as if she were chattel?

The same kind who could own slaves and never let it bother his conscience.

If nothing else, Bruce should have protected her. He should have made provisions for her, so that Rose wouldn't have to travel half a world away to gain some semblance of financial security.

Did Bruce know that his legacy would be forever tarnished by his cruelty? Rose had little to say in praise of her dead husband.

If he married, Duncan hoped his wife would say something pleasant about him after his passing. Something innocuous, if nothing else. *Duncan was very fond of his family. He was a good friend, a fair employer.* Would his own widow, should he ever have one, be as restrained as Rose? Was it because she was ashamed that she couldn't feel more for Bruce? Or because doing so opened up a wound?

The idea of Rose weeping for the bastard disturbed him.

He left the stateroom for the deck, needing to be in the company of something other than his thoughts. He nodded to a few of the seamen, listening to their conversation. On some nights they would probably bunk on deck, but as long as the weather had an early spring chill, their hammocks would be warmer.

What kind of man chose a seafaring life? One who was a great deal more comfortable with the ocean than he was. He'd never appreciated the sheer size of the Atlantic, being a lifelong resident of Glasgow and only familiar with the River Clyde.

He wasn't, if the truth be told, all that eager to become a well-seasoned traveler. He missed his home already and they'd been gone only three days. Perhaps he was a creature of habit or locked into a routine, but he got enjoyment from starting and finishing something tangible, a length of cloth, a sum of numbers, refurbishing an ancient piece of equipment. He liked planning, but more importantly, he liked seeing that plan come to fruition. Just like Lennox enjoyed laying out the design of a ship and then making sure it developed from an idea to a reality.

Being a sailor was less planning and more praying.

He stood at the rail, listening to the sound of the engines, watching as the paddle wheel turned. The ship was surprisingly quiet or maybe that was by design. Perhaps Lennox had made the engines as silent as he could, in preparation for running through a phalanx of Union ships.

At least after last night no one could say the *Raven* was cursed. She'd shown her true mettle.

He wanted to go home when this was done. He wanted to get mill number two cleaned out. Once the building was empty, he could have the smaller, more intricate looms delivered for use with the Indian cotton.

As a boy he discovered he had an affinity for machines. He liked figuring out what was wrong and fixing it. He was spending less time in his office and more on the floor of the mill and that was fine with him.

People weren't machines, however, but infinitely more complex and less understandable. Perhaps it was only women who confounded him. Or simply Rose.

He turned at a sound and saw the door to the stateroom open. A moment later she stepped out, nearly indistinguishable from the shadows in her mourning.

"Is it for him?" he asked. "Or do you wear mourning for your brothers?"

"My brothers."

He nodded, pleased in a way that disturbed him. But Bruce MacIain was not a man he admired and he wished the bastard didn't share his name.

"Why can't you sleep?"

"Perhaps my guilty conscience," she said.

Because of their kiss? That wasn't a question he would ask, not when someone might overhear them.

The moon was waning. A good thing, according to Captain McDougal. They'd timed their voyage right. They'd refuel at Nassau and leave for Charleston on a moonless night, the better to be unseen by Union ships.

She came and stood at the rail beside him.

"It's almost possible to believe that we're alone in the world, isn't it?"

One of her gloved hands was close to his on the railing. He wanted to put his hand on hers. He wanted to hold her, comfort her. Hell, he wasn't that altruistic. He wanted to hold her because holding her felt good. She fit against him perfectly.

The chilled breeze encouraged him to extend his arm around her and pull her close. What would she do? Instead of pulling her into his embrace, he touched her wrist, felt her shiver and withdrew his fingers.

"Forgive me," he said.

"No. No, it's all right. I just didn't expect it."

He was suffused with questions. Did no one ever touch her? Was she afraid to be touched? Had Bruce hurt her?

Turning, he faced her, wishing the moonlight wasn't so bright. In the darkness he wouldn't be able to see that she was looking away, her eyes on the distant horizon. The waves caught and held her attention as if she were a mermaid. A creature from the deep who'd agreed to be a guest aboard the *Raven* for only moments.

Daring himself, he stroked her cheek with two fingers, a slow journey from temple to chin. Her skin was so soft he wondered if he marked her with his callused touch.

She turned her head and looked up at him. Her eyes were wide and dark in the night. Her lips were slightly open as if about to speak. What was she going to say? *Please don't touch me. Please take yourself and your curiosity away.*

He was prepared for her rebuff. He had the words ready in the forefront of his mind.

You're sad and I don't know why. I can't leave you like this, as if you're about to cry. Can't I do something? Anything, even if that gesture angers you? Better your anger than your tears, Rose.

Instead, she confounded him by reaching up and placing her hand on his. Pressing his hand against her face as if she wished to mark his palm there permanently.

"You've been so kind to me, Duncan."

"How have I been kind?"

"You took me into your home. You listened to me when I came to you. You purchased Glengarden's cotton, and now, despite your misgivings, you're taking me to Nassau."

All of that was true, but he didn't want her thinking of him as kind. Any other label but that. He didn't want to be avuncular in her eyes. He didn't want her looking at him and thinking *friend*. He didn't want to be treated like her brother.

Her soft smile touched something deep inside him. He'd never thought himself as passionate as others in his family or even Lennox. Other than the MacIain Mill, he'd never devoted himself to a cause. He'd never been willing to give everything he had to ensure that someone else was safe or happy or pleased with life.

Lennox had been willing to give up his pride. So had Glynis.

Now was his turn.

"Don't make me out to be a saint, Rose," he said. "I'm not that unselfish."

He dropped his hand, suddenly angry at himself. Didn't she realize that he'd never acted the fool around another woman? He'd been pleasant and charming, but unapproachable.

She'd walked right into his life and stirred something in him, some base emotion that wasn't altogether pure. Something dark and forbidden, scary and uncontrollable, emotions he'd never felt before this moment.

How could he explain? Would words even matter?

He placed his hands on both her arms and pulled her gently toward him. She surprised him by remaining silent. Her eyes widened the closer she came. Those tempting lips opened a little more as if preparing for him.

There was no storm at the moment, no rocking of the ship to blame. She was fully attired and he was certain they weren't going to die at any moment.

He lowered his head slowly, giving her a small moment to protest. An instant of outraged virtue. A proper widow still grieving for her husband would surely have made some kind of sound.

The sailors could see them. The men taking a break from stoking the *Raven*'s fires, the pilot, even the captain, anyone could glance over and separate their shadows.

He touched her lips softly with his mouth, testing and tasting.

She moaned and freed her arms to reach up and entwine them around his neck. Her skirts billowed out behind her as she stepped closer.

He wanted to feel her. He needed to feel her. He needed to be as close to her as possible, damn all the layers of fabric between them. He could still remember the weight of her breast in his hand, hear her indrawn breath as his thumb teased her nipple.

Her corset guarded her virtue now, as well as the thought that they were being watched. If they'd been alone . . . If they'd been alone, he would have stripped her bare and had her there with her back to the rail, the waves and the wind as witness.

His tongue danced along her bottom lip, coaxing her mouth to open more fully. She pressed her body to his, startled him by tilting her head to deepen the kiss.

He should have gone to Edinburgh before this voyage. He wouldn't have been so controlled by lust if he had. He should have visited the friend he'd known for years, the woman who welcomed him whenever he appeared. If their union was more of friendship than lovers, he hadn't complained.

Nor had he known what he was missing.

The top of his head was about to explode and go sailing among the stars. He didn't think he'd ever been so hard. His toes curled. His heartbeat spiked. It hurt to breathe. His fingertips dug into Rose's waist, wanting to rip the damn corset from her, or that ugly black dress.

At least he could kiss her. He moved his hands to the back of her head, holding her steady for his assault. Let him kiss her until dawn appeared on the horizon, until his lips memorized hers. Let him feel this desire. Let him endure it and suffer it and experience it and know he would never feel this with anyone else.

"Duncan."

He heard her from far away, through the mist and haze of passion. He heard her as if in a dream, one he'd had as a boy when he first imagined being with a woman. He felt her lips against his, her palms on his heated cheeks.

"Duncan," she said again, softly and sweetly, calling him back to himself.

He was aboard the *Raven* and people were still on the deck. They weren't alone.

With difficulty, he pulled back, leaning his forehead against hers. He sighed, mustering up an apology.

"Forgive me," he said, his voice sounding rough.

"Must I? If you must be forgiven, then surely I must, also. Can we not simply dispense with forgiveness?"

He smiled and took a precautionary step back. "Perhaps it would be better if I weren't alone with you."

"I hope that's not true," she said, sending his heartbeat racing. "I like our conversations."

Damn it, she did put him in the category of friend.

"I like your kisses," she said, further confusing him. "But perhaps it would be better if we didn't kiss again."

"I'm not entirely certain I can promise that. I try never to make a promise I can't fulfill."

She sighed, turned and looked out over the ocean again. The darkness rendered her hair nearly black when it should have been aflame like the sunrise.

"If I were a cad, I'd blame you," he said.

"Me?" She turned to face him again.

"I'd say that it was your beauty that had me transfixed, that there was something about your smile that fascinated me. That even your conversation was like no other woman I've ever known. Of course I had no other recourse than to kiss you."

"But you're not a cad, so what do you say?"

"That I'm not entirely myself around you. I'm not

Duncan MacIain of MacIain Mills. I'm not responsible or sober or the man I've always known myself
to be. Instead, I'm just Duncan and I want to smile at
odd times. I think entirely too much about you, but
that's not your fault as much as it is mine."

He reached out and placed his hand over hers
where it rested on the rail.

"I have this wish to comfort you, as if I could take
your pain from you and magically erase it. I know
something is troubling you, but I don't know what
it is. If I could take the burden from you, I would."

"Perhaps you're the burden," she said softly.

He dropped his hand. "Am I?"

She didn't answer. Instead, she stood on tiptoe
and kissed him on the cheek.

"I'd better go to bed now, Duncan," she said.

In seconds she was gone, leaving him even more
confused than before.

Chapter 14

*N*assau was located on the island of New Providence, which was only about thirty miles in circumference. Paradise Island, a small island about two to three miles long, lay a half mile to the northwest. The channel between the two islands created a secure harbor for vessels with the freedom to enter from either end.

They'd flown the Union Jack approaching Nassau and hadn't been accosted. The British Commonwealth was officially neutral in the American Civil War. Another ship, the *Mary Jane*, flying no flag at all, hadn't been so fortunate. As they'd neared the port they saw a Union gunship fire at the smaller ship, water spraying from the bullets missing their target. She flew across the water like a goose, but the gunship had to abandon its pursuit once it entered Bahamian boundaries.

When they entered Nassau harbor, it was to find several steamers, screw and side-wheel, at anchor. The *Indiana*, a ship half the size of the *Raven*, was discharging her cargo of cotton at the wharf. According to Captain McDougal, she'd been successful in running the blockade more than twenty times. Other ships were in the process of being scraped, a process the captain said would make them faster.

"Anything to free the hull, sir. Remove any impediments to speed."

Another ship, the *Betty Anne*, smaller than the *Indiana*, was pocked with bullet holes, a warning about what they might face in the four day voyage to Charleston.

He was stunned by how active the city was and how filled with people.

"It's the blockade, sir," Captain McDougal told him. "The Bahamas have been made rich by the war."

Everything he saw seemed to verify that, including the fact that he wasn't able to procure rooms at the first two hotels they visited.

When he suggested to Rose that it might be better to deliver her to her friends, she shook her head.

"I couldn't possibly simply show up, Duncan. I haven't informed them of my arrival. I'll send word tomorrow."

"The Viceroy'll be available, sir," the driver of the carriage said. "They're the dearest on the island. None of the soldiers can afford them so they'll have rooms to let. For the toffs, it is."

He didn't consider himself a toff, and Rose only smiled when hearing the driver.

The Viceroy, they were told, had been finished only two years ago, billed as the most cosmopolitan hotel in the New World. Yet there was a tree house built around an old silk cotton tree whose branches curved low to the ground before soaring up into the sky. Surrounded by acres of tropical forest and perched on a hill overlooking the harbor, the hotel was truly beautiful.

The problem was, the Viceroy only had one room left. A suite, he was informed by the supercilious clerk. Unless, of course, the gentleman wanted to share the suite with the lady?

"I'm Mrs. MacIain," Rose said, coming forward to the desk. "This is Mr. MacIain. Of course we want to share the suite."

As the clerk apologized, Duncan turned to her, on the verge of stating that she could have the suite while he attempted to find accommodations elsewhere. The problem with that idea was while the Viceroy's rates might be out of the range of most people—and he could attest to the fact they rivaled that of any posh London hotel—evidently the Blockade Runner Bar was a popular spot.

He wasn't going to leave Rose alone in a hotel obviously favored by a great many men.

The lobby contained men in every type of Confederate uniform, from messengers to generals. Accents he'd never heard before filled the space, until it sounded like the Tower of Babel.

He suspected that those men not in Confederate uniforms were from the Union, but a little more discreet about their presence. Nassau was, after all, a hub of activity, a haven from which blockade runners made their way to Charleston and other southern ports.

No, he most definitely needed to protect Rose, even from himself.

Ever since their kiss, he'd been careful not to stand too close to her. Or to touch her, even in passing. He didn't want to give her the idea that he was always a lustful idiot around her. Never mind that he was thinking too much of her or that his dreams had become too heated of late.

There had been a humming tension between

them the last week, even during the dinners they shared with Captain McDougal. When she joined him on deck in the evenings, he had to restrain himself not to get too close.

Now he didn't have any other option but to sign the register as Mr. and Mrs. MacIain. Technically true, but not in the right sense.

Declining the use of a porter, he carried both of their valises to the second floor suite. After opening the door with the oversized key, he found himself in the largest hotel room he'd ever seen. Between the sitting room and the bedchamber, they could surely avoid each other well enough in the coming days.

He wouldn't be in Nassau long. Only long enough to ensure that Rose was safe with her friends, refuel the *Raven*, and take on additional cargo.

Behind the sofa was a long table on which was arranged a selection of pastries, a crystal decanter, and two glasses.

"That isn't going to be dinner, surely," Rose said, smiling at him.

He removed the stopper from the decanter and sniffed its contents. "It's rum. We'll both be tipsy in a minute."

"I hate to go down to dinner as wrinkled as I am." She stared down at her skirt with a frown.

"We're travelers," he said. "We're not supposed to look elegant."

"At this hotel?" she asked, smiling. "The Viceroy would accept nothing less."

She trailed her fingers across the tabletop.

"I'm sorry," she said, "I should have made the situation clearer at the front desk."

"It's better this way," he said. "I didn't like the

idea of you being in a room by yourself. Besides, we've made it this far being proper."

"Yes," she said, such a simple answer that he glanced at her.

Did she realize how much effort his restraint had cost him?

He deliberately looked away, studying the furniture. He was going to be relegated to the settee again, but at least this one was longer. Or he might just become accustomed to the floor.

He would not think of the bedroom with its huge bed. Nor would he envision her in it, her arms open wide for him.

Turning, he called out that he'd be back in a few minutes and left the room before temptation overwhelmed his common sense.

EVER SINCE that night on deck when he kissed her, Duncan had been a perfect gentleman. More than once she'd dreamed of him, and those nightly interludes had been sinful but utterly delightful.

As she watched the door close, she wondered if what she'd told him about Glengarden had repulsed him. Had she told him too much of the truth?

The sitting room was spectacular, with pale blue silk walls and upholstered furniture in ivory, matching the draperies. Mahogany tables dotted the space, arranged for a guest's comfort. An alcove overlooking the harbor held two chairs and a table and provided a spectacular view of not only the town, but the tropical forest around the hotel.

The bedroom was as luxurious as the sitting room, making her feel out of place. She didn't belong in this lovely room with its royal blue counterpane and four-poster bed hung with netting. The draperies were as sheer as the netting, but since the window faced the sea, who could look in?

A balcony off the window lured her. She opened the window and stood watching as night swept in with the tide.

Turning away from the view of the sea, she investigated the other items of furniture in the room: a secretary boasting stationery bearing the Viceroy logo, a large armoire smelling of cedar; a bureau of the same wood, highly polished, each drawer lined with a scented paper reminding her of patchouli.

She sat on the end of the bed, staring at the lovely carved long bureau with the rectangular mirror above it.

Duncan would sleep in the sitting room again, giving up the bed once more for her.

She'd never known anyone like Duncan MacIain. He was the most charming, generous, kind, witty, intelligent, and caring man she'd ever met. Although she'd no experience in kissing, she thought he must be a champion in it. Her blood always raced whenever she was near him and her chest felt tight.

Her emotions, however, were out of control. She wanted to cry, which was silly. At the same time she felt like she was filled up with bubbles, as if lighter than air. She wanted to smile whenever she saw him. If that wasn't foolish she didn't know what was.

Although she'd tried to tell him the truth when she could, the heavier lie sat on her shoulders. She had to tell him who she was. If, for no other reason, than because Duncan MacIain was a decent man.

Tonight, then. She'd tell him tonight. With any luck he'd understand that she had to protect the people of Glengarden. He had to go through with the sale. Once he understood, he wouldn't renege. A man like Duncan would always keep his word.

She stood and walked into the other room attached to the bedroom. It was a bathing room, but it was unlike any room she'd ever seen. Glengarden had hot and cold running water, but only when the boiler cooperated and there wasn't a hole in the cistern. Otherwise, they had to depend on the well to the side of the house. At night they used a chamber pot, discreetly emptied in the morning. Her bathroom had a basin and a tap, but little else.

This bathroom was like a dream, something from the future she couldn't even imagine. Were all hotel rooms similarly equipped, or only the rooms at the Viceroy?

There was an indoor commode, one made of polished mahogany. Beside it was a handle mounted on a glass dial. When she moved it experimentally, a gush of water splashed through the bowl, emptying it and refilling it. She twisted the handle twice more, just to see it work.

The bath was equipped with two taps, which meant she didn't have to wait for anyone to bring pitchers of hot water for her use. Mounted on the wall above was a shower head at least ten inches long. The sink was marble, set inside a grand mahogany stand carved with trailing flowers along each side. She turned on the hot water tap and in seconds the water was scalding.

She didn't wait, couldn't wait, but grabbed her other dress from her valise and hung it on the hook behind the door. Perhaps the steam would help with the wrinkles, much like an iron would. She didn't doubt that the Viceroy had maids to attend to their guests, but she didn't want anyone to see how faded her dresses were getting. The pattern of the material could be seen through the black dye if you looked hard enough.

The *Raven* had a bathtub, but she'd only taken one bath in her cabin, conscious of the limited water supply. With this tub, however, there were no such reservations. To her amazement, the hotel had even provided a container of bath salts that she used liberally.

For the next half hour she was purely hedonistic, smiling to herself as she bathed. Perhaps later she'd wash her hair, but for now she pinned it up out of the way.

According to the desk clerk, they had only a few hours to take advantage of the restaurant at the Viceroy.

She didn't want to be seen in public, as travel tired as she was, but there was no choice. Her stomach was reminding her that the last meal she had was at noon, before they entered the harbor.

Her steamed black dress looked as dreary as any mourning. She was tired of wearing black. Her grief for her brothers wouldn't ease if she were wearing another color. She would always remember Jeremy for his laughter and Robert for his somber attitude toward life and Montgomery for his charm. How could she forget any of the O'Sullivan brothers?

She combed her hair and repinned it. She wouldn't fare well against the other patrons of the dining room. The women would, no doubt, all be dressed in something fashionable, while the men would either be wearing uniforms that hadn't seen battle or black suits without a speck of dust.

Duncan would look his best, but he looked wonderful regardless of what he wore. One afternoon, as she'd come on deck to read, she spotted him with his jacket off, his white shirtsleeves rolled to the elbows and his collar open so that she could see the hair on his chest.

She'd stared. Whenever anyone glanced at her, she bent her head to her book again, intent on the words her eyes refused to read.

He wasn't the most attractive man she'd ever met. She remembered thinking, on meeting Bruce, that he was extremely handsome. She rarely thought of him that way anymore. But the longer she knew Duncan, the more good-looking he became, as if his character augmented his appearance. He was like a silver flacon inside a glass credenza. You paid it little attention at first glance. Then it became more interesting as you noted the curve of the handle and the embellishment of the spout. Finally, you recognized its perfection, how special it was from the more ostentatious pieces in the credenza.

She smiled at her thoughts and wished she could be pretty for tonight. She'd dress in a gown with a flowery print and put matching flowers in her hair. She'd wear something sparkly. Not diamonds, because she'd always been taught that diamonds were for older women. Pearls were considered unlucky. Garnets reminded her of death. What would be perfect for the night? Perhaps nothing at all.

She'd go to Duncan without ornament, simply herself. She'd gather up her hair and pin it in the back, allowing a few curls to fall near her face. She'd wear something soft on her feet so she felt lighter than air.

That dream died a cruel death as she surveyed herself in the mirror.

All she had was her day dress dyed black and her clunky, serviceable shoes that made a sound no matter how quiet she tried to be. And her hair? Oh, her hair was a mess and desperately needed to be washed.

She heard the door open and realized that Duncan was back. After taking another look at herself in the mirror, she wished she could have asked someone to bring a tray to her room. She wasn't ready to see the world or for the wealthy of Nassau to see her.

"Rose?"

"Coming," she said, pasting a smile on her face.

She would go because they both needed to eat and it would be nice to have a meal without feeling the ocean rolling beneath them.

Chapter 15

She opened the door to find Duncan standing there without his jacket, only his white shirt and trousers. At his side was a rolling tea cart, but instead of tea it contained plates. Two plates, to be exact, filled with steak and vegetables, and a bright red circular something that looked like aspic.

"Instead of going down to dinner, I brought dinner to us."

She could have kissed him. For a second she entertained a vision of doing just that, reaching up and winding her arms around him and kissing him to her heart's content. They might never get to eat the dinner he went to such an effort to obtain.

"I didn't think you'd mind," he said. "If you do, we can certainly go down to the restaurant."

"This is wonderful. More than wonderful. This is perfect."

She strode ahead of him to the sitting room and the alcove overlooking the harbor. Moving one of the tables, she made room for the tea cart as he rolled it closer.

"The restaurant is as well-patronized as the bar."

He sat and he passed her a plate.

"Is that steak?" she asked.

"Not just steak," he said, "but *filets mignon à*

l'americaine with sweet corn and asparagus tips, along with tomato aspic à la Viceroy."

After the entrée, a selection of cheeses and wafers completed the meal, along with coffee.

She hadn't eaten so well since Scotland, and told him so.

"Are you ready for the cake?"

"There's cake?"

He laughed. "Your eyes are lighting up like a child's."

Reaching to the bottom shelf, he pulled out the two plates piled high with coconut cake.

He filled her wineglass again, but she was concentrating on desert.

"This is wonderful, Duncan," she said. It was. She hadn't had coconut cake for months and this version was even better than the one Glengarden's cook had made.

"Would you like mine?"

She eyed it enviously for a moment then shook her head. "That would be unfair. It's truly a wonderful cake."

"It's a sacrifice I'm willing to make."

"Then, yes please, I'd love it."

He passed it over to her with a smile.

In minutes she finished the cake and took a sip from her glass. "Wine and cake. We are being decadent tonight, aren't we? Thank you, Duncan. How did you know that I didn't want to go to the restaurant?"

He smiled. "You're tired. So am I. It becomes tedious being around strangers when you're fatigued."

She looked at him. Two weeks ago he was a stranger, too. Now she'd always remember him.

He'd feature prominently in her memories. She almost wanted to tell him, to let him know how important he'd become. Recollections of him would make her smile. Some would make her wince with embarrassment, such as when she'd crawled on top of him with only her nightgown and wrapper on. But that had led to a kiss she would never forget.

And another on the deck of the *Raven*.

Would she ever have the courage to kiss him again?

A LOCK of her red hair had come loose from its cascade of curls. She fiddled with it for a moment, extracting a pin and putting it back in place to trap the errant curl.

A woman at her toilette was a fascinating sight, and here in this room, thousands of miles away from his role as mill owner, dependable, dedicated, and responsible, it seemed even more enchanting.

He grabbed the wine and poured both of them a full glass. After she took it from him, Duncan stared out at the harbor and its lights.

He felt curiously detached, but maybe it was the wine. Or the distance from Glasgow, allowing him to change from Duncan MacIain of MacIain Mills to someone different.

A man completely enamored of the woman who sat beside him.

"This has to be the most wonderful dinner I've ever had," she said, surprising him. "Other than in your house. I did like your home, Duncan. It's exactly the same kind of home I'd have if I'd been given a choice."

"And you weren't?"

She smiled. "Women aren't, all that much. Women are supposed to go along with a man, make a life where they dictate. Women are supposed to be meek and gracious, speak softly or not at all. We're supposed to know that the men in our lives are superior in every way."

He turned his head to study her. "Who told you that?"

"It's the code of the South. Or the code of women in the South. Or the code of the MacIains."

He smiled, thinking of his sister, Glynis. "I can tell you right now that it isn't the code of the Scottish MacIains. The women say whatever they wish whenever they want."

"It wasn't the code in my family, either," she said, holding up the glass and staring through the ruby colored wine. "I had a father and three brothers, and if I didn't speak up I'd never have been heard."

"What about your sister?"

"Claire? She was six years older than me and was always the sweet one. She talks very softly and everyone shuts up to listen to her. It's very annoying."

She stared at her glass as if to blame the wine for her honesty. What was that expression, *in vino veritas*? In wine is truth?

"She was always more feminine. Montgomery used to tell me that I should emulate her. That only made me stick my tongue out at him." She smiled, but the expression had a sad edge to it. "Jeremy, on the other hand, always said that I was best being myself."

"Jeremy sounds like he had a good head on his shoulders."

She nodded. "Do you ever get over missing someone? Sometimes I wake up from a dream and I could have sworn he was right there."

"I've only lost my father," he said. "But it was the same for me. For years I'd dream of him. Sometimes, in my dream, I'd tell him that he was dead, but he refused to believe it."

She looked surprised. "I've done the same with Jeremy, but then he stopped coming to me. Why is that?"

"Maybe there's something about the dead being given so many visits to the living. A way of saying good-bye when you weren't allowed to do so in life."

"I wasn't allowed to say good-bye to any of them, but you don't in war, do you?"

"No. How did you hear they were killed?"

"Susanna," she said.

He was left to imagine how her mother-in-law had known, and how, for that matter, the woman had transmitted the information to her. Had she done so with tact or cruelly?

Rose put her half full wineglass down on the table.

"Why do you want to go back to Glengarden?" he asked her.

"I don't," she said. "I despise the place."

" 'Love is sacrifice.' You said that to me once. Is that why? You have to be a martyr?"

She smiled. "I'm not the martyr type," she said.

"Do you have such loyalty to those people that you would endanger your own life?"

Wasn't that what she'd been doing for the past weeks? Yet it didn't sound as if anyone would reward her for doing so or even appreciate her effort.

"My niece is only five," she said. "She deserves a chance to grow up, even in the midst of war."

"And the others?"

"They would sit there and genteelly starve to death, never uttering a word of complaint to another soul. They would turn to skeletons while being perfectly dressed and coiffed. The perfect southern lady." She shook her head. "Someone needs to look out for them."

"Do you think yourself responsible? Is that why you're so dead set on doing this?"

"No," she said, looking at him. "I think it's the right thing to do, that's why I'm so dead set on doing this. Glengarden was built on all the wrong things, the belief that one man can enslave another, that any joy or happiness can come from that. But would I be any better if I ignored those people who need help? Wouldn't I be as bad as they?"

"You're an idealist, Rose, and the world isn't idealistic."

"No, it isn't," she said. "It's cruel and wrong, sometimes. Another reason not to ignore the right thing to do."

"Even if you're a Yankee?"

She smiled, and her expression held more amusement this time. "That's almost enough for them to refuse my help. But if you're hungry enough, you'll take a piece of bread from the devil himself."

He wasn't sure of that. Of course, he'd never been in the middle of a war, especially one that was dividing families.

A moment later she turned her head. "Why have you never kissed me again?"

He didn't know how to answer her. Perhaps the truth would have to do.

"Because I'm not a saint. Because I can't just keep kissing you without wanting more."

"*I DIDN'T* expect to see you here," Olivia Cameron said, after coffee have been served to her guest.

The meal had been an excellent one, but that was to be expected at Café Martinique, a restaurant known for its French chef. Most of the dishes were those that could easily be found in New Orleans or other southern cities, a wise move on the part of the owners.

Most of the inhabitants of Nassau were Confederates. Those who believed in the Union cause knew better than to broadcast it publicly, unless they wanted to be bodily detained en route to their hotel and beaten senseless.

The very city was a sea of gray, or men wearing light-colored suits and espousing southern sentiments with thick accents. She wasn't certain if all those men were simply Confederate sympathizers or very badly trained Union operatives.

Since the man sitting opposite her was responsible for those operatives, she doubted anyone he'd put in the field would be so poorly educated.

Matthew Baumann was a spider.

A very talented spider, but one nevertheless. He spun webs between people and events, places and things. She couldn't help but wonder if spiders saw patterns that were invisible to others. If so, that was another one of Baumann's skills.

"You're looking as lovely as ever, Olivia."

She smiled at him. He was very skilled at compliments. Even more so at determining which compliment would suit the recipient the most.

Perhaps he knew that she was feeling a little drab lately. Her latest relationship, if she might call it that, had faded until she'd taken pity on the poor man and ended it. She was currently without suitors, a fact that alternately amused and frightened her.

She'd known this day was coming.

Soon, Matthew would begin to compliment her on her skill at cozening someone, or her adept handling of a certain delicate matter between two of his operatives.

She was on her way to becoming his Mother Superior, while he had always been Machiavelli.

"I know why you're here," she said. "I saw her arrive."

"Ah, yes, the *Raven*. Your son's ship."

She would not allow him to see any reaction to his words. Instead, she sipped her coffee, wished him to perdition, and made sure her eyes met his over the edge of the cup.

"She's a beauty, isn't she?" she said, placing the cup on the saucer and reaching for her napkin. "But, then, Lennox was always a talented designer. He far exceeded William in that."

"I told him about you."

She didn't say a word. She'd had years of burying her emotions behind a calm facade. She was an expert at hiding strong feelings, especially those that would defeat another, less skilled actress.

That's what she was, when it was distilled to its finest drop. She was an actress on a stage of politics and upheaval and had been since she left Scotland.

Ten years ago she'd been living a relatively pleasant life in New York. She'd taken up causes that had been important to her while living in sin with a man five years younger. He'd been an artist, an impecunious one with a love of opium which he believed summoned forth the greatness of his talent. All it had done was make him a blithering fool who depleted their available funds and made it necessary for her to find employment.

She'd never been the millinery type. Nor had she any desire to work in a factory. She'd found herself in the curious position of becoming a whore.

Not a common whore, by any means, but one with a growing clientele, some of whom were active in city politics. The more exclusive she became, the more she was sought after. Evidently, men's egos were salved if they could say they'd bedded Margret, the name she'd taken in the role she played.

Nothing more than Margret. Her notes had a single M embossed on them. When she sent one of them to a man who'd solicited an evening, it was both an invitation and a bill.

She'd gotten rid of the artist, moved to a better address, and took up causes that interested her. The irony of working side by side in the abolitionist movement with the wives of some of the men she bedded amused her. So, too, the fact that occasionally she was invited to dinner, to sit at the table of a man who'd begged her to use a whip on him the last time they were together.

She might have continued as Margret had she not met Matthew Baumann.

He used blackmail like a woman used perfume. A spot of it there, a dot of it here. Despite her fluency with accents, he'd discovered that she was Scots. Her true name had taken longer, but he'd no qualms about using the knowledge to get her to work with him.

"Do you think I care what people think of me?" she'd asked on that long ago day.

She'd smiled at him, she recalled, amused that he thought she could be manipulated.

"I don't believe you give a good goddamn about the world, madam," he said, his mustache twitching with amusement. "But I think you care what your children think. Hardly fair for them to have a whore for a mother, is it?"

Time stopped in that instant, although such a thing was impossible, of course. Yet in those moments when she kept smiling at him and his agreeable expression hadn't altered, she envisioned his death at her hand. She'd stab him with something long and wickedly sharp, pierce the heart that existed only as an organ and not as a source of compassion or feeling. She'd watch him die in the ticking of a second and feel not one shred of remorse.

The only regret she had when leaving Scotland all those years ago was that she knew she'd never see her children again. A woman who abandoned her children, her life, and her husband had no rights. She'd never be able to explain that she was trapped in a marriage that could never be anything more than it was. William would never be a different man and she couldn't be the woman he deserved. She'd left. She'd left her darling son and daughter, knowing they'd be better off without her.

In that moment when time had simply stopped, she recognized that Matthew Baumann meant what he said. He'd have no difficulty telling either Lennox or Mary what she was, what she'd become. He might even take delight in it.

Perhaps she'd also recognized a kindred spirit in

him, a creature who would do whatever it must to survive and thrive.

Over the years, she'd passed on information from dozens of men. She'd even migrated to Washington, then to Virginia. With the war's escalation, she found it more amenable to move to Nassau, where the Confederacy maintained such an obvious presence. From here she learned all manner of secrets: which ships were bound for the still open southern ports, what their cargo contained, and who captained them.

Her penchant for bed sport, as he so charmingly called it, might have abated over time, but nothing had diminished her intellect.

She knew exactly why Matthew had suddenly appeared in Nassau, just as she knew that the long ago wish to murder him was once again at the forefront of her mind.

One thing he didn't understand. She might have left her children behind, but she would do anything to protect them.

Chapter 16

$\mathcal{R}$ose had always tried to look her best. She knew her hair was a drawback It was too brazen to be natural, too outlandish to be entirely proper. Her face was average, her nose and mouth neither too large nor too small. Her eyes were, perhaps, her best feature, but even they didn't make up for her hair.

She wanted Duncan to think her pretty, and the very thought made her feel silly and vulnerable.

"Do you think I'm vain?" she asked.

"You?" He studied her for a long moment. "I don't know of anyone less vain."

Warmth filled her at his comment. At least he thought her rational and practical, perhaps.

His hand cupped her cheek. "Especially as beautiful as you are."

She was being given her wish. Even if he didn't mean it, for a man like Duncan to say something like that was a gift she couldn't have expected and one she'd always remember.

She placed her hand on his, pressed against it as if to embed the texture of his palm on her skin.

"Thank you," she said softly. "You're very kind."

"I'm not exceptionally kind," he said. "I'm known as almost brutally honest."

"Not brutally, surely."

"I'm not talented in giving compliments. I should practice more. Shall I tell you about your gorgeous red hair? It reminds me of a sunrise. Or a sunset. Or your green eyes that always sparkle."

He was the one who was attractive. The kindest, most intelligent. She wanted to tell him the truth, to let him know everything. Perhaps then he wouldn't think her beautiful at all.

They were in Nassau. Close enough to the ending of it all that she could speak.

"Duncan . . ." she began, wondering how to start.

"Rose," he said, smiling. "You're as uncomfortable receiving compliments as I am in giving them."

She couldn't help but smile. "It's my upbringing. My three brothers were forever teasing me about my hair."

"Glynis made my life miserable following me around. Of course, it was Lennox she wanted to bedevil, but she was a pest."

"Oh, dear, I confess to being exactly the same. I think I was more obnoxious to Jeremy than to Robert or Montgomery." She shook her head. "Why do things have to change? Why do people have to die?"

"War," he said, extending his arm around her shoulders. "Chance. The ticking of the clock. A hundred reasons. A thousand. However many you want to claim. That's why life should be enjoyed each second, don't you think? Each moment. Each opportunity for happiness should be grabbed, and held onto for memory's sake, if nothing else."

For memory's sake, what a lovely way to say it.

She'd had few moments of happiness in the last two years. They'd come because of people she'd known, but not the ones she would have thought would bring her joy. Even her time with her niece was limited because of Bruce. He didn't want her to "corrupt his child." She recalled the laughter she'd shared with Maisie and the wisdom she received from Old Betsy. She'd received countless other acts of care and love from people who had nothing to give but the kindness in their hearts.

Yet the happiest she'd been was in the last two weeks. First, with the Scottish MacIains and then with Duncan. As her companion, he'd made her smile. Their conversations had left her with thoughts to ponder. Simply being with him had led to long stretches of contentment. Occasionally, she'd felt her breath catch on a perfect instant of joy.

Duncan MacIain had given her memories to seize and hold close.

She turned her head and knew that what she was going to do was possibly foolish and certainly scandalous.

She leaned nearer while still looking at him. Slowly, she closed her eyes and placed her mouth on his.

"Rose."

He spoke a caution against her lips, but she ignored it. She wanted more memories, wanted to grab everything she could in these days left to her. Give her something to hold onto in the dark times that were sure to come.

She placed both hands on either side of his face, held him still. His hands came up and removed hers. He held her captive, his eyes intent.

"Don't think me a saint, Rose, because I'm not."

"Good. I should think kissing a saint wouldn't be

at all enjoyable, do you? First, you'd have to apologize. Perhaps even say a prayer. I have no intentions of doing either, Duncan."

"I want you, Rose. If you start something, I may not be able to stop."

No one had ever wanted her before. No man had ever shocked her with those words.

Slowly, she pulled her hands free, and he let her. The next action should be that she stood and walked into the bedroom, shutting and perhaps locking the door behind her. Did the door even have a lock? She hadn't looked. If she used the lock, would it be to shut him out or to keep herself contained?

He was going to leave her here in Nassau. Or she was going to convince him to take her to Charleston. Either way, only days remained before she was back at Glengarden.

They were alone.

They were finally alone and no one knew. There were no seamen around or Captain McDougal. No friends to witness anything. No family to be shocked. No one either of them knew.

They were alone and the bed was huge and empty, beckoning to her.

She'd never considered herself wicked before. Nor did it feel especially wrong to consider loving Duncan. Only somehow right, as if this night, this place, this very hour was destined to happen.

She didn't know if they would, separate or together, make it through the blockade. Tomorrow was amorphous and uncertain. They might die. Or be caught and imprisoned. She might be put in a situation where she could be assaulted simply because she was an available woman.

She couldn't bear going back to Glengarden without memories. Scandalous memories, perhaps. Even shocking ones. Memories of her acting in a way she'd never thought to behave, shedding her virtue like an article of clothing.

Standing, she looked down at him. She'd never known anyone who could be so direct with a simple glance. It felt as if he peered into her soul, then swept the space to find anything she'd hidden there.

"Give me a few minutes," she said, uttering the words with a calm she didn't feel. She was trembling, either from fear or daring, she didn't know which.

Turning, she left him, feeling his gaze on her. When she closed the bedroom door, she leaned her forehead against it, her breath coming in dizzying gasps.

What was she doing?

Doing what she wished for one of the few times in the last year. Doing what she wanted from the depths of her heart. If she lived to be as ancient as Old Betsy, she would always remember moving to the armoire and removing her dress and undergarments, folding them away with a precision she'd never had before, as if to mark each separate act.

She donned her nightgown and walked into the bathroom. A little while later she removed the pins from her hair and brushed it slowly, watching herself in the mirror.

Would he come to her? If he didn't, what would she do? Go and kiss him again? Beg him with words she didn't even know?

How did you ask a man to love you?

If he didn't come to her, would she be able to face

him again? Perhaps it was best that he intended to leave her here to obtain her own passage back to Charleston. Most of the steamers running the blockade took passengers. The cost was prohibitive, but what was the price for humiliation?

She went to the bed, staring at it as if she'd never seen a bed before. Perhaps not one as ornately covered, with a coverlet sprinkled with silver thread. Netting hung from the ceiling and she pulled it free, stretching it around the mattress. Only then did she go to the door and open it wide, an invitation as blatant as calling out to Duncan.

Should she? Were words necessary right now?

Ducking beneath the netting, she pulled the sheets back, considered the open door and shocked herself by taking off her nightgown. Naked, there would be no doubt. Naked, words weren't necessary.

In seconds, it seemed, he appeared at the door, his shirt half unbuttoned.

Her heart was in her throat. No, it had fallen to her feet. She couldn't breathe for the excitement. Either that or terror. No, she wasn't afraid of Duncan, only what he represented, perhaps. The unknown. Masculinity defined by a towering frame, a broad physique and strength.

He'd extinguished the lamps in the sitting room. Only one light was left, the one on the low-slung bureau. Were lights left on when couples mated? Was that part of the ritual? She didn't know so many things, but she wasn't an innocent, either.

There was no privacy on a plantation. No discreet places for a couple to love when the mood struck them. She'd been an accidental voyeur on many occasions, enough to appreciate what was happening to her now.

Her mind didn't care that she was being unforgivingly brazen. Her body ruled, and it demanded that he join her, that he was the one she kissed, who felt her body, with whom she was intimate.

"Rose."

Don't speak. Don't spoil the moment. Don't lecture. Don't be wise or decent. Just come to me.

She didn't say a word, only pulled back the covers on the other side of the bed.

"Damn it, Rose."

She sat up, baring herself to the waist. His eyes feasted on her, heated her blood, tamed her fear and escalated her excitement.

Patting the mattress, she looked directly at him.

"I'm no damn saint," he said as he ducked beneath the netting.

"Well, thank heavens for that," she said as he came to her. "Because I'm no angel."

HE WOULD worry about going to hell later. He'd donate a wing to a church. He'd give to the poor. At the moment, his body was silencing his mind, and although he should walk away, he also knew he had no intention of doing so.

What man in his right mind would refuse the temptation of Rose, naked in bed, inviting him to join her?

Not him. Not when she'd been in his thoughts, his dreams, ever since he'd seen her.

This moment shouldn't be happening, though.

He should be counseling her on restraint. He should be sitting on the edge of the bed holding her hand, patiently explaining that the situation was impossible. He was about to run the blockade, and although he had faith in Captain McDougal, there was danger that he might be captured or killed.

He shouldn't be removing his shirt, shoes, pants, and underclothes in record time, sliding beneath the sheet and pulling her atop him. He certain shouldn't be kissing her until his head swam and any reasonable, rational thought was lost in lust.

He couldn't get enough of her. He wanted to kiss her everywhere but never leave her lips. He needed to touch her, his hands sweeping down her back to cup her buttocks, pull her hard against his erection.

She made a sound and wiggled closer and he was almost doomed. Too fast. They were going too fast. He wanted to savor her, have her hair draped over his chest, kiss her breasts and take his time.

He gently moved her off of him and rolled to his side.

"Did I do something wrong?" she asked.

"Wrong? You did everything right. You *are* everything right."

"Then why are you over there?"

"I don't have any control around you."

She raised up on her elbow, her glorious hair half covering her breasts. A nipple peeped out from beneath the reddish gold tresses to tease him.

He brushed two fingers against it, watched it harden with fascination. He couldn't resist and bent to kiss her there, pushing her hair out of the way. A second later his lips were tugging at it and she was flat on her back, her hands on his shoulders pulling him closer.

"Are you supposed to have control?" she asked, her voice faint and breathless.

"No. Yes. I don't around you."

"Thank you."

He raised up. "Thank you?"

She was the most beautiful woman he'd ever seen, graced by the light from the lamp, a study of porcelain, red hair, pink cheeks, and smiling lips.

"I like the uncontrolled you. It makes me feel the same."

Thank God for that.

He kissed her. He would always be inarticulate around her, he suspected, especially when she was naked.

Her breasts were plump, the areoles large and the most exquisite coral color. He saluted one nipple with a kiss, then the other before taking it into his mouth and sucking gently.

She moaned, her nails gouging into his shoulders, but he didn't complain. Nor did he when her hands began to explore him, sweeping down his arms, her palms planted flat on his chest.

"What a pity you have to wear clothes. You're so beautiful without them."

He was silenced again, this time by her words. He'd never been called beautiful before. Nor had a woman ever looked at him like Rose was looking now, her eyes sparkling as she explored him.

"May I touch you?"

He knew what she was talking about and he didn't know how to answer. *Please, for the love of God*, might be too abrupt. "Yes," didn't sound enthusiastic enough.

He rolled to his side, grabbed her hand and placed it on his penis. There, that was emphasis enough.

Her reaction stunned him.

She sat up, pulled the sheet back and stared. Now he'd wished he'd extinguished the light.

"Oh, my, Duncan. Perhaps it's a good thing you do wear clothes."

What the hell did that mean?

Her palm stroked up and down his length, only making his torment worse. She really shouldn't keep doing that. In a minute or two he'd tell her to stop.

He put his hands on her breasts, his palms brushing against her nipples.

When he'd thought of Rose in his bed, he'd never envisioned this. Not her delight or the pink cast to her cheeks, the soft smile she wore as she tortured him with her hands. Nor did he think that she would lean over him and in a voice as soft as the cooing of doves further tease him.

"Kiss me, Duncan. Please."

He wasn't a fool.

He moved one hand from her breast to place it behind her head and draw her to him. The other hand gently removed her fingers from his penis. He hadn't had enough of her, but if she didn't stop, he'd explode in her hands.

He wanted to love her for hours, but he knew he wouldn't be able to for this first time. He wanted to explain, to apologize, to say something, but kissing her was stripping every thought from his mind.

All he could think about was how she felt, warm and womanly, her hands on his arms, her breasts brushing against his chest, her mouth open above him, her tongue exploring his lips.

He reversed their places until he was over her, his hands sweeping over her breasts, stomach, thighs, that secret place that welcomed him with a widening of her legs. Her hips rose to meet his fingers, the wetness slicking his passage through the swollen folds, over the most sensitive places.

She moaned.

This should have lasted for hours. At least longer than it had. But he wanted her and it was evident she wanted him, too.

He rose up, supported himself on his forearms and guided himself into her. Her hips rose to meet him.

Words tripped on his tongue, were swallowed by astonishment as he met resistance.

She gasped, hands gripping his arms, nails gouging.

What had begun as something so magical, so perfect, so sensuous, was turning into a disaster.

He tried to pull out, but she locked her legs around his, wrapped her arms around his shoulders, her hips surging upward.

His body demanded release, bore down, pulled out, then back again, the endless rhythm impossible to stop. His vision grayed, his mind blurred as pleasure roared through him.

His hands dug beneath the pillow, his breath coming in hoarse gasps.

She turned her face to his, but he didn't kiss her.

Minutes later he pulled back, moving away.

He didn't let her escape, but rolled her to her side, facing him. She finally blinked open her eyes and looked at him.

He didn't know if he was angry or simply confused.

"Would you like to explain, Rose, how a widow is a virgin?"

DUNCAN GOT out of bed and went into the bathroom. She heard the water run, sat up and grabbed her wrapper. The blood on the sheet startled her. She covered it up with the top sheet and walked into the sitting room, tightening the belt on her wrapper as she did so.

Opening the door to the balcony off the sitting room, she stood there, buffeted by the breeze off the harbor. When she first came to Nassau, weeks earlier, she'd thought that it had to be one of the most beautiful locations in the world. Tonight was no different, with the twinkling lights from the ships, the dark water and, above, a sliver of moon.

She heard Duncan close the door, then his soft footfalls on the floor toward her. This confrontation was not going to be easy. She'd wanted to tell him the truth, but not exactly this way.

She hadn't even considered her virginity when she invited him to her bed. It had been like an old sweater she'd kept far past its prime, a garment that needed to be replaced. She'd chosen him, in a way, to end her maidenly state simply because she couldn't refuse the urge. She'd wanted to make love with Duncan. Did that admission make her a harlot? If so, then label her a harlot, because up until the last, it had been a glorious experience.

He came and stood directly behind her, so close he could hit her if he chose. But this was Duncan. He'd never strike her. He might yell at her but he would never hit her.

"What the hell is going on, Rose?" he said, his voice rough. "Bruce wasn't able to fulfill his husbandly duties?"

"I was never married to Bruce," she said.

She bent her head, studying the floor, waiting for him to speak.

"So you're not Bruce MacIain's widow?"

"No," she said.

"Just who the hell are you?"

"Rose O'Sullivan. Claire's sister. Claire is married to Bruce." She finally turned to face him. He was fully dressed, down to his shoes.

As he studied her, his face firmed until it looked like stone.

She knew how to look exactly the same. So many times over the last two years she'd had to mask her emotions or her thoughts. Bruce would use whatever she revealed as a weapon over her, so she vowed never to look weak to him.

Did Duncan feel the same way right now? No doubt he did, and she'd made him feel it.

The silence was suddenly more than she could bear.

"I couldn't tell you who I was. I assumed you would be like all those ignorant, small-minded factors here in Nassau, refusing to believe I had the rights to Glengarden's cotton."

She hadn't worn her gloves to bed, and in the sitting room light she extended her hands, palms down.

"You asked if I wore gloves because my hands were scarred by a fire. It wasn't a fire," she said. "It was from picking cotton. I thought they'd heal, but they haven't. A reminder of Glengarden that I'll carry with me forever."

"Why were you picking cotton?"

"The first time was one of Bruce's punishments. He said if I wanted to be with the slaves, I should act like a slave. I labored in the fields, alongside them.

For days I was bent over just as they were, learning what it was like to be treated as less valuable than a horse or a mule. I dragged a sack behind me, listening to the shouts of the overseer, waiting to be struck because I wasn't fast enough or too clumsy, or had looked up when I wasn't supposed to set my eyes on his privileged back."

She stared at her hands. "The second time was necessity. We didn't have enough people to harvest the cotton and we had to save it. Yet those idiotic men had the temerity to tell me I didn't have any rights to Glengarden's cotton."

When she'd left for Scotland, she never expected to find someone like him, a man of ethics and character, tenderness and honesty. How could she lie to him any longer?

"I always thought the scars would go away, but they never did. My face gradually got less tan, but that's because of the sour milk and something else Maisie made me use every night. I wasn't supposed to look like a slave, you see. I was only to be treated like one."

She couldn't bear it if his next words were cruel. She filled the silence with her own words, desperate to keep him silent and kind.

"I brought the cotton to Charleston myself," she said. "With two other people."

Benny, young and strong, had helped her, along with Maisie, older yet sturdy and just as stubborn as she had assisted her. They couldn't afford to hire men to help them, so the three of them had manhandled the bales themselves, with Benny doing most of the work. It had taken them four trips on the barge to Charleston.

She'd taken the precaution of doing business with those men who would give her a certificate for the cotton, both of which she'd kept in her valise.

He still didn't say anything.

She had to tell him the rest of the truth. "Bruce isn't dead."

His face didn't move.

"I pray for my brothers' souls every night. I pray for my father. But I can't push myself to pray for Bruce, God help me. I don't know where he is, but I don't want him coming back to Glengarden. The only reason the last year has been bearable is because he's been gone."

"Anything else?" he asked. "Any other secrets you haven't divulged?"

"I don't have friends in Nassau. I had to say something or you wouldn't have brought me here." She glanced over at him. "I hate lying to you, Duncan, and it seems I've done too much of it."

He turned and walked toward the door.

"Where are you going?"

"I don't know," he said. "Someplace other than here."

Chapter 17

Slavery had ended in the Bahamas as well as the other British West Indies around 1832. That point seemed to irk a few of the Confederate soldiers, who saw a freed black men as a personal affront.

Duncan encountered one of those angry young men as he descended the steps to the lobby. The man was making an ass of himself with his remarks and was being asked by the hotel manager to leave.

Since Duncan was in the mood for a brawl, he didn't mind adding his persuasion.

"Why don't you run along?" he said, hoping the man gave him a reason to take a swing at him.

He was upset because Rose had lied, angry because she'd been treated so badly, and confused because he'd been blindsided by her virginity. He, who had not been in a fight since he and Lennox got into it when they were thirteen, wanted to punch someone.

"You're English, aren't you?" the idiot Confederate asked.

"Actually, no. I'm Scot."

"Isn't that the same thing?"

"No," a woman said from behind him.

He turned to face her, but she addressed the man who'd inquired as to his nationality.

"A dog is an animal, but he isn't a cat. Never confuse a Scot for an Englishman."

Strangely enough, that silenced the officer—Duncan thought his insignia meant he was a colonel—and he pushed past all of them and headed for the door.

The woman, who smiled at him, looked to be in her fifties, but there was no fading of her beauty. Her hair was black with no hint of gray. Her eyes, a striking gray-green, held a hint of amusement. A mole on her cheek pointed to a perfect mouth, one wearing a half smile. Her neck was long and elegant, her shoulders without that crepe texture to her skin that older women sometimes have. Tall and resplendent in a dark green dress, she could have easily been a doyenne of society and perhaps was.

"I would like to speak with you," she said, surprising him. "Would you join me in the lobby?"

The Blockade Runners Bar was off-limits to women, even of a certain occupation, but this woman didn't look like a lady of the evening. In fact, she reminded him of someone familiar, though he couldn't place her.

He followed her to a set of two chairs and a table, one of several clustered in front of a now cold fireplace.

"You came in on the *Raven*, did you not?"

He nodded.

"The ship interests me."

A strange comment to make, followed by another statement that intrigued him.

"Tell me who you are. I haven't had a chance to make inquiries."

"Why would you want to know? I'm not averse to

giving you my name, but why are you interested in the *Raven*?"

"It's my son's ship," she said, tilting her head back and staring at him.

He was immediately reminded of Mary, Lennox's sister, how when she was pushed past politeness and stood up to someone her chin could look as pointed and the expression in her eyes as glacial.

"Mrs. Cameron," he said, "I'm Duncan MacIain, and the last time I saw you I was twelve years old."

He didn't know what he expected, but it wasn't delighted laughter.

"You're as handsome as you promised to be as a boy, Duncan MacIain. Are you as smart?"

He didn't know what kind of answer she wanted, but he gave her the truth. "I thought I was until about three weeks ago. Now? I don't honestly know."

"Well, I certainly hope you are because you and I both have a problem and we need to solve it."

HE HATED her. That was obvious. She knew he might be angry, but she'd never considered that he might be disgusted by what she'd done.

What did she do now?

She needed to find passage to Charleston on another ship, one where the price wasn't astronomical. She'd come to depend on Captain McDougal. Hopefully, the captain she chose would be as knowledgeable and lucky running the blockade.

She couldn't afford a room at the Viceroy, even if there was one available. She should go see the widow who'd rented her a room a few weeks ago. Perhaps she would have accommodations or might know where she could stay.

It wasn't going to be here, that was for certain.

At least she had the memories of being in Duncan's arms, having him touch her and kiss her.

If he'd known she wasn't a widow, would he have treated her differently? Would he have made love to her? Probably not. He would have stormed out of the suite just as he had now, only after a blistering lecture.

At least she wasn't a virgin anymore.

She'd been carried away by his kisses, intoxicated by his touch. She'd wanted him to do everything he'd done. If she left now, she'd never get the chance again, but it was clear he didn't want her here.

The shame that flowed over her was like boiling water, burning her skin. She felt her insides quiver and curl up, feeling the aching humiliation of her own actions.

Old feelings.

The thought came to her so suddenly she was startled. Those were old feelings. Old feelings spurred on by Bruce's words.

You're not a lady like your sister. Why can't you be more like Claire?

You shouldn't have made that remark at dinner, Rose. Next time, perhaps it would be best if you had a tray in your room.

My mother tells me you're being too familiar with your maid. You have to set a tone, Rose, and it's obvious you don't know how to do that.

Old feelings Bruce had made her feel, as if she weren't capable of a thought unless he'd given it to her. As if she were a poor shadow of her lovelier sister, a sister who'd become silent in the face of his constant criticism.

To hell with Bruce.

She wasn't going to feel those old feelings. Not now and not in the future. Very well, she might have done something shameful, but no one was going to take the memory of it from her.

She might be a doddering old lady or a matriarch like Susanna, a queen in her own carefully constructed kingdom, but she was always going to have the memory of this night to keep her company. Whatever happened to her from this point forward, however long the war might drag on and despite any privations it brought, she would know that for one night she was loved.

Even Bruce couldn't destroy that memory.

Only Duncan could.

WHEN HE was twelve years old Olivia Cameron scandalized all of Glasgow by leaving her husband. Not only did she abandon William Cameron, the owner of a prosperous ship-building company, but she left behind her two children, Mary and Lennox.

For years, Olivia Cameron was considered the most wicked woman in the history of Glasgow.

She didn't appear touched by her tarnished reputation.

He'd resented her, not for his own sake, but for Lennox's. His friend had never discussed his mother, her absence, or her once-a-year letters that had abruptly stopped when Lennox was sixteen.

"What do you want, Mrs. Cameron?"

"I knew the *Raven* was a Cameron and Company ship the moment she appeared in the harbor," she said. "I also knew that Lennox designed her. William's ships were more utilitarian. They didn't have that spark of beauty, that magic about them."

"How do you know? He was only twelve when you left Scotland."

She smiled. "I may not be in Glasgow, Duncan, but I know what goes on there."

"He's brilliant at what he does, Mrs. Cameron. He always has been."

"You're still friends, then."

He nodded.

"You're running the blockade, aren't you?"

"You surely don't expect me to answer that question, do you?" he asked, smiling.

She responded with a smile of her own.

"I was sorry to hear about your father," she said, surprising him. Evidently, she did know what went on in Glasgow. "You've inherited the mill, haven't you?"

He nodded.

"I understand my daughter's not yet married."

His mother had once confided in him that she and Olivia, who had been friends, thought a union between he and Mary would be a lovely thing.

"We're friends," he said. "But I rarely socialize with her. I understand, from Glynis, that she's seeing someone. Perhaps she's even contemplating marriage."

Olivia Cameron didn't say anything, even when a waiter appeared and he ordered tea for them both. He would have liked something stronger at the moment, but now was not the time.

"I'm glad Glynis and Lennox married," she said. "She was always taken with him."

"Don't believe all you hear about her from Matthew Baumann."

Her eyes widened just a little, enough that he could tell she was surprised.

"You know him?" she asked.

"He came to Glasgow," he said. "Made himself obnoxious enough that the whole city probably remembers him."

As they did her.

A comment that lingered in the air between them.

"Did you know she worked for him, was a Union operative?"

"Yes," he said. "I did. I also know that you work for him."

She smiled. The expression had a touch of malice to it.

"He told me he'd informed Lennox of that fact."

He nodded.

"And he, in turn, told you," she said.

"We're good friends."

"Will you tell Lennox that you saw me?"

"Do you want me to?"

"I don't know," she said.

"Neither do I. I guess that depends on what you've come to tell me."

She stared down at her hands long enough that he knew she was trying to gain her composure. When she looked up again, her green-eyed gaze was direct and her words startling.

"The *Raven* has a reputation for being one of the fastest ships built."

"Where did you hear that? Baumann again?"

She surprised him by nodding. "They knew you were coming here before you ever saw the last of Scotland," she said. "The Union wants her, badly."

"How badly?" he asked, getting a sour taste in the back of his tongue.

He waited until they were served before continuing their conversation.

"How badly, Mrs. Cameron?"

She smiled again. "I haven't been called that for a great many years, Duncan. People don't know me by that name."

"What name do you go by?

She shrugged, her smile altering character. "Any name that's convenient at the time."

"And now?"

"Peterson. Olivia Peterson."

"You still haven't answered me."

"I prize loyalty," she said, taking one of the striped biscuits from the plate. She ate it with delicacy, evidently savoring the chocolate.

He didn't have an appetite after his large dinner. "Do you?"

She nodded. "I find it very difficult to turn my back on a cause I believe in."

"Which is what?"

She took a sip of her tea before answering him.

"The sovereignty of the Union, Duncan. The survival of the United States. It's my adopted home and has treated me well. Better than I expected and possibly better than I deserved."

She put down her cup and studied him. "But there's something else I find more important than even the Union cause, something I never considered until I saw the *Raven*."

He remained silent. She had something to say and would take her own time in telling it.

"A mother's love."

She smiled, and it seemed to him the expression was sad rather than amused.

"Isn't that strange? I haven't seen my child for decades yet I will not allow his creation to be destroyed."

"What are they planning?"

"They can't fire on you in the harbor," she said. "But they can the minute you enter international waters. But that would damage the ship and they don't want that. How much better to simply board the *Raven* while she's in port and take command of her here."

That would violate a variety of maritime laws, but he knew Baumann. The man was ruthless. He'd already tried to sabotage the ship twice in Glasgow. He wouldn't put it past him to do the same here.

"When?"

"When the *Exeter* arrives in Nassau in two days. They'll use her crew to board the *Raven*."

They'd been planning on leaving Nassau in three days, timing their departure for when the moon wouldn't be visible. It looked like they'd just have to take their chances and leave as soon as possible. Hopefully, the coal could be loaded tomorrow, which meant they'd get a one day head start. He didn't have any doubts that if the Union couldn't capture the *Raven*, they'd try to blow her out of the water.

"If we were seen," she said, taking another sip of her tea and replacing the cup on the saucer, "it was to discuss old times. I asked about my children. You told me of them. Nothing else transpired."

"There's one other thing," he said, the idea only minutes old.

He wasn't going to leave Rose here to fend for herself. Nor did he want her to run the blockade with him. Olivia had arrived at the opportune time.

She frowned at him.

"Rose O'Sullivan," he said.

"Who is she?"

"A relative, of a sort," he said, smiling. Friend, lover,

stranger, enigma, confusion, all of these words could be applied to Rose and still not explain her. "I need somewhere for her to stay until I return from Charleston."

"You would trust me with the woman you love?"

For a moment he didn't know how to answer her. Words were occasionally inconvenient.

Her smile was kind, reminding him of when he was a boy and she'd been an impossibly beautiful figure to him.

"Oh, Duncan, why would you care about her safety unless you loved her?"

He wasn't going to discuss how he felt about Rose, not when he was confused about his emotions.

"Yes," he said. "I would trust you with her safety."

"Why?"

"Why?" He smiled. "Because when it came to making an important decision, you chose Lennox."

She didn't say anything for a moment, merely pulled out a calling card and wrote something on the back.

"My room number," she said. "I'm staying here as well. Send her to me, Duncan. I will take care of her. But leave before the *Exeter* arrives. Otherwise, there's nothing I can do to protect you or the *Raven*. You might be a Scot, but that won't save you from a Union prison."

MEETING OLIVIA had melted Duncan's anger and sharpened his confusion. He had two things to do: alert Captain McDougal that their timeline needed to be sped up, and convince Rose to remain in Nassau.

He didn't fool himself that running the blockade would be as simple as Captain McDougal had hinted. He couldn't subject her to the danger. Especially after all she'd already endured.

He made his way to the harbor, grateful to find a carriage to rent outside the hotel. Once aboard the *Raven*, he explained the situation to the captain.

"The coal won't be loaded until mid-morning, sir, but I'll make sure it gets done fast. Even so, it'll take hours. When did you say the *Exeter* is due in?"

"All the information I have is two days," he said.

"We won't be able to leave until tomorrow night at the soonest, but customs could slow us even further. They may hold us up until the day after tomorrow. I'll put in the paperwork change first thing in the morning."

"In other words, we might be getting out of here as the *Exeter* is entering the harbor."

"It might be a tight squeeze, sir, but I'll be damned if they're going to board the *Raven*. With your permission, I'd like to take on more crew. Just to be on the safe side."

He nodded. The extra expense didn't matter. He was responsible for the ship and he'd do what needed to be done to keep her safe. He was not going to return to Scotland and explain to Lennox and Dalton that he'd surrendered the *Raven* to the Union navy.

Once back at the hotel, Duncan climbed the stairs to the gallery on the third floor and stood looking up at the night sky. The heavens looked so close that it seemed he could almost reach up and pluck one of those stars.

He'd lived his life in order, a certain calm, structured peace. He was rarely tested, never physically harmed, and the only daily challenge he had was a financial one, keeping the mill running. His needs were always met, most of the time before he knew he had them.

The people in his life made no secret of their love and affection for him. He was applauded for drawing breath, for his efforts at the mill, for doing what he was expected to do. His family was loving. His friends were loyal. His employees were dedicated.

He'd seen, experienced, and lived with the best of human kind and had never truly appreciated any of that until now.

Or until a woman with bright red hair fell at his feet.

His life, in the last two years, had been idyllic compared to Rose's. She let slip details a little at a time, but enough now that a picture had emerged of her life at Glengarden.

She never stopped. She never gave up. She persisted and would probably always persist. He'd never known anyone with such tenacity.

Yet, somehow, he had to convince her to remain in Nassau.

Rose probably didn't have the right to sell Glengarden cotton. She wasn't Bruce's widow. The former fact disturbed him, but not the latter. He was damn glad she hadn't been married to the bastard.

He would go to Glengarden and visit with Claire. Her signature on the documents should make everything legal and aboveboard. As long as the rest of the paperwork was in order, and he'd examined it at home, he had no qualms about the transaction.

The day had been warm, warmer than he was used to, and now there was a soft humid breeze rustling the leaves of the trees surrounding the hotel.

The view of Nassau harbor was magnificent. He wasn't a seasoned sailor like Captain McDougal, and there were quite a few vessels he couldn't identify, ranging in size from small rowboats to steamers nearly the size of the *Raven*. If he used a spyglass, how far could he see? Would he be able to see the Union ships waiting just outside British waters?

Looking out over the harbor, he realized he couldn't pick out the *Raven*. She was one of the larger ships, if not the largest, and he should have been able to see her. A moment later he smiled, realizing that a few of the other steamers weren't visible, either. The *Raven* had been painted a particular shade of gray, a black line at the waterline marking the beginning of her iron hull. If she'd been painted black, which is what he might have done in his inexperience, she could be as easily seen as the other ships.

Lennox was a genius.

He knew that he'd tell Lennox and Mary about the meeting with Olivia. They deserved to know that their mother—if she could be called that after so many years—was alive and well.

A thought that brought him back to Rose. She wouldn't want to stay in Nassau, but he had to think of her safety.

He'd return for her. Would she care? Would she want him?

He came from a long line of Highlanders. Men who'd braved countless odds to fight for freedom. Men who'd been defeated time and again. He wasn't about to quit now. Not in his fight to save the mill or in his quest for Rose.

She might not realize she was being pursued. Perhaps that was another task he needed to put on his list.

He descended from the third floor and headed for their room. Now all he had to do was convince Rose that his plan was for the best. He didn't fool himself that it was going to be easy.

Chapter 18

$\mathcal{R}$ose packed her valise, wondering if Duncan would allow her to stay the night. Or would he make her leave the suite as soon as possible? If so, she'd give him the certificates for the cotton and directions to the warehouses.

Would he still consider their arrangement a valid sale?

She sat in the sitting room, staring down at the harbor. At least she got to know him. She wouldn't take back her actions, even with all her duplicity.

Had she known she would meet Duncan MacIain, she'd have left Glengarden a lot sooner than she had.

But then, he wasn't like most men she knew. No, that wasn't quite true. Jeremy, too, had a wonderful sense of humor. Duncan was loyal and devoted to family, like Montgomery and an obvious leader like Robert. Yet Duncan was his own man, stubborn and fixed when he was set on a point.

Determined, yes, he was that. Determined to make a success of his life, his heritage, and to win against all the challenges he'd been given.

What a pity Bruce couldn't have been more like him, but her brother-in-law always sought out someone else to blame for his own mistakes. Or he blamed nature, Lincoln, and the Yankees.

She wasn't sorry she'd gone to Scotland. She wouldn't have traded the chance to meet the Scottish MacIains for anything.

She heard the door open and held herself still as it closed.

"Rose? Why are you sitting there in the dark?"

"I wanted to see the harbor," she said.

"Why is your valise by the door?"

"I didn't know if you would want me gone tonight or in the morning, so I prepared for either."

"Are you daft?"

She turned and stared at him. "Do you not remember, Duncan MacIain, our conversation of a few hours earlier? When you stormed out of here?"

"You've never sounded Irish before," he said, smiling. "Is it because you're angry?"

She narrowed her eyes at him. "I'm not angry. My heart is broken, but I'm not angry. What right have I to be angry? I lied to you when I shouldn't have. And I didn't tell you I was a virgin, which isn't quite a lie, but isn't the truth, either, is it?"

"Why is your heart broken? And why is your hair wet?"

She decided to answer the second question since it was the easiest.

"I washed my hair. It smelled of the sea and was sticky. I'd rather not go out looking for lodgings with wet hair, but if I have to, I will."

"I repeat, are you daft? Why would you think I'd want you gone?"

He came around and sat beside her, not even giving her time to move her skirt.

"You were angry."

"Yes, I was, but that's no reason to think I want

you gone." Reaching out, he grabbed her glove, stripped it off her hand. She clenched her hand into a fist, but he extended each finger one by one, tracing the scars tenderly.

"I'm angry about the situation, Rose. I'm furious about the position you were put in. I'm angry that I wasn't a better lover, that I didn't treat you with tenderness."

"Oh, Duncan."

"You know, when I lived in Scotland, I was known as a very calm, rational man. I was always even tempered. I don't know what's happened since you came into my life, but you've changed me."

"I changed you?"

"I can't think of who else it could be. Do you see any other redheaded beauties around here?"

Her heart swelled. "I'm not beautiful."

"Of course you are. If you weren't, I wouldn't be an idiot around you. Or maybe I would be. I'm not sure."

She blinked back her tears. He really shouldn't say things like that.

"You're not an idiot."

"I wish I'd known you were a virgin. I wouldn't have seduced you."

She hadn't expected to smile.

"It was the coconut cake," she said, looking at him. "I think it cast a spell over me."

"Not the wine?"

"Perhaps a little of the wine," she admitted. "Or the kisses. You kiss like the Devil himself, Duncan MacIain. A woman should be warned not to trust your handsome face. You look so very kind and decent, but there's nothing decent about the way you kiss."

His face bronzed as if she'd embarrassed him. Didn't the man know how well he kissed? Evidently not, if his cheeks turned color at the mention of it.

"You're not going anywhere, at least not tonight," he said.

"Is that right?" Who was he to give her orders? Never mind that he said exactly what she hoped he'd say, there was the principle of the thing.

"Stay, Rose. Please." He pulled her into his arms. "But it's only fair to warn you. I have a feeling that I might be getting angry in the future. You'll have to get used to it."

"I will?"

"Or I might become temperamental. Passionate, perhaps."

"Will you? And this is all because of me?"

He nodded.

She didn't know what to say to him in response. She sensed it was a huge compliment he'd given her, one that made her feel humble and more than a little awkward.

It was only fair that he knew what he did to her in return.

"I've had the most delicious dreams about you. Last week you and the crew were dousing yourselves with water on deck and I peeked out the porthole. You really should go without your shirt more often."

"I should?"

His smile was charming and a little mischievous.

She nodded, then lay her head against his shoulder.

"What broke your heart?" he asked softly.

Should she tell him? If she did, she'd have no more

secrets. He'd know everything. Every insecurity she possessed, every vulnerability she had.

"The idea of leaving you," she said, taking a chance. "It was breaking my heart."

He didn't say anything for a moment, just hugged her tighter. His hands pressed against her back, his cheek was against hers. How odd to have a perfect instant in time after such a tempestuous evening.

"Now that I'm not a virgin, is there a reason not to take me to your bed? You were shockingly abrupt last time."

He pulled back and stared at her.

"I beg your pardon?"

"Well, I'd always thought that passion was supposed to be beautiful, and we hardly had a chance, did we? You were much too concerned about my virginity. Now that's done, we don't have to worry about it, do we?"

He continued to stare at her.

Oh dear, had she ruined everything?

DUNCAN WASN'T sure what he felt right now.

He knew she hadn't found any pleasure in their lovemaking and that he'd been a lousy lover. Part of that he put down to his surprise. No, shock. Hell, if he'd known she was a virgin, he wouldn't have been so eager to join her in bed. He would have kissed her on the forehead and locked and bolted her in her room.

Was that entirely true? Especially since she was looking at him in the same way she had earlier?

Where had his control gone? She'd somehow stolen it the moment she crossed his threshold in Glasgow. A red-haired seductress with cotton to sell.

"Damn it, Rose."

What was he going to do with her? The better question was: what was he going to do right now?

He stood, marched to the door, grabbed her valise and threw it into the bedroom. A moment later he entered the bathroom and began to remove his clothes.

A bath right now sounded like a fantastic idea. Maybe it would cool him off, give him time to return to his even-natured self. The water was boiling and that was fine. He'd turn it to cold before he got out.

She was right; she wasn't a virgin any longer, thanks to him. She, however, shared a bit of the blame since she'd invited him to her bed. The least she could have done was warn him.

If he made love to her again, he wouldn't compound his sin, but he might be able to make up for it, especially if he took his time and made sure she enjoyed herself.

He used the soap the hotel had provided, something that smelled of fresh breezes and the sea. He, too, washed his hair, standing under the shower with his eyes closed, thoroughly enjoying the moment.

Rose touched his back, making him jump.

He turned to find her standing there in her shift and nothing else. No mourning. No nightgown or wrapper. Just Rose in her shift with her nipples pressed against the thin fabric.

He was rendered entirely speechless when she removed the shift and stepped inside the tub.

She was going to do that a lot in the future, wasn't she? She was going to turn his life upside down. She was going to confuse him and bamboozle him and startle him endlessly. Why didn't the thought of that concern him one whit? Why, instead, did it make him want to smile?

"You're naked," he said, his gaze sweeping from the top of her head all the way down her curvy body.

"So are you," she said, giving him the same appraisal. "I understand it's something one does when one bathes."

"You're bathing with me?"

"I thought it would save time."

"Did you?"

She nodded. "Well, it's better than you taking a bath and me waiting and then me taking a bath and you waiting, don't you think?" She looked up at the shower and smiled at the water pounding down on both of them. "It's like rain, isn't it?"

He'd never bathed with a woman. He'd never before considered it or dreamed of a woman entering his tub, especially one as delectable as Rose.

He didn't know what to do first.

The old Duncan, the proper and restrained man of Glasgow, would have left, grabbed a towel, and possibly even been embarrassed over the lack of privacy.

He was no longer the old Duncan. Instead, he had begun to do things he'd never before considered. In this case, he grabbed the soap and began to wash her.

She liked it. He could tell because she closed her eyes when he began to massage her shoulders and smiled when his hands dropped to her breasts. They were very clean when he was finished, with their tips pointing directly at him.

He dipped his head and licked one, then began to soap it again.

Her hands were suddenly flat on his stomach.

He didn't know what to do about that, either, or the fact that her fingers were walking their way down toward his very hard penis. It, too, was pointing.

If she touched him, he'd be useless. Whenever he was around her, he wanted her, but this, this was too much. Her hands on him, soaping him? He'd erupt in seconds.

She deserved more from him this time. He was going to love her slowly, as she deserved, with patience and more skill.

He gently turned her so that her back was to him, wrapped his arms around her and bent to nuzzle at her neck.

"There are some temptations that should be delayed," he said.

He pulled back to wash her back. His hands froze in midair.

HOW STUPID to have forgotten. She'd been naked with him, but he'd not seen her back until now.

"He had you whipped?" he asked, his voice soft, his tone revealing none of his emotions. His trembling, soapy hands traced the lines of the scars from her shoulders to the middle of her back.

"Just twice," she said.

He turned her around and stared at her. "Just twice?"

She'd never envisioned a conversation like this while being naked. Nor had she expected him to reach out and pull her to him, muttering words she'd never expected Duncan to use.

Perhaps she anticipated that he'd be like her father and brothers and Claire. *Rose, if you'd bend more, the world wouldn't be so difficult for you. Rose, if you only cared less, things would be easier.*

Where did she bend? When a thirteen-year-old girl, barely more than a child herself, became pregnant? When it was all too evident that either Bruce or one of his friends had raped Phibba? When, one day, a month from giving birth, Phibba couldn't move as quickly as Bruce wanted so he struck her hard enough that she fell down a staircase?

Or did she care less when Bruce was bored or sotted and bet who could race faster, his prize horses or two male slaves, and the loser was sold to the winner as if he were an animal himself?

What about the time when Susanna's mourning brooch for her husband had gone missing and one of the maids was whipped, naked, for stealing. No one said a word when Maisie found the brooch under the dresser in Susanna's room where it had fallen.

Which part of any of that did she ignore? Who could?

"Why, Rose?"

She stepped away and grabbed a towel. "I told him I'd rather be a slave than his sister-in-law." She smiled. "That was before I learned to keep my thoughts to myself. He told me that if I wanted to be a slave, I should be treated like one."

"And the second time?"

"I helped a slave escape," she said. "A young man, barely a boy, he was planning on selling. If he had to be separated from his family, it was better that he go north."

She turned to look at him. He wasn't calm, as she'd thought. Fire blazed in his eyes, although his fingertips were gentle as they reached out and stroked her arm.

"I hope to God the bastard is dead," he said.

He stepped out of the tub and pulled her into his embrace again.

She went willingly.

"I'm sorry, Rose," he said softly. "On behalf of every MacIain who is turning in his grave, I'm sorry."

She didn't mean to weep, but her heart was pierced by his words, so effortlessly spoken and with such grace that she had no other choice. She clung to him, wetting his shoulder and his neck with her tears.

Even when her crying stopped, she kept her arms wrapped around his shoulders. She'd never had such a champion before.

How was she to have known that she'd give this man her heart along with her virginity?

HE GRABBED a towel and began drying her, taking longer in some parts than needed. The heat in the room was such that her hair felt damp, but he wasn't interested in her hair, only her shoulders, then arms, then a stop at her breasts. He dried beneath each one and carefully tended to their sloping curves. Her derriere, also, seemed to be of interest to him, as well as her legs. At one point he knelt in front of her, making her tremble.

He kissed her navel, making her smile, then breathed against her abdomen, changing the smile to shivers.

"Widen your legs," he said, and she did, allowing him to tenderly dry her there.

His breath made her insides flutter.

He startled her by carrying her in his arms to the bed. She'd straightened the bed earlier, and when he pulled down the sheet, he saw the bloodstain.

"I wish I'd known," he said, gently setting her down on the mattress.

"It wouldn't have mattered," she said, placing her palm on his cheek. "I didn't feel any pain, only a slight pinch."

He shook his head. "You weren't supposed to have any discomfort at all, Rose. You weren't supposed to be a virgin. Do you think I go around bedding virgins?"

"You don't?"

"I most emphatically don't."

"Then I'm most emphatically glad I didn't tell you," she said, reaching up and pulling him down to her.

She had wondered about passion from time to time, especially when reading. She occasionally thought about desire. But she hadn't missed either one.

You don't yearn for something you'd never known, like never tasting a lemon or smelling a rose. Life was plainer for the lack, but you never knew. Until you experienced it, you had no idea of the soft, sweet scent or texture of the rose, or how the oil of the lemon peel made your nose wrinkle.

Life was a series of experiences, a lesson Duncan had taught her. Or maybe she'd known all along and he just reminded her of it.

She knew now what his touch could do to her skin. The back of her neck pebbled when he kissed it. And that spot just beneath her ear made her moan if he nuzzled it softly. The backs of her knees, the inside of her elbows, it made her sigh in wonder that such places could welcome kisses and feel them so much.

He thumbed her nipples and they tightened and lengthened as if begging for his lips. When his tongue touched each one, she felt it deep inside. When he suckled her gently, her back arched, delight and wonder causing her to make a sound.

"Did I hurt you?" he asked.

"No, no. No."

She drew his head down to her breasts again, desperate to feel the sensation once more.

She was no longer Rose, but someone else. A wanton woman, perhaps, or one of experience, whose body was a temple to pleasure.

He wouldn't rush, but tortured her with slow and patient loving, as if to make up for their first time. She was being tormented by tender kisses and soft and delicate strokes.

She learned what desire was when he moved out of range of her touch and she couldn't feel him. She needed to hold him, to marvel in the size and the shape of him. She tossed on the mattress, every inch of her skin feeling like it was on fire, her body heating from within, melting in response to him, only him.

When he finally entered her and she gasped in wonder at their pairing, he did the same. When her back arched and she was propelled into a world of light flaring behind her eyelids, she learned something else: passion was a wondrous thing and she would never forget this night or him.

Chapter 19

The morning was a beautiful one, almost too pretty between the blue sky, the fluffy clouds, and the Bahamian seas. Several of the sailors had taken to swimming, and Rose smiled at their freedom and their laughter.

She felt the same sense of joy and delight. The world would see her as a fallen woman, but oh, from what heights had she fallen. She would never, ever be a spinster or a maiden. She'd known the taste of passion, the drive of desire, and would be able to recall her time with Duncan at any time and place and feel it warm her cheeks.

"I have to go see Captain McDougal," he said, "and then we need to have a talk about something serious."

She didn't want to have that conversation. She knew only too well what it was going to be. He wasn't going to take her to Charleston and she somehow had to convince him to do so.

"Do we have time to climb the tree house?" she asked.

"The tree house?"

"Didn't you notice? They've built a tree house in a silk cotton tree. You can have tea there if you wish."

"If that's what you want to do," he said, smiling.

"According to the pamphlet, the tree is almost a hundred feet high, although the top of it was felled during a storm a few years ago. Its trunk is ten feet in diameter above the buttresses." She looked up at him. "What's a buttress and why does a tree have them?"

"Support, I'd imagine," he said. "A tree that tall must need support."

"I think having tea in a tree would be a wonderful adventure."

She glanced up at him, wishing she had a pretty frock to wear, something with flowers embroidered on the gauzy fabric. Or a bright yellow dress to match the perfection of this sunny day.

As they made their way from the carriage to the *Raven*, she placed her hand on Duncan's arm, meeting the eyes of those Confederate officers who tipped their hats to her or nodded in a way of greeting. Here in Nassau, if a woman wore black, it was more often than not because of a loved one who'd fallen in battle against the North.

Her mourning was for her three brothers, all killed by men in the same uniforms she passed. Sometimes, she looked at those men who met her eyes in sympathy and wondered if he had been the one to kill Jeremy. If his gun had slaughtered Robert, or left Montgomery dying on the operating table.

Yet none of them had known her brothers as people. They were simply enemy combatants, a fact she found difficult to understand. How could you fire on someone from the same country? How could men who'd once been friends now try to kill each other?

Civil war? Was any war civil? You might as well call it family war. Her family had been affected by it. Claire had always supported the South because her husband did, while Rose desperately wanted the North to win so that slavery would be a thing of the past. How many other families were torn apart by similar thoughts? How many cousins fought cousins? At least her brothers had been on the same side.

More than once, Duncan was deliberately jostled. When it happened the third time, he stood his ground and faced the man who'd elbowed him.

"Is there something you wanted?" he asked.

"Just to know where you're from."

"Glasgow. Scotland. Before that, my family hailed from the Highlands. And yours?"

The other man surprised her by smiling. "Georgia. A little town you would never have heard of. Before that, England, I'm told."

The two men simply nodded at each other as if a safe passage had been issued.

Not even Nassau was exempt from small battles.

From here, the *Raven* looked to be the largest ship in port. Her lines were distinctive, making her appear slightly alien among the other steamships. Captain McDougal had gotten them through the monstrous storm leaving Scotland. According to him, the moon dictated the departure for Charleston. That meant time was running out.

Catch your joys where you can. A saying her father quoted often. How long had it been since she'd thought of it? Very well, she'd do exactly that. Perhaps she could even suggest to Duncan that they return to their room this afternoon. A wicked thought, one that set her cheeks to flaming. Could she truly do something like that? What would he think of her if she suggested such a thing?

She greeted the sailors while Duncan spoke with the captain. The ship was being loaded with coal and it looked like every able-bodied man was helping.

The discussion looked intent, and twice both Captain McDougal and Duncan looked over at her as if she were the subject of their conversation. She kept a smile on her face with some difficulty.

Would tears help? Would they change Duncan's mind about taking her to Charleston? She hadn't been that southern a lady on their voyage, had she? She couldn't recall one instant when she'd batted her eyelashes or tried to charm Duncan.

It was too late now.

When he joined her, she kept her smile in place. "Is your business finished?" she asked.

"For the moment."

His voice sounded somber, and she hoped he'd delay their conversation until they returned to the Viceroy. Otherwise, she was very much afraid she was going to cry. A lady, from South or North, did not weep in public.

"Are you ready to climb the tree house?" she asked. "They say the view of Nassau is spectacular from the top."

Once back at the hotel, they veered into the thick forest around the hotel, following the well-marked path. Climbing the steps arranged around the old silk cotton tree was a challenge. She was breathless by the time they made it to the very top and settled at a square wood table along the railing. She couldn't imagine how the waiters constantly carried trays up and down all those steps the whole day.

The bark of the tree looked to be smooth to the touch. Horizontal branches fanned out from the main trunk, some of them nearly skimming the ground. The leaves were large, nearly twice the length of her hand, with elliptical fruits, some of which had broken open. She was immediately reminded of a cotton boll, with the multitude of seeds and the white fibers filling the air.

The sweeping panorama of Nassau, the harbor and the houses, might have taken all her attention if she hadn't been so worried about their coming conversation. Part of her wanted him to just say the words: she was going to be left behind in Nassau.

Duncan settled in opposite her and ordered tea for both of them.

"Miss O'Sullivan, what a surprise to see you here."

Her thoughts stopped as she stared at the man who spoke. He halted beside the table, giving them no room to escape. She blinked a few times, but George Breton was still there, looking raffish in his grays, almost as if he'd never seen battle.

His blond hair was bright in the sun, his brown eyes filled with amusement. Not a mark appeared on his face, not a line or crease or sign of worry. A handsome man, she'd more often than not seen him laughing. Life was a source of humor for him, because he was as wealthy and privileged as her brother-in-law and one of Bruce's closest friends.

Had George's influential father found him some assignment here in Nassau to escape the fighting?

"Hello, Mr. Breton," she said, forcing a smile to her face.

"I saw you and couldn't believe my eyes. 'You must be mistaken,' I told myself, but no, here you are, Rose O'Sullivan. What are you doing in Nassau?

Enjoying the sights?" He glanced at Duncan. "Or even more than that?"

He'd been present at some events in her life she would like to forget. Like the first time she'd been forced to witness a slave being whipped. Had he been there when it happened to her the first time? Bruce had made her flogging public, an object lesson for both the slaves and the inhabitants of Glengarden. She couldn't remember, but she wouldn't have been surprised.

At least he hadn't stripped her naked to her waist, but allowed her to wear her shift. Not a blessing after all as it turned out, because it had taken hours to remove the bits of cloth from her flesh. Phibba had cried the whole time.

Duncan stood and moved to stand slightly in front of her.

"You'll show some respect, I'm thinking."

Duncan was a Scottish dragon with the burr of his homeland in his voice. A dangerous tone, and one she'd never heard from him before this moment. She hoped George had the sense to recognize his own peril.

George chuckled. "Who would you be to tell me what to do?"

"No one you know," Duncan said. "Perhaps it would be best if you were on your way."

The two men locked eyes. Duncan was taller, with broader shoulders, and a physique she knew well after last night. His arms were muscled, as were his legs, and his chest . . . she'd kissed every single well-defined muscle from his neck to his waist.

He was more than George's match and the other man seemed to know it.

He glanced at Rose. "You never answered me, Miss O'Sullivan. What are you doing in Nassau? Does Bruce know you're here?"

Time stilled. No, time disappeared. She was frozen, left to remain in this exact position for all of eternity. People might come and stare at her statue a hundred years hence, poking at her and wondering at the woman with the wide eyes and look of horror on her face. What was she doing here? Was she waiting for a ship to arrive? Had she just received news that a sweetheart she was desperate to welcome home would never be coming?

Duncan turned to her, his movements altered by time as well. She could see his frown, the questioning look in his eyes. See, too, his mouth open, but the words never made it to her ears.

She was going to faint again. This time not from hunger or exhaustion but from fear.

The words sat dormant on her lips, and she pushed them out, hearing them make their way to George.

"Have you seen Bruce recently?"

Please God, don't let him be in Nassau.

"He's back at Glengarden," he said. "Didn't you know?"

George was still talking. She was hearing the words, but they weren't making sense.

"He was injured?" she said.

George nodded. "He lost a leg."

With any other human being on the face of the earth, she would have felt instant compassion. With Bruce she felt nothing.

"When?" she asked, the word nearly impossible to say. She cleared her throat. "When did he return?"

"A few weeks ago."

She'd been in Scotland or on her way. She'd been blessedly ignorant. Thank God she hadn't known.

Soon, Bruce would know everything she'd done to free his slaves. Soon, he'd know about the cotton. Everything she'd done to this point had guaranteed her own destruction.

Without a word, she stood, pushed past both men and headed down the steps of the tree house and back to the hotel.

Glengarden Plantation
South Carolina

"NO, CHILD, don't pat them too thin. They'll burn when we put them in the oven."

Maisie smiled down at Gloria. The little girl was going to take after her Aunt Rose with her reddish gold locks, but her face was a combination of Claire's beauty and Bruce's determination. The child had her father's stubbornness, too, and if someone didn't curb her temper she was going to grow up to be as much of a devil.

Maisie had taken the last of the sugar she'd hoarded and made a sort of sweet hoecake for Bruce's birthday. Two years ago the whole plantation had celebrated as he'd ridden over his land like Jesus come again. The men who were smart put their hands over their hearts and bowed their heads. Those who hadn't yet learned either stared straight ahead or looked at their master. They didn't know it, but they'd just been marked as uppity and punishment was sure to come.

There wasn't anybody left to stand and worship Bruce. Nor was there a horse for him to ride. If somebody didn't do something soon there wouldn't be any food, either, except for charity or what Benny stole.

The Lord didn't like stealing, but she couldn't imagine that the Lord liked starving, either, so she only nodded last week when a hog appeared in the empty barn. Or a chicken or two found its way into their empty chicken yard. She didn't know if Benny was really that good at stealing or someone was giving them charity. Nobody at Glengarden ever said anything about the chicken stew or the fried chicken or the ham steaks. They just seemed to think she could pray on it and it would appear.

When they were lucky and they were biting, there were fish, too, but she was getting mighty tired of fish, especially without any cornmeal or flour to fry it up.

Bruce hadn't said anything about the food and that wasn't a good sign. Normally, he wanted to know everything, but he hadn't asked any questions. Not even about Rose, which worried her. He'd accepted the news that she'd gone off to visit friends. An out and out lie she'd told when Miss Claire just shrugged and said, "I don't know where Rose went. You know how she is, Bruce. She does what she wants when she wants."

The fact that Miss Rose had gone off to try to sell all the cotton they'd stored in the Charleston warehouses wasn't mentioned. Nor did anyone talk to Bruce when he stood on the veranda and stared at the fallow fields. This time last year the cotton had been halfway close to harvest.

She'd thought Bruce a cruel man before he left for war. She'd thought that war might purge him of some of his hate, but it seemed to have added to it. She avoided him when she could, and when she couldn't, she never lifted her eyes above the ground. She had learned over the years.

"I want one now!" Gloria said.

"You can't have one now, child, they're not finished cooking. Wait just five more minutes, that's all."

She leaned down and cupped the little girl's cheek in her hand. The contrast in their skin was remarkable, but other than that, there weren't too many differences between them. They lived on a plantation that was dying—anyone could see that. Their futures were uncertain. Soldiers might come invading any moment.

"Don't touch my child."

She looked up to see Bruce standing in the doorway of the kitchen. He leaned heavily on his two crutches. Pain had etched a story on his face, one that made him less handsome.

"Sorry, Master Bruce," she said, dropping her gaze to the kitchen floor. Made of dark red brick, she'd kept it spotless ever since she'd taken on the duties in the kitchen.

"You'll never touch my child again, do you understand?"

She nodded her head. "Yes sir, Master Bruce."

She didn't see the crutch until it struck her on the arm. Years of practice kept her from crying out and she didn't raise her head.

"See that you don't."

"Make her give me a hoecake, Papa," Gloria said. "She won't. She's mean."

"Give her what she wants."

She knew better than to argue, so she simply opened the oven, used a spatula to scrape the half-done hoecake from the pan and deposited it on a plate. Gloria took one look at it, wrinkled her nose, and immediately clambered down from the stool where she'd been sitting.

"I don't want it. It's ugly. I want oatmeal cookies."

"We don't have any oatmeal, child. Or raisins. Or sugar. Or flour."

Her recitation had fallen on absent ears. Gloria was off, racing after her father.

Perhaps the two were more alike than she thought. If that were the case, Glengarden was truly doomed.

Nassau, Bahamas

DUNCAN WATCHED as Rose walked away. Everything in him demanded he go after her and comfort her. First of all, he wanted to find out about Bruce.

"I've never seen you at Glengarden," George said.

"That's because I've never been there. I'm a relative, though. Duncan MacIain."

"Ah, the barbaric side of the family," George said. "I've heard tell of you Scots. All kilts and bravado. No wonder you and Rose were together."

He wasn't a violent man, but this was the second day in a row he was ready to fight. Something about George made him clench his fists and step forward, halting only when the other man threw up both hands, palms toward him.

"I didn't mean anything by it," he said. "It's just that you and Rose looked, what is the word, simpatico? A surprise, really, since Rose hasn't been known to be exceptionally friendly. Perhaps I misjudged her?"

At that point George made the bad mistake of leering. Duncan's fist was planted in the other man's nose so quickly it didn't even require thought. George staggered backward, both hands pressed against his face.

He turned and left without another word. So much for getting more information about Bruce.

Losing a leg wouldn't slow down a tyrant or make a kind man out of a bully. He'd known men who'd changed their trajectory in life, true. It's why he hired some of the men he had at the mill, trying to help them get back on the right path. A hand up didn't mean a hand out. A man had to want to try to better himself and participate in the process. If they didn't make every effort on their own, he had no patience with them.

Yet the men he'd helped, and the boys Lennox had made apprentice shipbuilders, weren't men without moral fiber. They'd either never gotten a chance to rise above their circumstances or they'd gotten turned around somehow. They hadn't been like Bruce MacIain, handed every advantage in life and never utilizing it for the benefit of others.

He swore as he felt his knuckles swelling. He'd see if he couldn't find some ice before returning to their room.

George's revelation had made the conversation to come even more difficult and Rose's cooperation urgent.

Chapter 20

"*A*re you all right?" Duncan asked when he entered their suite.

Rose was standing at the window staring out at the harbor.

"You have to let me come with you, Duncan. I have to get back to Glengarden."

"Why, especially now that Bruce is back? He'll blame you for his slaves leaving, Rose. He'll blame you for everything."

"I know." The barest smile curved her lips. "Me first, then the Yankees, and finally God. But I have to go back. I have to get Claire out of there."

"What if she doesn't want to come, Rose, have you ever considered that? What has she done to protect you? Why are you so determined to save her?"

"There's every possibility that Claire will refuse to leave, especially since Bruce was wounded, but I have to try. Wouldn't you do the same for Glynis? Wouldn't you insist on helping her no matter what she said or did?"

"I've never been able to change Glynis's mind about anything. In that, she's as stubborn as you."

He speared his hand through his hair, trying to find some way to explain what he was feeling to her.

"If you saw your child run out in front of a carriage, Rose, wouldn't you try to stop him? Or would you allow your son to be crushed to death because he wanted to cross the street?"

Her smile was fixed. "So that's what you think of me? That I'm a child?"

"No, of course not. I just can't see you returning to Glengarden."

"So you'll be like Bruce, refusing to hear my reasoning, refusing to allow me to do anything. Who's the tyrant now, Duncan?"

"If I promise to deliver the gold to Bruce, will you stay behind in Nassau?"

"No. I'll find passage somehow."

"What if Claire decides to come with you? Where will you go?"

For the first time she looked uncertain.

"You said yourself that you wouldn't be welcomed back in New York. Where will you live?"

"There's a second cousin in Massachusetts who once offered me a home. Maybe she'll take us in."

"Two women and a child? Isn't that pushing charity a bit far?"

"Maybe Ireland," she said, shocking him. "I've relatives of my father there. Somewhere."

"Come to Scotland," he said. "You could make your home in Scotland. You already know people. Family."

"I'm not your family."

No, not now, but he was going to do everything in his power to make sure she was.

He'd only known her for a few weeks. Was that long enough to know he was in love? How long does it take to know that his life would never be the same without her?

It would take him four days to run the blockade to Charleston and four days back, barring any bad luck like being intercepted by a Union ship. A day, perhaps two, to unload their cargo and the same amount of time to load the cotton. He'd be gone twelve days total.

"Wait for me here, Rose. I'll be back for you in less than a fortnight. Please."

Instead of answering, she turned back to the view of the harbor.

He walked to her side.

"I want you to stay with Olivia," he said, handing her the card.

"Olivia?"

"Olivia Cameron, although she's going by the name of Peterson now. She's Lennox and Mary's mother."

Her eyes widened.

"She left Scotland quite a few years ago. Evidently, marriage didn't agree with her."

"She was William's wife?" she asked, staring down at the card.

"She's also a Union operative," he said. "So be careful what you tell her, especially about the *Raven*. She warned me about the danger we're in, but she might be willing to tell the Union about other details of the ship."

"What danger?" she asked, frowning at him.

"The *Exeter* will be arriving in the next day or so. There are plans to try to take command of the *Raven*."

"That's why you and Captain McDougal looked so secretive."

He put his arms around her carefully, giving her

a chance to rebuff him, but she turned into his embrace and put her arms around his waist, leaning into him.

"I don't want to leave you, Rose," he said softly, "but I can't lead you into danger, either. Please stay here and wait for me. Please."

"When are you leaving?"

"The minute we have our customs papers approved."

She stepped back and looked up at him.

He thought they would have one more night together, but she walked away from him and into the bedroom. When he followed her, she was packing the last of her things into her valise.

"I'll go and stay with Olivia," she said.

She didn't look at him as she grabbed her valise, passed him and opened the hotel door.

"Will you wait for me?" he asked. "I'll come back for you, Rose. Will you be here?"

She turned and looked at him. He knew that he would remember the sight of her standing there for the rest of his life.

"Why?" she said. "Why would you come back for me?"

The words were pulled from him as if they had a life of their own.

"Because I care about you," he said. "I want to make sure you're safe."

She closed her eyes and then opened them. He hadn't expected her to shake her head or walk away in response to his declaration.

The sound of the door closing was too loud and too final.

Would she even be here when he returned?

HOW DARE he send her off with such a declaration. He cared about her? He wanted to make sure she was safe? How could he possibly have said such a thing to her?

She didn't know if she was angry or sad or simply confused. No, she was most definitely a combination of all three.

Rose knocked on the door of Room 115.

She held herself still, her face impassive. She would at least make an appearance of doing what Duncan wanted until she could obtain passage on another ship. Arguing with Duncan had only convinced her that he had a wall of stubbornness in him. Talking to him hadn't accomplished anything but make him even more certain of the rightness of his cause.

What Duncan didn't understand was that one person really couldn't protect another, especially in this time of war and destruction.

The only place to be perfectly safe was in a prison or a grave.

The door opened suddenly, revealing an older woman dressed in a gown of pale yellow with gold cording, the hoop so large that it occupied most of the doorway. The bodice was cinched tight, her bosom spilling over the décolletage. If she hadn't known that Olivia was Lennox's mother, Rose would have thought her much younger than she was.

"You're Duncan's Rose," Olivia said.

"I'm not sure I'm Duncan's Rose, but my name is Rose," she said. "Rose O'Sullivan."

Olivia smiled at her. "Thank heavens, a woman with backbone. I'd thought the poor boy had fallen in love with some foolish, helpless thing."

She was ushered into the room, motioned to a pale green upholstered settee, offered refreshments, which she declined, and divested of her valise.

"What do you mean, fallen in love?"

"Why else would he care so much about your safety?"

"Duncan's just that way. He's very responsible."

"Nonsense. There's being responsible and then there's being deeply in love. Have you ever seen the look on his face when he is watching you?"

She didn't know how to answer that.

"I saw you together today. At the tree house. He acted as if you were the only precious object in the entire world. You were the only focus of his attention."

Rose stared down at her gloved hands.

"And you, Duncan's Rose, looked at him in the same way. Almost worshipful."

How could she possibly deny that? Who wouldn't love Duncan?

Another thing he didn't seem to understand. She worried as much about him as he did her. He was sailing off into danger and he expected her to stay somewhere safe. How much better to be with him than remaining here without knowing what was happening.

"Please sit down, my dear. We'll talk of other things if the subject of love disturbs you."

It seemed to her that Olivia, like a great many southern women she had met, accomplished what they needed with a smile and a fan. They batted their eyes and southern men fell at their feet. They didn't treat southern women in quite the same way. Instead, they met their eyes directly as if looking for a secret knowledge or a wink and a nod.

God help you if you got on the wrong side of a southern woman, but they could be invaluable allies.

She had the feeling that Olivia could be the same.

"So, why does he want you to stay in Nassau? And where would you rather be?"

"With him," Rose said, so quickly that Olivia laughed.

The older woman sat beside her, regarding her steadily.

"Is there anything for you in Charleston?"

"Not at Charleston, but at Glengarden. My sister and my niece."

She told the older woman the expurgated version of the story of Glengarden.

Olivia took a deep breath when she was finished. "And you would rescue them?"

She nodded.

"What if they don't wish to leave?"

The same question Duncan had asked her, and one for which there was still no answer.

"I have to try."

"You're one of those people who are determined to be virtuous, aren't you? You'll always do the right thing, even when there isn't always a right thing to do."

She'd never been categorized in that fashion and didn't quite know how to answer. Making love with Duncan hadn't been the right thing, but it wasn't a response she was going to make to Olivia.

"Since you've been so frank, may I tell you a story?"

Rose nodded.

"Once upon a time," Olivia began, "there was a very vain woman. She would spend a great deal of time in front of the mirror, wondering how she could improve her looks. She'd been born to a good family. Her father was a physician. Her mother was a great beauty of her day. This woman, one might say, was touched with favor. She attracted the attention of a very fine man, a man on his way to being wealthy and famous. They wed and had a handsome son and a lovely daughter. The husband of this woman built her a house on a hill, something so splendid that all the inhabitants of the city below them remarked on it. 'He must love her very much,' they said. 'Look what he built for her.'

"As the years passed, the woman realized she was not happy. Yes, she was still beautiful and her husband adored her. Plus, she had the love of her two wonderful children. She could not help but wonder if there wasn't something out in the world that would make her happy. Someone she could love as she didn't love her husband, fine man that he was. Something that would make life exciting, as it wasn't now.

"Every day the thought stayed with her. Was this what her life was to be like? Always questioning? Always wondering? Always being dissatisfied? How was she to live like this? One day she took some money from her husband's money box. Not a tremendous amount, but enough for a sea voyage and to see her settled somewhere. She packed one trunk, arranged for the driver to take her to the train, and was away from the city in the blink of an eye.

"She had made a choice, you see, and as fate would have it, it was the wrong choice, but how was she to know it until she'd made it?"

"Why was it the wrong choice? Did she find that she loved her husband after all?"

Olivia smiled, but the expression held little humor. "Oh, no. She discovered that she didn't love herself. You can't truly love another person until you love yourself, you know, but that's not the moral of this story, Rose."

She remained silent.

"The moral is that there are always choices in life. Life is never black and white. Life is mostly gray. But in the grayness there are choices. Like the choice you have right this minute."

"What choice?" Rose asked.

"What do you want to do right now? If I could be your fairy godmother and help you do anything you wanted, what would it be? Make your choice wisely. It took me years to recover from the choice I made."

Rose sat there and regarded the older woman. Olivia was a surprise.

"Do you really want to stay with me until Duncan returns?"

Rose shook her head. "No. I want to get on board the *Raven* before she sails," she said. "Are you going to help me?"

"Of course I am, Duncan's Rose, but it's going to be dangerous, running the blockade."

She nodded.

"And I don't think it's going to be safe at that Glengarden of yours," she said.

"No, probably not."

Olivia studied her for a minute. "Don't let him go. If your sister won't leave, then don't be so foolish as to stay. Go with Duncan wherever he goes. Being together is so much better than being apart."

She couldn't agree more.

Fortified with a rum cocktail Olivia insisted she consume, and wearing one of Olivia's shawls to cover her hair, they descended the staircase and out the front of the hotel to hire a carriage. To her surprise, it wasn't at all difficult to obtain a vehicle at this hour and they were at the harbor in minutes. Nassau was like a city in the middle of a celebration. Even now she could hear music playing and people laughing.

DUNCAN WAS damned if he was going to sail away from the woman he loved without her agreement to wait for him, especially since it had taken him a lifetime to find her.

His valise in hand, he knocked on the door to Olivia's room, hoping that Rose would see him. He had to explain in a way that didn't insult her. He had to somehow find the right words. With any luck, Olivia might add her voice to his. She knew how dangerous their departure from Nassau might prove to be.

No one answered his knock. He knocked again and then once more before it was plain they weren't going to answer.

He wasn't deterred. Returning to his suite, he threw his valise down and sat at the secretary. He would quote Burns to her. She'd liked the man's poetry.

O my Luve is like a red, red rose
That's newly sprung in June;
O my Luve is like the melody
That's sweetly played in tune.

So fair art thou, my bonnie lass,
So deep in luve am I;

And I will luve thee still, my dear,
Till a' the seas gang dry.

There was more, but he couldn't remember it. He added his own postscript.

Robert Burns wrote that nearly seventy years ago, Rose, but he might have taken the words from my own thoughts. I love you as I've never thought to love anyone. My first wish is to keep you safe. My second is to come back to you.

He addressed the note to her, then returned to Olivia's room and slipped it beneath the door.

With any luck, Burns would do what his own words had not: convince Rose to wait for him.

FOR THE first time since she donned mourning for her brothers, Rose was grateful to be wearing it. The black dress and shawl made her blend into the moonless night.

"I doubt you'll have much trouble getting on board," Olivia said. "Ships are always scenes of chaos just before they leave port."

"Thank you," she said, turning the handle of the carriage door. "Thank you for everything."

"Just remember what I told you, Rose, and that will be thanks enough. Choose wisely, because you'll have to live with that choice forever."

She nodded, then leaned over and kissed Olivia's cheek. The look of surprise on the older woman's face made her smile.

Olivia did something to her décolletage that made her grateful Duncan wasn't anywhere near.

Lennox's mother or not, the woman had an astounding figure.

"What are you going to do?"

"People are often diverted, Rose. While you are gaining access to the *Raven*, I shall make a fuss about something. Maybe I'll claim a highwayman absconded with my jewels. Better yet," she said, "I'll claim my lover has been unfaithful and the rascal should be punished somehow."

She stared at Olivia, uncertain if the woman was jesting.

When the carriage stopped, she left the vehicle and made her way to the gangplank. At that exact instant Olivia began to scream.

The throngs of men and women crowded around the *Raven*, loading supplies, trunks, and other crates, turned to see what was the matter, only to be greeted by the sight of Olivia stepping out of the carriage, her hair askew, tears falling down her cheeks.

She was pointing to a nearby ship, and that's where everyone's attention was directed.

"How dare he leave me?" she shouted. "He promised me he would stay with me forever! Forever, until that Spanish whore lured him to her bed."

Rose was torn between wanting to stay and see Olivia's theatrics and getting to the captain's cabin.

The door to the stateroom wasn't locked. She entered the cabin, closed the door behind her, and sagged against it, her legs feeling wobbly. The faint lantern light through the porthole illuminated the space. She'd already considered where she would hide and realized there was only one place: one of the two wardrobes in the stateroom.

Both of them were empty, as she'd expected. She

removed her hoop, collapsed the foundation garment and stuffed it into the drawer below the bed. Putting the shawl next to the hoop, she grabbed her skirts and climbed into the wardrobe still smelling of Duncan's clothes and the scent of bay rum.

How much longer until they sailed? The voices from outside the cabin had faded a little. Leaning her head back against the wall of the wardrobe, she allowed herself to relax.

Duncan was not going to be happy with her, but his anger was nothing compared to what she'd face at Glengarden.

What had Duncan said? That he thought the journey too dangerous?

The voyage didn't hold as many terrors as facing Bruce. He would find some way to punish her, she was sure. No doubt he thought she'd dishonored the Confederacy by selling the cotton that would save them. He would have them all starve, waving the Confederate battle flag as they took their last breath.

What other alternative was there? He wouldn't care about Maisie or Old Betsy or Benny, but what about Claire? Or his daughter?

She leaned back and ended up dozing, waking to a lantern being lit. Footsteps moved around the bed, approaching the bureau. Suddenly the wardrobe door opened, a muscular arm reached in and put a garment on a hook.

She bit her lip rather than make a sound.

"Do you want to explain what the hell you're doing on the *Raven*, Rose?"

She sighed. "You can't possibly see me. It's black as pitch in here."

"Come out of there."

Bracing herself against the edge of the wardrobe door, she thrust her legs out, then pulled herself up by the door handle.

Standing was more difficult than she expected, because she'd been in an odd position for a few hours and her legs felt numb. She landed hard against Duncan, both of them toppling onto the bed with a thud.

He was warm and sturdy, like a tree trunk.

"How did you know I was here?"

"You smell of bath salts," he said.

"Oh."

She raised her head and studied his face in the light of the lantern. "You aren't surprised to see me here, either, are you?"

"I expected you would attempt something of the sort."

"If you think I'm going to be evicted from the *Raven*, I warn you, I'll cause a terrible scene. I won't go."

"No, you won't, will you?"

She frowned at him.

"Why are you being so agreeable?"

"I'm not being the least bit agreeable. I'm not feeling agreeable at all. I wanted to protect you, but I've also gotten to know you. I'm not so sure I would call it being opinionated or stubborn as much as I would having a strong will. You're probably the most strong-willed person I've ever known, and that's saying something, since I have a sister who has heretofore worn that label."

She didn't quite know what to say. To be compared to Glynis might be a compliment or it might not be.

"When you believe in something, Rose, I imagine it's impossible to turn you from your task."

She nodded slowly. That trait of her character had never before been considered an asset, but the way he was talking it seemed as if he thought it was.

"You must have driven Bruce to distraction. You were probably the only person who ever defied him, which makes the situation doubly dangerous."

He had always understood, so she wasn't surprised that he'd come to that conclusion.

"Are you very angry?"

"If I said yes, what would you do?"

She blew out a breath and thought about it for a moment.

"I would probably just leave you alone until you got over it. That always worked best with my father and brothers. However, I doubt most southern women would let you pout. They'd probably bring you a whiskey, flirt with you with a fan, and tell you how handsome you are."

"I don't pout."

She lifted her head and gave him a direct look. "I suspect you do, but in a Duncan-like way. All disciplined and professional. You'd remain very quiet and you wouldn't look at the other person. You'd ignore them until you were certain they knew how annoyed you were."

"I would?"

She nodded. "Then, and only then, you would say something innocuous, but in a very stern way. 'Terrible weather we're having.' It's the tone of voice, you see."

"You don't have a very good opinion of me."

"Don't be silly. You're the most wonderful man I've ever met."

"But I'm all disciplined and professional."

"Except in bed," she said. "There, you're not the least disciplined."

He put his arms around her.

"I wanted to make sure you were safe. Bruce is a tyrant and a despot. They don't change easily, if at all. I doubt the loss of his leg has made him a gentle creature who would understand your sailing to Scotland to arrange the sale of his cotton."

He was certainly correct in that assessment.

"I wanted to protect you, Rose."

She lay her head against his chest, listening to the thunderous beat of his heart, calming and reassuring her.

Her father and brothers had felt the same, trying to protect her from the consequences of her own actions. Then she'd learned, albeit a little later than she should, that every action has a reaction. Every gesture evokes a response.

"But it's only fair to warn you," he said, "that from this moment on, you won't be alone."

She raised her head to look at him.

"I have no intention of leaving you in Charleston or at Glengarden. When you're done with what you need to do, I'm hoping to talk you into coming back to Scotland with me." He smiled at her. "You see, I find I've developed an equally strong will."

The knock on the door stopped the conversation they desperately needed to have.

Chapter 21

*H*e opened the door to the stateroom and greeted Captain McDougal.

"The *Exeter* has arrived, sir."

Bloody hell. That was the worst news they could get.

"Good morning, Mrs. MacIain," the captain said, looking past him to where Rose was standing. "I didn't know you'd be traveling with us to Charleston."

"A change of plans," Duncan said.

The captain, a man with some degree of tact, said nothing in response.

An hour later the *Raven* left her anchorage, remaining just outside the lighthouse. According to Captain McDougal, the delay was because she was waiting for her clearance papers from the customs house. According to their official documents, the *Raven* was bound for Newfoundland. Instead, they'd be heading direct for Charleston, like most of the ships leaving Nassau.

The paperwork wasn't going to fool the *Exeter*. She'd be in pursuit of them the minute they left Bahamian waters. The *Raven* had been built as a blockade runner, one of the fastest ships in the Cameron and Company fleet. Today she'd come into her own.

They finally received clearance at noon, leaving the island slowly, as if time weren't important.

As long as they were close to land, they were safe. Three miles outside Nassau they'd no longer be in British waters.

Duncan stood at the rail and watched as the *Exeter* followed them. He didn't think Captain McDougal even blinked. Duncan sweated more than he'd ever remembered. Yet he was standing still, not working to clear out the looms or sweeping the production floor. The sun was grueling, the glare on the ocean so blinding he could close his eyes and still see the white gold of it.

His sympathies went to Rose. In order to be comfortable, she had removed her petticoats and hoop. The trade-off forced her to remain in the stateroom with the door propped open a little. At least on deck there was a hint of a breeze, if you could ignore the heat of the punishing sun.

Captain McDougal gave the order for the firemen to stoke the engines. The *Exeter*, a steamer only about half the size of the *Raven*, began to fall back a little at a time. They were no match for the *Raven*'s speed. Finally, the Union ship dropped out of sight.

Without Olivia's warning, they would have been boarded and captured. He didn't know if he was insulted or angered by Baumann's actions. The man couldn't firebomb the ship as he'd tried in Glasgow. Nor did he have a ship the equal of the *Raven*, so he had to resort to underhanded measures.

As night fell, so did the temperature. The breeze was cool, but there was an increased sense of danger.

He looked for traces of smoke as they sailed through the moonless night. Captain McDougal had been cautious there, too.

"It'd be suicide to run the blockade with soft coal as fuel, sir," Captain McDougal said that morning. "We might as well paint a target on the *Raven*'s smoke stacks. I'm not happy that we had to leave a day early, but we should be all right."

Talk on deck was forbidden unless it was the slightest of whispers. No light was allowed, even in the cabins. He couldn't see any of the other sailors, but he knew they weren't far away. The pilot stood not ten feet from him, but might as well have been invisible.

He peered into the night, feeling as if every nerve were concentrated on the blackness before him. He felt blind, rendered helpless by the absence of light.

If captured, he didn't know what their fate would be. It was entirely possible that the *Raven* would be seized first while explanations came later. He didn't fool himself that his Scottish nationality would save him. If nothing else, the contents of the hold—munitions from the London Armory Company—would demonstrate his intention to supply the Confederacy.

What would happen to Rose? She was from New York, but she'd been living in South Carolina for the last two years so she might be classified as an enemy to the Union as well. Most of the crew was Scottish born, but that hadn't helped his cousin's brother-in-law. Neville Todd had been English and yet was held in a Confederate prisoner of war camp for nearly a year.

He'd never thought himself selfish and perhaps that wasn't the word. Insular, then. His thoughts and concerns had always been narrowed to include his family and the mill. Maybe that's why he'd never married. He'd never found anyone important enough to take the place of either in his mind and affections.

What was it that Rose had once asked him? Something about a woman fascinating him enough that he'd do something contrary to his nature—that was it. Did this count? Almost every action he'd taken since meeting her had been contrary to the man he'd known himself to be.

All it had taken was a certain redhead with a determination to succeed to walk into his house and captivate him from the first look.

Yet until Rose, he'd never worried as much about what might happen. Borrowing trouble, that's what Mabel might say.

When a loom went down at the mill, no one got excited. No one panicked. It was expected that, at any given time, every loom would stop working. They kept extra parts on hand for just such a contingency. If he couldn't fix it, after a lifetime around looms, then another repairman could.

He handled the rest of his life like that, trying to plan for problems. He didn't have any idea how to do that now.

He'd thought that the best way to protect Rose was to keep her in Nassau. He was beginning to learn that whenever one of his plans came up against Rose's determination, it would be a challenge to see who was ultimately successful.

Now was not the moment to second-guess his actions, but he was doing so nevertheless. He was racing toward recklessness and he'd never been a man to do so. But from the very beginning, from the moment she'd come into his life, he'd begun to change.

He was no longer the level-headed MacIain. Look where he was now, creeping toward war, expecting cannon fire from shadow ships dotting the horizon. They were, perhaps, all fools to be on the *Raven*, but he was the biggest fool of all.

He'd always been the one to whom people had looked for guidance, for rational behavior. He'd plotted the course of his life with responsibility as the tiller. His heritage had been paramount. His word, his name, his promise, had meant something.

Glynis was no longer the rash one of the family. His sister had always had a core of practicality, one that was set aside whenever Lennox was involved. Then, she was passionate and feckless and irresponsible.

He was acting with the same idiocy about Rose, and it didn't look as if it were getting better.

He moved into the stateroom, only to find that she had gone into the parlor. The door was open there, too.

"I can't stand closed places," she said.

He knew why after her story about the cold house.

Without a light, the parlor was black as the grave. He made his way to the settee, grateful that he didn't trip over anything on the way, and sat beside her.

"My English cousin is blind," he said. "I never thought how difficult it must be for him to get around."

"By touch, I think," she said, reaching out her hand for him.

He clasped Rose's fingers, feeling the chill of her skin, wondering if she, too, felt the anxiety in the air. Their speed had slowed a little but they were still flying over the waves.

"Will it be like this all the way to Charleston?" she asked, her voice lowered so it didn't carry.

"I thought to ask you that," he said, smiling. "You've run the blockade once."

"The outbound voyage was almost dull," she said. "There wasn't even a hint of another ship."

"Then let's hope that it's the same for us. As dull as unbuttered toast."

"A boiled egg," she said.

"A politician's speech."

Her giggle made him smile.

"Oh, I couldn't top that one," she said.

She leaned against him and he put his arm around her. He was content to hold her for the entire night if necessary.

"If we had some light, we could play cards. Do you know any games we could play in the dark?"

"Hide and seek?"

"I'm afraid we'd both lose," she said. "We'd never find each other."

"Blind man's bluff? Grandmother's footsteps?"

"Stop. You'll make me laugh and then Captain McDougal will hear and be angry at me."

He took her hand and helped her stand.

"There's one way to occupy ourselves," he said.

"And what would that be?"

"Come to my bed, dear Rose."

He wished he could see her expression.

"Do you think that's entirely wise?" she whispered. "To lose ourselves in love when we're in such danger?"

"My dear Rose, I can't imagine a better time."

He placed a kiss on her forehead and went to the parlor door to close it.

They walked to the stateroom together, stopping for another kiss at the door. He shut the door to the deck, then came back to her side, wishing that he could see her.

Being with her, making love with her, meant more because it was Rose. He knew her heart, knew the depth of her courage, and the love of which she was capable.

How did he tell her that he admired her more than any woman he'd ever met? Or perhaps more than any other person?

He smoothed his hands from her shoulders to her wrists, then up again to her throat. He bent his head and kissed her cheek, finding his way to her lips unerringly, slowly, patiently.

When he pulled back they were both breathing quickly. He smiled as he began to unfasten the buttons of her dress.

"When it's time," he whispered, "and you put away your mourning, what color will you wear?"

"Yellow, I think. What's your favorite color?"

"Blue," he said.

"Then I'll wear yellow one day and blue the next."

"Right now I'd prefer that you weren't wearing anything."

"Oh."

She helped him remove the dress and he was grateful she'd already dispensed with the hoop and her petticoats. Her corset was loose, thank heavens. In minutes she was naked on the bed.

Turnabout was only fair play and he removed his own clothes in half the time it normally took him to disrobe.

He lay down beside her, propping his head up on his hand. They were in total darkness, but the memories from Nassau gave him sight.

"You are so beautiful," he said. "I love your breasts."

"Do you?" She sounded like she was smiling.

"And your feet."

"My feet?"

"Your feet," he said. "You have beautiful feet. I especially like your big toes."

She raised her head up as if to see her feet. "I don't think I've ever given my feet any thought at all."

"Well, you should. They're exquisite feet."

"Perhaps I should go without shoes."

"At the very least. Only when we're alone, however. I wouldn't want you to incite lust in other men."

She giggled again and he smiled.

"I like your chest." She placed her hand flat on his chest. "It's very manly."

"I should hope so." He cupped one breast. "You're very womanly."

"I should hope so," she said.

His fingers traced her smile. His hand stroked from her shoulder, down her arm to her hip. His fingers splayed across her stomach, up to rest between her breasts.

Her hand reached out and gripped his wrist.

"Kiss me, Duncan," she said. "I get lost when you kiss me. I forget anything and everything but you. Even running the blockade."

"It's the same for me," he said, bending his head and placing a soft kiss on her cheek. "You must be touched with Scottish magic."

"Irish," she corrected.

"I think you're more Scottish," he continued, smiling against her lips, "with red-gold hair and a temper to match."

He knew he would always remember these moments in the midst of danger. People were chasing them, obstacles lay before them, yet laughter tinted their lovemaking.

The night was touched by enchantment. Her body was so responsive to his. He'd never been as captivated by anyone or as concerned for her pleasure.

When she erupted in his arms, only then did he allow himself release, the effort of holding back making his heart race and his breath shallow. He calmed with her arms around him, her hands stroking his damp back, her kisses dotting his face.

He lay at her side, gathering her close.

"I love you, Rose O'Sullivan."

His declaration was met by silence.

In the past, whenever he thought about meeting the woman with whom he wanted to share his life, a moment like this had never occurred to him. Nor had he ever considered that his future wife would be complicated, complex, and unlike anyone he'd ever met.

Winning Rose's heart would not be an easy task and he didn't expect it to be now, even after making love to her.

Perhaps it was Fate's way of mocking him after so many years of not being interested in falling in love. His mother had hinted, more than once, that he might want to consider marriage. Glynis had been even more direct.

"You have to make yourself available, Duncan. How is any woman to know you're on the marriage mart if you make yourself a hermit?"

"I am not making myself a hermit, Glynis. I am simply doing what must be done. It's called the press of business."

She had folded her arms, frowned, and tapped

her foot on the floor. She'd done the same when she was eight and annoyed at him.

"One day it will hit you like lightning, Duncan, and you won't be able to think about the press of business. You won't be able to think about anything else but the woman you love."

He smiled and wondered what Glynis would say if she knew that day had come.

THE SECOND and third days of their voyage were uneventful. The pattern was the same. They occupied themselves during the day as best they could. The night shift of the crew slept belowdecks, preparing themselves for their silent watch.

Each night, he and Rose retired to their bed, taking advantage of the darkness. Pleasure had never bound him, but it was winding an inexorable ribbon around him now. When he thought back to this adventure, these nights with Rose would be the highlight, not the ever present sense of danger.

Tomorrow they would make Charleston, which meant that no one slept. Tonight the danger was at its peak.

The night was black, silent, and oppressive. The darkness pressed down against him, pushing him up against the rail. The only light to be seen was above him. Stars dotted the sky like sentient observers of human nature.

Rose stood beside him, his hand holding hers as if to keep a connection between them.

He nodded toward the sailors, silent and watchful.

Were they near the blockade fleet? Had they been surrounded by them? Or had Captain McDougal sailed around them? They'd seen three ships tonight, but he'd sensed that they had doubled back more than once, the route to the South Carolina port made longer because of their maneuvers.

The blackness of the ocean, combined with the darkness of the sky and the utter silence as the *Raven* slowed made him feel like he was entombed. The only life touching him was Rose's hand in his and her soft breathing.

Her mourning dress matched the night. He suddenly wanted to see her hair, a flame as bright as fire.

He wanted to speak to her, to reassure her in words that had not yet been born in his mind. Instead, he reached out and pulled her to him until he stood behind her, wrapping his arms around her.

Time inched by. Coal dust floated down on them in the calm, no doubt sticking to their skin and their garments. He didn't move or suggest they return to their dark and stifling cabin. He wanted to see what they faced rather than simply wait for it, unknowing.

He'd never known a night to be so long.

"The fleet is close," Captain McDougal had said a few hours earlier. "If we're seen, we can outrun them, but I'd rather we weren't seen."

So did he.

The sea wasn't as rough as it had been on the crossing to the Bahamas, but neither was it placid.

He didn't know how long they stood there watching, but finally the darkness seemed to lessen on the horizon, as if a reticent sun was being coaxed to rise. At the same time, he saw a trail of smoke, his eyes tracing back to its source, a steamer nearly as large as the *Raven* and clearly visible.

"I'm terrified," she whispered.

"Think of puppies or kittens."

"Puppies or kittens?"

"Something to take your mind off what we're doing."

She moved closer to him, and for an instant he wondered if they had the ability to read each other's thoughts. He knew exactly what she was thinking about, the last nights they'd spent in passion and then holding each other.

He tightened his arms around Rose, wished to hell she'd listened to him and remained in Nassau. How did he protect her now?

"Naught to worry over yet," said a voice at his side.

He turned to see the pilot, the man barely visible in the faint light of an oncoming dawn. The man would see them into Charleston harbor.

"Might be a ship just like us," he whispered. "A blockade runner, not one of the Federals."

"How will you know? Will you signal her?"

The pilot shook his head. "Any signal we'd send, a Federal ship could see as well. No, we'll just have to wait to see what she does."

The next ten minutes were tense, making him wonder if the crew on the other ship felt the same. When the steamer made no move to get closer and seemed to grow smaller, he realized she was sailing in the opposite direction.

"We'll have no problem making port now," the pilot said. "The captain's given the order to drive ahead. By dawn we'll see Fort Sumter."

As Duncan grabbed Rose's hand and left the deck, he supposed he said something, a polite word of thanks, a comment of appreciation for the knowledge the man had shared. He was conscious of two things: gratitude that they'd made it, and dread at the idea of finally meeting his American cousin.

Chapter 22

$\mathcal{T}$he pilot expertly guided the *Raven* into Charleston harbor. Within hours they were moored at a wharf and unloading their cargo.

He'd already made a profit on the voyage, given the munitions they'd brought in, most of which would be shipped by rail to either Augusta or Richmond, hubs for Confederate supply lines.

Duncan obtained a wagon, which was the only available means of transportation, and Rose gave him directions to the warehouse.

The destroyed lighthouse should have given him some clue, but Duncan's imagination had him think that Charleston resembled Nassau, a prosperous city made even more so by the success of the blockade runners. He'd expected strolling crowds, the sound of laughter, and signs of commerce.

What he got was a soot-covered scene out of a nightmare. Churches were gutted; buildings were razed. Sometimes, only a column was left from a structure that might have been a store or a bank. The roads were littered with broken bricks. Spires stuck up into the sky supported by two walls.

Life had ceased in this part of Charleston.

"I thought you said the war hadn't reached you," he said, looking around him.

"It wasn't the war," Rose said. "It was the Great

Fire of 1861. Two years ago in December. They say nearly six hundred buildings burned."

Everywhere he looked there was destruction. Some effort was being made to rebuild what had been destroyed, but it seemed a Herculean task needed to be performed instead of the efforts of a few people here and there.

He couldn't imagine war doing any more damage than the fire.

"A hundred fifty acres or thereabouts were destroyed, I heard," she said. "It ended when the spire from the new Cathedral of St. Finbar fell. Susanna said it was a sign that God was displeased with the way the city fathers had handled the war so far."

He glanced over at her. She returned his look with a wry smile.

"You'll find that almost every conversation is about the war."

He could understand it, especially for those living in Charleston. The city lay in shambles. The taste and smell of soot clung to his nostrils.

"What caused it?"

She shook her head. "Some say it began in a business. Others say slaves started it. There are as many stories as there are people in Charleston. No one is certain, only that it seemed to have begun in three different places."

"Which gives credence to the idea of a concerted effort to burn the place down," he said.

She nodded.

The wagon wheels rumbled beneath them, sometimes catching on the potholes left by the missing bricks. More than once he thought they might lose a wheel, but Rose never looked worried.

She seemed in her element as he led the horses down the ruined street. She was sitting up straight, her shoulders back, wearing a smile. Here was the woman who believed in freedom to the extent she helped slaves escape. Here was Rose O'Sullivan who would go head-to-head with Bruce MacIain despite the fact she'd always lost. Now she was determined and focused as she'd probably been dozens of times before. No emotion showed on her face other than fierce determination. She had a goal and she was damned determined to reach it.

A surge of admiration for her made him smile.

She caught his expression and frowned at him. "What?"

"Nothing," he said.

Of course she wouldn't have remained behind in Nassau. Of course she wouldn't have stayed at Glengarden with starvation and deprivation facing them. Rose would always do something, even if the action wasn't wise. She wouldn't be passive about life. She'd reach out and grab it with both hands, shake it until it surrendered or slapped her back.

When had he fallen in love with her? When had he realized that his life wouldn't be complete without her? Maybe that first day, when she'd taken one look at him and her eyes had widened before she fell at his feet.

Maybe when she'd argued with him about the price of cotton.

Maybe when he'd washed her back and realized that he would do anything to spare her from further pain.

Or maybe it was that first kiss, when she'd been cuddled on his lap and he was overwhelmed by lust and tenderness.

Whatever the timing, all he knew was that he wasn't leaving here without her. Even though each night when he told her he loved her only silence was his answer.

His patience could last as long as her stubbornness; at least, that's what he told himself.

He was going to have to handle one problem at a time. Right at the moment, he needed to figure out how to get the cotton to the *Raven*.

THE COTTON warehouse was located in a part of the city the fire hadn't reached. At first he thought that the three lines of dusty-paned windows meant the warehouse had three floors, but that wasn't the case. The windows were there to provide light to the cavernous one story space.

They were let in by a thin and grizzled man sitting just inside the front door in a small office that was as cluttered as the warehouse was empty. He'd perused Rose's certificate, then shrugged his shoulders.

"It's gone," he said. "Ain't here no more."

"Where is it?" Rose asked. "You promised it would be safe."

"It got took away. The owner came and got it."

"Did he have a certificate like mine?" She took back the paper from the man and waved it in the air.

"Didn't matter. The warehouse owner recognized him right away. Poor man, him with one leg gone in the war. Heard tell he was going to get a medal or something for bravery. Even helped him get the cotton back to his place."

For a moment Rose didn't say anything, and when she did speak her voice was hard.

"If he didn't have a certificate like I do, then you shouldn't have given him the cotton."

The look in her eyes gave Duncan the indication that she would fight this point until death. It didn't matter in the end, because the cotton wasn't there. Certificate or not, Bruce had taken it.

"It's all right, Rose," he said.

"No, it is very much not all right. It's theft."

She straightened her shoulders and marched out of the warehouse.

Rose might be incensed, but the fact was, the law stated that the cotton belonged to Bruce and there was nothing she could do about it.

She had already made it back up to the wagon seat when he returned, after thanking the man in the office, an innocent bystander in a war of two years' duration. Not the Civil War but the war between Rose and Bruce. In this battle, Bruce had won again, but at least he hadn't used force against her.

Nor would he ever, again, Duncan thought.

"I'd already decided to see my cousin anyway," he said, getting back on the wagon seat. "How far is Glengarden from Charleston?"

"A good four hours by land. Two by water."

"Then we'll go by water. Can the *Raven* navigate it?"

She nodded.

"It'll take another day to unload our cargo," he said. "We won't be able to leave until tomorrow at the earliest."

She stared down at her bare hands. She'd stopped wearing her gloves, but each time he saw her scars he was reminded of the cruelty of his cousin.

He'd once entertained the idea of a reunion of all three branches of the MacIains. He'd thought it fascinating, the different ways the three original brothers had decided to make their fortunes in the world. For the most part they all succeeded, which would have made their mother proud.

His family owned a mill that used to be the most prosperous one in Scotland. His English cousin was an earl. And his American cousin owned a plantation.

Yet the same man had seen nothing wrong with owning another human being.

The reunion would never take place; he knew that now. Nor would any meeting of the minds. They might be related, but they'd never be more than that.

THERE WAS nothing bright or beautiful about Charleston to show Duncan. The fire had destroyed more than a third of the city, most of the damage in the heart of it. They visited the ruins of St. Finbar, which gave a hint to how beautiful the building had once been. Other than that, there wasn't much to do but wait until the cargo was offloaded.

She spoke to the pilot about where Glengarden was located, and thankfully, he was familiar with the Wando River. They should be able to reach the plantation in two hours without any difficulty.

When they left Charleston, heading northwest, she continued standing at the rail. Speed wasn't of the essence now, so their navigation of the wide river was done slowly, to guard against debris that might harm the *Raven*'s iron-clad hull.

She didn't talk to anyone, not even Duncan, as she prepared to return to Glengarden. If she were courageous enough, she would have spoken of her fear that she'd wasted the time and resources of a man she admired, respected, and had come to love. How did she explain? How did she put her regrets into words?

Not for loving him. Not for even acting the harlot. Not even for bearing their child, if it came to that.

Please, God, don't let it come to that. How could she protect her child from Bruce?

She'd put Duncan in danger and she couldn't forgive herself for that. And she'd do so again, because the outbound voyage might not be as hazardous, but it would be more difficult for the *Raven* since the Union navy was on the lookout for her.

All for nothing.

She'd done everything for nothing. She'd traveled to Nassau, argued, cajoled, tried to convince various factors for no reason at all. She'd journeyed to London by ship, to Scotland by train, all to no avail.

Glengarden wouldn't be protected, unless Bruce agreed to sell his cotton. The future of the people who lived there would be just as bleak as the people once enslaved at the plantation.

She didn't know what to do, and the feeling of frustration was almost unbearable.

THE MAIN approach to Glengarden was from the river. The *Raven* lay at dock behind a wide barge with Glengarden's name painted on the stern.

"It's a cotton barge," Rose said, catching his questioning look. "It's how we take the cotton to Charleston."

"You took the barge to Charleston?" he asked.

He didn't know why he should be amazed. Rose was capable of doing anything she decided to do, even piloting a cumbersome barge down a river and into Charleston harbor.

"There was no one else to do it," she said.

That explained almost everything she'd done, didn't it? When no one else stepped up or stepped in, Rose had. She'd performed those tasks other people either couldn't or wouldn't do.

She was more a Highland woman than she was an Irish descendant.

He didn't know what was going to happen from this point forward, so he told Captain McDougal not to prepare to load the cotton until he returned.

He and Rose began to walk down the corridor of oaks. The tall trees met over the road, shadowing the approach, giving an appearance of peace and harmony on this warm afternoon. He didn't know what the weather was like in the winter in South Carolina, but if the branches overhead were filled with icicles, they'd be spectacularly beautiful.

The silence would have been enjoyable but it was overwhelmed by a peculiar and endless clicking noise.

"Those are the cicadas," Rose said, when he asked. "I'd never heard them before moving here. The sound goes on for hours, but you gradually get used to it. They're a flying insect, but they sometimes leave their shells on the bark of trees. Wait until you hear the tree frogs at night. Sometimes, they're so loud you can't sleep."

Charleston had been a disaster, but it was a city, one not appreciably different from any other city. Glengarden was another place entirely, almost otherworldly.

Every one of his senses were affected. The air was thick and warm, making him wish he hadn't worn his jacket. The perfume of heady flowers, none of which he could identify, seemed to surround them like a cloud. The day was bright, the sunlight glaring, but here beneath the branches of trees that must be hundreds of years old there were only shadows.

"Glengarden occupies all of the peninsula," Rose said. "You can't see the fields from here, but there are acres and acres behind the house. For the first time since MacIains came to South Carolina, there's nothing planted."

If Bruce agreed to sell the cotton, he'd have enough money to hire workers and buy seed so he could plant a crop next year, not to mention having the funds to sustain them for some time. Would he see the possibilities? Or only resent Rose's intrusion?

Duncan didn't know, but he wasn't feeling optimistic, given her tales of the man. Anyone who would lock a woman up, regardless of what she'd done, didn't seem the reasonable or rational type.

As they walked, she pointed out places that he might have seen but for the curtain of trees. To their right were a series of outbuildings.

"We don't buy many things," she said. "Cloth, shoes, flour, and sugar. Almost anything else can be made here."

As if she heard his curiosity, she pointed to the left. "The slave cabins are through there, beyond a small rise and behind a row of trees. They don't show."

THE CLOSER they got to the house, the slower Rose walked. Duncan reached out and grabbed her hand, holding it in his. She shouldn't think she was alone. He was here and he wasn't going anywhere.

Let the family think what they would.

They must have noticed the *Raven* on the river. Either that or the barking he heard must have alerted them. Three people were arrayed on the veranda, waiting for them. A daguerreotype of a southern family, one that wasn't particularly welcoming.

"Auntie Rose! Auntie Rose!"

A little girl with long curls of reddish gold stepped away from her mother. She might have flown down the steps toward Rose if her father hadn't held out his crutch in front of the girl and stopped her.

The little girl's face changed in that instant from joy to caution. A second later she slid back behind her mother's skirts.

"The man is Bruce," Rose said. "The woman is Claire, my sister. The little girl is my niece, Gloria. Susanna rarely makes it downstairs unless it's a special occasion. She's Bruce's mother. Maisie isn't allowed on the veranda. Neither is Benny. There's only one other person living here and that's Old Betsy. She rarely leaves her cabin."

She took a deep breath and stared up at the man in the Confederate uniform. He was using crutches, his left trouser leg pinned up as if to accentuate the loss of his limb. He was tall and slender, with brown hair that looked sparse but was left longer than normal, as if to make up for the lack. A chair sat behind him and Duncan knew it was for when he could no longer stand.

The compassion he would normally have felt for any man with his injury was missing. In its place was the memory of the whip marks on Rose's back and the scars on her hands.

Bruce reminded him of a Shakespearian quote: he had a lean and hungry look. The man had evidently suffered; the deep lines on the sides of his mouth belonged to a much older man. His face was nearly skeletal, marked by wrinkles radiating outward from his eyes and thinned lips. His eyes, tobacco brown, were narrowed, fixed on Rose as if he'd like to immolate her with his gaze.

The man looked exactly as he'd been in his letters: autocratic and overbearing. Evidently, there wouldn't be a welcome home speech forthcoming.

Beside Bruce stood one of the most beautiful women Duncan had ever seen. Her hair wasn't as bright red as Rose's, but darker, an auburn color with red highlights. Her face and Rose's had similar features, marking them as sisters, but hers were less lively and more patrician. The privations they must have endured in the last months had carved her face into a porcelain cameo complete with aquiline nose and sharp chin. Her smile was barely there, an infinitesimal curve of her lips.

Rose turned toward Duncan and smiled. Her courage was shining forth again, as was her daring. She might be terrified but she was not going to show it, especially to Bruce. Duncan kept her hand in his as they walked to the top of the broad steps of Glengarden.

"Duncan MacIain," he said, choosing to introduce himself before Rose could. "I'm your Scottish cousin."

Bruce didn't say a word, leaving his wife to lean toward him. "How very nice to meet you, Mr. MacIain," she said. "Welcome to Glengarden."

"You have a lovely home."

Bruce inclined his head in acknowledgment of the compliment, but that's where his politeness ended.

"Why are you here?" Bruce asked, directing his comment to Rose.

"I once lived here," she answered.

"You were never a welcome guest," Bruce said. "Only one I took in as a favor to Claire."

Rose's face didn't change.

Duncan wanted to push Bruce down the stairs, one leg and all. But what was worse was that Claire's expression didn't alter either. Nor did she say a word in her sister's defense.

No wonder Rose never considered Glengarden home.

ROSE WAS nauseous with fear and that made her mad. The anger steadied her, reminding her that Duncan was at her side. Thank God he'd returned with her. She didn't have to face Bruce alone.

"What did you do with the cotton, Bruce?"

"My cotton?"

She smiled. It was hardly his. He hadn't been there for the planting or the harvest. She and the slaves had picked it, ginned it, and packed it before taking it to Charleston.

But a glance from Duncan made her change her question.

"What did you do with your cotton, Bruce?"

"Brought it back to Glengarden," he said. "Not that it's any of your business."

"I've arranged to purchase it," Duncan said. "If you're willing to sell it."

He named the amount, but it didn't change Bruce's expression.

"That's more than the factors in Charleston or Nassau would have paid," she said.

"I'm not interested in selling it," Bruce said.

"What are you going to do for money, then?" she asked. "Is the Confederacy going to provide you with flour and sugar and meat? How are you going to support your family?"

"Tell your sister that she isn't welcome at Glengarden," he said to Claire before turning and making his way to the door. "Neither are you," he added over his shoulder to Duncan. "If you conspired with that conniving bitch. She can't sell what she doesn't own."

Claire grabbed her daughter by the hand and followed Bruce inside Glengarden. It was an early summer day, when all the doors and windows were normally kept open to allow the breeze to cool the house.

Instead, the door was closed firmly in front of them.

"I WOULD say that went well but I'd be lying," Duncan said. "At least we traveled here by the *Raven*. We won't have to sleep on the ground."

"There's always my cabin," she said. She waved her arm toward the east.

"With the slaves?"

She nodded, and he wondered why he wasn't surprised at her revelation.

He still held her hand, but before they descended the steps he grabbed her and hugged her. The meeting with Bruce had been difficult for her, especially in light of Claire's silence.

"I'm not willing to quit yet," he said.

She frowned at him. "What are you going to do?"

"Come back later and see if he'll at least meet and talk with me."

"In other words, without me."

"I think it would be best, don't you?"

She blew out a breath and nodded. "I should have said something about his leg. About how sorry I was."

"Are you?"

She looked sideways at him.

"Then don't practice being a hypocrite. Better say nothing than something you don't mean."

"How did you get to be so wise?"

He began to laugh, evidently startling her, judging by her expression.

"Here I am, standing on the steps of the oddest place I can imagine being, trying to figure out how to negotiate with a tyrant who bears my name. Not exactly a demonstration of wisdom."

"It's all my fault," she said, turning and taking the first step.

He accompanied her down the stairs.

"Yes, it is, and thank God. If not here, I'd be in Glasgow furiously working on plans for new looms and the import of Indian cotton. I'd never have experienced nearly dying in a storm at sea or Nassau and a certain tub, or being with you."

He sent her a glance. "I find I'm caring less and less about Bruce's damn cotton. You're the prize from this trip."

In full view of the house and probably as a gesture to annoy her brother-in-law, she raised up on tiptoe and kissed him.

"See, I told you that you were wise," she said, and smiled brightly at him.

Chapter 23

*H*alfway down the road she turned and stared back at the house.

"It's never been home for you, has it?" he said.

"How can it be, when I hated everything about it?" She glanced at him. "You realize that if something goes wrong in the future, it will be my fault. The Yankee in their midst. Perhaps even until his dying day, Bruce will blame me for something. For the Emancipation Proclamation, if the South loses, if they all starve—all of it will be my fault."

"You can't save him," he said. "Some people don't want to be saved."

"I don't want to save him," she said. "He never saw the brutality of slavery. Why should he see reality now? Unless the Confederacy paid him well, which I doubt, or gave him a stipend for his missing leg, he has no money. As for banning me from Glengarden, he told me, more than once, that he only tolerated me for Claire's sake. What he said today wasn't any different from what he's always thought."

"Show me your cabin."

She turned to him, surprised. "My cabin?"

He nodded.

She grabbed his hand and pulled him through the trees.

They topped a mound of earth that reminded him of a dike, then moved through a ditch and another line of trees. It was only then that Duncan could see the buildings. Each was long, with two doors but no windows. From what he could see, it looked as if there were four rows of six structures.

"How many are there?"

"Twenty," she said, her tone one of loathing. "Bruce would have built more, but the only slaves he could buy before he went off to war were skilled in rice, not cotton. He was very annoyed by that fact."

"But didn't you say there were over a hundred slaves here at one time?"

She nodded. "One hundred seventeen."

"That means every house had to accommodate five people."

"Or more," she said.

Some of the pine buildings were obviously older, but each was built the same. They were elevated slightly off the ground with one wooden step leading to a door.

She led him inside one of the pine structures. It was empty except for a cot with a blanket neatly folded at the bottom and topped with a pillow that was nearly flat.

There were no windows, so the door would need to be kept open for any light at all. And at night, would there be a breeze of any kind to ease the heat? If so, would they need to prop the door open then, too? Was there any kind of privacy? That question was answered with Rose's smile.

"The second thing you lose as a slave is privacy. The first is your freedom, of course. But everything you do is watched, either by the man who owns you, the overseer, or your fellow slaves."

She went to stand at the door.

"This is where I slept most of the time before Bruce went off to war."

"Why did he put you out of the house?"

She smiled. "A gesture to make me grateful for my blessings. He achieved his aim, but not in the way he understood."

She turned to him. "Have you ever been completely alone? Without one friend or anyone you knew?"

"No," he said. "I haven't."

Another blessing she pointed out to him if she but knew it.

"I learned so much from them. Sometimes I used to feel sorry for myself, but that only lasted until I came here. The slaves had nothing, yet they shared what they did have. They found joy in places I would never have looked."

She leaned up against the doorway, looking into the cramped and dark cabin. "I would hear them singing and wonder how they could find something to be happy about." She glanced over her shoulder at him. "It made me want to fight harder for them."

The structure was tiny and he could have crossed it in a few steps, but he wasn't going to chase her. Not after he'd been a satyr aboard ship. He didn't want her to think he was captivated by lust every time he was near her, although that might well be true.

"You're a Highlander," he said. "Never mind that your family comes from Ireland, you've the blood of warriors in your veins, Rose O'Sullivan."

"I doubt I'm that strong," she said.

"What would you call it, defying them all?"

"Doing what they should have been doing," she said. "Not brave as much as simply being human. Bruce and people like him are like children, I think," she added. "They believe that tomorrow will never come, that it's this far off thing that remains just out of sight. Tomorrow is here, Duncan."

Yes, it was, in more than one way.

"You said Bruce attended the Military Academy," Duncan asked. "Did he never serve in the military before the war?"

"Bruce resigned on his graduation leave. Two days after he and Claire were married. Said he didn't wish to be affiliated with his alma mater or most of his classmates."

"A man of expediency, then."

He tilted his head back to study the ceiling of the slave cabin. He could see chinks in the roof and the bright sky. Was she drenched when it rained?

"Is that what it's called, expediency? To wish the world the way you want it and refuse to participate unless it is? To me, it sounds like being a boy of five."

He smiled. "Perhaps it's that, too."

"What would you have done in his place?"

"Fortunately, I wasn't placed in that position."

"But what would you have done if you had been? If you'd been born into this world, if you were like Bruce?"

"I don't know," he said. "We're each dealt a role in life. Is it fair to say what a different person would do if given that card?"

"I don't see why not," she said. "I've been placed in Claire's position all my life, expected to deal with my circumstances exactly as she has. I've never had her dreams, her aspirations, her wishes. I never once wanted to marry a prince and go live in a castle."

"What did you want?" he asked.

"To be myself," she said, without a moment's hesitation. "To become eccentric, if I must. To be pointed out in the street. 'Oh, there's Miss O'Sullivan. Strange woman, she is. She has a liking for bean salad and apple bread. And cats. Oh, and dogs as well. She recites poetry to herself late at night and composes it when the mood strikes her, which it seems to do often of late. She likes thunderstorms and snow and can often be found staring at the lightning from her parlor window and out in a blizzard laughing like a demented child.'"

"All that?" he asked, smiling. "Perhaps you should think of it as exactly the opposite," he said. "Think how well or poorly Claire would deal with your life."

"It's no use," she said. "Claire would have been rescued, like as not, by some attractive man with a fortune at his disposal. She would have been whisked away to a faraway land to be worshipped as the beauty she is."

"Claire's a pale shadow to you, don't you know that? Claire's auburn hair is no match to yours." Especially now when flickers of sun were visible through the roof to light her red gold curls.

She threaded one hand through her hair self-consciously. "I've always hated my hair. My father said it was an indication of my temper. He said that God had given it to me to warn the rest of the world what I was like when I was angry."

"I've never seen you angry."

"You don't make me angry," she said. "But then

you don't own slaves and you don't abuse people who are powerless." She narrowed her eyes at him. "If you did, I'm certain Glynis or your mother would have warned me about you."

He smiled again. "I'm more than certain they would have."

"They didn't give me any warning at all. Nor did they recite all your virtues to me as if they were matchmaking. Why do you think that is?"

"I think they probably figured it out before we did," he said.

"What do you mean?"

"That I would fall in love with you," he said simply.

Her smile disappeared.

"Oh, Duncan."

"I've said it before and I'll keep saying it. However silent you remain."

He went to her, wrapped his arms around her and lowered his forehead to hers.

"Why are you so surprised? I've told you how I felt."

"But we were in bed," she said. "Isn't that part of making love, for a man to tell you he loves you?"

"I haven't bedded all that many women, but I've never said that to one. Ever." He pulled back. "Is that why you never said it in return? Or am I foolish to think that you don't feel the same? I've never been in love before, so I'm not very experienced at it."

"Oh, Duncan."

"Would you please stop saying that? It sounds like pity."

She closed her eyes, causing one tear to escape and slide down her cheek.

Do not try to talk me out of it. Do not give me words to ease my soul and make this moment easier.

He didn't want it easier. He wanted the passion and pain of it. He wanted to feel it all. If she was going to repudiate him, if she wanted to say something kind or sweet to ease his feelings, let her know the whole of it, how he truly felt first.

"I look at you and I lose my thoughts," he said. "And they might have been important thoughts like payroll or the loom maintenance schedule. Nothing seems as vital as simply looking at you."

He brushed away the tear with one finger, and thankfully, it wasn't followed by another. When she opened her eyes to look at him, he thought he could dive into those pools of green and lose himself. Who said that eyes were the windows to the soul? If that were true, Rose's eyes were a gateway to heaven itself, an oasis of comfort, joy, ease, and endless peace.

"When I'm near you, I wonder what your perfume is and where you've placed it. Then I find myself imagining being on a treasure hunt to find all those places. Behind your ear, your knee, the crook of your arm, your neck. All those lovely curves and hollows I discovered."

Her cheeks grew pink, but she didn't look away.

"When you kiss me, my mind dissolves. I no longer care who I am or where I am or how we've gotten there. Anyone could be watching or judging or ridiculing and it simply doesn't matter. All that matters is you, Rose, and the fact that you're kissing me."

He pulled back and looked at her, wishing he could always remember her as she looked right now, the shadows no match for the fiery color of her hair and the deep green of her eyes.

He didn't give a good damn where they were. All he knew was that she eased his heart and gave him hope and laughter. He admired her, lusted after her, respected her, and loved her with all the love he'd stored in his heart all these years.

"DO YOU think our children will have bright red hair? I suspect they will, just as I suspect they will be little hellions like their mother."

There was a twinkling in his eyes that was rarely there, which made her think she was being ridiculed, except that Duncan was not the type of man to make fun of other people.

She didn't know which part of that comment to address first.

It would be extraordinarily helpful if her heart would stop beating quite so fast and if her mouth wasn't suddenly dry. She might be trembling as well, but her hands were gripped so tightly together that she couldn't be certain.

"Are you offering me marriage, Duncan?"

"I am, Rose."

"Could you be phrasing it a little better, then?"

He didn't look the least disturbed by her words. If anything, his smile broadened.

"Would you marry me, Rose O'Sullivan? Would you do me the very great honor of becoming my wife? Would you come back to Scotland with me and live there the rest of your days?"

"Love frightens me."

"Why?" he asked. "The last thing love should do is frighten you."

"I don't want to change," she said. "Not like Claire has. It's like she doesn't have her own thoughts, her own feelings. Bruce is the filter through which everything she feels or thinks passes. If he doesn't approve, she doesn't speak or doesn't think or maybe even feel."

"Do you think I would do that to you?"

She glanced at him. "I don't know. I don't think you would, but what if you change? What if, a year after we're married, you suddenly decided that I shouldn't learn French?"

"I didn't know you were studying French."

She rolled her eyes. "I'm not. That's just an example."

"All right," he said. "So you're studying French, metaphorically, and I'm disagreeing. What happens next?"

"You would expect me to stop studying French."

"Would I?"

"Well, wouldn't you?"

"My name is MacIain," he said. "It's an old and venerable name in Scotland. There's a history to it. My family fought against the English. In 1745, they lost and Scotland was punished for its insurrection. Highland families that had gone against the crown were especially singled out to be punished."

She tilted her head and looked at him.

"Three brothers in our family left the Highlands to go and find their futures elsewhere. One went to Glasgow. That was my branch of the family. One went to England. That's Dalton's branch. You'll have a chance to meet him later. The third brother came to America, where he built Glengarden."

He walked to the door and stared out at the rows of slave cabins.

"I used to imagine that we must all somehow be alike. Dalton and I are friends. He's the one who financed this venture. We have the same tastes in whiskey. We laugh at the same jokes. But just because our names are the same doesn't mean we're identical. He's an earl and I'm a mill owner."

He turned to face her. "But Bruce? I don't even want to get to know Bruce. I find nothing about him to admire. Whatever he's done, you can't apply it to me. It's hardly fair and it's not applicable. I don't give a blazing bottom if you study French or practice the harpsichord or even sing. Whatever you want to do is fine with me, if it interests you and makes you happy."

"I can't sing," she said. "Well, not well. Would you really not forbid me to sing?"

"Don't you understand, Rose? I wouldn't forbid you to do anything." He shook his head. "No, I'm wrong. There's one thing I would forbid and that's staying here."

"Do you believe in fate?" she asked, coming to stand slightly behind him. She placed her arm around his waist and leaned against him. "Just think, if I'd never come to Scotland, we never would have met."

"I never have before," he said, "but perhaps I do now."

"I haven't anything to give you," she said.

"What?"

"You would give me a home and a family. You would give me a place to belong. I don't bring you anything. I'm not sure I can count Claire as family anymore, so I don't bring that. I have no place in the world. All I have is a valise, two dresses, my mother's hairbrush, and assorted other clothing and that's all."

"Take away the valise, the dresses, and the other odds and ends and that's all I want. You. Rose O'Sullivan, family or no. Alone or with a thousand people. Without a home or with a dozen. Do you think I care about any of that?"

He tipped her chin up to look at him. "All I care about is that I love you. I'm even willing to wait until you decide you love me, too. I have all the confidence in the world that you will, you see."

"I love you, Duncan. I'm not very experienced at love," she said, almost repeating his earlier words, "but I know how I feel about you."

He didn't speak, only pulled her into his arms and kissed her.

"I'll try once more with Bruce," he said, after she'd been thoroughly kissed. "But if he's as stubborn as before, I'm all for leaving Glengarden as fast as we can."

She lay her cheek against his chest, hearing the reassuring beat of his heart. Duncan had asked her to marry him. Not under a romantic looking tree. Not surrounded by rosebushes. Not even in a magnificent suite overlooking a harbor, but here, in this place that had known so much heartache.

It was somehow fitting and felt right.

"THERE'S SOMEONE I want you to meet," she said, "before we go back to the *Raven*. She's a hundred years old and she's been here longer than anyone."

She led him through the cabins. Some of them had tiny gardens attached. Some had porches added on. A man will provide for his family if it's possible. He couldn't help but wonder about the people who'd left Glengarden at night over the last few months, carrying their meager possessions. Had they found freedom? Were they safe?

The shame he felt was mixed with anger. He'd always been proud of his Highland heritage, but now he felt that he needed to do something to counteract his relative's actions. He wished to God that Bruce didn't bear the MacIain name.

The cabin Rose led him to was smaller than the others and at the end of the row. Characters that he couldn't read were scrawled on the door frame from the top crossbar to the ground. He sincerely hoped they were words wishing good fortune for the visitor and not some sort of curse. He didn't believe in such things, but he was a Scot. His culture was filled with fantastical creatures, myths, and legends.

Rose knocked on the door frame.

"Miss Betsy, is it all right if we come in? I'd like you to meet someone."

If Old Betsy claimed to be a hundred years old, he could believe it. She was a tiny, wizened woman sitting in a woven chair that looked to be nearly half her age and twice her size. Her skin reminded him of a walnut, hardened by years of working in the sun. Her hands were riddled with engorged veins traveling up her arms to disappear beneath the sleeves of the worn and patched patterned cotton of her dress.

Her eyes, white with cataracts, made him wonder if she could see.

"Miss Rose, is that you?"

"It is, Miss Betsy."

She clapped her hands together.

"I didn't think I'd see you again on this earth, child. You've come back, then?"

"Not to stay, Miss Betsy."

The old woman reared back in her chair and smiled, revealing only two teeth left in her mouth.

"Good. This place got no heart. My people's gone, but that's not the reason. This place never had no heart."

A wise woman, whatever her age.

"Who's that with you?"

"This is Duncan MacIain. He's from the Scottish branch of the MacIain family."

Betsy didn't say anything for a full minute, but she looked in Duncan's direction as if she were studying him.

"Thank you for coming to see me, Master Duncan."

"Just Duncan, ma'am. I'm master over no one but myself."

She smiled again and he had the feeling he'd given her the right answer.

"Then, Just Duncan, you got a home?"

"Yes, ma'am."

"It got heart?"

He smiled back at her. "Lots of heart. From generations of people loving each other. It hasn't always been easy, but the love has always been there."

She turned her attention to Rose, although she continued to speak to him.

"Are you going to take Miss Rose there?"

"Yes," he said. "I am."

"She'll make her home there with you? And you'll take care of her and protect her?"

"I will," he said, feeling as if it were a vow he gave her.

"Then go before the Devil does something to stop that."

There wasn't any doubt about whom she spoke.

Duncan stepped forward and placed his hand on the old woman's.

"There's nothing he can do to stop me," he said. "I promise that, too."

Rose bent and kissed Old Betsy on the cheek, gently enfolding her in a hug. He wasn't at all surprised to see tears on her face when Rose pulled back.

"How can I leave you?" she asked.

"You stayin' isn't going to change a thing. But if you go, I know that at least you'll be safe. You go on and have a happy life, Miss Rose."

Rose knelt at the side of the chair, bending her head at Old Betsy's knee. The elderly woman put both hands on Rose's head as if it were a benediction. Had she done so with all of the people who'd left her, off to find their freedom?

He realized why Glengarden disturbed him. It was the physical representation of arrogance and cruelty. Too many people had been brutalized here, and Rose had single-handedly done what she could to make amends. Yet one person's effort would never have been enough.

"You're a man who keeps his promises?" Betsy asked, raising her whitish eyes to him.

"Yes, I do."

"This is a good man you found, Miss Rose. Go on with him."

"I'll miss you," Rose said, standing.

"I'll be going soon myself, child. I'll be waiting at St. Peter's gate for you when it's your turn. You can tell me what you've been doing for the last fifty years. All of the details, now."

Her cackling laughter made him smile and they could hear it as they left the cabin.

"Miss Rose?"

A woman with a turban of black cloth wrapped around her head, her face the color of chocolate au lait, stood on the path. Her nose was wide, her chin squared, and her smile like a ray of sunshine as she revealed white, even teeth.

Rose startled him by starting to run. The woman who had called out to her placed the pot she had in her hands on the grass, then opened her arms.

"Maisie, oh Maisie, I've missed you so."

Maisie embraced her tightly. "Oh, child, I never thought you a fool. Why did you come back here?"

"I had to, Maisie. I sold the cotton," she said.

She motioned to him and he stepped forward, introducing himself to the woman.

Her eyes were brown, the brown of the fecund earth of dark woods, the bark of wet oaks, so deeply colored they appeared almost black. They were leveled on him, and he had the sense that she practiced hiding her emotions, but that her feelings sometimes escaped through those large brown eyes.

She took his measure in those short minutes and he couldn't help but wonder what she saw.

She held Rose away from her. "You should leave as soon as you can." She looked up at him. "This is not a safe place for Miss Rose. He's back and he'll hurt her if he can."

He had the same sense. As soon as he could finalize the sale of the cotton, they'd be gone. And if Bruce refused to negotiate with him, he'd just take Rose and sail away. He'd already profited from this voyage, and he didn't mean the cargo they'd unloaded in Charleston.

He had Rose in his life and he was going to do everything he could to protect her.

Chapter 24

*D*uncan wasn't going to leave without trying to make Bruce see reason. If that meant meeting with his disagreeable American cousin, so be it. He returned to the *Raven* with Rose, her silence unusual. He didn't attempt to breech it, didn't give her any platitudes.

He'd been briefed on the war by various people, from his English cousin to Captain McDougal. Up until the last few months the Confederacy had been faring well, but the tide was turning. He didn't know what was going to happen in the next year, but he didn't believe that Glengarden was exempt. Sooner or later the war would find them.

They walked side by side up the gangplank. Once aboard ship, she turned to him.

"Are you really going to meet with him?"

He nodded. "One last chance to get him to see reason."

"Be careful," she said before leaving him and walking to the captain's cabin.

"Will we be loading the bales soon, sir?"

He turned to find Captain McDougal standing there. The man's beard looked to have grown whiter in the days since they'd left Nassau. By the time they made it back to Glasgow all the hair on his beard and head might be as white as the clouds above them.

"Not yet, Captain. I've a visit to make first. Have we any good Scottish whiskey left in the crate we brought on board?"

McDougal grinned. "Aye, we do at that. I'll go and get it for you."

As he waited, he stared at the back of Glengarden. From here he could see the outbuildings and the stables. The trees on the banks of the river looked to be as old as those marking the formal approach to the house.

A man in the throes of patriotic passion sees only one thing, the love of his country. Yet shouldn't the love of family come before that? As much as he loved Scotland, his immediate family, which now included Rose, and his extended one of Lennox and his relatives, would always come first.

"Duncan."

He turned to find Rose standing there. Without a word she extended the drawstring bag that held the gold he'd paid her.

"Half down, half on arrival," she said. "It doesn't look as if you're going to get your cotton."

He shrugged. "It may be a matter of pride with him. He may not want a witness to him changing his mind."

"Here you go, sir," Captain McDougal said, coming to his side and presenting the bottle to Duncan. "Nothing but the finest Scottish whiskey."

Rose shook her head. "You intend to soften him up with spirits, Duncan?"

"They've been known to work before."

She glanced at McDougal. "I don't think we should

expect Duncan back any time soon, Captain. My brother-in-law has been known to like his whiskey."

"A wise man," McDougal said.

Duncan left the *Raven* with a smile, but it vanished as he followed the path back up through the oaks.

He hated Glengarden, and it was unlike him to judge something so quickly. He knew a little of its history, knew how Rose was treated, but it was something else about the plantation that disturbed him. An aura of tragedy seemed to permeate the place. Sorrow lingered in the dappled shadows. The breeze sounded a mournful wail in the branches.

He didn't know what its fate would be as the war progressed, but it seemed as if the house did and grieved for its passing even now.

At the steps, he didn't hesitate but climbed up to the veranda. Once there, he knocked on the door, still closed against them.

Maisie opened it a few minutes later. When he would have greeted her, she shook her head just a little, a clue that someone was listening.

Her brown eyes pleaded with him for kindness, for understanding, to be fair in his judgment of her, or perhaps not to judge at all.

"I'd like to talk to Bruce," he said, pretending they'd never met. "I'm Duncan MacIain."

"I'm to keep the door closed," she said.

"I've brought a present," he said, holding up the bottle with his right hand. In his left was the bag of gold.

"I'm to keep the door closed," she repeated, her eyes flickering to the left side of the door. "Master Bruce said so."

"I've come all the way from Scotland to see him."

"It's all right, Maisie. Let him in."

Behind her, in the shadows, he could see Claire descending a curving stairway. From what he could see of the inside of Glengarden, it was as prosperous looking as the exterior. At what cost? How many slaves had labored to build and maintain this place?

Maisie stepped aside.

"Bring us some mint tea, Maisie. You will join me, won't you?" Claire asked, sweeping her arm forward, evidently an indication he was to follow her.

He did so, feeling even more uncomfortable than while walking down the lane. Perhaps it was the otherworldly silence of Glengarden, like that of the grave. Perhaps the house was sentient and knew it was the last of its era, that it housed people whose time had come and gone. Or perhaps there were ghosts here with no knowledge of their mortality.

He couldn't rid himself of the feeling that this was a cursed place, one he'd give anything to leave as quickly as possible.

The parlor was filled with furniture he'd easily find in London, overstuffed settees and chairs with wood trim, pillows etched in delicate fringe, all in a restrained pattern of roses. The curtains were the same, now parted to reveal a view of the oaks and the long path to the river. Was the approach to Glengarden on the land side as formidable? Designed, no doubt, with a dual purpose: impress a visitor and hide the plantation's secrets.

"You're a very long way from Scotland, Mr. MacIain."

He smiled. Her voice held no trace of New York in it. Was her new South Carolina accent a practiced thing or had it simply come naturally over the years spent here? He suspected it was more the former than the latter.

She sounded nothing like her sister, but then Rose had only lived here two years. He wondered what her voice would sound like after a few years in Scotland.

"I am at that," he said. "Would it be possible to speak with your husband? I have a business proposition to offer him." He held up the bottle. "And a peace offering, of sorts."

She smiled, the expression only accentuating her beauty. He could well see why Bruce MacIain would marry Claire O'Sullivan and bring her back to Glengarden. Had he known he'd also acquire Rose, too?

He kept his smile in place as he waited for her answer.

"If you were a factor from Charleston, Mr. MacIain, my husband would be pleased to meet with you. If you were from Scotland and had come independently, the same would be true. But because you were accompanied by my sister, he's not disposed to give you any time. I'm sorry, but that's the truth of it."

"Not even if we're relatives?" he asked, wishing he had Lennox's charm. His brother-in-law was a great deal more diplomatic. "After all, we're descended from the same family."

Her smile was less charming and slightly thinner. He had the feeling that Claire demonstrated her moods not with words but with gestures.

"The fact that you are party to my sister's manipulations negates any familial feeling, at least that's how Bruce feels."

Was she being threatened by her husband or did

the words come of her own volition? He honestly
didn't know. Some women were terrorized by their
husbands, and it was easy to assume that was the
case here, but Claire might be the exception. She
might honestly feel that Bruce was justified in his
behavior.

"Your daughter is lovely," he said. "She resembles
you a great deal."

She inclined her head in acceptance of his compliment.

Maisie entered the room with a tray. He stood
to help her. The only response he got when he took
the tray from her was a widening of her eyes. She
glanced toward Claire, who nodded a dismissal.

When the other woman was gone, Claire spoke,
her tone soft, as if she feared being overheard. By
whom? Maisie or Bruce?

"You don't understand, Mr. MacIain," she said
softly.

"Since we are related, however distantly, would
you call me Duncan?"

She nodded, looking through the window. He
couldn't help but wonder what she saw. The past
with guests arriving for a ball at the grand house?
Or had Glengarden always been isolated, deliberately cut off from society?

"Rose has been a thorn in my husband's side from
the moment she arrived at Glengarden," she said.
"He was happy to give her a home when she had
nowhere else to live. She was, after all, my sister. But
instead of being grateful for his generosity and his
kindness, she sought to annoy him at every turn. He
forbid her to visit with the slaves, yet she was down
at the cabins every day."

She looked at her hands, the tips of her fingers meeting.

"If someone was whipped, she insisted on caring for them. If someone was cold, she took her own bedding to them. If someone was ill, she brought them medicine. I began to wonder if she did it out of a wish to genuinely help or only to annoy Bruce."

He wasn't often speechless, but Claire's words stripped a response from him. Rose had cared for their slaves and all Claire could think was that it was her way of irritating Bruce?

First of all, what kind of sister was Claire? Secondly, had she no humanity? Was that a prerequisite for living at Glengarden?

She was continuing to speak, which was a good thing because he didn't know what to say.

"She's pushed him into behaving unlike himself."

"He forced her to work in the fields, Claire."

She handed him his glass. He took it, thanked her, and waited for her response. When she didn't immediately answer, he took a sip of the drink. The mint tea was refreshing and would certainly be so on a hot summer day. Days like those Rose had spent in the cotton fields.

She finally nodded. "He believed that if she lived like a slave, she would come to appreciate her position as his sister-in-law."

"Instead, she endured."

She looked away again. "Rose is very good at endurance. If she'd only listened to him, if she'd only obeyed him, life could have been nearly idyllic."

Except for the slaves. Didn't she ever notice them? He decided the question would be foolish to ask. Claire was one of those people who saw what they wanted to see. When forced to visit reality, they pretended to be shocked by what was before them the whole time.

"She never once complained. Twice, she had to be brought in from the fields because of heat stroke, but she stubbornly went out the next day. It was a battle that raged between them until Bruce went off to war."

"Why didn't you leave him?"

Her eyes widened. The smile she'd fixedly worn disappeared.

"Why on earth would I leave him, Duncan? I love my husband. Besides, I'd taken a vow before God that nothing would separate us."

"Even after he treated your sister that way? Even with the slaves?"

A man doesn't take advantage of those who are weaker. A decent man doesn't own another. He had never felt this level of disgust, and what made it worse was the fact that Bruce was a MacIain. A distant relation, true, but a man who shared his name.

"My sister cares very deeply about people, Duncan. Too much. She didn't understand that slavery is a way of life in the South. When Bruce came home to find the slaves had disappeared, he was incensed. He knew immediately that she'd helped them." She took a sip of her tea. "How could he possibly have thought kindly of her after that?"

"Hadn't he heard of the Emancipation Proclamation?" he asked. Even he had learned of it, living in Scotland. President Lincoln's freeing of the slaves might not be recognized by the Confederacy, but the men, women, and children enslaved by "a way of life" had certainly understood it.

Hadn't she ever tried to help Rose? Hadn't she ever spoken up for her sister?

"Didn't he realize what she'd done in his absence? She worked hard to save Glengarden, to guard your last crop."

She looked surprised. "Not for Bruce's sake," she said. "But for the rest of us. Without cotton, there was no money."

"Yet your husband refuses to sell it."

She glanced over at him. Perhaps it was the look on his face, his inability to conceive of a man refusing to bargain out of spite that caused her to lean forward and place her hand on his arm.

"Rose believes in her cause. Bruce believes in his. That's why they hate each other as much as they do. If one succeeds, the other must fail. By selling the cotton to you, she'd won, in a sense."

"What about the war tax?" he asked.

Her eyebrows moved infinitesimally, evidently signaling her confusion.

He told her what he'd learned in Nassau. "I understand that the Confederacy is under some financial strain. They're taxing agricultural products at the rate of eight percent. So whatever he brought back from Charleston will have to be reported and paid for."

"Bruce will find a way."

As he sat there looking at the woman, he realized that Claire believed in her husband, rightly or wrongly. She was willing to take his side in blind trust. Such loyalty was to be commended to a point. Rose's mistreatment at Bruce's hands was that point, and Claire had gone beyond it.

He didn't know what to say to her. Or to Bruce,

for that matter. From what he'd learned, both from Rose and now Claire, the man couldn't bear to be bested. Yet his adversary, in this case, had been a red-haired termagant with a passion for justice.

A man who couldn't stand to lose was a very dangerous opponent.

ROSE WAITED until Duncan left the ship before slipping down the makeshift gangplank they'd erected.

How would she get in to see Claire? Had her sister been instructed not to talk to her? Probably, but she'd have to find a way.

Before coming to Glengarden, Rose had never been in a situation where someone hated her. True, she and her brothers had occasionally argued, but at the base of everything there was familial love. She'd had acquaintances in her youth, some of whom had drifted away. But no one had ever expressed his animosity toward her in such a direct and uncensored way as Bruce. He hated her and left no doubt about his feelings.

How had Bruce been able to change Claire's mind about her? How had he been able to sever the sisterly bonds? Granted, Claire was older than her, but they'd grown up in the same family, had the same father and mother, the same background. Even if Claire could dismiss the fact that Rose was her sister, how could she ignore everything else? Probably the same way she was so blithely able to ignore slavery itself.

Maybe it wasn't that Claire had changed so drastically. Maybe it was that she'd never truly known her sister.

She made her way through the copse of trees, just

far enough away from the back of the house that she could see the kitchen. From here she'd be able to signal Maisie, who could tell her when it would be safe to enter the house.

A voice spoke just behind her, causing her to jump.

"Child," Maisie said. "That's one mad man in that house and here you are running through the trees, just asking him to come out here with his whip."

Rose turned to face the other woman.

"I know," she said. "But I need to see Claire."

"You know he'll hurt you if he can."

"I know that, too, Maisie, but I have to talk to her."

"And what good would that do, child?"

"She has to leave here, Maisie."

The other woman shook her head. "You know she's not going to do that."

"I have to try, Maisie. I can't leave without trying."

She hugged the older woman and kissed her cheek. Maisie had been the closest to a mother she'd ever had. Maisie had protected her and warned her, just like today. More than once she'd looked Bruce right in the face and lied with a smile. The consequences of doing that were deadly.

"Master Bruce normally takes something for the pain in his leg right about now. Whatever's in that brown bottle puts him to sleep for a while. I expect you have two or three hours on the outside if you want to see Claire. No more than that, and for the love of the angels, don't try to see her when he's awake."

Rose nodded and followed Maisie into the back of the house.

The minute she was in the kitchen, she could hear the conversation in the Lady's Parlor, one of Claire's favorite rooms. She exchanged a glance with Maisie and walked through the hall, hesitating outside the door.

CLAIRE BEGAN to speak again, as if she'd come to grips with her confession, because that's exactly what it sounded like.

He wanted to counsel her that he wasn't sinless or blameless or a man filled with virtue. Once, he could have ascribed to those traits, but no longer. This voyage had taught him, as nothing else had, that he was all too human.

"Rose was always so strong, so certain of herself. She needed a strong hand, but my brothers spoiled her."

He pushed back his anger. Now was not the time to speak, not until she'd finished.

"I knew Bruce would give her direction, quell her more rebellious notions."

"She was an abolitionist," he said, biting out the words. "Is that a rebellious notion?"

She folded her arms in front of herself as if she were cold.

Slowly, she turned to face him, surprising him with her courage. He was not calm now. His anger was building as if it were a ladder. Each confession was a rung. This damnable place, Glengarden was a rung. Bruce was a rung.

"It wasn't just that," she said. "She defied him at every turn."

He would have done the same. Bruce MacIain was a tyrant. Yet the man would probably never accept that label about himself. He was simply living the life he was raised to appreciate. Scion of his own fiefdom. The Prince of Glengarden.

"Do you know why Rose came to Scotland?" he said. "Do you have any idea? To save you. To keep you from starving. Not for herself, Claire. For you and your daughter. For all the people who live here. But you've never done one thing to help her, have you? Not one time. When Bruce was using her as a slave, what did you do?"

"My sister has always been headstrong. I thought she needed someone to teach her a lesson."

He was beyond astonishment, or even rage, for that matter. He didn't understand, would never understand.

"Was it fear?"

He turned to see Rose standing in the doorway.

"Did you never say anything because you were afraid of Bruce?"

Whereas Claire had looked at him directly, she didn't glance at her sister. Instead, the carpeting beneath her feet suddenly held great interest for her.

"Fear should never be a greater force than love." Rose walked slowly toward her sister. "It should never be, Claire."

Claire finally looked up. He'd expected her to show some emotion, even tears, but no expression marred that beautiful face.

"Rose, don't be silly. He's my husband and I love him. If you'd only shown a little fear, he wouldn't be so angry at you. You're the one who never understood. You never listened. You never accepted being here or learning to live like us."

"How could I?"

"You could have, if you'd wanted harmony, Rose. But you never have. You wanted to stuff your principles down our throats."

Rose smiled, but there was no humor in the expression.

"If I'd known how you felt, I would never have come back for you."

"For me?" Claire laughed. "You didn't come back for me, Rose. You came back to rub it in Bruce's face. To make him feel even less like a man. You sold his cotton and he didn't."

IN THAT moment, Rose understood.

Claire still wanted to be the princess, reigning at her castle with the prince in attendance. The castle might fall down around her, the prince could be grievously wounded, but she was still the princess and always would be.

As long as that dream remained in her mind, she'd never see Glengarden as it truly was, just as she'd never seen the slave cabins, didn't want to talk about slavery, refused to discuss Bruce's punishments. Nor had Claire ever once mentioned Phibba or what had happened to her, or Maisie's constant unspoken grief.

In her way, Claire was as much a tyrant as Bruce, and it made her sick to realize it.

Claire had chosen to stand beside him all this time, regardless of what he'd done. Why had it taken her so long to understand that?

"May I say good-bye to Gloria?" she asked.

"I don't think that would be a good idea. I don't want her upset."

Gloria would be brought up in the same mold. Don't mind the slave cabins. Don't pay that any attention. Concentrate on the castle and growing up to be a princess.

She nodded and looked around her. What a grand and lovely place Glengarden was, designed by a famous architect, built by craftsmen. If the Union army didn't reach it, the house might stand for centuries. She wondered if the rest of the plantation would remain intact, all those cabins waiting to be populated with slaves again or the devil's post where slaves were whipped.

Her fellow Yankees might pull down everything, board by board. Hopefully, Bruce would be here to see it.

Having no knowledge of love until now, she'd accepted what she'd seen. But Duncan had promised more. Duncan had taught her, in these short weeks, that love meant joy.

Where had the joy been in Claire's life the last two years? Perhaps it was with Gloria that she saw her sister truly happy, those moments she shared with her daughter without the possibility of being interrupted by her husband. This last year, as difficult as it had been, had almost been blissful compared to when Bruce strutted around Glengarden like a prince. No, a king, one who had no power above him. Not even that of God.

You can't save people who don't wish to be saved.

She couldn't help but think of the men, women, and children she'd known at Glengarden, each one of whom desperately wanted their freedom. When the chance had come to escape, they hadn't hesitated. However frightening the future had looked for them, they'd taken their meager possessions, a hand-carved pipe, a doll made of straw, a cast-off brush, wrapped them in a piece of cloth and made their way silently and joyfully away from the plantation. Disaster might have awaited them, certainly privation had, but that didn't matter. Their lives lay before them to do as they would with them as free people.

And now was her chance to be saved.

She turned to Duncan and held out her hand, smiling brightly.

Just at that moment Maisie raced into the room. "The barn's on fire!"

ROSE MADE her way out of the house through the kitchen. Duncan found himself running to keep up with her. He didn't know if Maisie or Claire followed them; he was too intent on Rose.

The air was getting cloudy as she passed through the overgrown garden, veered to the left and took a path past the slave cabins and toward the smoke. At the end of one of the fields a barn was on fire. No doubt the structure was used to store farm implements, seed, or even cotton. Especially the cotton Bruce had brought back from Charleston.

If he were a painter of any talent, he would have immortalized the fire. The barnlike building with its gaping maw was now engulfed with flames like licking tongues, the roof pierced by swords of red and orange, and sprouting from all of it, billowing black clouds of smoke to announce the scene to everyone for dozens of miles.

He wouldn't have been surprised if the Union ships in the Atlantic could see the cotton burning. If the residents of Charleston saw the smoke, no doubt they remembered their own conflagration.

Maybe some of Bruce's neighbors would think that Glengarden was on fire. No, instead, its future was up in flames, thanks to the pride of its owner.

He'd never seen a grown man cut off his nose to spite his face before in such a spectacular way.

He'd come halfway around the world for Glengarden's cotton, and it was set ablaze in a petty act of what, revenge? Was Bruce determined that his family would suffer for the rest of the war? It wasn't enough for him to have lost a leg, did he want them all to starve now?

Bruce stood beneath an oak not far away. His face was solemn, while the expression on the face of the man beside him was alight with joy. As he watched, the man jumped up and down and waved, then crossed the dirt field to embrace Rose.

"Miss Rose. Miss Rose. Do you see? It's a fine fire, isn't it? I helped. I did."

"You're right, Benny, it's a fine fire," she said, patting the man on the shoulder. "You did good."

Duncan walked across the field, stopping when he was a few feet from Bruce.

"I would have bought your cotton," he said. "With gold."

"I don't want your damn gold."

"What do you want? Evidently to make a statement of some sort. How noble you are, how self-sacrificing. How loyal to your cause. Well, at least you don't have to pay the war tax this way."

"It's my cotton, damn it, and I'll do whatever I want with it. Throw it in the river. Give it to the army or set fire to it."

"Self-sacrificing behavior is fine if you're the only one doing it. But to make other people suffer along with you hardly seems rational."

"We'll be fine without your damn gold. Now get off my land."

He knew how expensive it was to maintain a household because he paid the bills. Maybe living in a city was more costly than being on a plantation, but he didn't think so. He hadn't seen any crops growing to feed the family, hadn't seen any animals that would provide meat or eggs. What about the rest of the taxes that would probably be levied against Glengarden?

Did Bruce think he could simply wave his crutch and some Confederate fairy godfather would provide all that he and his family needed?

"Get off my land before I get my gun and shoot you."

"As a gesture of hospitality, that's somewhat lacking, but I get your point."

He turned and walked back to where Rose was standing.

"It's only cotton, Rose," he said gently.

She nodded, then surprised him by wrapping her arms around his neck and standing on tiptoe to kiss him.

"It's only cotton," he said again when he felt her tremble against him.

He never wanted her to be afraid again. Or feel that she was alone. Most of all, none of the bullies of the world would be able to touch her or make her life miserable.

Without looking in Bruce's direction, they turned and walked away, heading back toward the *Raven*.

Chapter 25

$\mathcal{R}$ose left Duncan sleeping in the stateroom aboard the *Raven*. The night had been a sleepless one for her as she'd turned over scenes of the last two years in her mind.

Claire had never stood up for her or defended her, but she'd never considered that Claire thought she deserved the treatment she received. Or believed that Bruce had been justified in everything he'd done.

What had Claire called her? Spoiled? How had she been spoiled?

She had the strangest sensation of being pulled in two. What she'd always believed was being compared to the truth, and the truth was winning. Claire hadn't been a loving sister who was powerless to prevent her husband's actions. Instead, she'd agreed with every one of them.

Even the times when she'd been locked in the cold house? Even when Bruce had her whipped? Even those days when she'd worked in the fields alongside the slaves?

Inside, in some deep, hidden part of her she was probably preparing to grieve. At the moment, though, she felt nothing, and the absence of emotion was disconcerting.

She hadn't known Glynis very long, but she couldn't imagine the woman allowing something terrible to happen to Duncan without a loud and vehement protest. She'd expect the same behavior from Lennox if someone tried to harm Mary.

Nor could she imagine Jeremy or Robert or Montgomery refusing to protect her from any danger.

Why was Claire so different?

At least now, knowing the truth, she could walk away from Glengarden without a qualm. She would miss Maisie the most, Old Betsy next. Perhaps Gloria, although she was never allowed to be around the child that much. Anyone else? No, she wouldn't miss anyone else.

She'd not seen Susanna since returning, but because she and the older woman didn't have much of a relationship, she hadn't asked to see her. All the matriarch of the MacIains would do was castigate her in some fashion for her failures. How different she was from Eleanor MacIain. One was a bitter woman pretending that her world wasn't falling apart. The other was a generous, kind soul who, despite her own financial worries, still saw beyond her personal problems to help other people.

She wondered if Susanna had enough common sense left to realize what Bruce had done by burning their cotton. Did she see it as an act of revenge, patriotism, or outright stupidity?

Or Claire? Claire adored her daughter, but what kind of life would Gloria have in a world in which her father believed mostly in retaliation? What about survival? Wasn't that more important?

She'd talked to both Duncan and Captain McDougal last night. This morning she and two of the seamen were delivering what foodstuffs they could spare until they replenished their supplies in Nassau. She'd almost come to tears over their generosity. Despite the fact that Duncan had been so badly treated by his American cousin, he was all for settling as much as he could on them, bags of flour, sugar, potatoes, and salted meat.

They made their way from the *Raven*, past the barge she'd used to carry cotton to Charleston, and beyond to the path to the back of Glengarden. Anyone else would be grateful for their largesse, but Bruce would see it as charity. The last thing she wanted was to have him destroy the food. Maisie could make what they were giving her stretch for weeks.

She and the two seamen from the *Raven* stood behind the copse of trees. When she saw Maisie throw out the dirty water from the sink into the ruins of what had once been the kitchen garden, she waved her arms.

Maisie walked toward them slowly in a meandering way, as if searching for something on the ground.

When she reached Rose, she shook her head.

"Don't you have the sense God gave a mosquito, child? This is not a safe place to be."

"We brought you some food, Maisie. Not that much, but enough to get you by for several weeks."

Maisie's face didn't change, but her eyes softened.

"Do you want us to take it to the cold house?"

"Ain't nothing there, child. It'd be funny if I was seen going in there when everybody knows it's empty. Bring it into the kitchen. I'll find places to put it where no one will find it."

They followed her back to the house and as quiet as little mice laid the bags of food on the big oak table.

"Aren't they going to wonder where it all came from?"

Maisie shook her head. "No more than when Benny steals a pig or picks a few chickens from a neighbor's place. Sometimes I think they just expect food to appear on their plate like magic. Miss Susanna said she wanted some apple tarts the other day." Maisie sighed. "She doesn't seem to understand that I don't have anything to make apple tarts."

"Well, at least this way Benny doesn't end up getting shot trying to feed you."

"I expect some folks think they have a critter on the loose, one who steals their livestock."

Maisie hugged her when they were done laying out the food and gave her another warning.

"You go on now, Miss Rose. You deserve to have your own life. You've done as much as you can here."

Rose signaled to the two seamen. "Go on back to the *Raven*," she said. "I'm right behind you."

"We were told not to leave you, ma'am."

"I'll be right there. Just give me a minute? Please."

They left the kitchen, but they weren't all that quick about returning to the *Raven*. She watched them out the window for a little while, then turned her gaze to Maisie.

The older woman had always been a source of comfort, a gentle soul with endless compassion, just like Old Betsy. How could they care about others when they'd been treated so harshly? When they'd been *owned*?

"We're leaving this morning, Maisie. Won't you come with us?"

The other woman shook her head. "Not as long as my Phibba's here."

Rose nodded. She understood Maisie's devotion to her child even after death. Perhaps some of it was guilt, that she hadn't been able to save her. Or perhaps it was simply a case of Maisie still being protective about someone she loved.

"I'm sorry about the cotton," Maisie said. "I had to tell."

"I know you did and I don't blame you, Maisie."

She didn't know what kind of coercion Bruce had used, but it had been something. Otherwise, Maisie would never have told him about the trips to Charleston.

"But I didn't tell him about both warehouses."

She stared at the older woman. They'd had to divide the crop into two warehouses only because of space limitations. One of them held three hundred bales. The other seven hundred.

"How many bales did he get, Maisie?" she asked.

The older woman looked amused as she answered. "I imagine he burned three hundreds or thereabout."

It had never occurred to her that Bruce had been ignorant about the second warehouse. Nor had she bothered to check it because the same man owned both buildings. Surely he would have told Bruce about the rest of his cotton? Evidently he hadn't, because there were still seven hundred bales in Charleston.

She had to leave, but how could she possibly thank Maisie for everything she'd done? Her kindness, her wisdom, her steadfast guidance had been a mainstay. She couldn't have borne the last two years at Glengarden without her.

"I'll miss you, Maisie," she said.

"If you don't get going, you won't have a chance," Maisie said, her own eyes a deeper brown for her tears. "Go on with you now."

She did, walking away with thoughts not of what she was leaving, but what she was facing, a life of freedom and love.

"You just can't obey, can you, Rose? I told you to leave Glengarden, but of course you have to ignore me."

She shouldn't have been so occupied in her thoughts. If she hadn't been, she would have seen Bruce standing on the path to the river.

"What is it about your nature that makes you so stubborn? Claire isn't like you. Are you sure you're really her sister and not some foundling your parents found on the street?"

He leaned forward against his crutches, his smile eerie, as if an expression of welcome had been pasted over a face of evil.

She knew that look. Sometimes it had been the only warning prior to an act of cruelty.

The slaves of Glengarden were aware of that expression, had learned how to behave once they saw it. Then, a man's gaze never left the ground. His shoulders slumped. Men who were taller than Bruce bent their knees to equalize their heights or to appear shorter. Each person knew never to look up, and when addressed—if they were unfortunate enough to be known by name—they answered quickly, eyes averted.

She'd never learned the trait of being submissive, especially not to Bruce.

She should have been. She should always have

been more afraid. Fool that she'd been, she thought her safety lay in Claire. She believed that Bruce would never truly hurt her because she was Claire's sister. Knowing what she knew now, she realized the true extent of her past jeopardy. He could probably have killed her at any time and Claire would have somehow justified it to herself.

She straightened her shoulders, took a deep breath and addressed him.

"I'm leaving, Bruce. You'll get your wish. You'll never see me again."

"Ah, Rose. If only I believed you."

He took a few steps toward her. She had to stop herself from retreating. She wouldn't show fear now. The *Raven* was only a short distance away and so was Duncan.

"You see, I have some familiarity with your word, and it means nothing. 'No, Bruce, I won't talk to the slaves.' 'No, Bruce I won't teach my maid to read.' 'No, Bruce, I won't go down to the cabins.'"

He was within arm's reach now. She stepped aside, into the weeds and tall grass alongside the path.

"How can I believe you now, Rose?"

"Because I'm leaving," she said. "I'll never return to Glengarden."

The most incredible sense of freedom surged through her at those words. Was that how the others had felt when they left? As if a door to a prison had been opened? She would never have to see this place ever again. She wasn't going to think about it. If someone ever questioned her past, she would never mention Glengarden. Two years of her life would somehow have to be expunged.

He took another step toward her.

"I learned a great deal when I went to war. You never asked about my experiences. I was a little disappointed at that."

She had no desire to hear about the cruelties he'd inflicted on Union soldiers.

"Sometimes you just can't depend on circumstances. You have to manipulate them to your own desires. Otherwise, you're always taking a chance, and chance can be such a fickle bitch."

"I'm leaving, Bruce."

She wasn't listening to him. She didn't have to listen to him. Let him pontificate to his heart's desire to someone else. She never had to hear his voice again. Nor would she ever have to worry about Bruce MacIain.

He caught her as she moved past him.

"Let me go," she said, trying to pull away. His fingers dug into her arm until she was certain she'd have bruises from his grip.

"Always dictating to me. Tell me, do you never get tired of issuing orders? Do you tell your lover what to do, Rose? Does he listen, like a lapdog?"

"Let me go, Bruce," she said, trying to remain calm.

Despite being on crutches and having lost a leg, he was still a strong man. She tried to pull away, but his grip only tightened.

"Or you'll do what? Release my slaves? Try to bankrupt me? Sell my cotton to some trumped up nobody? Oh, that's right, you've already done that."

"I'm leaving. You can tell yourself that all your problems are my fault. I suppose you'll blame the loss of your leg on me, too. You'll figure out some way to do that, I'm sure."

"You've been a bitch from the day you arrived and you'll be a bitch until the day you die, won't you?"

She would never be his definition of a southern lady, one who accepted that a man was superior in every way. She and her brothers had had boisterous arguments. More than once she and her father had disagreed, but instead of castigating her for having an opinion, he seemed to enjoy their verbal sparring.

Even Duncan— Her thoughts came full stop. Duncan challenged her, goaded her, smiled when she lost her temper. He'd even laughed more than once when she argued a point, as if he were proud of her spirit.

Bruce, on the other hand, was almost petulant when he didn't get his way or when someone dared to venture a thought not in line with his, especially when a woman spoke up.

He grinned again, and she felt a premonitory shiver travel from the back of her neck all the way down her spine.

Duncan was only a little distance away. That's all she had to remember. Why hadn't she just run away from Bruce? He wouldn't have been able to catch up with her.

"You should have never come back."

"What was I supposed to do, Bruce, sit here and genteelly starve? We had no food or any way to grow any. Would you rather us depend on charity? We had a fortune in cotton in the warehouse. Why not sell it? But you chose to burn it. What a stupid thing to do."

She didn't see the blow before it came. He backhanded her so hard she fell to the ground, dazed. When he raised one of his crutches to strike her, she tried to roll away, but couldn't move fast enough.

He struck her with the end of the crutch, where bolts held the wood strips together. She could feel the blood trickle down from the cut on her cheek as he hit her once more.

His face was contorted into a mask of rage as he struck her again and again.

He was going to kill her unless she got away. She tried to get up, but a wave of dizziness made her fall back. She tried to call out but her voice sounded feeble. Wiping away the blood from her eyes, she finally made it to her knees.

When he came closer, she put up both her hands to ward him off, but couldn't push him away. Retrieving something from his pocket, he wound it around her neck and knotted it. A rope of some sort. No, smaller than a rope, but woven just the same. She raised her hands, trying to get her fingers between the rope and her neck.

He struck her again.

The battle between them was silent. No more insults. No more responses. She couldn't remain upright for long without being dizzy. He struck her again and she fell into the weeds. He jerked on the rope now tied to the crossbar of his crutch to rouse her.

This time he was going to kill her.

"I've been thinking about this ever since you came back, Rose. I have a certain disability, you see, but I thought there must be a way to get you to do what I wanted. What better way to treat a bitch than like a bitch? You put a leash on a dog, don't you? This is your new leash. I'm half tempted to parade you around Glengarden like this, but there are no more slaves to see you. Pity."

He began to walk, pulling on the rope and choking her with each step. Every time she resisted, the rope tightened, cutting off her air. She focused on the gravel path beneath her knees, wiping away the blood from her face. She couldn't speak, could barely breathe, but scuttled along the ground like a crab to keep up with him. Twice she lost her balance and fell over. He didn't stop, only jerked the leash even tighter. She had to keep up with him or be strangled.

"Please." The sound came out like a hoarse whisper.

"Please? Oh, I do please, Rose. I please myself in this instance. I please myself to rid Glengarden of you once and for all."

He raised the crutch and struck her again. For a few seconds, maybe longer, she managed to get to her knees again, inching along as he continued down the path to the east side of the house. She knew where he was going: the cold house.

It wasn't enough, then, that she wanted to be gone from here even more than he wanted her away from Glengarden. He was going to punish her for not being his slave, for daring to speak up, for thinking for herself. This punishment had nothing to do with being a woman and everything to do with not being in awe of Bruce MacIain.

Dear God, please let me live to see Duncan again, if only to tell him how much I love him.

Bruce stopped and both hands went to her throat to loosen the rope. He struck her again, smiling as he did so, chuckling when he heard her moan.

Then, from out of nowhere, he produced a pistol. Was he going to shoot her here? Please, no. Not now. Not when she'd been given a touch of joy. She'd been so looking forward to this morning, to finally leaving. Sailing away without a backward glance, her hand in Duncan's. All her secrets were out in the open and she'd been forgiven each one.

"Our favorite place," he said, waving the pistol at her. "You remember the cold house, Rose. It's empty now, all because of what you've done. But you know that, don't you? Did you give everyone food for their journey? Did you give them my money?"

He didn't let her answer. It didn't matter; he'd ignore anything she said. He'd made up his mind as he always had. What anyone said, or even the truth, was superfluous.

Murder was in his eyes. It was there in the twist of his lips as he removed the key from his pocket and inserted it in the lock. The iron-banded door was thick, both to keep in the cold and to prevent theft. Without the key it was impossible to open, and once the door was closed, the cold house was sound-proof.

"While I was off fighting the Yankees, Rose, you were doing your damnedest to ruin me and take away everything I had, weren't you? I should never have let you into my home. You were a bitch with rabies, weren't you?"

He pointed the gun at her. She'd been the object of his anger enough times to know this session was going to be bad. He couldn't be reached by words. He was a creature of rage, and until that rage was spent, he wouldn't leave her.

In the past, she'd learned to keep quiet, because it made the sessions shorter. What did it matter now? She knew that whatever she said or did, he was going to kill her.

"Get in there, Rose."

She turned and stepped toward the door. He suddenly pushed her the rest of the way. She tumbled down the four steps, landing on the soft dirt. With trembling hands she loosened the rope around her throat.

"This time, I'm going to make sure you stay where I put you. No one is going to rescue you, Rose. Not your lover, no one."

"You can't keep me here," she said, her voice hoarse.

"I'm your only male relative. I can do whatever I want, Rose, and there's no one to stop me."

"Duncan will."

"Your lover? What a slut you are, Rose. He'll be sailing away soon. You see, you decided to remain at Glengarden to stay with your sister and your niece."

Duncan wouldn't believe that. Duncan would never believe him.

"No one is going to release you, Rose. You can scream as long as you want. No one can hear you. Without water, you won't last long. Maybe a few days. Everyone will think you've gone off with your Scot. Only you and I will know the truth."

She remained silent.

The door closed, the darkness that of the grave. A moment later the key turned in the lock.

Duncan would save her. *Please God, let Duncan save her.*

MAISIE WAS putting away the food Miss Rose had brought, hiding it in corners and cubbyholes. As she was finishing up, she glanced through the kitchen window and froze.

Bruce was there, standing on the path in front of Miss Rose.

She left the kitchen and ducked behind one of the hedges that separated the garden from the rest of the back lawn, peering through the branches to see him strike her, then wind a rope around Miss Rose's neck.

The foolish girl had put herself in danger again, simply to be kind. When would she learn? Hopefully, never. The world needed angels like Miss Rose, the better to counter all the devils already here.

He had no right to treat the girl so badly. All she'd ever done was try to help those who needed help. But Bruce had never seen it that way.

He had to be stopped. And Miss Rose had to be saved.

Chapter 26

*R*ose hadn't returned.

Captain McDougal didn't say a word or prod him in any way, but the man had checked his pocket watch three times in the last fifteen minutes. Their route was back down the Wando River and the man was right to want to navigate it in the daytime.

The two seamen who'd helped Rose deliver the food were back. He'd told them he didn't want her out of their sight, but each man stated that she'd been adamant about speaking to Maisie alone.

He didn't know who he was angrier at, the two seamen or Rose.

That had been fifteen minutes ago.

When she still hadn't arrived a few minutes later, he knew something was wrong. He checked his own watch, caught McDougal's eye, and left the *Raven*, intent on finding Rose.

When he stepped up to the veranda, the door was open. He knocked on the door frame. No one answered, so he called out for Bruce or Claire. The child he'd seen before was suddenly there, racing through the foyer like a sprite.

"Hello," she said, stopping to stare at him.

He crossed the threshold to speak to her.

"Hello. Do you know where your Aunt Rose is?"

Her bright smile immediately vanished. "My daddy says she's done something wrong and can't come into our house anymore."

"So you haven't seen her?"

"Go to the kitchen, Gloria," Claire said, suddenly appearing at the door. "See if Maisie has anything for you to eat."

Gloria took one look at her mother, another at him, then was speeding down the corridor, her shoes making a tap, tap, tap on the wood floor.

"Where is she?" he asked.

"I have no idea where Rose is. I haven't seen her since she came into my house and insulted me. Nor do I intend to see her again."

"Won't you miss your sister?" he asked, genuinely curious. He'd missed Glynis those years she was away from Glasgow, and couldn't wait for another one of her letters to the family. But Claire didn't look like she gave a good damn.

"You don't wear mourning for your brothers," he said. "Why is that?"

"That is none of your business, Mr. MacIain. Now I'd appreciate if you would leave my home."

"Because they were Yankees and you've so fully embraced your husband's way of life that even a brother becomes an enemy?"

"This war has separated families, Mr. MacIain. Please leave my house."

"Not until you tell me what's happened to Rose."

"I don't know," she said. "It was my impression that she was leaving with you this morning."

Her patrician nose wrinkled a little, either at him because he was only Duncan MacIain of MacIain Mills, a man who worked for his living, or because

Rose was accompanying him without benefit of chaperone or companion.

He had a feeling it was equal amounts of both.

"Where's Bruce?"

"I don't know."

"What do you know, Claire?" He was annoyed, and he was rarely annoyed. That this vacuous woman had the ability to pull on his temper was another irritant.

He didn't like this woman with her air of propriety, who'd allowed her sister to be treated like a slave, to be whipped and degraded and hadn't lifted a finger to stop it.

She was just one of the reasons he'd be overjoyed to see the last of Glengarden. The other was Bruce, and it looked like he was going to have to go hunting for the bastard.

He turned and would have left the house, only to be faced with another woman, one he'd never before seen.

"You're a very rude man," she said. "You'll leave my house and never enter it again. Or if you must, use the back entrance so anyone with distinction will not be subjected to your ill humor."

She was standing, but not very well. She had a cane in one hand and was gripping a chair back with the other. He didn't know how old she was. The wrinkles on her face and neck could be from sudden weight loss or age. Her features—chin, nose, and cheekbones—were sharp. The dark blue dress she wore hung from her shoulders, and despite the hoop skirt, he could tell she was little more than a skeleton.

The bright pink circles on her sunken cheeks and

the pink color of her thinned lips didn't match her aristocratic expression. It was as if a painted doll had begun to speak like the Queen.

Susanna: she was the only one of the MacIains he hadn't met. Evidently, she wasn't disposed to like him, either. Maybe, at one time, he would have been concerned about the level of antipathy he faced from his American cousins. Now he accepted it as a badge of honor.

The more they hated him, the better he felt about himself.

But because he'd been reared to respect the elderly, he bowed slightly in her direction.

"I beg your pardon, ma'am."

"Who are you?"

He didn't bother answering. Let her son illuminate her. He had to find Rose.

Turning, he left the house.

He hadn't had time, or the inclination, to explore the whole of Glengarden, but he knew where the barn and the slave cabins were. A dozen other buildings were located to the west of the cabins, one of which was the stables. Each stall was empty, and from the number of industrious spiderwebs, he doubted if the building had had any occupants lately.

If he, as a Scot, would have been at war with England, would he have given all his horses to his fellow Scots? He couldn't say he would. Hopefully, he'd have retained some of his common sense and kept a few back for use on his own property.

Common sense, however, was something not to be found in abundant supply at Glengarden.

He walked the lines of cabins, his anger growing with each structure he passed.

If he'd been brought up here, like Bruce, would he have been a different man, or one just like his American cousin? The question was impossible to answer, but he hoped he would have had more compassion for his fellow man. Or had been able to learn from his mistakes. That, too, was unknowable, a hypothetical question that would never be answered.

Bruce seemed to be one of those people who enjoyed the suffering of others. Did each scream bring him pleasure? Did every moan make him feel more powerful? What kind of soldier had he been? Had he been a leader among men, or a sadist?

He found Bruce near a cluster of buildings closer to the house. He didn't know what they were used for and he didn't care.

Biting back his anger, he approached the other man.

"Where is she?"

"Who?"

He advanced on Bruce. "You damn well know who. Rose. Where is she?"

Bruce stood leaning against the wall of the building. He glanced around him, took a cheroot from his pocket and calmly lit it.

"You should look around the slave cabins for your lost little Rose. She was always mucking about with the slaves."

"She isn't there. Where is she?"

Bruce smiled. Did a man's character show on the outside? Had he always had that bitter look in his eyes or was that recent, after the loss of his leg? Had his mouth always turned down as if, despite all his advantages, he was somehow still dissatisfied?

He suspected that Bruce was one of those people

who were never happy. They could be wealthy, esteemed, and powerful, yet something would always be missing from their lives. Because of that, they resented those who found it. Maybe it was contentment. Or maybe the answer was simply love.

"You've done something with her. I know you have."

"She's changed her mind about leaving with you. Women like Rose do, you know. But they're too cowardly to come out and admit it. She doesn't want to go with you, but she'll never tell you. She's like that. Always running off when it's too difficult to stay in place. That's what she did in going to Scotland, you know."

He could see her standing in front of him in his imagination, her green eyes deep with emotion, her red hair a bright beacon.

Forgive me, Duncan. I couldn't say good-bye.

No, she wouldn't have done that. He knew she loved him. A woman like Rose wasn't fickle or faithless.

"She went to Scotland to save your family while you were off playing soldier."

Bruce's smile thinned.

"She had no need to do that. Or trying to run the plantation. There were men to do that."

"Until they left."

Bruce's smile disappeared.

"I don't know a damn thing about farming," Duncan said. "But even I know you can't harvest a crop unless you plant one. How did you expect her to buy seeds? Or till the soil without the horses you so kindly gave to your Confederate army?"

"Why use a horse or a mule when Rose would do?"

The smirk was visible; the sarcasm deliberate. He wasn't going to rise to Bruce's taunt.

"I heard about that. How you thought working in the fields might teach her a lesson. The problem was, Bruce, that she's the one who taught you. She took everything you doled out and threw it back at you."

"She's a thankless bitch who went behind my back to free my slaves. She gave them the money to leave. She showed them the way. She even forged my name to safe passage papers. Then she had the gall to sell cotton that belonged to me."

"I was willing to pay twice the price you could have gotten in Nassau because of her. Did you think of that when you burned it? Where are you going to get the money for seeds now? Who's going to see that your family is fed? Not Rose, because I'm not letting her stay here."

"Or maybe she's already made the decision," Bruce said, his smile back in place. "I'd be willing to bet she's run away again."

"Where is she?"

"I don't know and I don't care."

Bruce turned and would have walked away if Duncan hadn't grabbed him by the shoulder and jerked him around, causing the other man to almost fall. He didn't care that Bruce was missing half his leg. He could be missing both of them and he'd still want to lay him out flat.

Grabbing the man's shirt, he hauled him up until their faces were only inches apart.

"Where is she?" he asked, accentuating each separate word.

"In the cold house."

He turned to see Maisie standing there, her hands clenched in front of her.

"He dragged her all the way with a rope around her neck."

Her gaze moved from Bruce to meet Duncan's eyes.

"I don't know if she's still alive."

If she wasn't, Rose wasn't the only person who was going to die today.

"SHUT UP, Maisie. If you don't, I'll shut you up."

Bruce had that look in his eye. That look she'd seen in the kitchen, as if he wanted to whip her then. Or now. But if he thought she was going to tolerate a whipping, he was wrong.

She was free. She didn't care if the Confederacy accepted it or not, Mr. Lincoln had freed her. She stayed here to take care of Miss Susanna and she did so with more patience than anyone in this house. She cleaned up the old woman's messes, she calmed her confusion. She did errands for Miss Claire that she could easily do herself. She put up with every one of them, but she wasn't about to be punished for helping Miss Rose escape this place.

No. No more.

"He struck her, too. Her whole face was bloody."

"Where's this cold house?"

She turned to Duncan.

"I'll show you. He took the key from the pantry. There's only one."

Duncan still hadn't released Bruce, still had him by the shirt, but you would never know it from Bruce's smile. The Devil was on Bruce's face and in his heart.

Maisie began to lead the way to the east side of the house.

"You're dead, Maisie." Bruce's voice was like syrup, thick and sweet.

She was trembling, but she pushed down her fear. Miss Rose never did anything to hurt Bruce. She only tried to help other people, but that was enough for the man to hate her.

"Nobody goes in there anymore because it's empty. He would leave her to die."

"Where's the key?" Duncan asked Bruce.

The other man just shrugged.

She'd seen a lot of brutality in her life. Whippings, beatings, a man enraged and taking off after another man for stealing something of his, be it a brush or a wife. The blow she witnessed from Duncan MacIain ranked right up there at the top of brutal events.

His fist must have had the power of a boulder because when it connected beneath Bruce's jaw, the man's head snapped back. She heard something crack, saw Bruce's whole body fly up and then land flat on the ground as if he'd been felled by an act of God.

She stared at him for a moment, grateful that she'd been witness to such a thing.

Kneeling beside the unconscious man, she searched Bruce's pockets. To her great surprise, the first thing she discovered was a gun tucked into Bruce's shirt. She didn't try to pick it up, but only pointed to it. Duncan reached down and pocketed the weapon, which was a relief.

The key was located in the small front pocket of his trousers. She fished it out and handed it to Duncan.

The look on his face was that of an angel of retribution.

Her first thought was that Miss Rose certainly had picked right. Her second was that Bruce was going to be dangerous when he woke.

SHE WAS hoarse from where Bruce had choked her. She didn't bother shouting for help, knowing it was futile. She'd spent hours yelling for help and no one had ever heard her.

One by one she examined the shelves. There was nothing there. No bags of flour or sugar, no churned butter, no buttermilk, nothing. Their cook used to store food like chowchow, okra, pickles, and relish here in glass jars in the cold house, but there were none to be found now.

Nothing was on the topmost shelf, either. No old pots and pans not used but not discarded, either. Everything at Glengarden was saved, but the cold house had been stripped. The only things remaining were the shelves and the sounds, either industrious mice looking for any kind of scraps or spiders the size of her palm.

No one was going to come to the cold house. Their cook had been one of the slaves who'd slipped away from Glengarden at night. Maisie had taken on the task, but she knew there was nothing here. Claire, to the best of her knowledge, didn't even know the location of the cold house and wouldn't have been interested even if she knew. Old Betsy never left her cabin, and Susanna? Coming here would be beneath her. Benny was the only one who might wander by, but he wouldn't hear her.

She sat on the floor with her knees drawn up, trying to calm herself. She knew how difficult it was to figure out a plan when she was terrified. Instead, her mind was going in several directions at once. What if Duncan didn't find her? What if he sailed off without her? Would he?

No, Duncan was constant, of that she was certain. He was one of those people whose word was his bond. If he said something, you could believe it. You could trust him. You knew he was honest and decent.

Dear God, she wasn't worth him; she knew that. But she wanted him so much. She wanted a life with him where people were free, where war didn't threaten to overrun them. She wanted a life in a place like Glasgow, where people were friendly and smiling.

Her first day in Scotland had taught her that it was a different place. Even as a stranger, she'd been welcomed, treated like family, put to bed and fed.

The first day at Glengarden she'd been horrified. She could remember Claire showing her everything around the house and, later, the grounds. Her sister had waved her hand toward the fields and said something like, "Cotton is king at Glengarden. It's the only crop we grow." Only once on that day had she alluded to the one hundred seventeen people enslaved here, and that was with the same nonchalant dismissal, the same "way of the South" excuse.

She'd taken on a task that first day, to make the lives of Glengarden's slaves better. Some things she did, Bruce never knew about, like taking messages from one plantation to another, or ensuring that letters got to Charleston. Or seeing to it that a man who was talented in healing got the herbs and supplies he needed.

Anyone in the South would agree with Bruce,

that she deserved to be where she was, sitting in the dirt and the dark as punishment. She'd broken so many laws and so many societal edicts in the last two years.

Yet she wouldn't take back anything she'd done, even now.

Maybe being loved by Duncan and loving him in return was a reward for her small actions.

Wrapping her arms around her knees, she bent her head and prayed. A simple prayer, but a heartfelt one.

Please God, don't let me die here.

Chapter 27

Rose heard the key in the lock and braced herself. She had nothing with which to defend herself, only her body, and she was going to fight Bruce with everything she had.

He was going to have to shoot her to keep her in here.

"Rose."

She'd never been so grateful to hear a voice in her life.

She stood, nearly falling when a wave of dizziness hit her.

"My God, Rose, what did he do to you?"

She was, for the second time in her life, hefted in a man's arms and carried somewhere.

She glanced down on the ground at Bruce's unconscious form. "The question is what did you do to him?"

"A taste of what he truly deserves."

"He locked me in again," she said. "This time he was never going to let me out."

He glanced back at Bruce but didn't say anything. There was no love lost between the cousins. No respect, either. Duncan, honorable though he was, would not lift a hand to help Bruce, evident from the look he gave the man sprawled on the ground.

She would always remember what he did next. Duncan stopped in front of Maisie.

"Thank you," he said. "Without your help, I would never have found her."

Maisie ducked her head but didn't say anything.

"Come with us. Come to Scotland with us. You won't be safe here."

Maisie lifted her head and smiled at both of them. "You go on now. I'll be fine. Don't worry."

"Please come, Maisie," Rose said. "I don't feel right leaving you here."

Maisie shook her head. "I can't leave. This is my home. You go on now, the two of you." She glanced down at Bruce. "I'll clean up here."

"You risked your life to save Rose. I won't forget it, Maisie."

Maisie only smiled.

Duncan carried her all the way to the *Raven*, glancing at her occasionally, his frown growing as he did so.

"You have three gouges on your face. One looks deep enough to leave a scar. Hopefully, there's someone on the *Raven* with the skill to sew it shut."

"Do I get whiskey if he does?"

"All the whiskey in the world," he said, stopping to kiss her gently on her forehead.

She was not going to cry now. Not after she'd been rescued, but she was so grateful that she could have wept for days.

He glanced at her throat. "You're getting a bruise there. Did he strangle you, too?"

"He used a rope. He called it my leash."

Duncan stopped in the path as if he'd changed his mind about heading for the ship. Instead, it looked like he wanted to go back and pummel Bruce some more.

"Duncan?"

He blew out a breath. "I want to beat him, Rose. I've never wanted to beat another man in my life. I want to punish him for what he did to you. The faster we can get the hell out of here, the better," he said. "Which is another thing. I've never sworn as much as I have since I met you."

She didn't expect to be amused, not with her throat hurting so much, her knees skinned, and her head pounding. But he sounded so disgruntled, as if his behavior was her fault.

She knew exactly how he felt.

"I've never been as weepy as when I'm around you," she said. "Or emotional. I'm normally more focused. If I have a task, I plan it and execute it. Ever since I met you, I've been decidedly distracted."

He stopped again, staring down at her in what looked to be astonishment.

"Are you jesting? Surely you're jesting. I've never met a woman so intensely focused on an objective in my life. Who convinced me to sail to Nassau? Who got me to take her to Charleston? Why did I come to Glengarden? I shudder to think what you and my mother will be up to. No doubt the complete overhaul of Glasgow's tenements."

"You have tenements?"

"And it begins."

She bit back her smile.

"I have a problem," she said once they were back in the stateroom on board the *Raven*.

Captain McDougal had taken one look at Rose and volunteered the use of the ship's medical kit, which Duncan had accepted. He'd also suggested that they take advantage of the skills of one of the shipmen who had once been a sailmaker. Stitching her cheek closed did not sound like a pleasant experience, but it was better than dying in the cold house.

"A problem?" he said. "That's never a good start to a conversation."

She sat on the end of the settee as he cleaned the cuts on her face, all the while uttering a surprising array of oaths half beneath his breath.

Strange, but the stateroom and the parlor had become more home to her than any other place since she left New York. Even after the near disastrous storm, she still felt safe on the *Raven*. Granted, Captain McDougal was an exemplary captain, but she knew her comfort on the ship had to do with Duncan's presence more than anything else.

He made her feel not only safe, but cherished. She knew he would never do anything to hurt her. Nor would he tolerate her being mistreated by anyone else. She mattered to him, and that knowledge gave her a constant warm glow. Or maybe that was simply being in love.

Did love make you want to smile all the time? Did it make you wish to weep as well? Her emotions were all jumbled up, but a look from Duncan was all she needed to simplify everything. He mattered to her, too. What he wanted, what he thought, what he felt, were important to her, which was why she would bring the problem to him.

She'd never before had anyone with whom to share her concerns. Nor would she think of going behind his back. Duncan had a core of decency on which she could rely. Together, they'd figure out what to do.

"It's more in the way of a moral dilemma," she said.

He sat beside her, took her hand and squeezed it.

"You don't wear your gloves anymore."

"Why should I? You've already seen my hands."

He brought her to tears by what he did next. He kissed each separate finger as if anointing each one of her scars.

She cupped his cheek with her other hand, wishing she had the words to tell him what she felt. Were there words capable of explaining? He accepted her, all the scarred parts, all the flaws and failings. He didn't chastise her, didn't lecture, only listened in an attempt to understand.

That was Duncan. He heard people. He listened to what you had to say. He might not always agree, because they had challenged each other more than once. But he had never once ridiculed her ideas or refused to consider them because she was a woman. She wondered if it was being a Scot, or simply being Duncan.

"When we took the cotton to Charleston," she said, "the first warehouse we took it to only had room for three hundred bales. The second could accommodate the rest, seven hundred bales. Maisie said that she thought Bruce only brought home three hundred bales. That means there's still seven hundred in Charleston."

"Is she sure?"

"I don't think she counted it, but after the weeks of taking the cotton to Charleston, she'd have a rough idea of how many bales he had."

"Maybe he knows about the warehouse, but he has other plans for the cotton."

"I don't think he knows, not after what he said. He didn't have any idea of the size of the crop, so he wouldn't have known how many bales we produced."

"And your moral dilemma is whether you should let him know?"

"A little bit," she said. "I'm not inclined to tell Bruce anything. I never want to see the man again. Besides, if I tell him, there's no guarantee that he wouldn't burn them, too, to celebrate some Confederate victory. Or donate them to the Confederacy. In the meantime, everyone suffers."

She took a deep breath. "Here's what I want to do," she said. "You gave me enough to pay for five hundred bales up front."

"Which you've given back."

She nodded.

"Are you suggesting that I add to the gold to make it enough to pay for seven hundred bales?"

"Yes."

"Then what? Give Bruce the gold, but not tell him why we're giving it to him? He'd consider it charity, Rose, and I can almost guarantee that he's fool enough to dump it in the river. It seems like the only thing my cousin has inherited from his Scottish ancestors is his stubbornness."

"Not Bruce," she said. "Someone else. Someone with the sense enough to use it wisely, to get Glengarden through the end of the war."

"I don't like the idea of going behind anyone's back," he said.

She bit back her disappointment.

"Except in this case," he added. "I'd rather shoot my cousin than give him a helping hand, especially after what he did to you. How certain are you that the cotton is still there?"

"I know Maisie didn't tell anyone about the second warehouse. I know it's not here. So I'm relatively certain, but without checking, I can't guarantee it one hundred percent."

"What about the owner of the warehouse? Will there be any trouble obtaining the cotton?"

She pulled out the certificate from her valise. "This is my receipt. It's the only document we'll need."

"Bruce didn't need it."

"That's because the owner didn't follow the law. I can't see him doing it a second time."

"A lot of speculation, Rose."

She nodded.

"We can go back to Charleston and check ourselves," he said. "Or we can assume it's there and proceed in that fashion." He sat there silently for a moment before speaking. "If it were under different circumstances, I'd advise that we choose the former course of action, but I have the feeling that the faster we leave Glengarden for good, the better."

She nodded again.

"Who do you intend to give the gold to? Not Claire."

She shook her head. "Maisie. She's remained at Glengarden to care for Susanna. She's taken on the cooking and other duties on her own. If anyone could be said to be responsible for the house, it's Maisie, more than Claire or Susanna."

"After what she did today, I'm inclined to give Maisie anything she wants. Maisie it is."

Before she could thank him, he leaned over and kissed her. For a few moments all thoughts of cotton, Glengarden, and being stitched up flew from her mind.

MAISIE CIRCLED the body of the man she used to call Master. The blow Duncan dealt him had knocked him out all right. The rest was up to her.

In the year Bruce had been at war, life had gone on at Glengarden. It would never be idyllic. There were too many memories, like the grave beneath the old oak alongside the river. They had buried her daughter and her dead baby there, never even asking for permission. Some things should not have to be asked.

Some things should not happen.

By a shielded lantern, they'd dug the grave at midnight. They'd said their prayers as they lay Phibba in her shroud with her child in her arms. There she still lay, never disturbed, never discovered, until the day when the Earth would end and heaven's justice came to them all.

She visited the oak at least once a day. Sometimes she sat in the crook of the branches, in the hollowed-out spot where Phibba liked to sit sometimes, staring out at the river. Or when Rose had begun to teach her to read, to study the book that had become her prized possession. Once in a while Phibba had even read the story to her, and she'd nearly wept with pride that her daughter was being educated.

Had her daughter dreamt of freedom? She had it now, didn't she?

Sometimes she knelt on the other side of the tree with her hands pressed flat against the earth as if to absorb some of her child's and her grandchild's spirit into her soul.

She rarely prayed there, because God was already there. He'd given her the strength to stand in front of the man she called Master and give him the appearance of respect. He'd given her the power to live until this day.

The day she never thought would come to pass.

She grabbed Bruce's unconscious body by his lone foot. "You sure do weigh less without two legs. Maybe I should say a prayer of thanks to the Yankees?"

She dragged him backward to the door to the cold house. The key was still in the lock.

Bruce was stirring, his eyes opening and shutting as if he was having a hard time figuring out where he was. Once she dragged him down the four steps, though, his head bouncing on every one, he was out again.

She pulled him to the middle of the cold house, leaving his sprawled body on the dirt floor.

"Don't you worry, Bruce. You'll be feeling fine in just a little while. All the pain will be gone. Just like my Phibba."

She closed the cold house door and locked it. Bruce wouldn't be whipping anyone again. He wouldn't be threatening another human being. Nobody be calling him Master no more.

God forgive her, she couldn't prevent the surge of joy when she removed the key from the lock.

When he came to, he'd start to shout. He'd demand that someone come, but nobody would hear him. His mother wouldn't venture down from her room to look for him. Claire probably didn't even know where the cold house was. Little Gloria wasn't allowed near where the slaves used to be.

Nobody would hear him because the cold house was designed that way. Wasn't that why he shut up Miss Rose in there all those times?

She didn't know how long it would take for him to die. Maybe a day or two. Or maybe longer, like ten days. Maybe after that time she'd see a falling star, indicating that another soul didn't make it through the pearly gates. Maybe it would even be his soul she saw.

She knew she'd never see her Phibba again in heaven because of what she was doing. A thousand prayers would not make God forgive her. But some things needed to be done and even God knew that. He might not approve, but certainly He understood.

She walked slowly down the path to the river.

Something Michael had recited to her made her think of Bruce at the time. The deeds men do live after them.

In years, perhaps, or less than that, someone would find a way to open the cold house door. By then Bruce would be a skeleton. No one would know what happened to him, but surely everyone would remember why.

Chapter 28

They weren't going to leave Glengarden until morning, a decision Captain McDougal accepted with his usual tact.

Rose's injuries were treated all the while Duncan bit back his rage. She had only drunk about a quarter of the bottle but she refused to make a sound while the sailor sewed her face in two places, each tiny stitch causing Duncan to flinch. Then there was the matter of Rose's reaction to good Scottish whiskey. His soon-to-be-wife was very amorous when drunk, a bit of information he tucked away for later.

That afternoon, after she'd had time to sleep off her intoxication, he tucked her up in the chair in the parlor and handed her a pouch of gold.

The chair brought back memories of a night of terror and temptation. She'd been on his lap, all curves and warmth, clad only in a nightgown and wrapper. She'd kissed him or he'd kissed her or it had been a mutual decision based on carnal feelings and unbridled fear.

He'd not been able to forget the feel of her entwined around him for days.

"This is a great deal of money," she said, hefting it in her hand.

"Even if we lost it all, it's been a very profitable voyage."

"I know I trust Maisie, but you've only known her for a day."

"She saved your life. I'm inclined to give her the world for that. Besides, I wouldn't throw a bucket of water on Bruce if he was on fire. Nor do I trust your sister."

"Unfortunately," she said, "I think you're right." She frowned at him. "Remember, I'm not the least like my sister. Do not expect total obedience."

He grinned at her.

How had he managed to fall in love with a woman so like the other women in his family? Determined, perhaps stubborn, certainly opinionated. Odd, how she just showed up on his doorstep. Otherwise, he would have had to go halfway around the world to find her.

"I think the war is coming here," she said, staring down at the pouch.

"I'm surprised it hasn't already. The Union wants Charleston harbor very badly. It probably has something to do with Fort Sumter or maybe just to stop the blockade running."

"If the Union army came here, what would they do to Bruce?"

"I don't know. Maybe there's some honor among soldiers. Since he's been so grievously wounded in the war, perhaps they'll leave him alone. But Glengarden? I don't know what they would do to the plantation. War brings out the brutality in people. Maybe it provides them an excuse for it. Why preserve something when you can destroy it?"

She glanced up at him. "You don't think I want to marry you because I have nowhere else to go, do you?"

That idea had never once occurred to him.

"You can always go and live with your second cousin in Massachusetts," he said.

She nodded. "You're right. I could. Or I could get a job as a governess, even in England. People might consider it novel to have an American governess. Or I could go and stay with Olivia. She seemed very sympathetic."

"Especially since she helped you board the *Raven*."

"How do you know that?" she asked in surprise.

He shook his head, intent on returning to her more important question.

"I would hope that the only reason you would want to marry me is because you fell in love with me. But if it isn't, I still want to marry you."

"Well, you shouldn't," she said, frowning at him.

"I shouldn't?"

She shook her head. "You're a handsome man, Duncan MacIain, and a good one. Good right down to your toes. You care about people. You're concerned about them. You listen to them. I doubt if you've done anything mean or vindictive in your life. You're decent. You would never lie to get your way."

"You make me sound as proper as a bishop."

Should he tell her that he wasn't nearly as easygoing as he used to be? He'd found passion with her, and while it surprised him, he was also fond of the person he was becoming.

He felt fundamentally altered, as if a part of him, never given life, had been born over the last weeks. A better man, perhaps, one who felt more, experienced more. Colors seemed brighter. Smells were more distinct. Emotions were deep and there, right on the surface. All because of Rose.

"You shouldn't accept anything but the best."

"Oh, but I have. Her name is Rose O'Sullivan."

She looked up at him and he was startled to see tears in her eyes.

"I want to marry you because I love you," she said. "I love you more than I thought it was possible to love. I want to wake up beside you every morning. I want to ask how your day was, and if it was bad, to make it better. I want to laugh with you or just sit and hold hands. I want to forget everything that happened in the last two years and begin my life again."

He grabbed her, pulled her into his arms and held her tight.

"We'll marry as soon as we can," he said. The sooner the better, in a surprise he had planned.

She gave him a kiss, a habit they were getting into and one with which he heartily approved.

Before they left he would finish his final errand at Glengarden and see the last of this accursed place.

He couldn't wait.

DUNCAN INSISTED that Rose remain on the *Raven* to recuperate. To his relief, she didn't argue with him.

He took two firemen with him this time, men who were well-muscled from months of stoking the coal burning engine of the *Raven*. He'd already acquainted them with some of the events at Glengarden, and they marched off the gangplank behind him with resolve on their faces.

An angry Scot was a fine intimidation.

He found Maisie in the kitchen garden on her hands and knees, weeding the mint. The turban on her head was made from a brightly colored orange and yellow scarf, unlike the black one he'd seen her wear in the past.

"Are you celebrating?" he asked, pointing to the turban. "Rose's rescue or me hitting Bruce?"

Her bright white smile made him smile in return.

"It's a day of celebration," she said. "And here you are again. You need to leave, Mr. Duncan."

"I firmly agree," he said, "but we needed to talk with you first."

He moved closer so he couldn't be heard by the firemen.

She stood as he approached her, wiping her hands on her apron.

He gave her the pouch he'd carried from the *Raven*.

"This is the payment for the seven hundred bales of cotton still stored in Charleston," he said.

To his surprise, she wouldn't take it, even when he tried to hand it to her.

"Nobody ever gave me any cash money."

"It's gold, Maisie, and Rose and I decided you're the perfect person to have it."

"Me?" she asked.

He nodded.

"I don't trust Bruce to do anything to help anyone. He's eaten up by hatred, Maisie. I don't know if it's the loss of his leg or if he was that way before the war."

"He's been that way since he was old enough to walk," she said. "Dogs wouldn't have nothing to do with him and he abused every horse he ever had."

He wasn't surprised.

"Claire is too much like Bruce," he said.

She only nodded.

"I don't know Old Betsy," he said, "but I doubt she'll outlive the war. Benny doesn't have his wits about him. I've only seen Susanna once, but because she's Bruce's mother I don't trust her, either. She'll end up giving the gold to Bruce."

"Poor thing doesn't have her wits about her, either. Half the time she thinks the boys are little and wants to go looking for them by the river. I've had to set Benny to watching her."

"That leaves you. You seem to have some common sense, not to mention loyalty. You saved Rose's life even when you'll probably be punished for it."

"That won't happen, Duncan."

She met his eyes and he saw secrets there.

"I think you'll see that they all get through the war fine."

She finally reached out and took the pouch.

"There's a lot of money there, Maisie, enough to make it through several years. Bury most of it. Somewhere safe. Then, when things get bad, take a little out and tell them that I gave it to you before I left. They won't think to look for more."

She nodded.

"I never thought . . ." she began.

"That you might be the one to save Glengarden?"

"This place should not be saved," she said.

"Not the way it is. Or the way it was. But maybe you can make it different. Something better."

"I thought Miss Rose was an angel," she said, her voice halting and filled with emotion. "But I think you are as well."

"I'm not the least like an angel, Maisie, but I agree about Rose."

"You'll be happy, the two of you."

"Yes," he said, "we will."

He turned and left, then stopped himself, retraced his steps and hugged her. She stiffened, and he wondered when was the last time anyone had shown Maisie any kindness.

When he pulled back, he bent and kissed her on the cheek.

"Be safe, Maisie."

It was as much a blessing as he could give her.

THE PILOT carefully steered the *Raven* away from the riverbank and the barge.

Duncan stood at the rail with Rose beside him. They'd return to Charleston first, then run the damn blockade again.

They'd been in danger for so long that it felt almost commonplace. Did you ever get used to continually being cautious?

What would it be like to reach Glasgow again? He began to smile at the thought. By the time they got home, they'd be married. He wasn't taking any chances on Rose changing her mind or deciding she wasn't good enough for him.

How foolish.

He understood why she'd done everything she had. It had taken more than courage; it had taken a certain optimism, a fierce belief that everything would be fine in the end. Sometimes it wasn't; he knew that well enough.

This situation worked out better than anyone could expect. With any luck, he'd get his cotton.

The people of Glengarden had financial protection. And the most important result of all was that Rose O'Sullivan was in his life.

He glanced down at her.

He had watched her so intently for so long that he noted the look in her eyes and recognized it as regret.

"You can't change her, Rose. You can't make her more like you."

She surprised him by smiling. "I know. I figured that out. I guess I don't understand how you can love someone who is obviously a horrible person."

"To Claire, he isn't. To Claire, Bruce is merely a product of his upbringing."

She frowned at him.

"Is there anything in your life that's going to disturb me?" she said. "You don't impress mill workers, do you? You don't employ children?"

He smiled at her and wondered what cause she would champion in Glasgow. He had a feeling she and his mother would have a wonderful time occupied with helping the poor.

"No, no, and no. My only grievous sin, which has been repeated to me often enough, is that I haven't taken time to find a wife."

"Is that why you want to marry me?"

"Of course," he said dryly. "I crossed an ocean, nearly dying in the attempt, I might add. Was nearly captured in Nassau, ran the blockade, and endured being at Glengarden only so that people wouldn't badger me any further about being a bachelor."

"You can't blame me for the storm," she said, smiling. "Or Nassau."

He laughed and bent to kiss her, grateful that Glengarden was no longer in sight.

MAISIE WALKED slowly to the old oak.

She stood there for a few moments, watching as the mighty steamer made its way down the river, dwarfing everything in its path. It was only fitting that Mr. Duncan had come to Glengarden in such a magnificent ship.

When she was certain the *Raven* had gone far enough down the river and there was no one else who could see her, she knelt over her daughter's grave. She carved out a hole with her hands, deep enough that the pouch of gold couldn't be seen but not so deep that it would be hard to get to when she needed it.

Bad times were coming, she knew that. Bad times not like before, but different. She didn't know what would happen, but because of Duncan and Rose, they were going to be fine.

Maybe they'd grow cotton again. Or maybe they'd become like lowland planters and raise rice. For now, she'd take a little of the gold and buy enough seed for vegetables. Things to grow in the kitchen garden. Maybe a pig or two so Benny didn't have to be a thief.

Patting the soil down hard, she moved to the indentation on the other side of the oak where Phibba had often sat.

She took the key to the cold house lock from her pocket and threw it as far as she could into the river. It landed a fair distance from shore, making a splash as it sank to the river bottom.

Bad times were coming, but maybe good times were as well.

Maybe she'd wake in the morning not wanting to cry but thinking ahead to all that needed to be done.

And maybe God wasn't all that mad at her for what she'd done to Bruce.

After all, he'd sent her not one, but two angels.

Aboard the Raven
Nassau, Bahamas

ROSE MARIE O'Sullivan, spinster, of New York City, and Duncan Alexander MacIain, of Glasgow, Scotland, were married by Captain Angus Mc-Dougal aboard the blockade runner the *Raven,* just outside the harbor of Nassau, the Bahamas, in international waters.

The ceremony, witnessed by every member of the crew except for two firemen, was a raucous one. Rose had the feeling they were also celebrating the successful run into Charleston and out again, not to mention having seven hundred bales of cotton in the hold.

She didn't mind and had a few glasses of whiskey herself, just to toast the occasion and their success. The outbound journey had been similar to her first one, less fear and fewer Union ships.

They'd refuel here before making the journey across the Atlantic. The honeymoon was to be held in the Viceroy, in the finest suite they possessed, arrangements made by Duncan by a seaman sent on ahead.

Once they came into Nassau, the *Exeter* was nowhere to be seen, but neither Captain McDougal nor Duncan trusted the seemingly innocent ships in the harbor. They hired guards for the *Raven* in addition to continuing to employ the extra crew.

Would they like to see Scotland? It seemed that most of them would.

Duncan said that he wondered how many of them would settle in Glasgow, because just like a seamen considered himself a citizen of the world, there was a time and place to settle down. Glasgow was the perfect place for a man of the sea.

As far as she was concerned, anyplace Duncan was would be home.

As they left the *Raven*, she and Duncan smiled at each other. They were off to another grand adventure. Not running the blockade or loading cotton.

No, their great adventure would be life itself: Glasgow, family, and a future together.

Chapter 29

Glasgow, Scotland
December, 1863

"*We* might call this the dinner of the blind," William Cameron said.

"William!" Eleanor frowned at him, which was a wasted expression since the man would never regain his sight.

Dalton MacIain, the Earl of Rathsmere, seated on the other side of the table, smiled. He wore an eye patch, which made him look dashing and a little dangerous. But there was a twinkle in his good eye, one that warned Rose not to take him too seriously.

"On the contrary," he said. "I've begun to see in my left eye. Quite well, as a matter of fact. Well enough to tell you that my son is a worthy descendent of my Scottish heritage. He squalls when he isn't happy, is quite pleased to go around naked, and I wouldn't be the least surprised if he painted himself blue."

His wife, Minerva, only laughed, which gave Rose the impression that the heir to the English MacIains might be as incorrigible as the earl stated.

"Do get some sleep, my dear," Minerva said to Glynis. "You will need it. Babies never seem to sleep."

Glynis, who looked to deliver any second, had to sit with her chair some distance back from the table.

The occasion of this dinner, which was being held at Hillshead because of her condition, was to introduce the English branch of the family to Rose.

Dalton sat on the opposite side of the table with Minerva, whose smile was contagious. Rose found herself smiling along with her and laughing at the stories she told of excavating and exploring around the castle she'd inherited. She was an archaeologist, although she demurred at the title.

"I haven't the formal training," she said. "Not like my male counterparts. I like to think of myself as an explorer. Someone with curiosity."

"We might as well call ourselves Scots," Dalton said with a smile at his wife. "We've been living here more than in London."

"With a name like MacIain," Minerva said, "you belong in Scotland. London has never quite appreciated your Scottishness."

"My Scottishness?"

Rose suspected, from the glint in Dalton's eyes, that the conversation was one the couple had often.

Glynis looked gloriously happy and very maternal. Lennox wasn't faring quite so well. She'd never seen any man as nervous as he was. He was constantly asking if Glynis was tired, did she want something different to eat, if there was anything he could get her.

Didn't he realize that women gave birth every day? Or that women were stronger than most men gave them credit for? Women had kept their homes going when their husbands, brothers, and fathers had gone off to war. They hadn't crumbled to pieces when adversity struck. If the South lost the war, she suspected it would be southern women who helped it survive, the same women who once pretended to be helpless.

"I can also see well enough to tell my Scottish cousin that his wife is a redhead and quite beautiful," Dalton said. "I would even venture to say that she's more beautiful than you deserve."

"Nonsense," William said. "He ran a blockade for her."

"Did you?" the earl asked Duncan with a smile. "I thought you went for cotton?"

"The cotton was only secondary."

Rose felt her face warm. She really should be modest enough to tell Duncan that his constant praise of her was unnecessary. So, too, the compliments. But, oh, his kisses. His mother had gotten used to finding them engaged in torrid kisses in all parts of the house, and it had become a source of laughter for Mabel and Lily.

But she adored him for it, and it was quite pleasant to be so singularly adored in return.

As for the mill, it was running along at a higher capacity than it had in years. In addition, Duncan had won a contract for wicking, something she'd never considered before. Plus, he was going into specialty weaving, creating intricate patterns for the dressmaking trade.

The future looked bright, joyful, and glorious.

"I understand you were a prisoner of war," Rose said, leaning close to Minerva's brother so no one could hear her comment.

Neville Todd turned and looked at her, his expression one of surprise.

"I'm being terribly rude, aren't I? I am so sorry."

"No," he said. "You're not. It's just that you're the first person to come out and say something. Everyone else pretends it didn't happen."

She frowned at him. "How can they do that? Were you not missing for nearly a year?"

"Ten months," he said, nodding. "How did you know?"

She glanced over at Glynis. "My sister-in-law was married before, to a member of the British Legation. She was the one who let Dalton know where you were."

"A providential bit of knowledge, as it turned out," he said. "I understand they've stopped trading prisoners, but I was able to be ransomed."

For a good deal of money, if she wasn't mistaken.

Even if she hadn't known of Neville Todd's travails, she would have suspected that something terrible had happened to him. His face was lean, the cheekbones pronounced. There was a haunted look in his eyes, almost as if he saw horrible sights invisible to anyone else.

She wondered if she sometimes wore the same expression.

She knew that he'd been released from a Confederate prison camp and arrived in London barely alive.

"Was it very bad?" she asked.

"Yes."

She placed her hand on his arm, feeling it flex at her touch.

He turned and studied her.

"I understand you lived in the South," he said, his voice carefully neutral.

Did he think she was a Confederate?

"Yes, I did. Those two years will probably remain indelibly etched in my mind, unfortunately." She forced a smile to her face so that Duncan wouldn't notice her sudden somber mood. "But I'm from New York originally."

"Some memories shouldn't be wiped clean," Neville said, surprising her. "I think they should remain in the back of your mind to help you remember. Not only of what you survived, but most of all, to remind you to be grateful for what you have now."

"You're a very wise man, Neville Todd."

"I believe you're the first person to say that to me as well."

They smiled at each other, and she couldn't help but feel they'd been on a similar journey. With luck, the memories for each of them would fade until they were only a tiny postscript in their lives.

"You're next, Duncan," Glynis said, her eyes bright with mischief. "A little girl, don't you think, Rose?"

No one at the table said a word. For once, it was nice to know someone who occasionally spoke out of turn. Or to have people glance at each other at the table as if to say, *Can you believe she said that?* But she couldn't leave Glynis out there alone. She knew how that felt only too well.

"Twins, I think," she said, just to see Duncan's eyes widen. "They run in my family, I was told."

"Not only beautiful, but sassy," William said.

Rose smiled and wondered if it would be true this time. For now, she would hold her secret until she told Duncan. Would he be as nervous as Lennox? She hoped not, but people had been telling her how much Duncan had changed in the last months.

He and Lennox argued—loudly—and it seemed as though both of them enjoyed the exchanges. When he lost his temper, he didn't hide his anger behind a polite smile. He laughed a lot more, according to Mabel, and Lily said that he was forever giving her compliments. He always came home for lunch and sometimes they ate together in the garden and sometimes in the dining room. The time always passed so swiftly, but whatever she was doing with Eleanor, she always made sure she was home when Duncan arrived.

Every day was like a present, a gift she hadn't expected.

Eleanor smiled at her with fondness. Perhaps her news wasn't all that secret. She wouldn't mind if Eleanor had guessed. She'd come to love her mother-in-law, and respected her as well, and helped her in projects for the poor.

They'd told her the whole story of Rose's masquerade when they returned. Eleanor had enfolded her in a hug and wept a few tears, which had further endeared her to Rose.

She and Duncan hadn't told anyone about Glengarden. Not the true and awful story of the place. Perhaps history would treat it better. If the plantation survived the war and time, perhaps strangers would hold a fondness for it.

She'd take the lessons she'd learned there and use them for the rest of her life. Those who have little often gladly share what they have. Taking away a man's dignity does not alter his character. Those with power who abuse others who have nothing—not even their freedom—are the spawn of the Devil himself.

In the meantime, she would be about living her life in Glasgow, with the husband she loved and the child soon to come.

Duncan turned to look at her. In his eyes was a question. She answered it with a smile and a reassuring touch on his arm. She was fine. Better than fine. She was truly happy.

One day in the next few weeks, she'd take the path from the house down to the riverbank. The Clyde flowed fast there, off to the Atlantic. Like the women whose men went to sea, she'd give up something that mattered to her: a silver-backed mirror Claire had given to her when they lived in New York.

Not as a sacrifice, but in gratitude for all that she'd been given.

Author's Notes

Writing a book featuring slavery was a delicate task, to say the least. I hope I was true to the times, as much as research and a certain degree of sensitivity could make me.

Rose was born for me after I read two articles. The first was an account of an abolitionist society's meeting in New York City, held in 1860. I wondered what it would be like to be actively against slavery and then plunked down on a plantation. The second was the description of a wedding between a Connecticut woman and a graduate of the Military Academy, a resident of Georgia in 1859. One could only imagine how the war affected them.

Charleston didn't fall to the Union forces until February, 1865.

Many people, viewing the ruins of the city, thought the destruction was caused by the war. In fact, the fire of 1861 did more damage to Charleston than the war. Major rebuilding didn't begin until after the war ended.

The first luxury hotel in the Bahamas was the Royal Victoria, on which the Viceroy was modeled. It was built in 1861 and closed 110 years later. Although the hotel burned down in the 1990s, and was replaced by a parking lot, the original gardens of the hotel remain. I don't know what happened to the silk cotton tree on which the original tree house was built. The silk cotton tree is also known as a Ceiba. Oh, and they actually had a bar called the Blockade Runners Bar in the hotel.

Several photographs of the Royal Victoria are here: http://www.oldbahamas.com/id11.html

I confess to having a fascination with nineteenth-century plumbing, no doubt because I'm so grateful for twenty-first century plumbing. The accommodations described in the Viceroy were taken from the Davis family home in Natchez, Mississippi, where they not only had hot and cold running water in 1850, but a luxurious flushing toilet and a rain shower head.

The Bahamas were made wealthy by the blockade of the southern ports. Factors like Fraser Trenholm, who purchased the *Raven* originally in Book 1, *In Your Wildest Scottish Dreams,* realized just how much money independent ships were making. They set about buying their own ships and hiring their own captains to run the blockade. Percentage wise, they were more successful at evading capture than independently owned ships.

Determining how long it took to get from point A to point B has always been a challenge for me. This time, I tracked letters sent from the Bahamas to London. The longest travel time was nine days, which I thought was amazing.

The war tax was real. According to *Masters of the Big House: Elite Slaveholders of the Mid-Nineteenth Century South,* by William Kauffman Scarborough (Louisiana State University Press, April 1, 2006), in September 1863 one of the large plantation owners,

George W. Mordecai, paid the Confederate government seven thousand dollars in taxes on 87,000 pounds of cotton he'd purchased on speculation during the war.

A great many politicians maintained that, without Scotland's involvement in the Civil War, it would have ended in 1863. Blockade runners built on the Clyde brought in ammunition from the Bahamas that supplied the Confederacy and allowed them to keep fighting.

A fact that I discovered—and had never before known—was that America billed the UK for its part in continuing the war. The initial bill was eight billion dollars. The federal government reduced the bill to 3.5 million, and the UK paid the bill in 1871.

Welcome to the World of
Karen Ranney.
Keep reading to find out what other
wonderful romances Karen Ranney
has in store for you.

Scotsman of My Dreams

Once the ton's most notorious rake, Dalton Mac-Iain has returned from his expedition to America during the Civil War wounded and a changed man. Instead of attending soirees, he now spends his time as a recluse. But Dalton's peace is disturbed when Minerva Todd barges into his London town house, insisting he help search for her missing brother Neville. Though Dalton would love to spend more time with the bewitching beauty, he has no interest in finding Neville—for he blames him for his injury.

Minerva has never met a more infuriating man than the Earl of Rathsmere, yet she is intrigued by the torrid rumors she has heard about him . . . and the fierce attraction pulling her toward him.

Dalton does not count on Minerva's persistence—or the desire she awakens in him, compelling him to discover her brother's fate. But when danger surrounds them, Dalton fears he will lose the tantalizing, thoroughly unpredictable woman he has come to love.

In Your Wildest Scottish Dreams

Seven years have passed since Glynis MacIain made the foolish mistake of declaring her love to Lennox Cameron, only to have him stare at her dumbfounded. Heartbroken, she accepted the proposal of a diplomat and moved to America, where she played the role of a dutiful wife among Washington's elite. Now a widow, Glynis is back in Scotland. Though Lennox can still unravel her with just one glance, Glynis is no longer the naive girl Lennox knew and vows to resist him.

With the American Civil War raging on, shipbuilder Lennox Cameron must complete a sleek new blockade runner for the Confederate navy. He cannot afford any distractions, especially the one woman he's always loved. Glynis's cool demeanor tempts him to prove to her what a terrible mistake she made seven years ago.

As the war casts its long shadow across the ocean, will a secret from Glynis's past destroy any chance for a future between the two star-crossed lovers?

Return to Clan Sinclair

A Novella

When Ceana Sinclair Mead married the youngest son of an Irish duke, she never dreamed that seven years later her beloved Peter would die. Her three brothers-in-law think she should be grateful to remain a proper widow. But after three years of this, she's ready to scream. She escapes to Scotland, only to discover she's so much more than just the Widow Mead.

In Scotland, Ceana crosses paths with Bruce Preston, an American tasked with a dangerous mission by her brother, Macrath. Bruce is too attractive for her peace of mind, but she still finds him fascinating. Their one night together is more wonderful than Ceana could have imagined, and she has never felt more alive.

But when the past reaches out in the form of an old foe, Ceana's life is in danger. Now Bruce must fight to become her savior—and more—if she'll let him.

The Virgin of Clan Sinclair

Ellice Traylor has a secret. Beneath her innocent exterior beats an incredibly passionate and imaginative heart. She has been pouring all of her frustrated virginal fantasies into a scandalous manuscript. But when her plans for her future are about to be derailed by her mother's matrimonial designs, she takes matters into her own hands.

Ross Forster, the Earl of Gladsden, has spent his life creating order out of chaos. He expects discipline and calm from those around him. What he does not expect is a beautiful, thoroughly maddening stowaway in his carriage.

But when Ross discovers Ellice's secret book, he finds he can't stop thinking about what other fantasies the disarming virgin can dream up. He has the chance to learn when a compromising position forces them to wed. But can the uptight earl survive a life with his surprising new wife? And how will the hero of Ellice's fantasies compare to the husband of her reality?

The Witch of Clan Sinclair

Logan Harrison is looking for a wife. As the Lord Provost of Edinburgh, he needs a conventional and diplomatic woman who will stand by his side and help further his political ambitions. He most certainly does not need Mairi Sinclair, the fiery, passionate, fiercely beautiful woman who tries to thwart him at every turn. But if she's so wrong for him, why can't he stop kissing her? He's completely bewitched.

Mairi Sinclair has never met anyone like Logan Harrison, the perfect example of everything she finds wrong with the world. He's also incredibly handsome, immensely popular, and impossible to resist. His kisses inflame her and awaken a passion she can barely control.

Can two people who are at such odds admit to a love that would bind them together for life?

The Devil of Clan Sinclair

To Dance with the Devil . . .

For Virginia Traylor, Countess of Barrett, marriage was merely the vehicle to buy her father a title. Widowhood, however, brings a host of problems. For her husband deliberately spent the money intended for Virginia and her in-laws, leaving them penniless—unless she produces an heir. Desperate and confused, Virginia embarks on a fateful journey that brings her to the doorstep of the only man she's ever loved . . .

He's known as the Devil, but Macrath Sinclair doesn't care. He moved to a tiny Scottish village in hopes of continuing his work as an inventor and starting a family of his own. He bought the house; he chose the woman. Unfortunately, Virginia didn't choose him. Macrath knows he should turn her away now, but she needs him, and he wants her more than ever. Macrath intends to win—one wickedly seductive deed at a time.

The Lass Wore Black

Third in line for an important earldom, Mark Thorburn is expected to idly wait to take up his position. Instead, he devotes himself to medicine, a life's work that leads him to the door of famous beauty Catriona Cameron.

The victim of a terrible accident, Catriona has refused to admit even the most illustrious physicians to her lush Edinburgh apartments. But what if a doctor were to pose as a mere footman, pretending to serve her every need . . . would she see through such a ruse?

Entwined in the masquerade, Mark manages to gain Catriona's trust, only to find that somehow she has captured his heart at the same time. But when their passion becomes the target of a madman bent on revenge, Mark will have to do more than heal her body and win her love . . . he'll have to save her life as well.

A Scandalous Scot

One scandal was never enough . . .

After four long years, Morgan MacCraig has finally returned to the Highlands of his birth . . . with his honor in shreds. After a scandal, all he wants now is solace—yet peace is impossible to find with the castle's outspoken new maid trying his patience, challenging his manhood . . . and winning his love, body and soul.

Jean MacDonald wants to leave her past behind and start anew, but Ballindair Castle, a Scottish estate rumored to be haunted, hasn't been the safe haven she envisioned. Ballindair's ancestral ghosts aren't as fascinating as Morgan, the most magnificent man she's ever seen. Though their passion triggers a fresh scandal that could force them to wed, Jean must first share the secrets of her own past—secrets that could force them apart, or be the beginning of a love and redemption unlike anything they've ever known.

A Scottish Love

Shona Imrie should have agreed to Gordon Mac-Dermond's proposal of marriage seven years ago—before he went off to war and returned a national hero—but the proud Scottish lass would accept no man's charity. The dashing soldier would never truly share her love and the passion that left her weak and breathless—or so she believed—so instead she gave herself to another. Now she faces disgrace, poverty, and a life spent alone for her steadfast refusal to follow her heart.

Honored with a baronetcy for his courage under fire, Gordon has everything he could ever want—except for the one thing he most fervently desires: the headstrong beauty he foolishly let slip through his fingers. Conquering Shona's stubborn pride, however, will prove his most difficult battle—though it is the one for which he is most willing to risk his life, his heart, and his soul.

A Borrowed Scot

Who Is Montgomery Fairfax?

Though she possesses remarkable talents and astonishing insight, Veronica MacLeod knows nothing about the man who appears from nowhere to prevent her from committing the most foolish and desperate act of her life. Recently named Lord Fairfax of Doncaster Hall, the breathtaking, secretive stranger agrees to perform the one act of kindness that can rescue the Scottish beauty from scandal and disgrace—by taking Veronica as his bride.

Journeying with Montgomery Fairfax to his magnificent estate in the Highlands, Veronica knows deep in her heart that this is a man she can truly love—a noble soul, a caring and passionate lover whose touch awakens feelings she's never before known. Yet there are ghosts in Montgomery's shuttered past that haunt him still. Unless Veronica can somehow unlock the enigma that is her new husband, their powerful passion could be undone by the sins and sorrows of yesterday.

A Highland Duchess

The beautiful but haughty Duchess of Herridge is known to all the ton as the "Ice Queen." But to Ian McNair, the exquisite Emma is nothing like the rumors. Sensual and passionate, she moves him as no other woman has before. If only she were his wife and not his captive . . .

Little does Emma know that the dark and mysterious stranger who bursts into her bedroom to kidnap her is the powerful Earl of Buchane, and the only man who has been able to see past her proper facade. As the Ice Queen's defenses melt under the powerful passion she finds with her handsome captor, she begins to believe that love may be possible. Yet fate has decreed that the dream can never be—for pursuing it means sacrificing everything they hold dear: their honor, their futures . . . and perhaps their lives.

Sold to a Laird

Lady Sarah Baines was devoted to her mother and her family home, Chavensworth. Douglas Eston was devoted to making a fortune and inventing. The two of them are married when Lady Sarah's father proposes the match and threatens to send Lady Sarah's ill mother to Scotland if she protests.

Douglas finds himself the victim of love at first sight, while Sarah thinks her husband is much too, well, earthy for her tastes. Marriage is simply something she had to do to ensure her mother's well-being, and even when her mother dies in the next week, it's not a sacrifice she regrets.

She cannot, however, simply write her mother's relatives and inform them of her death. She convinces Douglas—an ex-pat Scot—to return to Scotland with her, to a place called Kilmarin. At Kilmarin, she is given the Tulloch Sgàthán, the Tulloch mirror. Legend stated that a woman who looked into the mirror saw her true fate.

Douglas and Sarah begin to appreciate each other, and through passion, Douglas is able to express his true feelings for his wife. But once they return to England and Douglas disappears and is presumed dead, Sarah has to face her own feelings for the man she's come to respect and admire.

A Scotsman in Love

Running from their pasts . . .

Margaret Dalrousie was once willing to sacrifice all for her calling. The talented artist would let no man interfere with her gift. But now, living in a small Scottish cottage on the estate of Glengarrow, she has not painted a portrait in ages. For not even the calming haven in the remote woods can erase the memories that darken Margaret's days and nights. And now, with the return of the Earl of Linnet to his ancestral home, her hopes of peace have disappeared.

From the first moment he encountered Margaret on his land, the Earl of Linnet was nothing but annoyed. The grieving nobleman has his own secrets that have lured him to the solitude of the Highlands, and his own reasons for wanting to be alone. Yet he is intrigued by his hauntingly beautiful neighbor. Could she be the spark that will draw him out of bittersweet sorrow—the woman who could transform him from a Scotsman in sadness to a Scotsman in love?

The Devil Wears Tartan

A Man in the Shadows

Some say he is dangerous. Others say he is mad. None of them knows the truth about Marshall Ross, the Devil of Ambrose. He shuns proper society, sworn to let no one discover his terrible secret. Including the beautiful woman he has chosen to be his wife.

A Fallen Woman

Only desperation could bring Davina McLaren to the legendary Edinburgh castle to become the bride of a man she has never met. Plagued by scandal, left with no choices, she has made her bargain with the Devil. And now she must share his bed.

A Fire Unlike Any They've Ever Known

From the moment they meet, Davina and Marshall are rocked by an unexpected desire that leaves them only yearning for more. But the pleasures of the marriage bed cannot protect them from the sins of the past. With an enemy of Marshall's drawing ever closer and everything they now cherish most at stake, he and Davina must fight to protect the passion they cannot deny.

The Scottish Companion

Haunted by the mysterious deaths of his two brothers, Grant Roberson, tenth Earl of Straithern, fears for his life. Determined to produce an heir before it's too late, Grant has promised to wed a woman he has never met. But instead of being enticed by his bride-to-be, Grant can't fight his attraction to the understated beauty and wit of her paid companion.

Gillian Cameron long ago learned the danger of falling in love. Now, as the companion to a spoiled bluestocking, she has learned to keep a firm hold on her emotions. But from the moment she meets him, she is powerless to resist the alluring and handsome earl.

Fighting their attraction, Gillian and Grant must band together to stop an unknown enemy from striking. Will the threat of danger be enough to make them realize their true feelings?

Autumn in Scotland

Abandoned by a Rogue

Betrothed to an earl she had never met, Charlotte Haversham arrived at Balfurin, hoping to find love at the legendary Scottish castle. Instead she found decaying towers and no husband among the ruins. So Charlotte worked a miracle, transforming the rotting fortress into a prestigious girls' school. And now, five years later, her life is filled with purpose—until . . .

Seduced by a Stranger

A man storms Charlotte's castle—and he is *not* the reprehensible Earl of Marne, the one who stole her dowry and dignity, but rather the absent lord's handsome, worldly cousin Dixon MacKinnon. Mesmerized by the fiery Charlotte, Dixon is reluctant to correct her mistake. And though she's determined not to play the fool again, Charlotte finds herself strangely thrilled by the scoundrel's amorous attentions. But a dangerous intrigue has drawn Dixon to Balfurin. And if his ruse is prematurely revealed, a passionate, blossoming love affair could crumble into ruin.

An Unlikely Governess

She had no recourse but to accept the position . . . and no choice but to fall in love.

Impoverished and untitled, with no marital prospects or so much as a single suitor, Beatrice Sinclair is forced to accept employment as governess to a frightened, lonely child from a noble family—ignoring rumors of dark intrigues to do so. Surely, no future could be as dark as the past she wishes to leave behind. And she admits fascination with the young duke's adult cousin, Devlen Gordan, a seductive rogue who excites her from the first charged moment they meet. But she dares not trust him—even after he spirits them to isolation and safety when the life of her young charge is threatened.

Devlen is charming, mysterious, powerful—and Beatrice cannot refuse him. He is opening new worlds for her, filling her life with passion . . . and peril. But what are Devlen's secrets? Is he her lover or her enemy? Will following her heart be foolishness or a path to lasting happiness?

Till Next We Meet

*In a departure from her nationally bestselling Highland
Lord series, Karen Ranney brings us another emotionally
intense and passionate story that will speak to her fans.*

When Adam Moncrief, colonel of the Highland
Scots Fusiliers, agrees to write a letter to Catherine
Dunnan, one of his officers' wives, a forbidden cor-
respondence develops and he soon becomes fascinated with her even though Catherine thinks the
letters come from her husband, Harry Dunnan.

Although Adam stops writing after Harry is
killed, a year after his last letter he still can't forget
her. Then when he unexpectedly inherits the title of
the Duke of Lymond, Adam decides the timing is
perfect to pay a visit to the now single and available Catherine. What he finds, however, is not the
charming, spunky woman he knew from her letters,
but a woman stricken by grief, drugged by lauda-
num, and in fear for her life.

In order to protect her, Adam marries Catherine,
hoping that despite her seemingly fragile state, he
will once again discover the woman he fell in love
with.

So in Love

The Highland Lords: Book 5

Jeanne du Marchand adored her dashing young Scotsman, Douglas MacRae, and every moment in his arms was pure rapture. But when her father, the Comte du Marchand, learned she was carrying Douglas's child, Jeanne was torn from the proud youth without a word of farewell—and separated not long after from her newborn baby daughter. Jeanne feared her life was over, for all she truly cared about was lost to her. Can the power of love prevail?

Once, Douglas believed his lady's loving words—until her betrayal turned his ardor to contempt. He cannot forget even now, ten years later, when destiny brings her to his native Scotland, broken in spirit but as beautiful as before. His pride will not let him play the fool again, although memories of a past—secret, innocent, and fragile—tempt him. Can passion lead to love and forgiveness?

To Love a Scottish Lord

The Highland Lords: Book 4

A Lord Not Meant to Marry

Hamish MacRae, a changed man, returned to his beloved Scotland intending to turn his back on the world. The proud, brooding lord wants nothing more than to be left alone, but an unwanted visitor to his lonely castle has defied his wishes. While it is true that this healer, Mary Gilly, is a beauty beyond compare, it will take more than her miraculous potions to soothe his wounded spirit. But Mary's tender heart is slowly melting Hamish's frozen one . . . awakening a burning need to keep her with him—forever.

A Lady Who Dares Not Love

Never before has Mary felt such an attraction to a man! The mysterious Hamish MacRae is strong and commanding, with a face and form so handsome it makes Mary tremble with wanting him. Already shadowy forces are coming closer, heartless whispers and cruel rumors abound, and it will take a love more pure and powerful than any other to divine the truth—and promise a future neither had dreamed possible.

The Irresistible MacRae

The Highland Lords: Book 3

To avoid a scandal that would devastate her family, Riona McKinsey has agreed to marry the wrong man—though the one she yearns for is James MacRae. Had she not been maneuvered into a compromising position by a man of Edinburgh—who covets her family's wealth more than Riona's love—the dutiful Highland miss could have followed her heart into MacRae's strong and loving arms. But alas, it is not to be.

A man of the wild, tempest-tossed ocean, James MacRae never dreamed he'd find his greatest temptation on land. Yet from the instant the dashing adventurer first gazed deeply into Riona's haunting gray eyes, he knew there was no lass in all of Scotland he'd ever want more. The matchless lady is betrothed to another—and unwilling to break off her engagement or share the reason why she will marry her intended. But how can MacRae ignore the passion that burns like fire inside, drawing him relentlessly toward a love that could ruin them both?

When the Laird Returns

The Highland Lords: Book 2

Marriage He Never Wanted

Though a descendant of proud Scottish lairds, Alisdair MacRae had never seen his ancestral Highland estate—nor imagined that he'd have to marry to reclaim it! But the unscrupulous neighboring laird Magnus Drummond has assumed control of the property—and he will relinquish it only for a king's ransom . . . and a groom for his daughter Iseabal! Alisdair never thought to give up the unfettered life he loves—not even for a bride with the face of an angel and the sensuous grace that would inflame the desire of any male.

A Passion They Never Dreamed

Is Iseabal to be a bride without benefit of a courtship? Though she yearns for a love match, the determined lass will gladly bind herself to Alisdair if he offers her an escape from her father's cruelty. This proud, surprisingly tender stranger awakens a new fire inside her, releasing a spirit as brave and adventurous as his own. Alisdair feels the heat also, but can Iseabal win his trust as well as his passion—ensuring that both their dreams come true . . . now that the laird has returned?

One Man's Love

The Highland Lords: Book 1

She swore to hate him . . . but he knew her heart was his.

He was her enemy, a British colonel in war-torn Scotland. But as a youth, Alec Landers, Earl of Sherbourne, had spent his summers known as Ian, running free on the Scottish Highlands—and falling in love with the tempting Leitis MacRae. With her fiery spirit and vibrant beauty, she is still the woman who holds his heart, but revealing his heritage now would condemn them both. Yet as the mysterious Raven, an outlaw who defies the English and protects the people, Alec could be Leitis's noble hero again—even as he risks a traitor's death.

Leitis MacRae thought the English could do nothing more to her clan, but that was before Colonel Alec Landers came to reside where the MacRaes once ruled. Now, to save the only family she has left, Leitis agrees to be a prisoner in her uncle's place, willing to face even an English colonel to save his life. But Alec, with his soldier's strength and strange compassion, is an unwelcome surprise. Soon Leitis cannot help the traitorous feelings she has when he's near . . . nor the strange sensation that she's known him once before. And as danger and passion lead them to love, will their bond survive Alec's unmasking? Or will Leitis decide to scorn her beloved enemy?

After the Kiss

The promise of a single kiss . . .

Margaret Esterly is desperate—and desperation can lead to shocking behavior! Beautiful and gently bred, she was the essence of prim, proper English womanhood—until fate widowed her and thrust her into poverty overnight. Now she finds herself at a dazzling masked ball, determined to sell a volume of scandalous memoirs to the gala's noble host. But amid the heated fantasy of the evening, Margaret boldly, impetuously, shares a moment of passion with a darkly handsome gentleman . . . and then flees into the night.

Who was this exquisite creature who swept into Michael Hawthorne's arms and then vanished? The startled yet pleasingly stimulated Earl of Montraine is not about to forget the intoxicating woman of mystery so easily—especially since Michael's heart soon tells him that he has at last found his perfect bride. But once he locates her again, will he be able to convince the reticent lady that their moment of ecstasy was no mere accident . . . and that just one kiss can lead to paradise?

My True Love

Anne Sinclair has been haunted by visions of a handsome black-haired warrior all her life. His face invades her dreams and fills her nights with passionate longing. So the beautiful laird's daughter leaves her remote Scottish castle, telling no one, to search for the man called Stephen—a man she does not know but who fights in war-torn England, a place she has never seen.

Stephen Harrington, Earl of Langlinais, never expected to rescue this unexplained beauty from the hands of his enemy. And yet, when their eyes first meet, he feels from the depths of his soul that he should know her . . . that he needs to touch her, and keep her by his side forever. For unknown to both of them, they are in the center of a centuries-old love . . . a love that is about to surpass their wildest dreams.

My Beloved

They call her the Langlinais Bride—though she's seen her husband only one time . . . on their wedding day, twelve years ago.

For years, naive, convent-bred Juliana dreaded being summoned to the side of the man she wed as a child so long ago. Now her husband, Sebastian, Earl of Langlinais, has become ensnared in his villainous brother's wicked plots—and has no choice but to turn to his virgin bride for help.

Juliana now finds herself face-to-face with a man so virile and so powerful that she's fascinated by him—just as he asks her to go against everything she holds true. Sebastian never counted on being enchanted by the beauty of this innocent angel he intended to keep as wife in name only—and he dares not reveal to her the secret reason why their love can never be.

The Glenlyon Bride

from the Scottish Brides Anthology

A Novella

A land of legend and wild beauty—of clans, lairds, honor, and passion—Scotland forever stirs the soul of romance.

Now, in one incomparable volume, four of Avon Romance's best-selling authors present stirring tales of hearts won and weddings to be, featuring a quartet of unforgettable heroines about to discover the rapture of love in a world as untamed as the men they will one day marry.

Upon a Wicked Time

He was her ideal husband, and she should have been his perfect bride . . .

Tessa Astley is everything a duke should want in a wife. A breathtaking beauty with a reputation that is positively above reproach, she desires nothing more than the love of her husband, the man she's long pined for.

Only Jered Mandville doesn't want a soul mate, just a proper duchess hidden away on his country estate to beget heirs. He certainly doesn't see a place for his bride in his decadent life in London.

Tessa won't let her fairy tale slip through her fingers. She'd do anything to win Jered's heart. So Tessa starts a campaign to win her husband's heart by invading his home, his reckless adventures, and his bed—all to prove to her cynical duke that even a happy ending can be delightfully wicked.

My Wicked Fantasy

An Explosive Encounter

Mary Kate Bennett was married too early, widowed too young, and left to fend for herself without a penny. Her path was never meant to cross with Archer St. John's, except for a terrible carriage accident with the wickedly handsome Earl of Sanderhurst. Mary Kate awakens in a mysterious lord's bed to a life more luxurious than she could have ever imagined, facing a man she's never met before, but instinctively knows . . .

A Heart Held Hostage

The whispers about Archer follow him wherever he goes. Had the reclusive nobleman murdered his unhappy countess? When Mary Kate enters his life so unexpectedly, the bold earl is convinced that she has all the answers he has been searching for. So why can't he think of anything else besides her decadently red hair, her luminescent skin, and the feelings this vibrant, spirited beauty evokes within his masculine soul?

A Wicked Fantasy

Their love can be a fantasy, or it can be strong enough to entwine their destinies forever.